The Rage of
Dragons

The Rage of Dragons

THE BURNING: BOOK ONE

Evan Winter

www.orbitbooks.net

ORBIT

First published in Great Britain in 2019 by Orbit

1 3 5 7 9 10 8 6 4 2

Copyright © 2017 by Evan Winter

Map copyright © 2019 by Tim Paul

The moral right of the author has been asserted.

A CIP catalogue record for this book
is available from the British Library.

HB ISBN 978-0-356-51294-5
C format 978-0-356-51295-2

Printed and bound in Great Britain by Clays Ltd, Elcograf S.p.A.

Papers used by Orbit are from well-managed forests
and other responsible sources.

Orbit
An imprint of
Little, Brown Book Group
Carmelite House
50 Victoria Embankment
London EC4Y 0DZ

An Hachette UK Company
www.hachette.co.uk

www.orbitbooks.net

To my father for showing me how to work hard;
To my mother for her daily lessons in infinite love;
To my wife for being a better partner than any man deserves;
To my son, this story is for you.

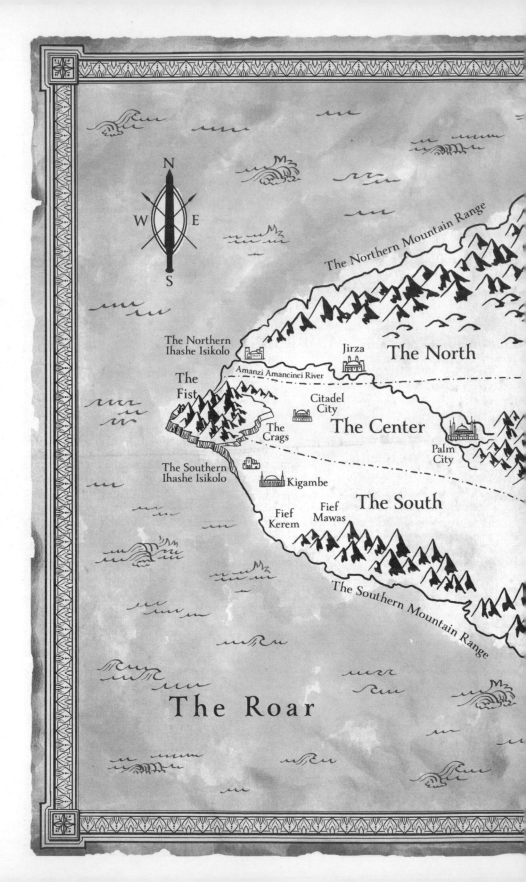

The Northern
Fortress

The Front Line

The Central
Mountains

The Southern
Fortress

Fief
Dakur

The Curse

PROLOGUE

LANDFALL

Queen Taifa stood at the bow of *Targon*, her beached warship, and looked out at the massacre on the sands. Her other ships were empty. The fighting men and women of the Chosen were already onshore, were already killing and dying. Their screams, not so different from the cries of those they fought, washed over her in waves.

She looked to the sun. It burned high overhead and the killing would not stop until well past nightfall, which meant too many more would die. She heard footsteps on the deck behind her and tried to take comfort in the sounds of Tsiory's gait.

"My queen," he said.

Taifa nodded, permitting him to speak, but did not turn away from the slaughter on the shore. If this was to be the end of her people, she would bear witness. She could do that much.

"We cannot hold the beach," he told her. "We have to retreat to the ships. We have to relaunch them."

"No, I won't go back on the water. The rest of the fleet will be here soon."

"Families, children, the old and infirm. Not fighters. Not Gifted."

Taifa hadn't turned. She couldn't face him, not yet. "It's beautiful here," she told him. "Hotter than Osonte, but beautiful. Look." She pointed to the mountains in the distance. "We landed on a peninsula bordered and bisected by mountains. It's defensible, arable. We could make a home here. Couldn't we? A home for my people."

She faced him. His presence comforted her. Champion Tsiory, so strong and loyal. He made her feel safe, loved. She wished she could do the same for him.

His brows were knitted and sweat beaded on his shaved head. He had been near the front lines, fighting. She hated that, but he was her champion and she could not ask him to stay with her on a beached ship while her people, his soldiers, died.

He shifted and made to speak. She didn't want to hear it. No more reports, no more talk of the strange gifts these savages wielded against her kind.

"The *Malawa* arrived a few sun spans ago," she told him. "My old nursemaid was on board. She went to the Goddess before it made ground."

"Sanura's gone? My queen...I'm so—"

"Do you remember how she'd tell the story of the dog that bit me when I was a child?"

"I remember hearing you bit it back and wouldn't let go. Sanura had to call the Queen's Guard to pull you off the poor thing."

Taifa turned back to the beach, filled with the dead and dying in their thousands. "Sanura went to the Goddess on that ship, never knowing we found land, never knowing we escaped the Cull. They couldn't even burn her properly." The battle seemed louder. "I won't go back on the water."

"Then we die on this beach."

The moment had arrived. She wished she had the courage to face him for it. "The Gifted, the ones with the forward scouts, sent word. They found the rage." Taifa pointed to the horizon, past the slaughter, steeling herself. "They're nested in the Central Mountains, the ones dividing the peninsula, and one of the dragons has just given birth. There is a youngling and I will form a coterie."

"No," he said. "Not this. Taifa..."

She could hear his desperation. She would not let it sway her.

"The savages, how can we make peace if we do this to them?" Tsiory said, but the argument wasn't enough to change her mind, and he must have sensed that. "We were only to follow them," he said. "If we use the dragons, we'll destroy this land. If we use the dragons, the Cull will find us."

That sent a chill through her. Taifa was desperate to forget what they'd run from and aware that, could she live a thousand cycles, she never would. "Can you hold this land for me, my champion?" she asked, hating herself for making this seem his fault, his shortcoming.

"I cannot."

"Then," she said, turning to him, "the dragons will."

Tsiory wouldn't meet her eyes. That was how much she'd hurt him, how much she'd disappointed him. "Only for a little while," she said, trying to bring him back to her. "Too little for the Cull to notice and just long enough to survive."

"Taifa—"

"A short while." She reached up and touched his face. "I swear it on my love for you." She needed him and felt fragile enough to break, but she was determined to see her people safe first. "Can you give us enough time for the coterie to do their work?"

Tsiory took her hand and raised it to his lips. "You know I will."

CHAMPION TSIORY

Tsiory stared at the incomplete maps laid out on the command tent's only table. He tried to stand tall, wanting to project an image of strength for the military leaders with him, but he swayed slightly, a blade of grass in an imperceptible breeze. He needed rest and was unlikely to get it.

It'd been three days since he'd last gone to the ships to see Taifa. He didn't want to think he was punishing her. He told himself he had to be here, where the fighting was thickest. She wanted him to hold the beach and push into the territory beyond it, and that was what he was doing.

The last of the twenty-five hundred ships had arrived, and every woman, man, and child who was left of the Chosen was now on this hostile land. Most of the ships had been scavenged for resources, broken to pieces, so the Omehi could survive. There would be no retreat. Losing against the savages would mean the end of his people, and that Tsiory could not permit.

The last few days had been filled with fighting, but his soldiers had beaten back the natives. More than that, Tsiory had taken the beach, pushed into the tree line, and marched the bulk of his army deeper into the peninsula. He couldn't hold the ground he'd taken, but he'd given her time. He'd done as his queen had asked.

Still, he couldn't pretend he wasn't angry with her. He loved Taifa, the Goddess knew he did, but she was playing a suicidal game. Capturing the peninsula with dragons wouldn't mean much if they brought the Cull down on themselves.

"Champion!" An Indlovu soldier entered the command tent, taking Tsiory from his thoughts. "Major Ojore is being overrun. He's asking for reinforcements."

"Tell him to hold." Tsiory knew the young soldier wanted to say more. He didn't give him the chance. "Tell Major Ojore to hold."

"Yes, Champion!"

Harun spat some of the calla leaf he was always chewing. "He can't hold," the colonel told Tsiory and the rest of the assembled Guardian Council. The men were huddled in their makeshift tent beyond the beach. They were off the hot sands and sheltered by the desiccated trees that bordered them. "He's out of arrows. It's all that kept the savages off him, and Goddess knows, the wood in this forsaken land is too brittle to make more."

Tsiory looked over his shoulder at the barrel-chested colonel. Harun was standing close enough for him to smell the man's sour breath. Returning his attention to the hand-drawn maps their scouts had made of the peninsula, Tsiory shook his head. "There are no reinforcements."

"You're condemning Ojore and his fighters to death."

Tsiory waited, and, as expected, Colonel Dayo Okello chimed in. "Harun is right. Ojore will fall and our flank will collapse. You need to speak with the queen. Make her see sense. We're outnumbered and the savages have gifts we've never encountered before. We can't win."

"We don't need to," Tsiory said. "We just need to give her time."

"How long? How long until we have the dragons?" Tahir asked, pacing. He didn't look like the man Tsiory remembered from home. Tahir Oni came from one of the Chosen's wealthiest families and was renowned for his intelligence and precision. He was a man who took intense pride in his appearance.

Back on Osonte, every time Tsiory had seen Tahir, the man's head was freshly shaved, his dark skin oiled to a sheen, and his colonel's uniform sculpted to his muscular frame. The man before him now was a stranger to that memory.

Tahir's head was stubbly, his skin dry, and his uniform hung off a wasted body. Worse, it was difficult for Tsiory to keep his eyes from the stump of Tahir's right arm, which was bleeding through its bandages.

Tsiory needed to calm these men. He was their leader, their inkokeli, and they needed to believe in their mission and queen. He caught Tahir's attention, tried to hold it and speak confidently, but the soldier's eyes twitched like a prey animal's.

"The savages won't last against dragons," Tsiory said. "We'll break them. Once we have firm footing, we can defend the whole of the valley and peninsula indefinitely."

"Your lips to the Goddess's ears, Tsiory," Tahir muttered, without using either of his honorifics.

"Escaping the Cull," Dayo said, echoing Tsiory's unvoiced thoughts, "won't mean anything if we all die here. I say we go back to the ships and find somewhere a little less...occupied."

"What ships, Dayo? There aren't enough for all of us, and we don't have the resources to travel farther. We're lucky the dragons led us here," Tsiory said. "It was a gamble, hoping they'd find land before we starved. Even if we could take to the water again, without them leading us, we'd have no hope."

Harun waved his arms at their surroundings. "Does this look like hope to you, Tsiory?"

"You'd rather die on the water?"

"I'd rather not die at all."

Tsiory knew where the conversation would head next, and it would be close to treason. These were hard men, good men, but the voyage had made them as brittle as this strange land's wood. He tried to find the words to calm them, when the shouting outside their tent began.

"What in the Goddess's name—" said Harun, opening the tent's flap and looking out. He couldn't have seen the hatchet that took his life. It happened too fast.

Tahir cursed, scrambling back as Harun's severed head fell to the ground at his feet.

"Swords out!" Tsiory said, drawing his weapon and slicing a cut through the rear of the tent to avoid the brunt of whatever was out front.

Tsiory was first through the new exit, blinking under the sun's blinding light, and all around him was chaos. Somehow, impossibly, a massive force of savages had made their way past the distant front lines, and his lightly defended command camp was under assault.

He had just enough time to absorb this when a savage, spear in hand, leapt for him. Tsiory, inkokeli of the Omehi military and champion to Queen Taifa, slipped to the side of the man's downward thrust and swung hard for his neck. His blade bit deep and the man fell, his life's blood spilling onto the white sands.

He turned to his colonels. "Back to the ships!"

It was the only choice. The majority of their soldiers were on the front lines, far beyond the trees, but the enemy was between Tsiory and his army. Back on the beach, camped in the shadows of their scavenged ships, there were fighters and Gifted, held in reserve to protect the Omehi people. Tsiory, the colonels, the men assigned to the command camp, they had to get back there if they hoped to survive and repel the ambush.

Tsiory cursed himself for a fool. His colonels had wanted the command tent pitched inside the tree line, to shelter the leadership from the punishing sun, and though it didn't feel right, he'd been unable to make any arguments against the decision. The tree line ended well back from the front lines, and he'd believed they had enough soldiers to ensure they were protected. He was wrong.

"Run!" Tsiory shouted, pulling Tahir along.

They made it three steps before their escape was blocked by another savage. Tahir fumbled for his sword, forgetting for a moment that he'd lost his fighting hand. He called out for help and reached for his blade with his left. His fingers hadn't even touched the sword's hilt when the savage cut him down.

Tsiory lunged at the half-naked aggressor, blade out in front, skewering the tattooed man who'd killed Tahir. He stepped back from the impaled savage, seeking to shake him off the sword, but the heathen, blood bubbling in his mouth, tried to stab him with a dagger made of bone.

Tsiory's bronze-plated leathers turned the blow and he grabbed the man's wrist, breaking it across his knee. The dagger fell to the sand and Tsiory crashed his forehead into his opponent's nose, snapping the man's head back. With his enemy stunned, Tsiory shoved all his weight forward, forcing the rest of his sword into the man's guts, drawing an open-mouthed howl from him that spattered Tsiory with blood and phlegm.

He yanked his weapon away, pulling it clear of the dying native, and swung round to rally his men. He saw Dayo fighting off five savages with the help of a soldier and ran toward them as more of the enemy emerged from the trees.

They were outnumbered, badly, and they'd all die if they didn't disengage. He kept running but couldn't get to his colonel before Dayo took the point of a long-hafted spear to the side and went down. The closest soldier killed the native who had dealt the blow, and Tsiory, running full tilt, slammed into two others, sending them to the ground.

On top of them, he pulled his dagger from his belt and rammed it into the closest man's eye. The other one, struggling beneath him, reached for a trapped weapon, but Tsiory shoved his sword hilt against the man's throat, using his weight to press it down. He heard the bones in the man's neck crack, and the savage went still.

Tsiory got to his feet and grabbed Dayo, "Go!"

Dayo, bleeding everywhere, went.

"Back to the beach!" Tsiory ordered the soldiers near him. "Back to the ships!"

Tsiory ran with his men, looking back to see how they'd been undone. The savages were using gifts to mask themselves in broad daylight. As he ran, he saw more and more of them stepping out of what his eyes told him were empty spaces among the trees. The trick had allowed them to move an attacking force past the front lines and right up to Tsiory's command tent.

Tsiory forced himself to move faster. He had to get to the reserves and order a defensive posture. His heart hammered in his chest and it wasn't from running. If the savages had a large enough force, this surprise attack could kill everyone. They'd still have the front-line army, but the women, men, and children they were meant to protect would be dead.

Tsiory heard galloping. It was an Ingonyama, riding double with his Gifted, on one of the few horses put on the ships when they fled Osonte. The Ingonyama spotted Tsiory and rode for him.

"Champion," the man said, dismounting with his Gifted. "Take the horse. I will allow the others to escape."

Tsiory mounted, saluted before galloping away, and looked back. The Gifted, a young woman, little more than a girl, closed her eyes and focused, and the Ingonyama began to change, slowly at first, but with increasing speed.

The warrior grew taller. His skin, deep black, darkened further, and, moving like a million worms writhing beneath his flesh, the man's muscles re-formed thicker and stronger. The soldier, a Greater Noble of the Omehi, was already powerful and deadly, but now that his Gifted's powers flowed through him, he was a colossus.

The Ingonyama let out a spine-chilling howl and launched himself at his enemies. The savages tried to hold, but there was little any man, no matter how skilled, could do against an Enraged Ingonyama.

The Ingonyama shattered a man's skull with his sword pommel, and in the same swing, he split another from collarbone to waist. Grabbing a third heathen by the arm, he threw him ten strides.

Strain evident on her face, the Gifted did all she could to maintain her Ingonyama's transformation. "The champion has called a retreat," she shouted to the Omehi soldiers within earshot. "Get back to the ships!"

The girl—she was too young for Tsiory to think of her as much else—gritted her teeth, pouring energy into the enraged warrior, struggling as six more savages descended on him.

The first of the savages staggered back, his chest collapsed inward by the Ingonyama's fist. The second, third, and fourth leapt on him together, stabbing at him in concert. Tsiory could see the Gifted staggering with each blow her Ingonyama took. She held on, though, brave thing, as the target of her powers fought and killed.

It's enough, thought Tsiory, leave. It's enough.

The Ingonyama didn't. They almost never did. The colossus was surrounded, swarmed, mobbed, and the savages did so much damage to him that he had to end his connection to the Gifted or kill her too.

The severing was visible as two flashes of light emanating from the bodies of both the Ingonyama and the Gifted. It was difficult to watch what happened next. Unpowered, the Ingonyama's body shrank and his strength faded. The next blow cut into his flesh and, given time, would have killed him.

The savages gave it no time. They tore him to pieces and ran for the Gifted. She pulled a knife from her tunic and slit her own throat before they could get to her. That didn't dissuade them. They fell on her and stabbed her repeatedly, hooting as they did.

Tsiory, having seen enough, looked away from the butchery, urging the horse to run faster. He'd make it to the ships and the reserves of the Chosen army. The Ingonyama and Gifted had given him that with their lives. It was hard to think it mattered.

Too many savages had poured out from the tree line. They'd come in force and the Chosen could not hold. The upcoming battle would be his last.

INGONYAMA

Queen Taifa rushed from the main room of her cabin on the ship. Her vizier had interrupted a meeting with the Ruling Council, ushering her to the foredeck. Somehow, the savages had gotten around the Chosen's front lines and the Omehi were under attack.

The news had shaken the Ruling Council. They'd harried Taifa about her promise of dragons and she'd told them the coterie was nearing the end of its work. She reminded them she was a queen who kept her promises, hoping they couldn't tell how worried she was about keeping this one.

So as Taifa hurried after her vizier, she prepared herself. She would do what she could to win the battle, but she was no fool. If they survived the day, her council would look to leash her ability to rule. Then the real tragedy would come.

In all likelihood, the council would order the higher castes back to the remaining seaworthy ships. They'd try to save themselves by flee-ing, by abandoning the Lessers and leaving her people to their fates.

This, Taifa would not allow. It was not her way, but in a time of war, she could rule by fiat. She was no tyrant, but a good ruler would not stand by and watch her people be destroyed. A good ruler would not allow frightened fools to turn fear into folly.

The council needed leadership, not discussion, not consent, not compromise. Wasn't that how the military worked under her champion? Wasn't that how wars were won? Weren't the Chosen at war?

Her thoughts brought Tsiory to mind. She'd need him more than ever if she defied the Ruling Council. She'd need him, but he hadn't come to her after her decision to form the coterie.

She didn't want to think his absence a punishment, and she could order him back, but she wouldn't. Doing so would violate their unspoken rules. She was his queen, but he was her lover. With him, she wasn't looking for a subject. She wanted an equal. He couldn't be that in public, but in private they could blur the lines.

He's too stubborn, she thought, stepping onto the deck of the ship and wondering how he'd take it if she disbanded the council. He'd have to accept it, she decided, he'd have—

Queen Taifa Omehia of the Chosen didn't finish the thought. She was looking at her worst nightmare, made real.

The beach was overrun and her enemy was everywhere. She couldn't understand how so many of them had gotten past their front lines. She couldn't—a Chosen man died on the beach, his chest opened up by a heathen's spear. She looked away from the gruesome scene and saw two women, two of her people, run down by the natives.

"What happened?" she asked. Her Queen's Guard, her vizier, and her Ruling Council, trailing her, said nothing.

She heard a war cry and the thunder of hooves. It came from the far side of one of her broken ships, the ones foraged for wood and resources. From the ribs of the scavenged vessel pounded a dozen horses ridden by a unit of Enraged Ingonyama, and her heart stopped.

Tsiory was leading them. Tsiory was enraged.

"No," she said, her voice a whisper.

The Ingonyama smashed into the thickest fighting and cleaved through their enemies like a machete through grass. Savages scattered and died, but there were too few Ingonyama and too many savages.

"Gather the Gifted," Queen Taifa told one of her messengers. "I want Enervators down there. Have them hit as many of the savages as they can. Bring the KaEid to me. We need the dragons, now."

The messenger, an Edifier, entered a trance and sent out the orders.

"Oh Goddess," moaned Lady Panya as she took in the battle. "We're undone."

"Panya, you are a member of the Ruling Council," Queen Taifa told the Royal Noble without taking her eyes from Tsiory. "Carry yourself like one."

She couldn't believe he was doing this to her. Every time he engaged the enemy she died a little. If he fell...

"Where are the Enervators!" she yelled.

"There, Queen Taifa," Lady Umi said, pointing with one of her long-fingered hands, and Taifa saw them.

The Gifted were gathered too close together. Their positioning would reduce their effectiveness, but they were young, not fully trained. Her battle-tested Gifted were on the front lines. The same front lines that had been bypassed.

Taifa watched as the young women tried to spread out. She couldn't hear the call to attack. They were too far for that, but she felt hope when she saw their arms snap up with military precision. They might be young and untested, but it wasn't fair to think them unready.

The wall of protective soldiers surrounding the Gifted flowed to the sides, leaving the path between the women and their enemy clear. Even with the distance, Taifa saw the Gifted stiffen as their powers were made manifest and wave upon wave of shimmering energy sprang from their fingers to sweep toward the savages.

The heathens raced to the attack, colliding headlong with the enervating wave. All struck were felled, dropped to their knees, bellies, or backs, and made helpless. Instantly, the Gifted cut the flow of enervation, allowing their soldiers to charge and fall on the savages, hacking them apart. Taifa leaned forward, distaste for her bloodlust warring with gratification as she watched some of her enemies destroyed.

In the first days after landfall, it had been the Gifted, specifically the Enervators among them, who had won the beach for the Chosen. The savages had not seen gifts like enervation or enraging and didn't know how to fight against them.

It was different now. The enemy soldiers, having been taught many deadly lessons, were clever students, and one of their leaders split her fighters into several prongs and rushed her warriors into and among the Chosen soldiers. The young Enervators were inexperienced, scared. After their first successful attack, they splashed waves of enervation everywhere, often hitting their own men.

Chosen soldiers, the ones not immediately overcome by the savages' numbers or incapacitated by poorly aimed enervation, fought bravely and died badly. After that, it didn't take long for the savages to reach the Gifted. The women fled and were run down, their screams carrying across the sands to Taifa as barely heard cries that still felt loud enough to deafen.

Tsiory wasn't faring much better. Most of the Ingonyama who had ridden out with him were dead, and more savages spilled from the trees and onto the beach.

"Call for a surrender," Lady Umi said. "It might not be too late."

"We are Chosen," Taifa told her.

"Is that what they'll call us when we're all dead?"

Without sparing her a glance, Taifa said, "Guards, place Lady Umi under arrest. Throw her in the ship's prisons."

Two of her guards grabbed the ancient Royal Noble, her eyes wide with surprise.

"Are you mad?" Umi said, struggling against the iron grips of Taifa's guard. "Queen Taifa, what is this? Are you so determined to rule over the end of your people?"

"Remove her," Taifa told the guards, letting her gaze flicker over the faces of the remaining members of the Ruling Council. The council members remained impassive, but Taifa could tell her message had been received.

She returned her attention to the battle, despair ripping through her at a new threat. Savages had emerged from the tree line riding massive beasts. The beasts were blue-skinned, tusked, and horned, and they moved about on six tree-trunk-thick legs.

"What demon-spawn are those?" said Panya, her face filled with fear.

"Don't do it," whispered Taifa to the battlefield, to the Goddess, to Tsiory. "Please, don't."

Tsiory and his remaining Ingonyama charged.

"Queen Taifa," said the KaEid, leader of Taifa's Gifted. She was out of breath and accompanied by sixteen other Gifted. They must have run the entire way. "We're ready."

Taifa wasn't listening. She watched the charge, saw the collision of horse and horror-beast, Ingonyama and savage. Her nearest soldiers, both the gray-uniformed Ihashe and the larger black-garbed Indlovu, joined the fight.

Swords flickered, flesh and bone broke, men died, and their blood filthied the sands of this alien shore. The few Gifted near the fight, low-level Entreaters, did what they could. They grabbed hold of the minds of the six-legged beasts, turning them against their riders and the other savages.

The creatures bucked their riders, goring and trampling the tattooed savages. They stampeded, breaking the natives' war formations and giving Tsiory's Ingonyama brief reprieve. Still, the enemy was too numerous and Taifa could do nothing but watch as Tsiory fought and fought, until he took a horrible cut and went down.

"The dragons, my queen," said the KaEid.

"We call to them," Taifa ordered, weak with worry as she flung her soul to Isihogo, latching onto the KaEid and the rest of her Hex. As one, they sent out the distress call, and a breath later, she felt the dragons stir and take flight.

Hurry, she thought to herself. Hurry.

Tsiory was back on his feet. She wished she could see him more clearly. Hurry. Was that blood on his face?

A savage riding one of the six-legged monsters threw a spear, bone white and long hafted, at him. He slapped the projectile away and stabbed the monster in its foremost leg. It reared and threw its rider. Behind Tsiory, a savage stabbed for his spine. Taifa screamed, close to coming undone, but an Ingonyama protecting Tsiory knocked the attack wide and chopped the offender in half.

Hurry. In her mind, Taifa could feel wings beating through the thick and hot air. She could feel the dragon's blazing anger, its worry, its bitter hate. Hurry.

In Isihogo, where half her mind was, she saw the dim glow of a shrouded soul. It was not one of her Gifted. It was a savage, drawing energy to bring to bear on the battlefield. Using her real body, her real eyes, Taifa searched and found him. He was just inside the tree line, not far from where Tsiory fought. The heathen aimed his hands at the battle and the savages doubled in number.

Seeing this, one of Taifa's guards, breaching protocol, shouted in surprise. Taifa couldn't blame him. She'd never seen such a powerful gift. It had created new life, new warriors to fight for her enemies. The battle was lost. They could not win.

"There!" It was the same guard. Taifa looked where he pointed. One of the Enraged Ingonyama was slashing at the savages around him, his sword tearing through the hordes like they were nothing but air.

Taifa closed her eyes, blocking out the things her senses told her, so she could see with her soul. The Gifted savage was there, in Isihogo. He was pulling incredible amounts of energy and his shroud was about to collapse, but she couldn't wait for that.

It would have been impossible for any in her Hex, for any of her Gifted, but Taifa was of royal blood and it was not impossible for her. She split her mind in three, one-third watching the battle, one-third calling to the dragon, and the last third she used to attack the savage.

She drew more energy into herself and took aim. Across the distance, through Isihogo's mists, she fired. Her bolt burned a path through the underworld's fog like a comet across the night sky. It struck the heathen and, before he could react, expelled him from Isihogo, his link to the energies there broken.

Taifa heard shouts and gasps around her. She opened her eyes. The illusions of women and men that the Gifted savage had created were gone, but the enemies that remained, the ones of real flesh and blood, were still too many.

On the sands, Tsiory yelled something to his men. He was calling a retreat before they could be surrounded. If they could get to the ships, they might be able to reorganize.

A group of savages attacked. Tsiory fought them off, still yelling orders. He was hit once, twice, a few more times, and then he did something Taifa would not forgive for the rest of her days. He severed his connection to his Gifted and lost the enraging.

Taifa knew he did this to save the Gifted. She had seen him take blow after blow. She knew the amounts of energy the Gifted would have needed to pull from Isihogo to keep Tsiory safe. She knew he'd saved his Gifted's life by cutting the connection, and she didn't care.

Tsiory took a spear through the back. Taifa screamed as it went in and was still screaming when the head of the spear burst through his chest and leather armor. Taifa saw the look of surprise on her lover's face and saw it turn to pain, his mouth open, gasping for air that his torn lungs could no longer breathe.

The spear was ripped free, and he looked—she swore he looked right to her. Then she watched him fall, fall onto this cursed land's unnaturally white sand. There to stay, there to die.

Dimly, Taifa knew she had not stopped screaming, but that part of her felt far away when compared to the overwhelming presence of the dragon that had come into her range. She merged with it.

MONSTER

Taifa's vision, sense of self, and purpose split. She could see the battlefield from the air. The women and men, dying by the scores, looked small and insignificant.

She could see the two and a half thousand ships of her people, most of them cannibalized for parts, lying on the beach like the half-eaten quarry of some greater predator. She could see Omehi women and men scurrying from the makeshift shelter of those broken ships to the sand to the battle. She could see the ocean behind them all, stretching beyond the horizon, endless.

But it wasn't endless. She'd crossed it with what was left of the Chosen of the Goddess. She'd saved her people from eradication, and it was not their fate, having found this distant land, to die on its sands. Her people's sacrifice, Tsiory's sacrifice, would have purpose, and the natives, heathens one and all, would learn what it meant to oppose her.

The merging completed, and the dragon's power, its fury, flowed into Taifa. Quickly, she coiled these thick tendrils of consciousness and fashioned them into the ropes that would hold her tight to it.

It was then the savages on the beach spotted the creature, and through its eyes, she saw them turn and point. She could see their fear, smell it, and Taifa tapped the dragon's anger, stoking it, fueling it, turning the creature's need for vengeance into a compulsion.

It dove, spiraling toward the beach, and, using its gift, drew more from Isihogo than any human ever could. The dragon took its power from there, from the Goddess, and brought it into the world, igniting its blood. The beast burned, and when the heat threatened to overwhelm it, it blew fire, lighting the world ablaze.

Two dozen women and men, people of this strange land who thought to defend its shores from her, erupted in flame beneath the blast of Taifa's first attack. She could hear their screams as their lives ended in suffering. Her dragon, twice the size of her warship, with scales harder and sharper than bronze and blacker than tar, swept down and snatched two more of the heathens from the beach, slicing them to pieces in its massive claws, before landing on the sand. The dragon blew fire again, arcing the inferno across the gathered enemy horde.

Those hit by the blast were incinerated, and that was a mercy. The women and men on the attack's edges were seared by the heat, their flesh bubbling and sloughing off their bones. The ones this didn't kill choked to death on the fumes of the creature's acrid blood.

The daughters and sons of these white sands and withered trees, once so fearless in battle, mounted no more attacks. They fell back in terror, scrambling to flee, and in retreat, they faced the rest of the rage.

Taifa's Entreaters, the most powerful of her Gifted, merged with the two other dragons that answered their call. Together, the rage blew fire so hot that Taifa, only half in her body, still felt its heat from her warship.

The savages, the ones not dead or dying, ran for the safety of the trees, but Taifa pushed her dragon to follow. It rose into the air, chasing those who fled, burning down the tangled foliage that hid her enemies from her. The heat of its fires melted white sand to black glass and where the flames fell left nothing but ash.

As her dragon scorched the earth, Taifa prayed. She prayed to Ananthi, the Goddess, for two things. The first was forgiveness. She begged for it, knowing no mortal would have the grace to offer it, given what she was going to do to the people of this land. After that, after forgiveness, she asked for the power to destroy and the will to see it done.

"My queen," Taifa heard the KaEid say through the fugue of the merging. "They're retreating. We've won."

But Tsiory was dead and Taifa would honor him with a funeral pyre built from the corpses of her enemies. She urged her dragon on. She killed and killed, until her wrath cost the lives of most in her Hex, and until there was no one left to burn.

Exhausted, and with the shroud that masked her soul's light collapsing, Queen Taifa Omehia sacrificed one more Gifted, released the dragon, and folded back into herself. The beach was a smoldering ruin, and with a remnant of the creature's senses, she could smell the charred flesh, death, and stink of fear that suffused the sand.

She looked skyward as her dragon beat its way higher into the cloudless dusk, making for its nest. As it went, it belched a twisting column of flame, bright as the sun, and let out a mournful keen that almost started her crying. She refused to shed a single tear. The day was won, and though there were many more to come, the Goddess had already answered one of her prayers. Queen Taifa had the will to do what must be done.

Striding past the bodies of the Gifted she'd sacrificed and ignoring the horrified faces of her Ruling Council, Taifa turned away from the foreign land that would be her people's new home. She quit the ship's deck, descending stairs that took her from light to dark, and, finding herself alone in the false twilight, placed a hand to her stomach. She had so little of Tsiory left, but what she had she would protect.

"Let them think me a monster," the Dragon Queen thought. "I will be a monster, if it means we survive."

CHAPTER ONE

HEIR

One hundred eighty-six cycles later

Tau stumbled as he avoided the Petty Noble's swing. He tried to regain his footing, but Jabari was on him and he had to hop backward to survive the larger man's attack.

"Come on, Tau! You can't always run!" Aren yelled from outside the fighting circle, the words made indistinct by the booming of the ocean below.

Tau's sword arm was numb and he couldn't wait for the day's training to be done. "I'm baiting him," he lied as Jabari pushed him closer to the cliffs. Another step and Tau would be out of the fighting circle, losing him the match.

For Aren's benefit and to prove he'd learned something that season, Tau made a halfhearted attack, cutting for Jabari's leg, but Jabari bashed the sword aside and launched a counter, catching him on the wrist.

Tau yelped and, having had enough, was about to step out of the circle when Jabari leapt forward, swinging for him. Tau threw himself back, hoping to avoid being hit again, but his heel hit one of the stones marking the circle's boundaries and he went down with enough force to wind him.

He was on his back, near the cliff's edge, and the ocean was loud enough to set his teeth chattering. He glanced down and wondered if rolling over and letting himself fall could hurt any worse than his wrist and bruised ribs already did. Far below, the water roiled like it was boiling, crashing against itself and spewing froth. Tau knew falling into the Roar was death.

"Get up, Tau," Aren said.

He did, slowly and without enthusiasm.

"Look," Jabari said, pointing to the water.

Tau saw it then. From the ground, he'd missed the boat.

"Are they mad?" asked Jabari.

"What is it?" Aren asked.

Jabari pointed again. "A boat."

Aren Solarin, Tau's father and the man in charge of Petty Noble Jabari Onai's training, walked over. The three men watched the small watercraft bob in the churning waters. "They'll be lucky if they don't drown," Aren said.

"Can you tell who they are?" Jabari asked Tau.

Tau was known for his sharp eyes. "Doesn't look like one of ours…"

Aren looked closer. "Hedeni?"

"Maybe," Tau said. "I don't see anyone on it. It's heading for the boneyard…"

Waves drove the abandoned ship against the group of rocks, and it was dashed to pieces.

Jabari shook his head. "How did we do it?"

"Do what, nkosi?" said Aren, using the Petty Noble's honorific as he scanned the sinking wreckage.

"Cross it," Jabari said. "No ship we make now can sail more than a few hundred strides from shore. How did we cross all of it?"

"Nkosi, perhaps we should save the deep thinking for your tutors," Aren said, still trying to pick out details that might identify the boat as theirs or the enemy's. "My concern is your sword work. Let's go again."

Boat forgotten, Jabari smiled and moved to the opposite side of the circle, swinging his sword in looping circles. He loved fighting and couldn't wait to join the war effort.

Aren walked over to Tau, grabbed at the sword belt he was wearing, and pretended to be adjusting it for him. "You need to give everything to this," he said, almost too quietly for Tau to hear.

"To what end?" Tau asked. "I won't win. It'll only drag out the loss and end the day in pain."

"I'm not asking you to win. That's not solely in your control," Aren said. "I'm asking that you fight to win. Anything less is the acceptance of loss and an admission that you deserve it."

As Tau nursed his wrist, already swollen and likely to welt, his father finished tightening his sword belt, then stepped out of the fighting circle.

"At the ready!" Aren shouted.

Tau looked to the man he was about to fight. Jabari was taller, stronger, faster. The Petty Noble was born that way, and Tau couldn't see the point in giving his all to a game he knew was unfair.

"Remember, both of you," Aren said, "by attacking, you push your opponent to defend."

Tau wasn't listening. He'd spotted Handmaiden Zuri. She'd just crested the hill, arm in arm with Handmaiden Anya, and he was caught in the sway of Zuri's hips. It didn't hurt that the knee-high slit in her dress offered glimpses of calf. Tau smiled and Zuri's brown eyes danced as she raised a questioning eyebrow at him. Anya squeezed Zuri's hand and giggled.

Aren raised his fist. "Fight!"

Wanting to impress Zuri, and against his own better judgment, Tau ran at Jabari. The Petty Noble looked surprised by the aggression, but he rose to the challenge and attacked high, too high.

It was a rare opening, and thanking the Goddess for his luck, Tau lunged, sending out a strike that would have disemboweled Jabari if they were fighting with real swords instead of dulled practice ones. The attack didn't land. Jabari had baited him, expecting the reckless thrust, only to whirl away and off the killing line.

Hitting nothing, Tau stumbled forward and was still trying to get his feet under him when Jabari's sword belted him below the armpit. The blow knocked Tau further off-balance, drove the air from his lungs, and sent him tumbling, his fall accompanied by Handmaiden Anya's tittering.

Embarrassed and battered, Tau looked up to see that Zuri, though not laughing, hid a smile behind her hand. Worse, his audience had grown. A High Harvester was standing with the young women.

"Nkosi," said the Harvester to Jabari, sparing not even a glance for Tau. Tau thought this one's name was Berko. He was from the mountain hamlet of Daba, where they grew potatoes, tiny, mis-shapen potatoes. "I've come from the keep. Umbusi Onai as well as your father and brother are looking for you."

Jabari grimaced. He wasn't close with his older brother and Tau couldn't blame him. Lekan was self-impressed, condescending, and the single best argument against making firstborns heirs to anything.

"I'm training," Jabari told the Harvester.

"It's news from Palm."

That caught Tau's attention. News from the capital was rare.

"From Palm City?" asked Jabari.

"Yes, nkosi. It's the queen... She... Well, she's dead."

Anya gasped, Zuri covered her mouth, and Jabari looked dumb-founded. Tau turned to his father but found no comfort there.

"W-who leads the Chosen now?" Jabari asked.

Berko, rail thin but paunchy, with a patchy gray beard, stepped closer. "Princess Tsiora, the second, will be queen."

"Then, Palm City seeks ratification for her ascension," said Jabari.

Though it hadn't happened since he'd been born, Tau had heard of this. New queens asked the Petty, Greater, and Royal Nobles to accept their rule. It was a formality. The Omehia line had ruled since before the time of the Guardians.

Jabari looked to Tau's father. "Apologies, Aren. I have to go."

"Of course. Goddess guide you and may She also embrace Queen Ayanna in Her glory."

Jabari marched for the keep, and Anya, eager to hear the gossip, rushed after him, dragging Zuri with her. Tau didn't even have a chance to say goodbye.

"She's a child," said Berko.

Aren gave the man a look. "What?"

"Queen Ayanna's granddaughter? She's a child."

"Princess Tsiora is of age," Tau's father said.

"Cancer." Berko hawked and spat on the packed dirt of the fighting circle. "Hard to believe things like that can kill royalty. First Princess Tsiora's mother; now her grandmother. The line grows thin and the princess will need an heir or it'll be the end of the Omehias."

Tau spoke up. "There's her older brother, Prince Xolani, and there's the younger sister too."

"Brother doesn't count and Princess Esi is…unsettled," Berko told him. "Add all the raids to the balance and it's not a good time for a child queen." Berko lowered his voice. "Let's not forget, it's been a long time since our queens have been gifted." Tau had to lean in to hear the last part. "A bit strange that the Omehias can no longer call the dragons themselves, neh?" Tau saw his father stiffen. Berko saw it too. "I'm just saying, is all," he said, turning to call down the hill to the two Drudge waiting there near a ration wagon. "One Low Common portion and one full portion for Aren."

"I'm High Common," Tau said, annoyed he had to correct the man.

Berko shrugged. "And one High Common portion!"

One of the Drudge took two sacks from the wagon and tried to run up the hill. The scrawny man, dressed in little better than rags, couldn't keep the pace and slowed to a hurried walk before getting to them. Breathing hard from the brief run, he placed the sacks by Tau's feet and waited to see if the Harvester needed anything more to be done. He kept his head down and Tau couldn't blame him. The Drudge would be beaten if he met the eyes of his betters, and Tau wasn't sure the thin man could survive that.

The Drudge's skin was dark, almost as dark as Tau's, and his head was a mass of kinked hair. It was forbidden for them to shave their heads like proper men, and his poor state made it hard for Tau to tell what Lesser caste he'd originally come from.

"Tau," his father said.

Tau gathered up the sacks, making a show of examining their contents, but when the High Harvester looked away, he placed two potatoes near the Drudge. The man's eyes widened at the unexpected offering, and, hand shaking, he snatched them up, tucking them under the folds of his rags.

"Coming," Tau said to his father.

The man looked half-starved. He needed food. Tau did too, though. He trained most afternoons and that was hard to do on an empty stomach.

Jabari would have called him softhearted. He'd have said the man's lot was his own doing. The only Lessers who became Drudge were the ones who didn't make it into the real military and still refused to join the Ihagu.

Survival rates for Ihagu, the low-level, unskilled fighters who made up the front lines of every battle, were abysmal. Yet, most would say being a Drudge was a worse fate than an Ihagu's near certain death. When given the choice, almost everyone chose to fight. After all, a lucky few were assigned defensive duty and stationed near the fiefs or cities.

As Tau walked past with the rations, his father put a hand on his shoulder. "Kindly done," Aren whispered, little escaping his notice. Then, louder, he said, "Take the food home. I need to see the umbusi. With this news from Palm, we'll want to add more patrols."

Tau nodded and went to do as he was bid. He made it three strides when he heard Nkiru, his father's second-in-command, shouting from down the mountain. The muscular man, along with a full unit of the fief's Ihagu, was running. He was drenched in sweat, his sword's scabbard slapping at his thigh. It would have been humorous if not for the look on his face. He was terrified.

"Raid! Raid!" he yelled, struggling to be heard over the ocean's roar. "The hedeni are raiding!"

DUTY

Tau moved to his father's side as Nkiru arrived.

"Signal smoke, near Daba," Nkiru said, blowing hard.

"Daba?" asked the High Harvester. "Daba?"

Nkiru ignored him. "'Hedeni crossing fields,' that's the message. They must have landed a war party and climbed the cliffs. If they're in the farming fields it won't be long before they're in the hamlet."

Tau thought about the wrecked boat. It had been an enemy ship. He marveled at the stupidity and courage of sailing the Roar. How many had they lost to the waters in order to mount the raid?

"Did the message say anything about numbers?" Tau's father asked.

"No," Nkiru said. "But if they've come this far—"

"Send men. Send everyone," Berko pleaded. "You can't let them reach Daba."

Aren gave orders to the gathered fighters. "Nkiru, Ekon, take the men you have and head for the mountain barracks. Empty it out."

"Yes!" said Berko, frantic. "I'll go too. I have to get back home."

"I'll make for the keep," Aren said. "I'll gather the men there and ask the umbusi's Gifted to send an edification. We have to call in the military. This isn't a normal raid. If they've come this far, they've come in force. The fighters at the mountain barracks won't be enough."

"Aren . . . it's just us," Nkiru said. "Lekan won't let the keep guard come to Daba's defense. I just left him and he says it's too risky to send everyone. He's worried that the hedeni might also send raiders here, to Kerem."

Aren closed his eyes, drawing a slow breath. "Lekan is not right in this," he said. "If the hedeni sailed the Roar to get to us, they've come to do damage in force. They won't split their fighters and pick at us. They'll attack as one. They'll destroy Daba." He looked down the mountain, in the direction of the keep. "I have to speak with Lekan. We need the Gifted to call the military and we need enough men to defend the hamlet until the military arrives. We can't do that with just the men from the mountain barracks. We need the keep guard."

"He won't . . . ," Nkiru said, trailing off and knuckling his sword's pommel. "Lekan has already called for the military, but he also ordered me to tell you to lead Daba's defense. He says he'll see to the keep's safety. . . . Aren, he won't go to Daba, and he won't let the guards go either."

Berko shot looks at the men discussing the fate of his home. "What does this mean? What do we do?" he asked.

Aren looked to the sky. It was a cloudless day, merciless in its heat. "We defend Daba," he said. "That's what we do."

Nkiru's forehead was crinkled with lines of worry, but he turned to the men and did his best to sound eager. "You heard the inkokeli. Move!"

The fighters, Berko, and the two Drudge went up the mountain, making for the Taala path. It was the quickest way to the barracks and to Daba.

"Go home," Aren told Tau, placing a hand on his shoulder. "I'll see you when it's done."

He squeezed Tau's shoulder, patted it, and left. Tau stood there and watched his father follow the rest, the lot of them racing against what little time the people in Daba had, before the hedeni were among them.

He'd not seen his father that concerned in a long time. It meant Aren didn't think they'd hold Daba. It meant there was a damned good chance they'd all die.

"No...," Tau said. "Not because of Lekan. Not because of that coward."

He rushed to the closest bit of brush and hid his practice blade and ration sacks. He belted on his sharpened bronze sword, the one that had belonged to his father's father, and gripped its hilt. He felt the etchings his grandfather had made, spelling out the family name in a spiral that wound its way from pommel to guard. "Solarin," it read.

Steadied and feeling ready for the task ahead, Tau ran down the mountain, in the opposite direction his father had gone. He went to find Jabari. Lekan might be craven, but Jabari was as decent as Nobles came. He'd help. He'd tell his mother to order the keep's men to go to Daba, and that would stop Tau's father from getting killed.

Before long, the Onai's keep, the largest building in Kerem, came into view. It was two floors tall, had a central courtyard, and was surrounded by an adobe wall that was nine strides high. The adobe was smooth and that spoke to the Onai's wealth.

"Eh, what're you about, Tau?" a reedy voice asked from above.

Tau looked to the top of the fortifying wall. It was Ochieng, one of the Ihagu assigned to be a keep guard. Ochieng had always been a blustering oaf, and, a full cycle older than Tau, he'd already reached manhood. He hadn't passed the test to be part of the real military and had come back from the southern capital with his head low and prospects grim.

He'd been lucky; Tau's father spoke on his behalf, and on the strength of Aren's word, the keep guard took Ochieng as one of their own. Most of Ochieng's family were either dead or Drudge, and if Aren hadn't vouched for him, Ochieng would have followed in their footsteps. As it stood, Tau felt owed.

"Open the gate, Ochieng. I don't have time."

"Don't have time, neh? Where's your hurry?"

"Hedeni raid," Tau said, hoping the news would shock the guard to action.

"Just heard. What's it got to do with you?"

"I have to see Jabari."

"He know you're here?"

"What do you think?" Tau said.

"Don't know what you're fooling about," Ochieng muttered, disappearing behind the wall. A moment later, Tau heard the heavy latch on the bronze gate swing up and away.

"Hurry. In you get."

"Thanks, Ochieng."

"Didn't open the gate for you. Tell Aren I said hello."

Leaving the gate behind, Tau came to a juncture in the keep's paths and stopped. Jabari could be almost anywhere, and, worried he was making the wrong choice, he went toward the keep proper and Jabari's rooms.

He moved through the keep's yards at a brisk walk, head down, trying not to draw the attention of any of its handmaidens or administrators. Lessers in the keep tended to be women or, if male, they were higher caste than Tau. He'd stand out and didn't want to be stopped or, worse, prevented from getting to Jabari.

He sped up, eyes on the dirt, anxious to get where he was going, which was why he came near to knocking his younger half sister on her ass.

"What in the Goddess's... Tau?" said Jelani, unable to keep the surprise from her face. "Why are you here?"

"Hello, Jelani."

"Don't 'hello' me."

"Uh...how's Mother?"

"That'll depend," Jelani said, glaring at Tau like she'd found a maggot in her rations, "on what I tell her about seeing you here."

"I'm looking for...Jabari asked to see me."

Jelani squinted at him. "Jabari?"

"Yes, there's a raid in the mountains...the hedeni—"

"He's in the bathhouse. Find him and leave, before I tell my mother."

Our mother, Tau thought, inclining his head and hurrying back to the path he hadn't selected. He swore he could feel Jelani's beetle-black eyes on his back as he went. She hated having a half-low as a sibling. That's how she thought of him, half-low.

It made Tau want to yell that he was as High Common as she was. Status came from the woman who bore you, and his name was

Tafari, just like hers. It wouldn't have done any good. Jelani knew their mother wouldn't have anything to do with him, or Aren.

Pushing his sister out of mind, Tau stepped up to the bathhouse, opened its door, and was hit by a blast of hot scented air. "Jabari?" he said into the fog. He didn't dare go in. "Jabari?"

"Tau? That you?" said a familiar voice. "What are you about?"

He'd have only one chance to convince Jabari to help. "There's a fight coming," Tau said, "and if we don't do something, the people your family pledged to protect will die."

Tau heard water slosh around, and then Jabari appeared through the steam, towering over him, stark naked.

"What's this?"

Lekan hadn't told Jabari about the raid. Tau corrected that, telling him everything, then begging him to act. "Go to your mother," he said. "She's the umbusi; tell her the defense of Daba will fail without more men."

"Tau, I'm the second son. Lekan's the one being groomed to command our fief's men. She won't go against him on my word."

"Jabari—"

"She won't, Tau."

"We have to do something!" Tau said, struggling to keep his voice respectful.

"I know, I know. There's a fight coming and my family must protect the people of Kerem." Jabari clapped Tau's chest with an open palm. "I have it."

"Have what?"

"A plan," Jabari said.

RAID

"There," Tau said, pointing at a flickering light in the distance. "Do you see it?" The light was bright against the evening's darkness, but he was never sure how far Jabari could see.

"I see it," Jabari said. "They're burning Daba."

He picked up the pace, and Tau, lungs raw from running, struggled to keep up with his friend's longer strides.

He couldn't believe he'd gone along with Jabari's plan and tried not to think about what they'd find when they got to the hamlet. "What if this doesn't work?" Tau asked. "What if they don't come?"

"They'll come."

Before leaving the keep, Jabari had gone to its barracks and told everyone he was going to Daba to defend the hamlet. The highest-ranking guard in the room tried to reason with him, but he wouldn't be swayed.

It was clever. Jabari couldn't countermand Lekan's orders, but the guards were bound, on pain of death, to protect every member of the Onai family. By letting them know he was putting himself in harm's way, Jabari was forcing them to organize and send an honor guard to protect him. Tau hoped the extra men would be enough.

"Swords out!" Jabari said as they came over a hill. Tau pulled his weapon free, looked down on the hamlet, and froze.

Daba sat on a plateau with natural borders. The most obvious border was four hundred strides directly ahead. There, the plateau became mountainous again and the rock continued its climb to the clouds. To Tau's right, and roughly eight hundred strides away, was the hamlet's central circle. Beyond it, the plateau ended in a series of steep but scalable cliffs that dropped toward the valley floor. On Tau's left were the raiders.

The hedeni had come from the paths leading to Daba's growing fields, and they had burned half the hamlet already. The flaxen roofs of the larger houses were on fire, and in the night's dark, the flames silhouetted the fleeing women, men, and children of Daba.

The Ihagu, Aren's men, were fighting a series of skirmishes between the hamlet's tightly packed homes and storage barns. They were out-numbered and losing ground but could only go so far. The hedeni were herding everyone to the cliffs.

Tau didn't know what he'd expected, but this wasn't it. Scarred and disfigured, marked by the Goddess's curse, the hedeni held either bone spears or bone-and-bronze hatchets and chopped at the Cho-sen like woodcutters. They used no recognizable fighting stances and their attacks followed no rhythm or sequence. Worst of all, the Ihagu had been reduced to fighting just as savagely. Both sides hacked at each other, and every so often someone fell back, dead, wounded, or maimed.

"What is this?" Tau asked, his voice too low for Jabari to hear.

"There," Jabari shouted, running down, not waiting to see if Tau followed.

Tau tracked his path and saw three of the raiders harrying a woman and child. Jabari yelled, charged in, and Tau chased after him.

By the time he reached the flats, Jabari had already engaged two hedeni. They were circling to his sides, trying to get between him and the woman and child.

Tau went for the third savage, arcing his sword in a blow meant to decapitate, but the wretch brought up a hatchet and blocked the strike. The raider, a mass of dirty hair and mud-caked skin, blundered forward, swinging the weapon low, aiming for Tau's thigh.

Tau leapt back, fear lending him speed, and the hatchet's blade hissed past his kneecap, a hairsbreadth from taking his leg off at the calf. Blood pumping and desperate to shift the fight's momentum in his favor, Tau attacked. He stabbed out with his blade, aiming for the heart, and, as he'd been taught, kept his eye on the target, ready to react when the hedena dodged.

The collision, then, was a surprise. Tau's blade plunged from tip to hilt, into and through his opponent's chest. The savage had made no move to avoid the sword's point at all.

Tau didn't understand. The lunge had been obvious. It wasn't a serious killing blow. Anyone with decent training would have avoided it.

He looked into the face of the person he'd stabbed. The woman's eyes were big and wide, staring off at something in the distance. Her mouth, full-lipped, formed a gentle O, and the raider's hair, dreaded by lack of care, hung down her scarred face.

Tau pulled back in revulsion, but his blade wouldn't come free. The woman—or girl; he couldn't tell—cried out as the bronze ripped her insides.

She reached for Tau, perhaps to hold him close, hoping to halt the blade's bitter exit, and her fingers, bloody already, touched his face. She tried to speak, lips flecked with spittle, but her life ran its course, and she sighed before the weight of her lifeless body pulled Tau to the ground.

"Tau!" Jabari's voice sounded far away. "Are you hurt?"

"No...I—I hurt her, I think," Tau heard himself say.

"Get up. More are coming. We have to make it to the rest of our men," Jabari said. "Is that your blood?"

"Blood?"

"Your face."

Jabari and the woman and child were staring at him. The two hedeni men who had faced Jabari were dead.

"It's not me," Tau told them. "Not my blood."

"We have to go," said Jabari.

Tau nodded, struggled to jerk his blade free from the hedena woman's body, took a step, doubled over, and retched. Nothing came up. He retched again, his stomach still heaving when he forced himself upright. The child was staring at him. He wiped his mouth with the back of his blood-streaked hand. "Fine," he said. "I'm fine."

Jabari looked Tau over and began moving. "We have to go."

Tau followed, looking back once. The woman he'd fought lay in the mud like a broken doll. He'd never killed someone. He was shaking. He'd never—

"This way," said Jabari as the four of them weaved between huts and buildings, doing their best to avoid the fighting all around them.

Jabari was heading toward the barricade that the Ihagu had set up at the edge of the hamlet's central circle. They'd used overturned wagons, tables, even broken-down doors to block the paths that led to it. They were making a stand. They wouldn't last. There were too many hedeni.

"In here!" Jabari shoved the woman, who had picked up and was carrying the child, through the open door of a hut. He dashed in after her and Tau was right behind.

The hut was far larger than the one Tau shared with his father. It must belong to a High Harvester. Maybe even Berko, he thought, as the first hedena warrior burst through the doorway.

The man, hatchet out, made for Jabari. He didn't see Tau and Tau sliced at him, cutting into his arm. Hollering in pain, the raider stumbled into the nearest wall, and Jabari stabbed him in the gut.

The next hedena through the door had a spear. It was a woman. Tau knew the hedeni fought women alongside men. He knew it like he knew he had ten toes, but seeing a second female fighter gave him pause.

He should attack. He didn't. She thrust her spear at him and it would have taken out his throat if Jabari hadn't reacted, knocking it from her hands.

She drew a dagger from her belt. Tau remained rooted, noticing instead that she wore no armor. She had on an earth-toned wrap that covered her breasts and looped round her back, where it dove into loose and flowing pants. She was sandaled and her hands were bangled, the golden metal bouncing on slim wrists as she flicked her dagger at Jabari.

Jabari danced back. She came forward and Tau saw his chance. He was behind her. He just had to kill her.

On weak knees, Tau stepped forward and swung his sword as hard as he could, sending the flat of his blade hammering into the side of her head, knocking her down. Jabari followed up. He kicked the dagger from her hand and leapt on her, pressing his sword to her neck.

"You speak Empiric?" Jabari snarled. "How many ships did you land on our shores? How many raiders?" He pressed the point of his sword into her neck, drawing blood. "Speak or die!"

She looked frightened but spat in Jabari's face, closed her eyes, and began to spasm. Jabari scurried back, making distance, as her skin, already scarred by the Goddess's curse, bubbled and boiled. Blood erupted from her nose, ears, mouth, and eyes, and she began to scream and scream and scream. Then, like a candle blown, her life was gone, snuffed out.

The Lesser woman let out a choked gasp and turned away, holding the child closer. The child was crying. Jabari was still as stone, watching the dead savage with wide eyes.

He turned to Tau, mouth open, brow furrowed. "Demon-death," he said. "Your father told us it's what they do when captured. I didn't believe it."

Tau could think of nothing worth saying.

Jabari stood, wiped the savage's spit from his face, and stumbled away, using the wall for support. Tau, along with the woman and child, followed. Jabari bashed out a shuttered window at the back of the building and they crawled out of it, emerging in the middle of a circle of tightly packed homes.

In front of them was a storage barn, and they were still a hundred strides from the Ihagu's barricade. Jabari tried the barn's door. They hadn't been seen and could go through the long building. With luck, they'd come out a short run from the barricade and the rest of their people. Jabari broke the door's lock and they went in.

The storage barn was large, but its interior was tight, crammed with shelves, most empty. That was bad. It was almost Harvest, and if the storehouse was any indication, the Omehi would have trouble feeding their people.

As they slunk through, Tau began to have trouble breathing.

"What are you doing?" Jabari asked.

He couldn't stop panting and felt dizzy. "Too close," he said about the shelves and walls.

"What?"

Tau squeezed his eyes shut. It didn't help and he couldn't get enough air. He stopped moving, unable to keep going, when a cool hand slipped into his.

"It's a few more steps," the Lesser woman told him. "Keep your eyes closed. I'll guide you."

Tau nodded and stumbled after her.

"Ready?" asked Jabari.

Tau, still nauseous, opened an eye. They'd walked the length of the storehouse and were at its front doors. "Hurry," he said, wanting nothing more than to be outside.

"If the Goddess wills, we'll have a clear run for the barricade," Jabari said. "We make it there and we're safe."

Tau wasn't sure anywhere in Daba could be called safe. He'd seen how many hedeni were out there.

"Ready?" Jabari asked again.

The woman, eyes wide, nodded.

"Go!" Jabari yelled, kicking the door open.

Tau pitched his way through, fixated on being free of the barn, and ran into a startled hedena. He bowled the man over and Jabari stabbed the downed savage. There were four, maybe five other raiders, but they were fighting Ihagu. Jabari joined the fight, and Tau, head spinning, grabbed the woman's hand, pulling her away.

The barricade was just ahead and he made for it. The woman, carrying the child, was slowing him, and he could picture raiders running them down. Gritting his teeth, he tightened his grip on the woman's hand and pulled her after him. The men behind the barricade saw him coming. Tau thought he recognized one of them, but the blood caked on the man's face made it hard to tell.

As they hit the barricade, the man shoved aside a pile of over-turned chairs, making a climbable path for Tau and his two charges.

"Your turn now," the bloody-faced Ihagu yelled, after the woman and child were behind the ramshackle wall.

"Tendaji?" Tau asked.

"Tau?" said Tendaji. "What are you doing here? Never mind, climb up!"

"Can't. Jabari is still out there."

"Jabari's here?" The shock in Tendaji's voice spoke volumes.

Tau nodded, and with fear grasping at his guts, he forced himself to turn and run back to the fighting. He didn't have to go far. They were coming to him.

Jabari was bleeding through the arm of his gambeson and the other warriors carried one of their own.

"I'm well," said Jabari, waving off Tau's concern. "Let's get behind the barricade."

Tau helped carry the wounded Ihagu to the wall.

"Jabari?" Tendaji said, mouth dropping open. Tau had warned him, but actually seeing one of the heirs to the fief in the middle of a raid must have been too much for him to accept.

Tendaji helped lift the wounded man and then helped Tau and Jabari. Once the last fighter was over the barricade, they shifted the rubble back in place, blocking the way.

Behind it, Tau had hoped to feel safe. He didn't. Most of the Ihagu were injured, the ones fighting at the contested sections were being overwhelmed, and the townspeople were frantic.

Looking beyond the barricade, Tau saw that the hedeni were being heavily reinforced, and possibly a hundred more of them were racing down the paths and into the flats. Tau looked to Jabari, and for once, the optimistic second son looked worried. This was not a battle they could win. Even Jabari's honor guard, if they made it to Daba before everyone was dead, would only slow the inevitable.

"Get back, nkosi," Tendaji cautioned, remembering Jabari's hon-orific this time. "They're coming."

"Let them," Jabari said, stepping up to the barricade.

Tendaji looked like he would say more. Instead, he shifted, making room.

Tau stepped up on Jabari's other side. "For the queen," he said with little conviction, which was still more than he felt.

"For the Goddess," intoned Jabari and Tendaji together. The three men hefted their weapons. The barricade wouldn't hold and they wouldn't last, not against the number of hedeni coming for them, but they'd give a good accounting of themselves.

GUARDIANS

The first wave of hedeni hit the barricade, and it was madness. Tau stabbed and swung at limbs and faces. He sliced away someone's fingers, praying they'd come from an enemy's hand; was almost scalped by one of the raiders; and barely managed to push away a third before she could climb onto his side of the barricade.

It didn't matter. There were too many. There had always been too many. It was why the Goddess had blessed her Chosen with gifts. It was why she had given them dragons.

The burst of fire exploded a hundred strides in front of the barricade, singeing Tau's eyebrows. He threw himself back, away from the searing heat, and as soon as he regained some semblance of sense, he saw that Jabari and Tendaji were on the ground too. Tau tried to speak. His spit had been cooked away.

"Guardians!" yelled a hoarse voice from farther down the barricade. "Guardians!"

His vision swimming, Tau looked up and saw his first dragon up close. The behemoth, its body a mass of pure-black scales that drank in light and twisted the eye, ripped through the air. Tau watched it course toward the hedeni, sinuous tail trailing behind, lashing the smoke from Daba's fires to hazy shreds.

When it was close enough, the black creature opened its maw

and lit the evening with a twisting pillar of sun-bright flame, thick as three men. Tau tottered to his feet and climbed the barricade, watching the dragon's chain of fire explode against the ground. The hedeni who were hit were vaporized, and the dragon flew on, past Daba's plateau, turning for another pass.

"Tau?" said a voice he would recognize anywhere.

"Father," he said, turning to face Aren Solarin.

"Why, Tau?" his father asked. "Why?"

Tau's mouth opened and closed, no words coming.

"After I heard about the raid, I sought him out and ordered him to accompany me," Jabari lied. "It's my duty, as son of the umbusi, to fight with my mother's men. I know I'm not yet an Indlovu, but this is my place, and I couldn't come alone."

Aren eyed Jabari and shouted to the nearby listeners. "Shore up the barricades! The Guardians won't do us any good when the hedeni are mixed in with our own people." The gawkers snapped into action. "Jabari, as inkokeli of your mother's fighters, your place is best decided by me. By coming here, you've risked your life."

Jabari was forced to nod, accepting as strict a chastisement as Aren could give him. Tau looked down and away. The words were also meant for him.

"Please, Aren, accept my apologies," Jabari offered. "I'm only doing what I believe I must." He lifted his chin and seemed to stand straighter. "I also went to the keep barracks. The guard knows I'm here. They'll send men."

Aren grunted. "Ill-advised, but smartly done. My men and I thank you for it. Now, stay back from the fighting." He marched away to give his men more orders. "It would break my heart to have to tell your mother that you'd died." More words meant for Tau.

"Ihagu," Aren shouted. "Form up and help the townspeople carry what they can." Everyone began moving. "If the Gifted have enough reason to call the Guardians, it means we must run."

"Run?" Jabari asked Tau.

The roar of several hundred foreign voices answered in Tau's place, and the two men stepped onto the barricade in time to see the full force of hedeni raiders charging in their direction.

"Goddess...," said Tendaji, his voice little more than a whisper against the howling tumult racing their way.

"Away from the barricade," ordered Tau's father. "Run. Now!"

Jabari was off the barricade first, Tendaji and Tau right behind. Needing little encouragement from the Ihagu, the townspeople abandoned everything but their loved ones, and they ran too.

"We're being herded," shouted Jabari. "When the flats end, we'll hit the cliffs. There are no paths this way."

The raid had been well planned. The initial attacking force was large, but not too large. The Ihagu and townspeople had been led to believe they could hold Daba and had willingly trapped themselves with their backs to the cliffs. Once they'd done that, the hedeni launched their real attack, proving Tau's father's worst fears. This was no raid; it was an extermination.

The Guardian made a difference. It would thin the hedeni's numbers, but like Aren had said, if the savages got in among the Chosen, the dragon would have to hold its fire or burn the people it had come to save. Tau thought this through and knew what would come next.

"Ihagu," his father shouted. "Form up, battle lines."

It was the only reasonable choice. The Ihagu would stand and fight. They'd slow the hedeni enough to allow the townspeople some chance at escape.

Tau stopped running and turned to face the horrifying mass of enemy flesh, with their sharpened bronze and bone. Tendaji was beside him, his presence a surprising comfort. His father ran up as well.

"Jabari, Tau," he said. "I need you to guide the townspeople down the mountain. Take them to safety."

"You ask too much, Aren," Jabari replied. "I'll be no help to them and you can't save me from this fate. I'll stay, just like every other fighter here."

Conflicting emotions played across Aren's face. Tau saw pride and fear warring with each other. He'd been trying to save them.

"We'll show them what it means to be Chosen, Father," Tau said, his hands shaking.

"So we will," Aren said, holding Tau's eyes with his, before turning to yell his orders to the rest. "Tighten the lines. Stand firm.

Remember, the men to your left, to your right, they're your sword brothers. Keep them safe and they'll do the same for you."

Aren stopped there, waiting for the right moment. It came quickly. "For the Goddess!" he bellowed.

"For the Goddess!" they screamed back as the hedeni front lines smashed into them.

WARRIORS

The fighting was a nightmare of bronze and blood. Weapons flashed in and out of Tau's sight; he fought wildly, yelled himself hoarse, received a shallow but biting cut to the leg, and was pulled back by Nkiru, his father's second-in-command. Tau tried to thank him, but the older warrior had moved on, his sword swinging at anything not Chosen.

Tau spotted his father and Jabari, and, slowed by his weakened leg, he pushed his way back to the front lines. Tendaji was beside him, until he wasn't, the bitter fighting splitting them up.

Afraid of being separated from the Ihagu, Tau tried to get closer to his father and slipped. He went down and was nearly trampled by the press of women and men trying to kill one another. He pushed himself to a knee, the head of a spear whizzed past his ear, and, blindly, he punched his sword at the spear holder, missing his mark but coming close enough to make the fighter curse and fall back into the clot of hedeni.

He scrambled to his feet and glanced down at what had made him fall. It was Tendaji, his head crushed. Tau's stomach lurched and he stumbled away from the body, bumping into one of Aren's men, who sliced him across the arm with an errant swing.

The cut was not a bad one, but Tau's arm lit up in a line of pain. He hissed at the sting of it and found he was taking rapid, shallow breaths that didn't help at all. His sight also seemed to be going, his vision closing in at the edges with black and red.

Panicked, in pain, and afraid he was going blind, he pushed back and away from the thickest fighting. He was about to flee, run down the mountainside with the townspeople, when a hedena attacked the Ihagu beside him.

The Ihagu was wrestling a hatchet from another raider and didn't see the spear coming for his spine. He'd die without even knowing what killed him. Tau tried to call out a warning as he leapt forward, but nothing came out. His voice was gone.

He crashed into the spear-wielding savage and they went down, struggling, teeth bared, growling; then a sword flashed over Tau's shoulder and into the hedena's cheek, tearing the man's face in two. The hedena gurgled, scrabbled at him, and went limp as Aren took Tau's arm, hauling him to his feet.

"Back," his father said, his sword point dragging in the dirt. "Their attack is failing."

Tau, blood and muck coating him, looked for the man he'd tried to save. He found him nearby, on the ground and dead. Tau stared at the body. It didn't make sense. He'd been alive a breath ago.

"The Ihashe and Indlovu are here," his father told him. "Goddess be praised."

Tau looked past the skirmish seething around him, and out there among the savages, he saw them—the might of the Chosen military.

Battling the hedeni were Ihashe, the elite fighters drafted from the Lesser castes, and Indlovu, the larger and more powerful Noble caste warriors. They all fought fiercely, but the main prong of the Chosen counterattack was led by a giant. He wore bronze-plated leather armor painted red and black. He had a shield on one arm and a shining bronze sword in the other hand. He was an Enraged Ingonyama.

The Ingonyama was close to twice Tau's height, his arms bulging with muscle, and he moved faster than should have been possible for someone his size. He fought like a god.

"Hold the line," Tau's father ordered the Ihagu. "The military are here!"

In the time it took Aren to speak, the Ingonyama had cut his way through an entire line of hedeni, whipping his sword around hard enough to slice through two men in a single blow. Three more savages attacked and he belted the first away with his shield, kicked the next in the chest, and with the pommel of his sword, cracked the third's skull like it was a rotten nut.

"Everyone, toward the Gifted! Move!" shouted Tau's father, and the Ihagu beat a hasty retreat, running to the grouping of women in black robes near the cliffs.

"Incredible," Jabari said, pointing to the Ingonyama. "He's incredible."

As kids, they would play at being Ingonyama, and Tau hadn't forgotten Jabari's heartbreak when Lekan, catching them at it, taunted his younger brother with the truth. Jabari's blood, like that of all Petty Nobles and lower castes, was too weak to enrage.

"Faster!" said Aren, yanking on Tau's gambeson.

They were near enough to the Gifted that Tau could see them, though not well. There were eight of them, in their traditional coal-black and flowing robes, and they were guarded by a ring of warriors. The Gifted had their hoods up, and the gold necklaces they all wore shimmered with light from the hamlet's guttering fires.

Having reached a measure of safety, Aren's men let their exhaustion take hold. Some dropped to their knees, and one scrawny Ihagu sat on the ground, staring at nothing. The man beside him had his sword up, as if expecting his companions to turn on him.

Tau sought out the Ingonyama. He was there, in what was left of Daba, destroying all he faced. Around him, his Indlovu dealt death like it was a choreographed dance. They, along with the Ingonyama, were the Chosen's most devastating fighters.

Tau glanced at Jabari, who had found water and was drinking, spilling much of it. It was hard to believe that nothing more than a test and time separated the optimistic young Noble from being a full-blooded Indlovu. Jabari would test soon, and if he passed, he'd become an initiate of their citadel, train for three cycles, then go to war as one of them.

Tau's father wanted the Lessers' equivalent for him. He wanted Tau to test for the Ihashe, train at the closer of the two fighting schools reserved for Lessers, and serve in the military, just like he had. Aren's service was what made it possible for him, a Low Common, to lead their fief's Ihagu.

Before Tau was born, his father had trained to be an Ihashe and had fought as one, serving the military's mandatory six cycles. It was in his final cycle of service that he met and fell in love with Imani Tafari, a beautiful, strong-willed High Common. He wooed her, and with his service complete, they ran away to Kerem, to escape her father's wrath at the poor match.

In Kerem, Aren's Ihashe background was valuable and he was made second-in-command of Umbusi Onai's Ihagu. His wife did even better, landing a position in the keep.

Tau was born soon after, but in the first few cycles of his life, Imani grew weary of living like a Common. She left Aren. She left Tau too.

With the woman he loved lost to him, Aren gave himself over to two things: raising Tau and being the best fighter in the fief. In time, he came to lead the Ihagu, and when Jabari was old enough, the umbusi asked Aren to train him.

After Lekan, her firstborn, failed his testing, she couldn't afford to hire an Indlovu teacher for Jabari. Tau's father, though a large step down from an Indlovu, was the next best thing. Aren accepted without hesitation. Teaching Jabari meant he'd have time to train Tau as well.

Tau knew it was the best Aren could do to give him a solid start toward a good future, but in a burning hamlet, surrounded by the dead and dying, he was having a difficult time believing there was anything good about the violent path his father had prepared for him.

Zuri would have sucked her teeth, rolling her eyes at him. Since becoming a handmaiden, she had little time and less patience for Tau's bouts of self-pity. Still, a smile would have followed the eye roll, and that would make everything better. She always made everything better, he thought, as a horn sounded across the flats, snatching him away from her memory and returning him to the nightmare of Daba.

At the far edge of the hamlet, a hedena held a horn. He blew it again, three short blasts followed by a longer one, and Tau prayed it was a call to retreat. Something felt wrong, though. It was the man beside the horn blower.

"What is it?" asked Jabari, startling Tau. He hadn't heard him approach.

"The man beside the one blowing the horn," Tau said. "I think that's their inkokeli."

"What does he look like?"

"He's tall, almost the height of a Petty Noble, and well built. He's wearing more than they usually do, and he's carrying one of those bone spears. He's... he's burned, not just cursed. It looks like he's been through a fire. Half his face is a ruin."

"They aren't leaving."

Jabari was right. They weren't. They were doing the opposite.

The hedeni, hearing the horn's notes, came together but did not rush the barricade or the military men facing them. As one, they attacked the Enraged Ingonyama, ignoring the fighters around him.

"Stop them, Amara!" the Gifted nearest to Tau said to another black-robed woman.

The one named Amara lifted her hands, aiming past Tau at the charging hedeni. "They're too far. It'll splash," she said.

"Try, damn you!" said the first Gifted, and Amara did.

Energy, like pulsing waves of heat, began to radiate from her fingers, thickening as it flew out and away. Enervation, Tau thought with wonder, before the edge of it struck him and the world disappeared.

VICTORY

Once, when he was younger, Tau climbed down the cliffs of Kerem to the beach below. He was with several other boys, and one of them dared him to go into the ocean, up to his waist. He said no and they called him a coward.

Tau made it four strides in and, with the water swirling around his knees, was swept off his feet and dragged out.

He was sucked under, pummeled and crushed by the ocean's fury. He lived only because it was low tide and the water so close to the beach was shallow. The other boys had made a chain of arms to reach him, pulling him from the churning swell.

Being blasted by the Gifted felt like drowning in the ocean. It was as if Tau's body was being dashed to pieces while the world around him warped and spun, and when the spinning stopped, things got worse.

Tau saw Daba, but everything was different. The colors had been torn away, leaving the hamlet, earth, and sky in shades of gray. An unnatural wind buffeted him, shrieking, burying the other sounds, while impenetrable mists obscured anything farther than twenty strides away.

Tau could see what had to be the other men who had been standing near him, but he couldn't make sense of what he saw. The men, all in varying degrees of distress, were glowing with golden light. Tau looked down at himself. He was glowing too, and the glow had attracted something from the mists.

The creature was hidden and indistinct, but Tau could see more than enough. It moved in a lurching run on two feet, its balance aided by club-like hands on arms so long they could touch the ground. It had a flat face, red eyes, and a slavering mouth, and its skin seemed diseased.

The monster had Tau in its crimson gaze and roared. Tau couldn't make himself move, and it came for him, careening out of the mists, reaching for him with misshapen hands. Tau's legs gave out, and he opened his mouth to scream, fell and kept falling, through the ground, beyond the mists, beyond its grasp.

Pulling in air, ash, and the stench of blood, Tau reeled. He was on his knees, his mind on fire as fear unlike anything he'd ever known thundered through him. He felt warm wetness soak his trews and soiled himself. He didn't care, couldn't care. It was enough not to collapse into the battle-churned muck.

The men around him were similarly affected, and from the corner of his eye, Tau saw that many of the hedeni were also down.

"Tau?" It was his father.

"Da?" Tau said.

"Be at ease. It'll pass. It'll pass."

Tau's head pounded, but he looked to the Gifted anyway. Amara was still pushing out the wave of twisted energy. His father had pulled him out of the way and, Tau realized, he'd done it just in time. Amara's wave of enervation had forced Tau's soul into the underworld, where one of its demons had almost gotten him.

His head was a muddle, but Tau thought he understood. The Gifted was trying to disable enough of the hedeni to allow the Ingonyama to flee. Her efforts weren't enough. She'd missed too many with her powers, and the Ingonyama, bleeding from a hundred cuts, found two attackers taking the place of each one he killed.

"I can't hit more of them," Amara said. "I can't!"

"He has to drop the enraging," the other Gifted said, "or Nsia dies."

The Gifted needn't have worried. The Ingonyama bellowed, killed another man, and stepped back, and then there were two flashes of light. The first flared around his body, and when it vanished, so did the effects of the enraging. The man shrank into himself, diminishing in height, bulk, and strength.

The second flash of light came from farther up the flats, in the half-closed doorway of one of the abandoned homes. As if waiting for this, the horn blower fired off two sharp blasts and a group of hedeni made for the house.

The ones who remained finished off the Ingonyama. He was stabbed by spear and hatchet. They opened his belly, then cut his head from his shoulders and held it aloft.

Amara had tears in her eyes and the Gifted woman beside her cursed, raising her hands to the sky. Her robes fell back from her wrists and Tau heard the dragon roar.

It circled, the Gifted twitched her fingers, and, blowing fire, the dragon dove for the hedeni who were running for the home. The slower among them died in the inferno as the beast careened past, but the rest made it, went inside the home, and came out with what they sought. The hedeni had captured a Gifted.

"Nsia!" the Gifted communing with the dragon shouted.

Nsia, being dragged from the building, pulled something from her robes that glinted. It was a knife. There were too many for her to fight off, but it still surprised Tau when she didn't try.

Instead, she reversed her hold on the blade and made to plunge it into her chest, but one of her attackers was too quick. He slammed a spear into her arm and the knife fell from her deadened fingers. She tried to fight then, mouth open to scream, but one of the hedeni struck her across the temple, she went limp, and they carried her off.

They rushed her toward the warlord with the burned face, and Tau checked the skies. The dragon was turning for another pass but wouldn't make it in time. The horn blower, standing beside the warlord, lifted his instrument and blew a final note, and the hedeni retreated, ending the raid on Daba more suddenly than it had begun.

A few of the Chosen sent up a cheer. Most of the townspeople were safe, the Ihagu had held until the real military arrived, and, once again, the Chosen had beaten back their enemy. The cheer was almost loud enough to drown out the sounds of choking.

It was one of the Gifted. Not the one who had skimmed Tau with her enervating blast and not the one directing the dragon. This Gifted had stood quiet and still, surrounded by soldiers, and far from combat. She was convulsing and coughing up blood, her skin bubbling and bursting. It looked like she was being torn to pieces from the inside out. It looked like what had happened to the hedena Jabari had captured and questioned.

A soldier took hold of her and, with tenderness, helped her to the ground. The other soldiers tightened the circle around her, blocking Tau's view. He could still hear, though. He could hear her dying, and he started toward them, thinking to help, when a hand fell on his shoulder.

"No," his father said. "That's Gifted business."

"She's dying."

The choking Gifted had gone quiet.

"Come," his father said. "We won."

CHAPTER TWO

PLANS

Tau saw the hedena's face, reliving the moment he killed her. In his dreams, she did not die silent. She screamed, deafening him, crushing him with her hate. He woke near midday, unsure he'd slept at all.

"You'll feel raw," his father said, stoking their hut's cook fire. "During a fight your blood's up and your body does everything it can to keep going. When the danger passes, it shuts down." He offered Tau the vegetables he'd boiled. Tau waved them off.

"Eat," Aren said. "You'll be training today."

Tau didn't feel like training and thought that if he never touched a sword again it would signal a life lived well.

Aren must have seen something in his face, because he looked away from Tau and stared into the pot's murk. "I wish I could give you more," he said. "I wish..." His voice broke, and he rubbed the back of his hand against his mouth, clearing grime that wasn't there. "Tau... you need to know I'm going to push you. You test for the Ihashe soon, and that's what I thought I was preparing you for, a test. I'd forgotten how bad things can get. I'd forgotten how little of this has to do with sword forms, exercises, or techniques."

Aren reached out, coming close to putting a hand on Tau's shoulder. He let it fall short, making a fist.

"I'm teaching you how to kill," he said. "And I need to teach you how to be good enough at it to survive."

Tau nodded. It was what his father wanted.

"It'll be twice the training sessions from now until the testing. We'll add mornings to our normal afternoons. I have my duties, so your mornings will be with Nkiru and some of the other men, the ones with a good head for sword work." Aren stood, reminded Tau to eat, and left.

Tau didn't eat. He was supposed to meet Jabari and went to buckle on his sword belt and sword. Aren had made him clean his gear before letting him sleep, but Tau could still see it on the bronze. He could still see all the places the blood had been.

When he arrived for his afternoon training, Jabari was already in the fighting circle. "Tau!" he said.

"Well met, nkosi."

"I feel like a mountain fell on me. Could hardly get out of bed. I've pain in places I didn't know were there." The Petty Noble smiled. "I nearly didn't have to worry about any of that, though. I had to face my mother this morning. I thought she'd kill me."

"Guess not?" Tau said, earning a laugh.

"She'd heard Aren's report before seeing me. She was angry, very angry, but proud. You should have seen Lekan! He had to stand next to Mother, listening to her praise me. He looked like he'd be sick." Jabari's eyes glittered. "I could get used to this hero thing. Jabari Onai and Tau Tafari, the Chosen's most feared warriors!"

"From your lips to the Goddess's ears," Tau told him as he lifted his practice sword and stepped into the fighting circle.

Jabari smiled. "May we always be pleasing in Her eyes," he intoned. "At you!" he said, attacking.

No one came to instruct them. Aren and his men would have a busy few days as they and the rest of the fief recovered from the raid. Aren always said the toughest part of a battle was afterward.

Part of his duty as inkokeli was to travel to the homes of the men who'd gone to the Goddess. Tau didn't want to think about him visiting Tendaji's family. He couldn't imagine having to tell Tenda-ji's wife she'd never see her husband again.

"What whirls in that head?" Jabari asked.

They were sitting and sweating on the edge of the fighting circle. Jabari had gotten the better of Tau. That was normal. The ease with which he had done it was not.

"I can't get past last night," Tau said.

"Of course not."

"Did you sleep?" Tau asked.

"Barely," Jabari said. "The rush hadn't left me. I actually considered waking Lekan to talk to him about the battle. Can you believe that? Lekan!"

Tau slumped. "Not sure he would have appreciated it."

Jabari laughed again. "As you say! Well, I'm not sure I could swing a blade of grass. I'm for the keep. Father suggested to Mother that Lekan and I should help the rebuilding effort at Daba. She agreed and I need to figure out when works best."

"I'd like to help, if you don't mind," Tau said.

"Kind of you. We'll do it together." Jabari stood. "I'll let you know when we make the first trip over."

"Do you think...Will they come back?"

"Don't know. They don't usually attack the same place, but they don't usually raid with that large a force either. Not a good start to the new queen's reign. It's also..." Jabari's hesitation was unusual. He was always certain. "When Aren reported to my mother, he told her they'd identified five hedeni tribes among the dead, but the tribes don't raid together. They join forces in the Wrist out of necessity. It's the front line of the war. In raids, though, the tribes go it alone." Jabari shook his head. "I'll never understand the savages. They're separate races. They feud with each other. But, they also cooperate and...mix." Jabari's distaste dripped off the last word.

The Chosen had been surprised when they'd discovered the hedeni were several races of man, each with unique gifts. They'd been shocked to learn that the races mixed, polluting their bloodlines, risking those gifts. Some in the Sah priesthood preached that it was this profane behavior that caused the Goddess to curse them.

"They're allying for raids now?" Tau asked.

"Let's hope last night was unique."

"From your lips," Tau said, eliciting a nod from the Petty Noble.

Jabari reached over, placed his hands behind Tau's head, and pulled him close. Their foreheads touched. "Whatever comes, we're sword brothers. We'll face our tests as the Chosen have always done, with sharp bronze." He let go, slapped Tau playfully on the back of the neck, stood, and walked off toward the keep, whistling.

Tau prepared to leave. His body ached, but there was a nervous energy in him that wouldn't let him rest, and as much as he didn't feel like "playing sword," he welcomed the distraction the exercise would give.

Groaning, he limbered up and pulled his blade free of its scabbard. He went through his forms, trying to be as perfect as possible, and, blinking sweat from his eyes, he made himself move faster and faster.

Tests, he thought, always tests. So much of Chosen culture revolved around fighting and tests, but he didn't want to spend a cycle of his life at the Southern Ihashe Isikolo, sparring with other wood-headed brutes, just so they could all spend a tenth of their lives on the front lines of an unending war. He didn't want to kill women and men he'd never met and, equally important, he didn't want them to kill him.

He'd never even... Well, he shouldn't imagine Zuri like that. He did, though. He did some nights, picture them married, behaving as married people might. Tau's face felt hot, hotter than the sun's heat seemed to merit.

Imagining would be all he'd ever get, if he went to war and couldn't come back for six cycles plus one more for training. Seven cycles away, would Zuri even remember him? Even if she did, Ihashe weren't known for making the best husbands, and after one battle and all the nightmares that had come with it, Tau could understand why. It didn't mean he was about to forgive his mother for leaving them for a pretty-faced and soft-handed man from the Governor caste, but he couldn't pretend he didn't understand why she'd done it.

There was no love lost between Aren and Makena, his mother's fancy husband, but the man did make his mother happy, and Tau didn't want to begrudge her that. Being happy was all anyone wanted. He wanted to be happy. He thought he could be, if Zuri would have him.

He swung his dull practice sword harder, trying not to envy Makena. The man was several castes above Tau, and it always seemed like his life had been easy. He hadn't even had to fight in the war or be made a Drudge. The lucky bastard passed his Ihashe testing but was injured badly enough to be dismissed. He was allowed to go back to his home to serve as an administrator instead of a warrior.

Of course, Aren didn't think it was luck. He said the way Makena limped and the kind of break in his leg wasn't the sort you got from training or a fall. It was, Tau had heard Aren say after a few drinks, the kind of injury a man got when he felt a crippled leg was a better thing than honorable service.

Tau swung for the neck of his pretend opponent. His father could look down on it all he liked, but the outcome didn't seem so bad. Makena got to avoid the war and marry the woman he loved. As much as Tau admired his father, given a choice, he'd take Makena's life.

Tau stumbled and almost fell as the realization hit him like a thrown rock. He did have a choice. His best friend was the umbusi's second son. His mother and her husband were two of the umbusi's chief administrators. So long as Tau passed the Ihashe test, he would have fulfilled his duty and could not be made a Drudge.

And if he happened to be horribly injured shortly after the test... well, that would be a shame. He'd have to come home to Kerem, his family... and Zuri.

Tau exhaled, releasing tension he'd held for so long he'd forgotten it was there. He had a plan that could solve all his problems, and the thought filled him with relief and peace. It didn't last long.

Shame chased away the sense of calm he'd only just found. He was Aren Solarin's son, and avoiding his duty through deceit and selfishness was beneath him. His father had taught him better. That should have been the end of it, but he remembered the young woman he'd murdered in Daba, and the shame lost its grip.

He would not kill women and men in a war with no end. He would not be part of the madness. Tau had a way out and, by the Goddess, he'd take it.

He thrust a lethal blow at an illusory enemy, imagining it to be the life he'd been expected to lead. "I'm done with killing!" he said.

"You killed someone?"

"Cek!" he swore, swinging round to see another face from his dreams.

It was Zuri.

COURAGE

Zuri? I-I didn't…" He bowed his head, his face burning at the thoughts he'd just been having. "Apologies," he said.

"No, I shouldn't have startled you," she said, her arched eyebrow letting him know that, startled or not, she had not expected to hear such language. "I was watching you train. You're good."

"You're kind." Tau sheathed his sword. He wanted to add that she was beautiful. He didn't have the courage. "I'm not that good," he said instead. "I just have the benefit of my father's training. Jabari is better." What made him say that? "I mean—"

Zuri raised a hand above her head, as if measuring a tall person. "He's Noble," she said. "Did you really kill someone?"

Tau went cold. "It was one of the hedeni." He didn't want to say more but was still recovering from the shock of it and couldn't help but speak. "She was with two others. They tried to hurt a woman and child."

"I'm prying—"

"It's fine. I just…" Tau struggled to even out his emotions. "I killed her."

"You were defending Chosen lives."

"It doesn't feel that way."

"If you didn't fight, she'd have killed a woman and child. Would their deaths be a fair price for a clear conscience?"

That didn't seem fair. "You came to argue?" Tau asked.

She looked hurt. "Is that what we're doing?" She shook her head. "I came to see you," she said, lifting her chin and taking a deep breath. "I came to..." She gave him a nervous smile, the edges of her mouth fluttering. "I came to..."

"What?" asked Tau, confused.

"Ah..." Zuri was steeling herself for something, then seemed to lose her nerve. "I'm surprised Aren didn't whip the skin from your back," she said.

Tau wasn't in the mood for her teasing. "Jabari asked me to accompany him."

The smile slipped from her face. He'd been too terse with her. He was an idiot.

"I saw Jelani," she said. "She told me she saw you yesterday, before the battle. She told me you were on your way to find Jabari."

"Jelani, her mouth has always been too large for her face."

"Tau, Jabari is many things. He's bold, handsome, tall—"

"Is he?" Tau asked.

"But he's not impulsive. That characteristic I'd lay at someone else's door."

"What do you want me to say?"

"I don't want you to say anything. I came to...I wanted to see you." Zuri had that strange look on her face again. "I wanted to make sure you were well. I needed to know that."

"I am."

She stepped closer, within arm's reach, and suddenly, his arms felt heavier than boulders. She raised a hand and, hesitating, laid it on his chest. "Would you tell me, if you weren't?"

Tau's scalp beaded with sudden sweat. She's being friendly, he told himself. She's worried about a longtime friend. He looked down at her hand and back to her face. She was so close. He could almost—

"The battle, w-we...I thought we had no hope," Tau stammered.

"You fought. You kept us safe," Zuri said, stepping closer.

Tau could feel her chest against his. "They had us. There were too many." He couldn't keep his mind on his words. Every time Zuri took a breath it was...distracting. "The hedeni were about to over-run us when the military arrived, with Guardians."

Zuri's eyes widened. "You saw dragons?"

Dragons. That was something he could talk about. "I've never seen one up close before."

"I've never seen one at all," Zuri said.

"They're enormous. Black as shadows. I felt their fire. It's...Well, it's indescribable. And the Gifted controlling it—"

"An Entreater."

"What?"

"Entreating. Gifted don't control the Guardians, they call to them," Zuri said. "How did she do it?"

"Eh...she lifted her arms and waved them around," Tau said.

"She waved her arms around?" Zuri pursed her lips at him.

"I'm telling the truth."

"I believe you."

"No, you're teasing me again," Tau said, trying not to stare at her mouth.

"Never," Zuri said, full lips curving into a bright smile, eyes spar-kling. "Well, it sounds funny to think of a Gifted guiding Guardians by waving her arms around."

"It doesn't look like the way you're saying it. It...You can feel their power."

"Go on," said Zuri, still close.

"There were other Gifted, like the one with the Ingonyama. The hedeni captured her when—"

"What?" Zuri's smile vanished.

"They killed the Ingonyama and took the Gifted."

She stepped back.

Why had he told her that? Did he want to describe the way the dead had looked too? "I shouldn't have said anything."

"It's my fault," Zuri said, voice soft. "I'm asking about it like a child, imagining it's all honor and glory, brave warriors and won-drous Gifted. It isn't, is it?"

"No," said Tau. "It isn't."

"No," Zuri echoed, lowering her eyes.

Silence, and Tau had no clue how to fill it.

"Tau, I came here for a reason. When I heard you went to Daba, I was so worried I . . . Tau, we don't have long before you leave for Ihashe training, and I won't look back with regrets. I'd rather live with a thing done poorly than do nothing and always wonder how things could have been."

He should have told her she was beautiful when he had the chance.

"Tau?"

"Yes?"

Zuri stepped in and kissed him. His entire body tensed with the shock of it. Her lips, first pressing softly on his mouth, became insistent, and his pulse pounded in his ears as his scalp tingled.

He didn't know what to do with his mouth, or his hands, and it felt like a warm fire lanced across his skin in the places where their bodies touched. Tau put his arms around her, holding her, pleading to the Goddess to let this moment last forever. He wanted to die like this, with her in his—She ended the kiss.

He opened his eyes, surprised to see the sun still shone. For a few precious breaths nothing but Zuri had existed.

"We should stop," she said, her voice deeper than usual. "We don't want to go too far."

Tau's mind felt stuffed with grass. "Zuri . . . ," he said, astonished at how needy he sounded. He was close to begging and wasn't sure what for.

Her eyes danced. "I did it," she said. "I wasn't sure I'd have the courage." Her smile was a new day's dawn. "I'll see you soon, Tau Tafari."

She slipped out of reach and walked away. Tau watched her go, the most perfect being who had ever existed.

"We have the rest of Grow and Harvest before the testing," she called to him, before disappearing below the rise of the mountainside.

Tau stood there, trying to understand some part of what had happened. He couldn't make sense of it, but somehow, his life had become better.

PATHS

The next morning, Tau woke before sunrise. He was still sore from the battle, but the nightmares had lessened, and as the sky brightened, his head filled with thoughts of Zuri.

"You're up," Aren said, eating cold lentils and potatoes.

"I'm up."

Aren watched him. It was the same look from training, when he was worried Tau was about to get hurt.

"I'm well," Tau said.

"Didn't say anything."

"Were about to," Tau countered.

"Maybe, but you'll never know now."

Aren got up, buckled on his sword, and went outside to relieve himself. Tau heard him greeting someone and then his name was called.

"Coming," Tau said, pulling on his worn boots and going outside. Jabari was there.

"Well met, Tau."

"Well met, nkosi." Tau knew Jabari didn't like it when he used the Noble honorific to address him, but Aren was there, and Tau would get an earful for being too familiar if he didn't.

"I'm for Daba. It's just me. Lekan won't come."

"Well, we'll do the work of three," Tau said, glad Lekan wasn't joining them. It gave him the day with Jabari, and that was an opportunity for Tau to tell him his plan. It was a chance to ask Jabari for his help.

His father stood outside the hut, watching them leave. He liked seeing them together and had always encouraged Tau to spend time with the umbusi's second son. Tau waved and Aren gave him a nod in return. He was playing the part of the stoic, but Tau knew he was proud that the two of them were lending aid to Daba.

"It'll take most of a season to make Daba what it was," Jabari said as they walked. "I'll go up for the first few days, but then it'll have to be training all morning and afternoon."

"The testing."

"It'll be here before we know it, and Father is relying on me." Jabari kicked at the dirt. "It still shames him that he failed his."

"Your father has done well by Kerem," Tau said. "Besides, he's an umbusi's husband. That makes him military."

"Honorary. He hasn't trained a day and the mandatory military status does him no favors. It means anyone in the service, even Lessers, can challenge him to a blood-duel." Jabari shook his head. "The Ruling and Guardian Councils give military status to men like my father to keep them in line. It's no compliment or benefit."

Tau was half listening. He'd never cared much for politics and was worrying over how to tell Jabari his plan. He figured he'd start with his feelings for Zuri. Jabari would understand that, he hoped.

Truth be told, Tau would have preferred not to involve his friend at all, but he needed his support. It was the only way he could guarantee himself a position in the Onai keep, once he was . . . injured.

Jabari picked up a small rock and began tossing it from hand to hand. "It didn't help when Lekan was rejected either," he said, still going on about the family's failings. "Now I'm the last hope. My mother is the umbusi and the war needs warriors. I have to pass the testing and become an Indlovu. If I don't, none of the men in the Onai family will serve and the fief will face tithes we can't pay."

Jabari pulled out a hand's span of dried meat from his pack, and Tau's mouth watered. "You'll make the citadel," Tau said, trying not to stare.

"From your lips to the Goddess's ears," Jabari said as he broke off some of the meat and offered it to Tau.

"Thank you, nkosi," Tau said, bowing his head.

"Don't call me that."

Tau had trouble listening. He was focused on the meat. It had been a long while since he'd tasted some. He'd have to take it slow or his stomach would toss like ocean driftwood. He took his first bite and the taste was the Goddess's own gift.

Jabari took a bite of his half, speaking as he chewed. "It should be fine. I've trained hard. We both have. You'll make the Ihashe for sure."

Tau swallowed, trying not to sigh with pleasure. Root and soft vegetables had their place, but meat was something else. "Beg pardon?" he asked.

"You'll make the Ihashe and be a great addition to the war effort."

Tau refused to let the words spoil his last bite or weaken his resolve to go ahead with his plan. He plopped the meat into his mouth and chewed slowly, savoring its texture and flavor. When the last of it was gone, it was time.

"I hope to make the Ihashe," he said, "but I won't serve."

"Neh?" Jabari turned to him, mouth full and an eyebrow raised.

Tau dove in, deep and fast. "I'm in love with Zuri Uba, and I'm not a killer. I want to marry her, but I can't if I have to leave her to fight in the war as an Ihashe or Ihagu. And if I refuse either option, I'll be made a Drudge and we'll never be together."

Jabari had stopped walking and tilted his head to one side, staring at Tau. He was completely still, except for his mouth. It continued to move, chewing. "What now?" he asked.

"I have to pass my testing for the Ihashe. After I do, I'll be sent to complete my training. I'll . . . I'll be injured badly and have to come home."

"Injured? You can't know . . ." Jabari's eyes went wide. "Oh . . ."

"When I come home, I hope I can work in the keep. It's better than I deserve, but . . . Jabari, I'm begging. . . . I'm . . ." Tau sighed. "Will you help me? When I'm back? Will you put in a good word?"

"You're joking." Jabari's face remained still, and Tau couldn't read it.

"I'm not," he said.

"Tau, don't let Daba define you. It was your first battle, you can't—"

"Nkosi, I'm not a killer."

"Don't 'nkosi' me. We're friends. Sword brothers..." Jabari swallowed the last of the meat. "You're serious about this?"

"I am."

"How do you know Zuri will even ask you to marry her?"

"I...I don't know, but she came to me yesterday."

Jabari shrugged. "And?"

"She kissed me."

"Oh..." He rolled the stone around in the palm of one hand. He seemed to have forgotten he was holding it. "Did it seem serious?"

"Ah..."

"She kissed you? On the lips?"

Before Tau knew it was coming, he'd broken out into a cheek-straining grin. "Yes. Yes, she did."

"Nceku!" Jabari swore, grinning too. "How was it?"

"Jabari..."

"If I'm going to help you, I deserve every detail of this kiss."

Tau's breath caught. "You'll help me?"

"Sword brothers, that's what I said...even if you're being stupid enough to think your life will be better without the sword part." Jabari sniffed. "Anyway, we've a while before you test and head to the isikolo."

That was it, then. Jabari believed Tau would change his mind. He probably thought the kiss had done this to him and that a little time would undo it.

"You'll put in a good word for me, if I come back?" Tau asked again.

"If you come back looking for work in our tiny keep, I'll feel sorry for you, but that won't be what I'll tell my mother. I'll tell her Tau Tafari is the best, hardest-working Lesser I know."

"Thank you."

"Nceku! I can't believe Zuri Uba kissed you." Jabari laughed and started walking again. "We're talking about the same person, right? The pretty handmaiden?"

"She's the beautiful handmaiden," Tau said.

SONS

Tau and Jabari returned to Kerem that evening, exhausted but satisfied. The Lessers in Daba had lost much but refused to surrender to despair. The hamlet would survive.

As they approached Tau's hut, Tau noticed light from the fire pit. Aren never lit it at night. Tau ran the rest of the way. They found a bleary-eyed Zuri inside the home.

"Tau!" she said.

"My father—"

"Aren is well. It's not him. It's Anya."

"What's this?" said Jabari, squeezing his way into the hut, making the tight space feel oppressive.

Zuri struggled to find the words. "Nkosi Jabari," she said, addressing him formally, "it's my friend's father...ah, Aren's second-in-command....He's been accused of attacking a Noble."

"Nkiru?" Jabari asked. "No. Why?"

Zuri's mouth opened and closed, like the words wouldn't come. "Your brother was...I mean to say, Nkiru struck him when he—"

"Why in the Goddess would Nkiru..." Jabari's face went slack. He'd pieced it together at the same time as Tau.

Zuri still had to say the words, though. "Lekan was forcing... Pardon me. Nkiru found Nkosi Lekan with his daughter, Anya."

"Cek!" Jabari swore.

Zuri winced. "Your brother wishes for the laws to be upheld, but Aren refused."

Tau slumped against the nearest wall. There was no way Aren would order, or allow, the killing of Nkiru and his family.

Jabari paced, or tried to, in the tiny home. "Lekan, that half-witted fool." He stepped outside. "Let's go. This has to get sorted before it gets worse."

They sped down the mountain. It was late, but the closer they got to the keep, the thicker the crowd.

Lekan, along with his family's guard, stood in the center gateway to the keep. The guards held peat-moss torches that illuminated both their faces and the worry on them. Ochieng was one of the guards, and like the others, he looked forlorn. They faced a crowd that was two wrong words from becoming a mob.

Standing opposite Lekan were Tau's father, a few of the men under his command, and Nkiru.

"Give him to me, Aren," said Lekan. "Don't make me say it again."

"Nkosi Lekan, I only ask that we take time to discuss this with Umbusi Onai," Aren said.

"My mother is resting, and this is not a matter that needs her attention," Lekan said. "You have my orders. Carry them out!"

Tau, along with Zuri and Jabari, pushed their way through the crowd. Tau watched Lekan the whole time.

Lekan was taller than Jabari and heavier, though not from muscle. The umbusi's eldest son was known for his appetite and, in a land where food was rationed, it sat ill with many that he could grow so large. The Petty Noble also enjoyed his drink, and it was said, behind hands, he drank more olu than water.

"Nkosi Lekan," Aren said. "I believe we can solve this without death, and I invite your counsel, in addition to your mother's."

"In addition? Damn you, Lesser! Send over the man!"

Nkiru looked miserable and Anya was beside him. She was a wreck. Her eyes were bloodshot and she had bruises on her arms, visible even in the dim torchlight. Her dress was torn. Zuri went to her.

"Well met, brother," Jabari said, pushing through the crowd to stand beside Tau's father.

Lekan did not look pleased. "Jabari."

"What's this, then?"

"I was accosted," Lekan said, lifting his square chin.

"Accosted? How?"

"It's not a matter for public discussion."

"Surely, an attack on a Noble is the exact type of discussion to be had publicly. If a punishment that destroys an entire family is to be meted out, we must know the story."

Lekan glared at his sibling. "I was accosted. Is a Noble's word no longer enough in Kerem?"

Tau saw Jabari's hand tighten around his sword hilt. That was bad. In a fight, Lekan would lose, but that would do less than nothing to help Nkiru and his family.

"Nkosi," Aren said, addressing them both. "I have had time to interrogate the accused."

Tau figured that, at most, his father had had Nkiru drink a cup or two of masmas to calm his nerves.

"Nkiru was looking for his daughter," Aren said. "He—"

"I won't have my name slandered!" Lekan said.

"He came upon his daughter and—"

"I'm warning you, Aren!"

"And saw her enticing a man."

Lekan's eyes went wide and he cocked his head, as if trying to hear a far-off noise. Anya began to sob and Aren told the awful lie that was the only chance he had to save Nkiru, Anya, and the rest of the family.

"Nkiru was incensed with his daughter's lewd behavior," Aren said. "He struck out at the unknown man and, when his attack was repelled, realized his grave error." Aren spoke louder, telling the story for the crowd, making it easy for Lekan to let this tale become the official one. "Nkiru snatched his daughter and drew her from the keep in shame. He came straight to me to admit her sins and to atone for his part in shaming the fief."

"The fief was shamed!" said Lekan.

"If it please the nkosi, I was dragging this man and his daughter to Umbusi Onai to tell her that I would ask for their banishment."

"Yes!" said Lekan. "Wait, banishment?"

"Yes, Nkosi Lekan!" said Aren. "We cannot allow such diseased behavior to continue unchecked. A Noble with a Lesser? A Common! Disgusting and disgraceful. Who would believe it possible, except that the wretch of a woman did all she could to beguile you."

"Yes…" Lekan was catching himself up to the fable.

"Nkosi Jabari," Aren said, "if you and your elder brother agree to banishment, there is no reason to bring this before Umbusi Onai. All gathered here already know Nkosi Lekan's character. We know what is likely, were he found in a room alone with a Common like Anya."

Aren was running along a ridge here, and the crowd, knowing Lekan's character well, began to murmur.

"We can imagine what took place," Aren continued. "So, why waste the umbusi's time? I have sworn, here among my peers and betters, that Nkiru acted in fear for his daughter. We would be unjust to punish him and his family for a child's behavior."

"That's no child," said Lekan, looking at Anya sideways, as if he could see scales, fangs, and venom.

"Even better," said Jabari, seeking to help Aren get his way. "Let us excise the evil from our midst. I agree with Inkokeli Solarin's advice. The family will be banished from the fief." Jabari spat the distasteful words like the rot they were.

"My Noble person was offended." Lekan still wanted blood.

"Unknowingly," Aren reminded him.

"Unknowingly." Lekan gnawed on the word. "Yes, the fool must not have known who it was he attacked. He wouldn't have dared, if he knew."

"He wouldn't have dared," said Aren.

"I was wearing my sword. If he'd seen me clear, he'd know that to face me is to die," said Lekan, glaring at the crowd. "Yes, banish the scum. Know this, though," Lekan said, placing a hand over his heart. "If I see any of their kin within the boundaries of Kerem after morning's light, they will be eviscerated."

"What could be more just?" Aren said.

"What's that?" asked Lekan.

"Your word, my will," intoned Aren.

"By the Goddess," said Lekan, turning on his heel and striding into the keep, the visibly relieved guards in tow.

The gate clanged shut and the noise seemed to cut the invisible strings holding Nkiru aloft. The man collapsed to the dirt.

Tau felt hollow. Nkiru was a good man. True, Anya could be a pain, but that was as bad as she got. There was no chance she had tried to seduce Lekan.

"I'll talk to my mother," said Jabari.

"It's done," said Aren. "Lekan won't stop if Nkiru or his family stays in Kerem. He was out for blood tonight."

"Lekan is an oversized—"

"Nkosi...," said Aren, shifting his eyes toward the gathered crowd, drawing the Petty Noble's attention to the listening Lessers.

Jabari pressed his fingers against his temples, massaging them. "As you say. I won't try to stop the banishing, if that's what you wish, Aren."

"Nkosi Jabari," Aren said, "I thank you for your help. It's frightening to think what could have happened if you hadn't come." Aren put a hand on Nkiru's back. He was still on the ground. "We Lessers will do what must now be done." Aren helped Nkiru to his feet, Zuri stayed by Anya's side, and the crowd dispersed.

The rest of the night was longer than Tau's day. He went to Nkiru's hut with his father, Zuri, and Anya. Several Ihagu were waiting when they arrived, and everyone gave a hand in the packing. Nkiru's wife, still suckling Nkiru's youngest, acted brave but couldn't hide her fear, not really.

It was near morning when they saw the family off. They would travel east to Dakur. The borderland fief suffered many raids, but that meant there'd be a place for a competent Ihagu.

Aren gave Nkiru a few names to call on, and then there was nothing left to say or do. Zuri hugged Anya, holding her tight, reluctant to let her go. Anya looked numb, and Zuri cried for both of them when the family trudged away.

Aren began the walk back to the keep. He had more to do. It was a new day.

Tau stood next to Zuri, and they watched the rising sun turn their friends into silhouettes that became hazy with the morning's heat and then vanished as the mountain swallowed them behind its curves. She slipped her hand into his and leaned her head on his shoulder. They stood like that, silent but together, for a span. She was still crying.

MEN

The days that followed were hard. Zuri made it a point to spend as much time with Tau as their duties allowed, but Anya's fate weighed on her. It hurt Tau to see Zuri so melancholy, and it didn't help that his nightmares about the raid hadn't stopped. Still, they found quiet moments to sit and talk, to laugh, sometimes for Zuri to cry.

Tau tried to be her mountain and found that she helped him more than he could her. She was everything he hadn't known was missing. She was his first thought in the morning and his last at night. He had trouble considering anything but her smile, her eyes, her voice . . . her.

Still, he did what he could to remain focused. He promised himself he'd repay Jabari for helping protect Nkiru's family and for being willing to help him make a better life for himself with Zuri. The thing Jabari needed most was training for the upcoming Indlovu testing. So Tau spent every day sparring with his friend until they both collapsed. It was in this way that the final days of Grow ended, the early days of Harvest flitted by, and the ceremony for manhood arrived.

The male Lessers born in the same cycle as Tau were to be made men. The local Sah priest attended the ceremony, reeking of olu. He spoke of the tests facing all women and men of the Chosen. He encouraged the newly made men to be righteous and hoped their deeds would bring pride to their families, as they served the Omehi people, the queen, and the Goddess.

Then the new men were given gaum. It was Tau's first time tasting the yellowish sludge, distilled from scorpion poison. He downed his cup and the drink blazed its way across his throat, burned his nostrils, and seared a path up and over the back of his scalp. He gasped and gagged, to the enjoyment of everyone come to see him and the others made into men.

Tau couldn't understand why anyone would choose to drink something so vile, though once the taste had passed, he did notice that the following feast of boiled cabbage, sea-salted potatoes, and long beans tasted more flavorful than usual. Also, jokes were funnier, he couldn't feel his teeth (had he ever been able to feel them?), and every woman he saw was almost as beautiful as Zuri.

He celebrated into the night with the other new men, and sometime during it all, Jabari had shown up and gifted Tau a brand-new pair of boots. Tau hugged him for a long time and invited the Petty Noble to join him for the best drink in all the peninsula. Jabari smiled, waving off the proffered cup.

The rest of the evening raced, then crawled, in turns. Tau's father congratulated him and even sat with him for a time before leaving for some duty or other. Zuri came and he told her she was the Goddess on earth. She looked at him, an eyebrow arched, hands on hips. He thought this made her more lovely and wanted to kiss her, but people were around. He tried anyway. She didn't let him and said she was there to take him home.

Tau was not ready and tried asking Zuri to dance, but his tongue felt fat. No matter; he took her by the hand and guided her to the dancing circle. They danced and it was marvelous, until Tau's stomach began to heave. He excused himself, pointing to his stomach and mouth before stumbling off to the nearest brush, where he returned his dinner to the earth.

He stood like that for a while, amazed so much could come out of him. When he was done, he looked for Zuri, so they could continue dancing. She thought it best they head home. Tau thought that nonsense, but Zuri impressed him with her strength when she pulled him away from the party.

Tau yelled he had to get his new boots, and Zuri pointed out he was holding them. He said she was the Goddess on earth and was told he'd already said that.

Aren was at the door waiting, and he helped Tau to bed. Tau didn't need help. He could take off his own trousers. He pulled one leg free and tumbled to the ground. He should get his other leg free, he thought, closing his eyes.

It was the shouting that woke him. His mouth tasted like he'd swallowed a fistful of sand, his stomach rolled, and his head boomed like the inside of a beaten drum.

"Where is he now? I'll kill him!" It was Aren.

Tau jumped to his feet and fell over. He had just one leg of his trousers on.

He heard his father storming away, the footsteps heavy, angry. Tau jerked the trousers the rest of the way on, snatched his tunic from the night before, and saw it was filthied with vomit. He found another shirt, torn but serviceable, pulled on his new boots, grabbed his practice sword, and dashed out of the hut into a painfully bright new day.

Aren was with Ekon, the tall and wiry fighter he'd made his second-in-command after Nkiru's banishment, and Aren was furious.

"Father? What's going on?" Tau asked, squinting against the sun.

"Go back inside."

"What's going on?" Tau demanded. He'd never seen his father like this.

"He had them killed!"

"What? Who?"

"He had them killed, that nceku!" Aren marched off.

Tau jogged after. "Who!"

"Lekan," Aren growled.

Tau didn't want to know. "W-who...who'd he kill?"

"Ekon's patrol found them. Their bodies had been thrown from a cliff. Nkiru, his wife, Anya, her brother...the baby...the baby." Aren drew his sword, moving faster.

Tau ran to catch up. "Father, what are you going to do?" He grabbed his father's arm, forcing him to stop. "Father!"

"I'm going to kill him." Aren pulled his arm free.

"Ekon!" Tau said. "Do something!"

Ekon, hands fidgeting with the ties on his tunic, tried to talk sense into Aren. "Inkokeli, uh...Aren, we...we should think about this. We don't know for sure it was—"

"Don't!" Aren said, rounding on Ekon, making him cringe. "We know who did this. We know! A baby, Ekon. Nkiru's baby girl!"

"You can't fight him," Tau said, joining Ekon in front of his father, blocking his path.

"I'll kill him."

"He's a Noble," said Tau.

"Mka! He'll die the same as a Lesser when my sword is through his neck."

Ekon looked about them, head jerking left and right, to see if anyone else had heard that.

"Father—" Tau started, but Aren pushed past.

"They'll hang Tau if you kill him," Ekon said. "They'll hang him and then his mother. They'll cut their bodies open and leave them in the sun to rot. Aren, they will."

Tau's father was no longer moving.

"They'll hang Tau," Ekon said again. "You know it."

Aren sat like the bones had gone out of him. He dropped his sword in the stunted grass and placed his head in his hands. Tau went to his father and Ekon followed. Aren's shoulders bounced up and down. He was crying, without sound. Tau couldn't remember the last time his father had cried.

"Da," he said. "Da." Tau knelt nearby and put his arms around him.

"I'm sorry, Aren," Ekon said. "I'm sorry." He kept saying that, over and over. Like the thing that had happened was uncontrollable and inescapable, like it was something more than the act of one man.

"We'll give them a proper burning," Aren said a while later. "We'll do it in secret. Lekan mustn't know we found them."

Ekon nodded.

"Tau, Jabari will come up to train. He'll wonder where you are."

"I'm with you," Tau said.

"Go," Aren said, standing. "And don't tell Jabari about this."

Tau glanced at Ekon. He didn't like the look on his father's face.

"I won't do anything. I can't." Aren choked on the word. "Lekan isn't military and Ekon is right. I can't kill him. They'll come for my family, for you and Imani, for Imani's daughter.... Go, train. I'll be in the hut."

Aren strode away and Ekon placed a hand on Tau's shoulder. "I'll stay with him," he said. "I'll stay as long as it's needed."

When Tau got to the fighting circle, Jabari was already through most of his forms. He saw Tau and his face stretched into a wide grin. "The boots look great!"

"Thank you," Tau said, feeling sick to his stomach.

"Ready to fight?" he said.

"In a while," Tau told him.

"No chance. We're well into Hoard. No days off with testing so close. And you missed even bigger news by sleeping in."

Tau looked at Jabari, muscles tensed.

"The queen is coming," Jabari said.

"What?"

"The queen! She's coming to Kerem. Well, more to say, she's passing through Kerem on her way to Kigambe. Still, she arrives this afternoon."

The queen visited the northern or southern capital every fifth cycle to personally present the citadel's highest honors. The ceremony also honored the women who had tested as Gifted. The Chosen tested every woman. It was a rite of passage, announcing the transition from girlhood to womanhood.

And, with only one in ten thousand possessing the gift, their abilities marked them as part of a caste of less than five hundred. They outranked all but Royal Nobles and were duty-bound to serve. Tau had heard stories of the citadel catching women who held back in their testing, failing on purpose. They were branded, then taken to serve anyway.

Tau pulled his practice sword free of its scabbard, wishing he could plunge the blade into Lekan's seeds. "I guess we'd better get started if we're to finish in time to see the queen."

Jabari let him get a toe into the fighting circle before engaging. The first round was painful, the second excruciating, and Tau had to concede the third so he could throw up his breakfast.

"The gaum?" Jabari asked as Tau wiped half-digested cabbage flecks from his mouth.

He didn't answer. He saw Jabari, but not really. He was focusing on the features his friend shared with his brother, Lekan. "Let's go again."

The two men battled back and forth in the fighting circle, and Tau caught out the Petty Noble every eighth or ninth match. It wasn't enough. Tau wanted to teach Jabari a lesson, because he would never have the chance to teach one to Lekan.

He moved through an offensive form as fast as he could, forcing Jabari back. Then Tau caught Jabari on the thigh with a glancing strike that would leave a welt. The contact encouraged Tau, and he brought his sword up and around to slam the blade into Jabari's side.

The swing was clean and fast, but Jabari was faster. The Petty Noble whipped his sword at Tau's legs, smashing his ankles together and dropping him in the dirt.

Tau groaned. His head had hit the fighting circle's floor and there were spots blinking in front of his eyes. Beyond the spots was Jabari, standing tall, his sword tip pressed against Tau's throat stone.

"Goddess's mercy," Tau said, ceding the match.

Jabari stood down. "Cek! You nearly had me. You're faster than a desert scorpion."

Tau was angry. "I'm done."

Jabari didn't notice his tone. "After that last match, I'm good for a break too. You really went for me. Hey, let's get down to the keep. I'll get changed and ready for the queen's procession. Tau, come with me. Be my aqondise for the formal nonsense where I'm expected to have one?"

"Your aqondise?" Tau said. Jabari was honoring him, giving him a chance to act as his most trusted. As Jabari's aqondise, Tau would be as close as a Lesser could get to the royal procession. On any other day, Tau would have been overwhelmed by the gesture. "Yes, of course...nkosi."

"Don't call me that. And I need you. Standing beside Lekan for that long, without anyone else to talk to, is torture." Jabari was grinning like a fool. "Will you come?"

Tau nodded, face grim.

PROMISES

Tau accompanied Jabari to the keep. It was filled with people and everyone was frantic, doing their best to prepare. Kerem had not expected the royal visit, and it had been a surprise when the queen's vanguard had arrived, requesting an evening's accommodation for the queen and her retinue.

Jabari went to bathe and prepare, telling Tau to ask the keep guard for a proper aqondise's tabard. This meant Tau had time, time enough for an unpleasant task. He went looking for Zuri.

He found her in the keep's courtyard, near the bathhouse. She was cleaning linen with a dozen other handmaidens. When she saw him, her face lit up and she ran over, hugging him. It was more than she'd ever done in public.

"I've never seen such chaos," she told him. "Can you believe she's coming?"

The other handmaidens kept at their work, but Tau could feel their eyes on him, and the courtyard had gone quiet. "Handmaiden Uba, I've a request from Inkokeli Solarin. May I speak with you a moment?" he said.

"Of course, Common Tafari," Zuri replied, thinking his formality a game.

When they were out of sight, she kissed him.

He fell into the moment, anything to avoid what was to come. "I've missed you," he said.

"It's been such a day," Zuri told him, her face little more than a handspan from his.

Tau took a breath. He had to tell her, but there was a tightness around her eyes. "What's happened?" he asked.

She touched his face. "Am I so easily read?"

She was worrying him.

"My testing day has been set," she said.

"It has? Goddess, when?"

"The new moon."

"Oh—"

"You'll be with Jabari for his testing on the same day. I know."

"The fighting circles aren't far. I'll see you in the evening."

"Of course."

"You'll be a woman."

"I'm not already?"

"You're the most beautiful woman in the world," Tau said.

Zuri punched his arm. "Common Tafari, a proper compliment must be reasonable if it is to be believed." There was that tightness again.

"Zuri?"

"It's almost over, isn't it?" she said. "Common Tafari..." She picked over each word. "It'll be Ihashe Tafari soon enough, and it'll be that for the next seven cycles as you train and then fight."

"Would you prefer something else?" he asked.

"Don't tease. I know what has to be."

Tau took her hands in his. "It doesn't have to be," he said. "We can make a few choices of our own. We wouldn't have much, but we could try to be happy together." He hadn't meant to say all that. "Maybe I won't have to fight. Maybe I can contribute elsewhere."

"Tau..."

"I'm glad your testing is coming," he told her. "I'll help Jabari get through his, and I'll come back to you—a newly made woman." He forced a smile, wanting a moment more of peace, of happiness. "Maybe you'll even give me proof?"

Zuri laughed out loud, covering her mouth at such scandal. "I think not!"

"Not yet, then," he said.

Zuri tilted her head at him and Tau could tell she'd heard the intent in his words.

"The seven cycles will pass," she said, forcing a smile as tears filled her eyes.

"I'll come back to you." It was as close to a promise as he could make.

Her eyes searched his face, pupils large and deep, and he could have lived in that moment forever, but he had to tell her about—

"Zuri! Zuri, where are you?" called a handmaiden. "Mistress Chione will be back any minute. I won't do all your work for you, you wretch."

"Who's that?" Tau said, stepping forward.

"You're going to defend me against fearsome Kesi now?" Zuri asked, eyes twinkling. "She's about this high"—she pointed to Tau's shoulder—"and has a dangerously sharp tongue. I should leave now, before it comes to violence. Against Kesi, I'd fear for you." She paused, letting the weight of the earlier moment return. "I'll see you, Tau Tafari," she told him.

Tau hated himself for being weak. He hated himself for the rush of relief he felt, knowing the tale of Nkiru's family would have to wait. "I'll see you, Zuri Uba."

"Coming, Kesi! I'm coming!" Zuri hastened her way to the courtyard, stealing a look at him as she went.

Tau smiled at her, still upset with himself. He was a coward. He'd stolen a kiss and stayed silent instead of telling the woman he loved the truth about her friend's death. And soon he'd be standing within arm's length of the man responsible for the murder, and he would do nothing. He was a coward.

QUEEN

Thousands lined the main path to the keep. The gates had been thrown open, and Jabari's family, the Onai, stood beneath the keep's walls, ready to welcome their queen. Tau was with the family, wearing the aqondise's tabard that had been loaned to him.

He was two strides back from a bathed and scrubbed Jabari. Jabari, in turn, was one stride back from his father and his mother, Afia Onai, the umbusi of Kerem. Lekan was there too, mirroring Jabari on their mother's right-hand side. Tau did his best to ignore him, though his hand twitched near his empty scabbard. Jabari's father fidgeted too. The gouty old man was nervous.

To avoid having Lekan in his field of view, Tau stared at the press of people stretching into the distance. Aren was beyond the gate, dressed in full fighting gear. He had his men standing at attention along the sides of the path. They were there to keep the crowd a respectful distance from the queen, but like the keep guard spaced out across the top of the keep's walls, it was for show. Afia Onai was doing her best to impress her monarch.

Tau saw dust rising. The queen's procession had come to the last rise before the keep. His heartbeat quickened and he told himself that he was a man now, not a child to be excited by nonsense. The dust cloud grew bigger, the first men of the Queen's Guard marched into view, and Tau's pulse raced.

The Queen's Guard was outfitted in maroon, a blend of red and black, the royal colors, a dragon's colors. They marched in lock-step, and behind them were some of the peninsula's most powerful. Queen Tsiora Omehia, her champion, the Gifted Leader, and Abasi Odili, the current chairman of the Guardian Council, rode down the path to Kerem on horses.

Tau had heard of horses, but he'd not expected to see any. The animals were huge, though a dragon could eat one of them in two bites. But people didn't ride dragons, and here were four Chosen moving across the earth on horses, as if it was the most natural thing.

Voices thundered, drawing Tau's attention, as the people of Kerem cheered their new queen. They pushed against Aren's Ihagu, trying to get closer, making Tau think that perhaps lining the path with fighters had been for more than show.

As the procession neared, Tau made out more details. The first, and most astonishing thing, was the queen. She was young and couldn't have had her testing for womanhood more than a cycle ago. That wasn't it, though. It wasn't her youth. It was her beauty.

Her skin was dark as a moonless night and she had lips like the sunrise. Her face was framed by delicate cheekbones, and beneath long lashes she had eyes shaped like almonds. She wore a black and red riding dress, cut to be formfitting, but flowing in the arms and legs. It also had a neckline that exposed enough skin to be gossip-worthy in a small fief like Kerem. She gazed out at the crowd, smiling as if pleased to see an old friend.

"Goddess be praised," Jabari muttered.

The queen's procession came to a halt, and her champion, Abshir Okar, stood up from atop his horse. Tau saw that the champion, armored in the red of blood, fire, and mourning, had his feet in a rope contraption that wound its way around the horse's body, forming a seat on the animal's back.

"Queen Tsiora Omehia," said Champion Okar, his voice deep as a mountain well, "second of her name, first among the Goddess's Chosen, and monarch of the Xiddan Peninsula, seeks Kerem's hospitality."

Okar was no longer young, but only a fool would underestimate a man who looked like he was carved from rock. The champion, Tau remembered, had placed first in all three cycles at the Indlovu Citadel. Upon graduation, he was made an Ingonyama and had fought in countless campaigns. When old Queen Ayanna's champion had died in battle, she'd asked Abshir to take up the mantle.

It was the umbusi's turn to speak. "I, Afia Onai, umbusi of Kerem and vassal to Queen Tsiora, would consider my house and lands blessed by the Goddess, if my queen permitted me to wait upon her."

There was no higher honor, or status, for a Chosen male than to be made champion. It meant access to the queen, a seat on the Guardian Council, and other privileges.

It wasn't forbidden, but queens did not marry. They were wedded to their people and loved none more than the Goddess, so the saying went. Instead, queens took great care in the selection of their champions. The queen's champion was more than a military leader. He was also the seed for the next generation of royalty and, in ideal circumstances, a true partner.

It was awkward, then, the transition from one queen to another, if the old champion was still in place. Before long, Queen Tsiora would need to graciously retire Abshir and select a champion of her own. Monarchs must have heirs.

The greetings done, the procession wound its way into the keep, and Tau was close enough to see that Abshir wore the two guardian daggers and guardian sword he'd won from his time at the citadel. The dragon-scale weapons were incredible, none more than the sword.

The black blade was belted at his side. It had no scabbard and was dark enough to have been shaped from obsidian. But, even from a distance, there was something alien about the weapon. It drank in the light, and no matter how hard he looked, Tau was unable to make out any details on its surface. It was as if the weapon hid in plain sight, like he could see its outline rather than its whole.

It reminded Tau of what it had been like to watch the Guardian at Daba. Dragon scales stymied the eye, tricking it into underestimating the dragon's position and speed. The eye-bending properties were useful to a massive flying predator, more so to an accomplished swordsman.

"Did you see?" asked Jabari. "She's . . . she's . . ."

"Perfection?" offered Tau.

"Yes! Well said. Perfection."

"You'll sit near her at dinner?" asked Tau.

"Not too near," Jabari said, chewing his lip. "She'll be closest to Mother and Father. Lekan as well. I'm a second son. I'll be farther back."

"Don't worry, I can speak to her on your behalf," Tau told him.

Jabari laughed. "Point taken. I'll be closer than most. I just . . . Did you see?"

"I did."

"Then you know." His eyes followed Queen Tsiora as she rode her horse down one of the paths inside the keep. A keep Common, looking ready to wet himself, led the entourage to the hastily constructed stables.

Tau took the opportunity to examine the rest of the queen's party. The KaEid, riding close to the queen, was the leader of the Gifted and served as both a military and religious official with powers that paralleled the guardian councillors'. "What's the KaEid doing here?" Tau asked.

Jabari's head swayed in sync with the queen's body as she rode. "The who? Oh, KaEid Oro? She'll make the opening statements at the awarding ceremony."

"In the southern capital?"

"No, on a boat on the ocean. Of course in Kigambe."

Tau waited until the queen disappeared around the bend before asking his next question. "Beside them, was that the Guardian Council's chairman?"

"Hmm?" The queen was lost to sight, but Jabari had his neck craned, trying to catch one last glimpse.

"Was that Abasi Odili with them?"

"Yes," said Jabari. "He'll be watching this cycle's testing."

"You didn't tell me the chairman of the Guardian Council will be at the testing." Tau tossed the concept around in his head.

"I don't tell you everything," said Jabari, accepting that there was no more of Queen Tsiora to see. "Hey, did you notice the two beside him?"

"The hulks?" Tau said. He'd noticed.

"The bigger one is Dejen Olujimi. He's Abasi's Body, his personal Ingonyama."

"Goddess," muttered Tau. The man was a behemoth. Tau couldn't fathom what he'd look like when enraged.

"He's supposed to be the best fighter in all the peninsula."

"You could handle him," Tau joked.

"Easily," Jabari said with a crooked smile.

Tau grew serious. He was thinking about Lekan and about how Aren had actually considered fighting him. "Jabari, how exactly do the blood-duels work?"

"Blood-duels? What's this about?"

"Nothing, my father... uh... one of his men mentioned them," said Tau.

"Why?"

Tau shrugged.

"They don't happen often, but any full-blooded military man, any Ihashe, Indlovu, or Ingonyama, can challenge any another. Caste makes no difference."

Tau found the idea ridiculous. The average Noble was bigger, stronger, and faster than the average Lesser. And if a Noble was in the military, it meant he was an Indlovu or Ingonyama. They would destroy any Ihashe.

"Most blood-duels happen when two soldiers are drunk and one gets caught with the other's woman," continued Jabari. "There's too much to lose for reasonable men to go around compelling people to fight them to the death. And they almost never happen among Royal Nobles."

"The Bodies," said Tau.

"Challenge a Royal and they can have their Body fight in their stead. Hence, Dejen. Councillor Abasi Odili prides himself on having the most deadly Bodies in the queendom. It's the reason he has that slightly smaller beast in tow. He's grooming him."

"Who is he?"

"Greater Noble Kellan Okar. He won his first cycle at the citadel and that won him Odili as a patron. This cycle, he placed first again."

"Okar? He's Champion Abshir Okar's son?" asked Tau.

"The champion has no children. Kellan is his nephew."

"Then . . . Kellan is the coward's son?" said Tau, remembering the Greater Noble hanged for treason.

Jabari hissed, looking around them.

Tau leaned in, whispering. "His father was the one they hanged?"

"The Battle of Kwabena," Jabari said. "One of our worst losses. Coward Okar was inkokeli for an entire wing. It was his responsibility to defend the rage's flank. When the hedeni attacked, he panicked and ran. He said he was engaged by an overwhelming force and had no choice."

Tau sucked his teeth.

"Without his soldiers defending the flank, the hedeni cut through the rest of the rage. Four thousand men and nine Gifted died that day. Nine Gifted, Tau."

As he told the story, Jabari's voice lost its whisper, becoming a growl instead. "At the trial and under oath, the other inkokeli swore that coward Okar's account was a lie. The force that engaged him was a fraction of the size he claimed. Then the idiot argued that the hedeni had gifts, that they appeared out of thin air and disappeared the same way. He—"

"Gifts?" said Tau.

Jabari cupped his hands near his crotch. "He had big bronze stones, to stand in front of the Guardian Council and tell them—"

"At Daba, the tribes were working together. They never do that. Something's changed or is changing. Maybe—

"Don't be foolish. They—"

"Maybe their gifts really have returned," Tau finished, unwilling, that day, to be called foolish without some small counter.

Jabari gave Tau a hard look. "Don't interrupt me," he said, pausing, making it a point to hold Tau to silence. "The Goddess weakened the hedeni gifts for their mixing and blasted them away entirely when they decided to fight against us."

Tau had known Jabari his whole life. He knew when the Petty Noble was on the cusp of anger, and Tau was good at turning his frustrations into a smile or even a laugh. It was one of the reasons they were close.

That morning, though, with Nkiru and his family dead, Tau couldn't play the part. He shook his head, suggesting he didn't agree with Jabari. It was a little thing, a small act of defiance. It turned the taller man's face sour.

"You think it matters to Nobles," Jabari said, "whether the hedeni miraculously had gifts that day? We didn't hang Kellan Okar's father for lying. That wasn't his crime. We hanged him for cowardice, for proving himself unworthy to be treated or judged like a man." Jabari stepped close, until he was looking down at Tau. "We hanged him for behaving like a Lesser."

Heat swept up Tau's neck and he stared up at Jabari, unwilling to step back or look away. He didn't care about coward Okar or his crimes, but hearing Jabari compare and weigh a Lesser's life so lightly hurt. If Jabari felt this way, it must have been so simple and uncomplicated for Lekan to have an entire family of Lessers murdered.

"We are Chosen," Jabari said, still standing too close. "We fight, we don't surrender, and we don't run. The Nobles have tried to teach that to Lessers for generations."

Tau couldn't stop himself. "If we don't run, then why are we on Xidda instead of Osonte?"

Jabari's face twitched and he balled his right hand into a fist. Tau braced for the hit, but the blow didn't come.

"I'm going in," Jabari said. "I have to change for dinner."

"Of course . . . nkosi."

"I'll see you tomorrow for training, Common Tafari. Be ready. I can't afford to go easy on you anymore. The testing is close."

CHAPTER THREE

TEST

Queen Tsiora left for Kigambe the next day, and her beauty was the topic of conversation for the rest of the moon cycle. She had captured the hearts of Kerem's men and the imagination of its women. Tau could tell Jabari was particularly smitten, but they hadn't spoken more than was needed as they beat and battered each other in preparation for what was to come.

The training left Tau with little time to spend with Zuri, and Aren had asked him not to tell her the truth about Nkiru's family. Tau argued she had the right to know, but he felt relief that the burden of telling her had been taken from him. And yet, holding the secret didn't help. The closer he got to Zuri, the more he wanted to tell her everything. Instead of making things better, keeping the secret tainted his time with her and left him guilt-ridden.

So on the morning of Jabari's testing, as they marched to the fighting fields on Kerem's borders, Tau was unsettled. He was worried about his future with Zuri, about his friendship with Jabari, and about having Lekan join them, instead of Jabari's father, who, suffering an attack of gout, had remained in Kerem.

The march to the testing was the first time Tau's father had been so near Lekan since learning the fate of Nkiru's family, and that, along with everything else, had Tau feeling like he was walking through a nest of scythe ants. True, he hadn't been bitten yet, but each step brought with it a fresh opportunity.

Head heavy with troubles, Tau stole a look at Jabari. The Petty Noble had to feel the day's pressure. At the testing, he'd hold his sword and Kerem's potential for prosperity or poverty in his hands.

"I'll be fine," Jabari said, noticing the glance.

"Soon you'll be crossing blades with some of the best Noble fighters in the South."

"I know," Jabari said. "I'm ready. Aren made me so...with your help."

The words were kinder than any Jabari had spoken in days, and it was more of a peace offering than a Lesser had any right to expect.

"You are ready. I know it," Tau said, hoping it was true.

Aren drew apace with them. "How's the knee?"

The day before, Tau and Jabari had collided in practice and Jabari had fallen.

"It's strong," Jabari said. "The swelling is gone. I feel fine."

"Eyes on the Goddess," Aren told his student.

"Always. I'm ready," Jabari said, echoing Tau's words and shooting him a smile. "I'll not fail."

"It's luck that determines who you draw in the first rounds," Aren told him. "Remember what I said."

Jabari tapped his temple. "I have it. If I face Lanre, I'll watch his overhand swing."

"You'd better. It's a feint, and he'll crack those pretty teeth of yours with his shield while you gawp at his sword. And?"

"And Sizwe is quick."

"Quick? That skinny bastard...Uh, no disrespect to his Noble person, but that skinny bastard is an inyoka, except he strikes twice as fast."

Jabari laughed. He was always quick to laugh, thought Tau, but this was serious. He looked up and wiped sweat from his shaved head, more forming the instant the first swath was whisked away.

They were still a few thousand strides from the fighting circles, on the flat and fallow fields between Kerem and Mawas, and the sun was nearing its zenith. The testing would begin at midday and it was

Hoard: too hot to grow, too hot to harvest. It would be horrible to fight in this swelter, which was the point.

He heard more laughter. Jabari was joking with one of the Ihagu. If all went well, the Petty Noble would be a full-blooded Indlovu in three cycles. Tau worried Jabari wouldn't laugh as much after he'd spent time fighting the hedeni. He wanted nothing but the best for his Noble friend, truly, but he was glad he'd found a different path for himself.

"Keep your head straight too," Aren said to Tau. "Watch Jabari and the other Nobles. This is a great opportunity. You'll get to experience a testing before your own."

Aren put his arm around Tau's shoulders and squeezed. "It makes a difference, seeing how desperate fights get when something is on the line."

Tau nodded and let his head hang, facing the dirt. It would break Aren's heart if he knew what Tau was planning. "I've experienced something similar," he said, reminding his father he'd fought in Daba.

"Yes, I think I try to forget you have..." There was a pause. It looked like Aren wanted to say more. "Still," he said, "even though you're not fighting today, keep your sword nearby. Warm up with Jabari and put yourself in a fighting mind. Give your body the same feelings and stress. It'll help when it's your turn. Trust me."

"Always," Tau told his father as the column of men slowed to a stop.

"The testing," Aren said. "We're here."

SHARP

Below them were flat fields sitting in a small depression in the otherwise hilly scrublands that Kerem shared with Mawas. The Drudge, who had prepared the fighting circles, had done an excellent job. The stones that made up each of the ten circles were pressed into the earth and painted red. They would catch the eye but were sunk low enough to avoid catching anyone's foot.

In each fighting circle, the scrublands' silt-like soil was covered with clay, carried all the way from Mawas. The clay had been laid, smoothed, and allowed to harden under Xidda's sun. It was a perfect fighting surface.

Up and down the length of the fallow fields, the black flags of the Indlovu Citadel flew above their sand-colored tents. The flags had been wired with bronze to look as if they moved on the currents of a strong wind.

Tau scanned the fields. Many Nobles had already arrived, and Tau knew Aren would have preferred to have done the same, but it was customary for the more influential Nobles to take their time, and Lekan, in his conceit, had dallied.

The umbusi's firstborn stood at the head of the column, hands on hips, looking down on the assemblage as if they were all Lessers. In truth, the Nobles, come to watch their sons test, were Lekan's

peers if not betters. A few of them, like Greater Noble Thabo Ogh-
enekaro, husband to the umbusi of Kigambe, greatly outranked fief
Kerem and its Petty Nobles.

Still, the victory, however minor, was Lekan's. The sun was
almost at its zenith and the journey had been well timed. They were
last to arrive. Even Ogozi of Mawas was already on the field.

"Let's go down and get started," said Lekan. "Where's our spot, Aren?"

Tau's father didn't speak to Lekan, opting to point to a cordoned-
off area close to the center of the field. Aren had sent several Drudge
and two Ihagu a quarter moon early, to stake and hold their spot.

Lekan shaded his eyes. "Good. We'll have a view of nearly all the
fighting circles."

The column started down and Aren turned to Jabari. "We'll set
up, and Tau will see to your armor and helm. I want you to stretch
and run through your forms. Nothing fancy. People will watch to see
what forms you tend toward. Don't give them that, just the basics."

"Your will, Inkokeli Solarin," Jabari said. His eyes narrowed as
he chewed the inside of his cheek. The testing had become, Tau
thought, a little too real for Jabari as well.

After that, things moved fast. The Drudge and Ihagu settled in
and Jabari warmed up, then dressed. Tau did the same and the two
men sparred. Aren didn't watch them as much as glare at them. He
corrected this and that, hovering like a mother over a newly walking babe. Tau did what he could to keep his "head straight," but the
energy on the fields was distracting.

Lessers scurried back and forth, attending to their betters. Ihagu
were either set as guards or found spots to cheer on their Nobles.
The Drudge dug out latrines, carted foodstuffs, or offered the young
fighters gulps of water, cooling wet cloths, and even boiled mashed
potatoes, for quick boosts of energy. Meanwhile, full-blooded Indlovu wandered the fields like they owned the earth beneath them.

The Indlovu were titans, every one. Most were head and shoulders taller than Tau, all of them were more muscular than he could
ever hope to be, and quite a few looked like they could crush rocks
with their bare hands. He watched them in awe.

"I have to go with your brother," Aren told Jabari, avoiding

Lekan's honorific. "He'll sign the official documents for your testing, and I'll be back. The fighting will begin soon. Be ready." But before Aren could leave, Lekan strolled over with an older Noble and a young man of age with Tau and Jabari.

"Aren," Lekan said. "I have a task." He indicated the Noble beside him. "This is Nkosi Izem Okafor and his second son, Kagiso."

The difference between man and son couldn't go without remark. Izem Okafor was gaunt and tall, even for a Noble. He had a stern face and long fingers, and his skin was well oiled, despite the heat. He was shiny but wasn't sweating, and Tau wondered how the man managed that trick.

The son, on the other hand, wasn't much taller than Tau. He was pudgy, his eyes were set deep in his moon of a head, and his skin was the color of light topsoil, rather than the deep-earth dark that was characteristic of the Chosen.

"Kagiso has drawn one of the first matches," said Lekan, "but has no one with whom to warm up."

Aren glared, his look a clear warning.

"I believe," Lekan went on, "that your son could step in and serve Kagiso in this regard."

"I would be indebted," Izem Okafor said, his voice melodic, a surprise given his ascetic appearance. "I wish to give Kagiso every opportunity to succeed."

"Indeed," said Lekan.

Aren was furious. He hid it, thought Tau, but he was furious.

"Tau, warm up with Nkosi Kagiso," Aren said, managing to obey the order without speaking to Lekan. "Nkosi Jabari, please do not interrupt your forms. I'll return once your documents have been registered with the citadel."

Aren strode off without excusing himself and without waiting for Lekan, causing the older Okafor to raise an eyebrow.

Lekan struggled to keep his composure. "Yes, yes. Always such a rush at these things," he said, as if he attended a testing every cycle. "Shall we, Izem?"

Izem Okafor inclined his head and, together, they left. Izem, Tau noticed, did not exchange any words with his son.

"Well met, Jabari," said Kagiso, his voice, like his father's, defying expectation. For all his girth, Kagiso spoke like his seeds had yet to drop.

"Kagiso . . . ," Jabari said, continuing his forms.

"Haven't seen you since the Grow festival in Mawas."

"Has it been so long?" Jabari said, showing his back to the heavy-set Noble as he worked through a thrust, low-cut, and riposte combination.

"We should get started, nkosi," Tau said to Kagiso.

Kagiso turned to Tau, looked him up and down, and turned back to Jabari. "What a horror show, this testing. The life of a Noble son, yes?" Kagiso's grin revealed a row of teeth yellowed with calla leaf stains.

Jabari replied with a grunt.

Kagiso, disappointed, switched his attention to Tau. "Well, Lesser, let's get this over with."

Tau moved them back a few paces from where Jabari was working. "Nkosi, would you like me to fetch your practice sword?" he asked, seeing Kagiso wearing sharpened bronze.

"It's light sparring," said Kagiso, "and it'll take too long to get it. My match is coming up. Let's go."

Tau wanted to protest, but Kagiso had his sword out and was already swinging. Tau backed off, and, worried about getting hurt, he fought defensively. Kagiso took this as a chance to push the pace, increasing the strength of his swings.

Tau made sure to be aggressive enough to keep him at bay. If he took an unblocked blow, the injury would be serious. He considered asking again if Kagiso would use his practice blade, but after their first few engagements, he realized Kagiso was no swordsman.

The discovery turned Tau's concern to surprise. The only other Noble he'd crossed swords with was Jabari, and he'd believed all Nobles to be as capable. Kagiso's hack-and-slash style flew in the face of that belief, and Tau wondered if the man he faced was a poor fighter or a more accurate representation of the abilities of his kind. If the latter was the case, Jabari would make short work of the men he faced.

More likely, thought Tau, Kagiso was simply a Noble son who

had never taken to his duties. It would hurt Izem Okafor to have a son who failed to make the citadel. It would also hurt Kagiso's chances at a good marriage.

"Hey, Tau!" Jabari said, followed with a reluctant, "Kagiso."

Jabari didn't break his form or momentum but indicated a direction with his head.

"See there," he said, "that's Jayyed Ayim, the ex-adviser to the Guardian Council."

Tau looked and saw him. Jayyed Ayim was a Lesser dressed in the grays of an Ihashe warrior. He was in his middle years, almost as tall as a Noble, and nearly as big. Tau whistled to himself and looked back to Jabari.

His friend was smiling, and even from several strides away, Tau could see the mischief in his eyes. "The way my father tells it, he's probably a match for many Indlovu."

Kagiso took the bait and scoffed. "A Lesser as good as an Indlovu?"

"Perhaps that's too far a walk down the path," Jabari said, "but given the swordsmanship I've already seen today, I'm certain he'd make short work of at least a few of us."

Kagiso's mouth tightened and his nostrils flared wide as a rock lizard's frill, but Jabari ignored him, speaking to Tau instead. "After your testing," he said, "do everything you can to get into Jayyed's scale. You want to train under a man like that. . . . He might even make you change your mind about the Ihashe."

Tau nodded agreeably and gave the ex-adviser turned fighting instructor another glance. He had a square jaw and a heavy brow and walked with the sure movements of a fighter. It wasn't hard to imagine him as skilled with a blade.

Beside him were two bigger men, and without their formal attire, it took Tau a breath to recognize them. Jayyed Ayim was with Dejen Olujimi and Abasi Odili, the chairman of the Guardian Council.

"He's with Councillor Odili and—" started Tau, before lurching aside to avoid a wild swing from Kagiso.

Off-balance, Tau blocked another strike, turned the third, and had to drop to his knees to duck the fourth, aimed for his neck.

"Char and ashes!" shouted Tau, standing up. "Are you mad . . . nkosi?"

"Pay attention, Lesser! You're sparring against a Noble."

"Easy, Kagiso," said Jabari. He'd stopped his form work and was watching the two of them. He'd seen Kagiso swing for Tau's head. "This is sparring. Why do you have a sharp blade?"

Kagiso didn't answer. Instead, he pressed Tau, swinging like a drunk trying to catch a fly.

"Calm yourself!" Jabari hissed. "They're walking this way."

Tau risked a look behind him, almost got his nose chopped off, and had to bring his full attention back to Kagiso. There was bloodlust in the fat man's eyes as Kagiso came at him again, and Tau wasn't about to risk injury.

He blocked the Petty Noble's swing and stepped in, throwing his body weight against him, shouldering him aside. Kagiso staggered back, tripped, and fell to the dirt.

Jabari started to laugh but stifled it. From his ass, Kagiso glared. Then his eyes flickered past Tau's shoulder and his face went blank. Tau worried he'd hurt him and was about to beg forgiveness, when Kagiso bumbled to his feet and charged, his razor-sharp blade leading the way.

"Blood will show!" Kagiso yelled.

Tau had no idea what the idiot was doing, but he was done playing. He sidestepped Kagiso's lumbering charge and smashed the flat of his blade into the Noble's back. Kagiso was launched from his feet and hit the ground hard, skipping across it like a poorly thrown stone in a pond.

"By the Cull, man, what are you doing?" said Tau, his blood redhot, all thoughts of begging for anything burned away.

Kagiso moaned, then lifted his head, and blood gushed from his nose. It was broken, and that was when Tau became worried. Heart hammering, he looked up from Kagiso, and his worry turned to terror.

The chairman of the Guardian Council and the Ingonyama that was his Body, as well as Jayyed Ayim, Lekan, and Kagiso's father, were there. Tau looked to Jabari for help, but Jabari was staring at him like he was covered in curse scars.

The fighting fields were silent, no one moved, and Tau felt like he was in a nightmare. It got worse when the guardian councillor began to clap.

DONE

"Well, this is an interest," said Abasi Odili, walking to Kagiso and bending over the downed man. "Who are you?" His Palm accent made the words glide together like they'd been greased. Kagiso moaned and Odili kicked him. "Speak up."

"Kagiso, Kagiso Okafor," he managed.

Tau had never seen a Noble treated this way and looked to Kagiso's father. The man was only a few steps from his son but came no closer. He stood still and straight-backed, staring at his boy as he struggled.

"Kagiso . . . ," said Odili, straightening and turning to take in the growing crowd. "Well, we should thank Nkosi Kagiso. He's saved us a lot of time."

The crowd murmured.

"Kagiso," said Odili, "was bested by a Lesser." He examined Tau, his pupils black and face hard under the midday sun. "A Low Common." Odili picked up Kagiso's sword. "He fought him with sharpened bronze and the Common has a practice blade." Odili clucked his tongue and turned the edges of his mouth up. It wasn't a smile. It couldn't be called that. "Indlovu, we leave for Kigambe. If these southern Nobles can be bested by Commons, then none are fit for the citadel."

Odili began to walk away, and the murmuring gave way to shouts of protest. Tau saw his father in the crowd. Aren looked near to panic.

Nearby, Lekan was trembling, he was so angry. Tau was about to go to Aren, thinking to explain about Kagiso, when Jabari threw down his sword in disgust. It had all gone wrong, and it was Tau's doing.

"Councillor Odili," he yelled, trying to be heard over the protesting crowd and hoping his form of address was an appropriate one. "Councillor Odili, please. Nkosi—"

Aren was on him then, pulling him back, trying to get him away. Tau resisted. He had to fix this. Odili stopped. There was a chance.

With his back turned, the councillor spoke. "You, little Common, are lucky I don't have you hanged for attacking and injuring a Noble. Scurry back to your mud hole now, before I change my mind."

Tau couldn't believe the man's words. Hanged? Attacking a Noble? He let his father pull him back.

"Your indulgence with that Low Common offal did this," Lekan hissed at Jabari.

Tau didn't think; he reacted. He turned to Lekan, the man who had tried to force himself on Anya and then had her entire family murdered. "I fought Kagiso fairly," he said, seething, "and, Common or not, I was the better man. I'm a better man than you!"

Tau's hand went to his sword hilt, and Lekan stepped back, sputtering. Everyone who'd heard Tau's words spoke at once, shouting over one another until Odili raised his hand in the air, commanding silence. When he had it, he poured slippery words in its place.

"Kellan," he said, letting his voice carry into the crowd behind him, "this Lesser has the dangerous idea that he knows the sword."

Like the sea before a ship's prow, men parted and Kellan Okar stepped forward. A sculptor could have carved the champion's nephew from granite and the likeness would have been too soft.

"He seems to know the sword as well as he needs to," said Kellan. "Is a future Drudge worth our time?"

Tau bristled, the insult cutting too close to truth. His father clutched his upper arm hard enough to crush it.

"You mistake me," said Odili. "I'm not asking."

Kellan looked down at Tau and back to Odili. Jaw flexed, he locked eyes with the councillor. A breath passed and Kellan looked away. Taking his time, he unsheathed his sword and stood across from Tau.

It didn't feel real, none of it. From the crowd massed around him, to the mountain of muscle facing him, to Lekan's sneering face, none of it felt real. Tau's heart began to pound, his hand tightened on his practice sword, and he looked to his father. Aren paid him no mind. He had a tight grip on Tau's arm, but he was facing Odili and Kellan.

"Councillor Odili, this is my son. He's barely a man and has not yet tested. I'm a full-blood Ihashe, with military status. I take his place."

Aren pulled his sword free and shoved Tau toward his Ihagu. The men grabbed and held him as Aren strode over to Kellan Okar.

"Father!" Tau shouted, finding more arms had joined the others to hold him back.

Odili opened his mouth. It seemed he would deny Aren's request to fight in Tau's place. Aren didn't give him the chance. He threw himself at Kellan and they crossed blades in a crash of metal and sparks. The crowd roared, its ranks swelling to form a wall of human flesh, and Odili's protest died on his lips as the fighters circled.

Kellan was the bigger man, much younger too. However, he was an initiate, only two-thirds through training. Tau knew the Indlovu Citadel's reputation, everyone did, but his father was the best fighter in Kerem.

Kellan struck, swinging his sword in a flashing arc. Aren blocked, point down, but Kellan's attack had enough power to knock Aren's blade back. Neither man was dressed for combat and Aren's blade rebounded, cutting Aren in his side. Tau's father gasped in pain and shuffled back, and Kellan was on him, swinging, cutting, and stabbing, using forms Tau had never seen and couldn't have identified, given their speed.

Aren stumbled into the wall of people and they shoved him back toward the circle's center. He was bleeding from his arm, side, and leg, and Kellan came at him again. Aren took a slash to the face, a sword pommel to the gut, and was sent to one knee by the flat of Kellan's sword.

"They're cheating. They're using gifts," Tau said, looking for the Gifted, the Enrager hidden in the crowd.

"No, they're not," said one of the Ihagu.

"End it," said Abasi Odili, and Tau finally understood. This was a blood-duel, a fight to the death.

Tau strained against the men holding him. He shoved and pushed at them until a hand slipped off. He slapped one of the others and head-butted the last. He was free and ran for his father, who, in that short moment, had been beaten to both knees.

Tau was three strides away. His father was dazed and bleeding, sword down by his side. Kellan raised his weapon and swung.

"No!" Tau screamed, running, watching the bright blade burn through the air.

Aren lifted his sword to defend. Kellan adjusted, hitting him on the wrist, separating hand from forearm. Tau saw his father's sword drop to the dirt. None of it felt real. His father screamed and collapsed.

Kellan stepped away and said to the crowd, "It's done. I've taken everything from him that made him a man. The son's offense is paid in full."

With nothing on which to clean his sword, Kellan held it out from his body and walked back the way he had come.

"Stop!" said Tau. He couldn't remember picking it up, but he was holding his father's sword, its hilt red and slick in his hands. He had the weapon pointed at Kellan's back.

"Put it down, boy." It was Jayyed Ayim, the onetime adviser to the Guardian Council. "That's a Greater Noble you're threatening."

Kellan turned to face Tau and Tau had sense enough to be afraid. Aren, with the hand remaining, clawed at Tau's leg, trying to pull him to safety, but it was too late. Councillor Odili spoke.

"Dejen," he said, calling his Body.

Face placid, Dejen drew his midnight-black sword and strode into the circle.

"Clemency!" Jabari pled.

"I stand for fief Kerem here!" Lekan shouted. "Councillor, I back your will."

"Odili, it's done," said Kellan, arms wide.

Odili inclined his head and Dejen surged, driving his black sword so deep into Aren's chest it tore open his back. Aren stiffened in shock, mouth open, and there was no time to move or breathe before the Ingonyama ripped the blade free, swinging it at Tau, spattering him across the face and body with his father's lifeblood.

"Now it's done," Odili said.

BRAVE

The sword slipped from Tau's fingers as he dropped to the earth beside his father.

"Councillor, it goes too far!" said Jayyed Ayim over the crowd's din.

Tau held Aren, speaking to him, speaking words that made no sense. He spoke for no better reason than to hold his father's attention, because as long as his father listened, his father was with him.

Aren's eyes were unfocused. They fell on Tau, fell away, and returned with difficulty. His mouth moved, but he said nothing. He couldn't, not over the horrible sucking sounds that came from his chest with every breath.

"Father? Father! Da...," Tau said, as the man who had always cared for him convulsed, drowning in a sea of his own blood. "Da!" But it was too late. Tau's father was gone and could not hear.

The noise of the fighting fields came back in a rush. It seemed everyone was shouting, until Odili's voice cut through.

"This Common, a military man," he said, pointing at Tau's dead father, "fought a blood-duel on behalf of his son. The same son who assaulted one Noble and later raised his sword to another."

The tumult did not settle.

"I see you are not satisfied," said Odili, walking to Tau, sword in hand.

Tau watched him come. He didn't move. Jayyed Ayim did. He

stood over Tau with one hand near his sword hilt and the other raised to the councillor, blocking Odili's way.

"Nkosi—" he began.

Odili brushed past and swung a killing blow. Tau didn't flinch until the metal shrieked, Odili's blade brought to a screeching halt by Jayyed's sword.

"Peace," said Jayyed, his sword arm quivering with the strain of holding the edge of Odili's weapon away from Tau's head.

Tau didn't know when the large man had moved, but Odili's Body had the point of his sword pressed into Jayyed's cheek, dimpling it, drawing a bright flower of blood from the skin there.

Councillor Odili lifted his sword and stepped back. Dejen pressed his blade deeper against Jayyed's face, forcing him away.

"Peace, again? Do you only play one note, Jayyed?" Odili asked. "You're no longer an adviser to the council, and no matter how you preen, the Goddess and world can see you're a Lesser. You think you've fallen far? There is so much farther to go."

"Councilman Odili is willing to be merciful," shouted Jayyed to the crowds without taking his eyes away from Odili and ignoring the Ingonyama looming over him.

Odili laughed, jerking the muscles of his face into an empty smile. He sheathed his sword and waved Dejen back. Dejen let his sword dip until it aimed for Jayyed's heart, but moved off.

Odili kept his voice low, speaking to Jayyed alone, though Tau could hear. "Have this peace, Jayyed." Odili's grin stretched as if pulled by hooks. "It's the most you'll get." Raising his voice, he addressed the crowd. "Clemency asked, clemency granted. The Lesser's father has been punished. I'll leave the boy to his fief."

He said it like it was worth a cheer. The southern crowd did not oblige. Unfazed, Odili clapped Jayyed on the shoulder as if they were great friends and whispered, "You've been a pest. The old queen would not let me swat you, but the old queen is dead. Get in my way again and it'll be the last thing you do."

Odili slapped Jayyed's shoulder a second time, laughed like they'd shared a jibe, and left. The enormous Dejen, Odili's Body, followed. Trailing the two, disgust on his face, was Kellan Okar.

Tau didn't understand. His father could help. He tried to wake him. After long days, Aren would often fall into deep slumbers.

A hand fell on Tau's shoulder. "He's gone." It was Jayyed.

Tau looked up. "My da..." Tau couldn't feel the ground beneath his knees or the sun's heat. He glanced around. Jabari was there; so was Lekan. Tau saw Kagiso on the ground. The fat Noble, nose still a bloody mess, was nursing the spot where Odili had kicked him.

Thought of the councillor roused Tau. He placed his father on the ground, letting him rest, and reached for Aren's sword. A strong hand with rough fingers fell on Tau's wrist.

"I am sorry for this loss," Jayyed said, taking the sword from him. "Your father was very brave. He knew if he stepped in the circle to fight Kellan, he would never leave. The Chosen are made less by his passing." Jayyed called out to Aren's Ihagu. "Come, take your man. Take him home for his burning."

The Ihagu, glad for instruction, did as they were bid. Tau wanted them to leave his father alone. He wanted to snatch the sword from Jayyed and hunt down Odili, Dejen, and Kellan. He did nothing.

"Nkosi," Jayyed said, addressing Lekan, "this Common is from your fief?" He was asking about Tau.

"Yes. Yes, of course," Lekan said.

"He'll be cared for?"

"What? Yes, yes. You can trust I'll take care of him," Lekan said. "And the testing?"

"Nkosi?"

"My brother is here, we all are, for the testing."

Jayyed didn't answer. He gave Aren's sword to Tau and walked away.

"Who does that cursed Lesser think he is?" Lekan said to the Kerem men around him, low enough that Jayyed would not hear.

The Ihagu took Aren's body away and Tau would have knelt in the dirt till the sun fell from the sky had Jabari not come to take him away as well.

"I will kill them," Tau told him through tears. "I swear it to Ananthi and Ukufa, I will kill them all."

BANISHED

The journey home was made in silence. Jabari sent runners to alert the keep that the ritual burning for Aren would be performed that same night. Tau marched without marking where they were or how much farther they had to go. He marched with Jabari beside him and marched when Jabari wasn't. He marched as the sun beat down and kept going when it didn't. They marched past nightfall, into the low cliffs of the Kerem mountains. None of it mattered.

"The pompous ass," Lekan said, walking up to Jabari. "Does Odili even have the power to cancel the testing? Blasted Palm Royals all act like they're birthed from the Goddess's twat covered in gold." Lekan barked at his own joke, no humor in the sound. The Onai family was in a perilous position as long as Jabari remained unconfirmed for the citadel. "What about you? We need you in the military. We can't pay higher tithes."

"I'll travel to the North," Jabari said. "They test later than we do."

"How much later? This season's tithes are due in—"

"It's not the time, Lekan."

"Why not? Because your pet Common got above himself and got his father—"

Lekan didn't finish. Tau leapt on him, bore him to the ground, and struck him in the face. He raised his arm to hit him again, but Jabari shoved him away. Tau rolled to his feet, ready to attack.

"Kill him!" Lekan yelled, his left eye swelling shut. The Ihagu surrounded Tau, keeping him away from the frantic Noble.

"Kill him!" Lekan shrieked.

"They'll do no such thing," said Jabari.

"He attacked me. I'm heir to Kerem."

"Get up."

"He attacked me. He cost you your testing. I'll have—"

"Shut up!" Jabari shouted, startling his brother, before turning to Tau. "High Common Tau Tafari, you have attacked my brother, a Noble, and the punishment for that crime is death by hanging."

"Fine, I'll do it myself!" said Lekan, reaching for his blade.

"Everyone here knows the crime and its punishment," said Jabari to the Ihagu and Drudge with them, as much as to Tau. "We also know what this day has cost you, and, for the love I bore your father, I will both honor and consider that in rendering judgment over you."

Tau felt cold. He knew Jabari was talking to him but couldn't make himself care.

"I cannot ignore your crime, but as the second son of fief Kerem, and as a neutral Noble, not the aggrieved party, I commute your sentence." Jabari swallowed and cleared his throat. "Tau Tafari, you may attend your father's burning this evening, but when the sun rises, you will no longer be welcome in Kerem."

Lekan was only a few strides away when he pulled his sword from its scabbard. "No more banishments, Jabari. I'll take my own justice."

Jabari was in his brother's way. "Another step and you'll need to take it over my blade."

Tau looked at the two Nobles posturing in front of him. One of them, his friend since childhood, had just banished him from the only home he'd ever known.

"You may appeal my decision, taking up the crime and offered punishment with Umbusi Onai," Jabari told Tau without taking his eyes off Lekan. "Be warned, she may look less kindly on a Lesser having struck her heir than I have."

"Jabari...," Lekan growled, his voice aggressive, predatory, in stark counterpoint to his lowered sword and reluctance to step closer.

"Get on, Tau," said one of the Ihagu, one of his father's men. "Get on."

Tau looked for the speaker, couldn't find him, and turned back to Jabari and Lekan, hating them both with enough force it had his hands shaking, hating them all.

"Get on..."

A hand touched his shoulder, encouraging him to move, and Tau's vision began to blur with tears. His father was dead. The tears came faster, and refusing to shame himself further, Tau shook the hand loose and left.

His gait was jerky, almost a stagger, like he'd had too much gaum to drink and couldn't find his balance. He half expected the Ihagu near him to reach out, steady him. Instead, they moved away, letting him leave, and Lekan, perhaps realizing that demands to stop Tau would go unanswered, held his tongue.

A span or two later, Zuri found him in the home that was no longer his. Tau didn't have much, but what he had, he was packing. She ran to him and held him.

"Tau," she said, "I'm sorry. By the Goddess, I'm so sorry."

Tau couldn't stand to be touched but couldn't summon the will to move away.

"We'll attend the burning tonight and then we'll go," she said. "We'll leave Kerem and all of this behind."

"I have nothing to give you," Tau said.

"Give? I want to be with you. I won't stay in Kerem without you, and I won't let them take me." She was breathless, wide-eyed, skittish. "I-I had my test, but it doesn't matter. Tau, they don't deserve either of us. We'll—"

"Test?" Tau found there was enough in him to feel surprise. "You're...you're Gifted?"

She didn't answer, didn't need to. "If we leave now, if we leave together—"

"Gifted. I knew you were special."

"We can—"

"No," Tau said. "We can't. They'll hunt to the ends of Xidda to get you back."

There was no argument against that. It was a truth neither could deny.

"Gifted," he said again, the word feeling foreign. Tau turned away, closing his eyes. His head was pounding. "I'm going to kill them, Zuri. I'm going to kill the men who did this."

"Who? The Nobles?"

Tau gathered up the last of his things.

"Tau, if you kill a Noble, they'll execute your sisters, your mother, your mother's husband. They'll find out if you have cousins, aunts, uncles, they'll kill everyone they can, and once that's done, they'll hang you, cut your body open, and leave it in the sun to rot."

Tau strapped his father's sword and his sword, the one that had belonged to his grandfather, to his belt. He walked out of the tiny hut, into the twilight.

"You're letting them take your life too," Zuri said.

He kept going and she ran up behind him, taking his arm and pulling him so he was facing her.

"Don't do this," she said. "Come with me to your father's burning. You . . . you don't have to be with me," Zuri said, "but don't lose your life and everything you are to this."

Tau took Zuri's hand off his arm. Gifted, he thought. The Nobles weren't satisfied with wiping out Nkiru's family or the murder of his father. They'd taken Zuri too.

"Goodbye, Lady Gifted," he said, using the title that would become hers, the title that placed the woman he loved in an elite caste outranking all but Royal Nobles. Zuri Uba had gone farther from his reach than the stars.

Zuri shook her head. "Tau, please, don't do this."

He left her there and took the path to Daba. He would circle back when he was lost to sight. He didn't want Zuri to know he was going to the keep. He didn't want her to know that he was about to pay Lekan Onai a visit.

LEKAN ONAI

Lekan was angry. The day had been exhausting and the evening worse. He'd had to explain the events at the testing to his mother and father with Jabari present. Everything he'd said, Jabari had undercut. His mother had been furious and his softhearted father had mourned Aren's loss, excusing himself to get ready for the burning.

Lekan didn't believe the Lesser worth the bother. Aren had grown too bold and his end was the natural outcome of an unworthy man caught up in his unnatural pride. If Aren had been more humble, his son would be too, and the boy wouldn't have tried so hard to show up Kagiso. If both Lessers had better known their place, the morning's unpleasantness could have been avoided.

As it stood, Lekan had been castigated by his mother. He'd been made to suffer for the mistakes of others. They'd have to find a new inkokeli for the Ihagu, she'd said, and without Jabari in the citadel, the fief was in a difficult enough position. She'd cursed the stupidity of men, claiming the Goddess had forsaken her by sending her sons.

Lekan, knowing his mother's moods, took it in silence. Jabari had tried to argue. She'd sent him from the room.

When it was just the two of them, she'd given Lekan the one positive thing to come from the day. She wanted him to arrest Tau

Tafari at his father's burning. They'd hang him the next morning for attacking a Noble. That's what Lekan admired about his mother. She knew when a firm hand was needed.

Later that night, hundreds of women and men came out for the burning, many weeping and sobbing like they'd lost a war hero. Lekan was there with several keep guards, but the Tafari boy did not show his face. Refusing to have another failure on his hands, Lekan sent men to Aren's hut. The boy wasn't there either.

Empty-handed and with the evening growing late, Lekan had given the men, the ones who had dealt with the Common whore and her family, the duty of finding Tau. That done, Lekan went to the cellar. He picked a well-aged jug of olu. His mother would lash him with her tongue if the Lesser slipped through his fingers, and that, when added to the rest of his day, had earned him the expensive liquor.

He downed it, and when it didn't soften the world's edges or dull the pain around his eye where Tau had struck him, he'd taken a second jug to his chambers along with a bowl of half-ripe avocados from the kitchens.

The second jug helped. He'd also enjoyed cutting up slices of avocado, imagining his dagger digging into Aren's son's flesh. Warmed by the olu and stomach full, he'd tumbled into bed, falling asleep with his breeches and tunic on.

Lekan was a deep sleeper, but that night it had begun to rain, an uncommon event in any season and rare during Hoard. On a normal night, the rain wouldn't bother him. His chambers were on the second floor, where he couldn't hear it pitter-pattering against the ground, and Lekan's room had thick shutters. No, Lekan could sleep through a thunderstorm, but he couldn't sleep through being rained on.

He spluttered awake, slapping at his wet face. It was raining in his chambers, which didn't make sense. Then he saw the shutters were open. Lekan sat up. He was going to close them, but there was a demon at the foot of his bed.

He squealed and scrambled back, about to shout for the guards, though what they could do against a demon he did not know, when the shadowed creature moved into the light. Lekan relaxed, then went tense again. It wasn't a demon, but seeing Jabari's pet Common at the foot of his bed wasn't much better.

"What are you doing here?" Lekan hissed.

"I'm not here to kill you," the filthy and wet Common told him.

"Kill me?" Lekan said. "You dirty cek!"

"That's all we are to you, neh? Nceku? Not men, not people. Is that why you threw my father's life away?"

Lekan didn't like the boy's tone and looked him over for weapons.

"I'm not armed, nkosi. I'm not here for your life, yet."

Lekan risked a glance to the night table beside his bed. His dagger was there, its blade hidden among the avocado skins.

"I'm here to tell you how you'll die," Aren's son said, making Lekan's arm hairs stand on end. "I'll join the military as an Ihashe initiate. I'll pour my soul into the craft of killing, and I will wait for you to rise to fief leadership. Palm will give you military status, and you will know despair."

"Despair?" Lekan forced a chuckle as he shifted closer to the table.

"Every day, every season, every cycle, you'll live in fear, unable to enjoy the taste of food, the sun's warmth, or the night's breeze, because one day I'll come. I'll challenge you to a blood-duel, Petty Noble Lekan Onai, and you will die on the end of my father's sword."

The Lesser had gone mad, Lekan realized, and his mother had the right of it. Aren's son needed to be put down.

"I am your curse," the Lesser said. "I am your end."

"Are you?" Lekan asked, snatching the dagger from the table and lunging, slashing the madman across the face and feeling the blade bite into skin and skitter across bone.

The Common squawked and fell back, blood spraying across the floor in a staccato line of red as Lekan threw himself on the small man, bearing him to the ground. He weighed more than sixteen stone and the Lesser couldn't have been a sand-grit over eleven. With the dagger in both hands, Lekan pressed it toward the fool's blood-covered face, using his weight to drive it downward.

"Kill me? Kill me!" Lekan said through clenched teeth as the wretch wriggled beneath him. "I'm going to burn your whole family. You have sisters?" he spat. "Yes, Jelani? I'll have her with this knife!"

Pain erupted in Lekan's seeds, seared through his crotch and into his gut. He gasped, his strength gone, as he succumbed to the agony the Common's knee had caused. The Common slapped the dagger from his hand and pushed him away, using the space to scuttle to his feet.

Lekan stood, swinging for the Lesser's face, but his target ducked and tackled him, driving the air from his lungs and carrying them back to the ground. They knocked over the bedside table, the dregs from the jug of olu spilling on them. They wrestled there, beneath the open window, as the storm raged.

Lekan used his greater strength to beat and batter Tau. He rolled on top, hit the Common, disengaged, and kicked him in the thigh. He'd aimed for the bastard's ribs but missed.

Tau began to rise and Lekan dashed to retrieve his dagger. He plucked it from the stone floor, put his back to the wall, and turned in time to see the Lesser running for him. He thrust his arm forward, to skewer the scrawny man, but the Common tripped on the fallen jug of olu and stumbled, making Lekan miss and causing his blade to tear through Tau's dirty tunic instead of his belly.

The two men slammed together, becoming entangled. Lekan sliced at Tau but couldn't land a killing blow, his knife trapped in torn cloth. Fumbling with the dagger, he tried to work it free, as the Lesser's fingers scratched their way round his neck. He made to shout, ready to call in the guards, ready to end the farce, but his head was smashed into the wall.

Lekan saw bursts of light flare in his vision, and before he could recover, his head was whipped against the unyielding adobe again. He scrabbled at the bastard's arms, couldn't get a grip, and his head was slammed a third time, turning the light bursts into suns.

Remembering the dagger, he tried to stab Tau, but the blade was still trapped in the mess of torn fabric and Lekan couldn't get a clean thrust. Desperate, he cut away from his assailant's body, freeing the short blade. He cocked his arm, ready to plunge the knife into the Common's heart, when his head was blasted into the wall, and something cracked.

Lekan's legs went limp and he tried to yell at Tau to stop. His mouth wouldn't work and he couldn't see anything from his left eye.

He patted at Tau's face, his hand coming away wet and sticky. Lekan didn't know where he was or what he was doing. He didn't—

The back of Lekan's head crashed into the wall again, and he saw his mother's face. She was young, leaning over him. He was in the bed he'd slept in when he was a child and she was cooing. He reached up to touch her and she shattered into a million pieces as time stopped and pain unlike anything Lekan had ever known consumed him.

FALLEN

Tau's face burned where Lekan had slashed him. The cut was deep and went from the bridge of his nose down to the middle of his right cheek. He was lucky he hadn't lost an eye. He was lucky Lekan hadn't killed him.

Tau looked down at the Petty Noble's body and his stomach heaved. The back of Lekan's head was collapsed inward. There wasn't much blood, but the man was dead.

Tau began to panic. He could leave, but the body would be discovered and he'd be suspected. They'd search for him, find him missing, and punish his mother, his sister, his mother's husband. The only option was for all of them to flee.

They wouldn't get far. The umbusi would have them hunted. They'd be found and executed. He'd ruined everything. He'd murdered his own family.

The door to Lekan's chambers flew open, and a keep guard, wild-eyed and sword at the ready, burst into the room.

"Hold!" the guard ordered. "Tau?"

"Ochieng," Tau said. He'd been caught by the man his father helped place on the guard.

"What are you...Goddess wept!" Ochieng said, seeing Lekan's body. "What have you—"

"I didn't come to kill him." Tau shut his mouth. What could he say that would matter?

"Why me? Why tonight?" Ochieng muttered. "Why, Goddess?"

Tau hung his head, and blood from the wound on his face dripped on the floor. He wouldn't fight, not against Ochieng.

"Get on, then," Ochieng said.

"What?"

Ochieng indicated the open window. "Get on. I'll close it behind you."

"I...I can't. They'll know it was me. My family—"

"They won't know, Tau. Get, now, before I change my mind."

Tau didn't know what to say, could think of nothing to say. He got onto the windowsill, found the handholds he'd used to climb up, and stopped, locking eyes with Ochieng.

"Go on. Quick, now."

Tau nodded, began to make his way back down the wall, and Ochieng got to work, picking up one of Lekan's shirts, balling it up, squatting down and wiping at the blood in the room. He swished the scrunched cloth back and forth, diluting and scrubbing the blood into the rain-dampened floor. Then, when he got close, Ochieng paused, crouching over the Noble's body before hawking up phlegm and spitting on Lekan's face.

"That's for Anya, for Nkiru's family, and for Aren, you heartless cek," he said.

It was slow, slower going down than up, and Tau's heart hammered in his chest. He worried about being seen, and when he heard a bang and clatter from Lekan's room, he came close to falling off the wall.

Ochieng's voice followed the tumult. "Guards! Guards! Goddess, no! He's fallen down the stairs! Nkosi Lekan needs help, please!"

Tau moved faster, as fast as he dared, and his heart didn't slow till his feet touched the ground. He stepped back, taking his hand from the wall of the Onai's keep, where his mother, her husband, Tau's sister, and Jabari were sleeping, and he considered turning himself in.

He couldn't imagine Ochieng's ruse would work, and though he'd be killed if he surrendered, he could beg for mercy for his family. It was a child's hope, he knew. Ochieng would be executed for trying to fool the Onai, and Tau's family had a better chance in the hands of Ochieng's story than in mercy from Nobles.

Tau closed his eyes and prayed to the Goddess. Prayed she would see fit to spare his family. Prayed Ochieng would be believed.

He hadn't finished the few muttered words when he heard more voices from the keep's second floor. He needed to hurry; the incomplete prayer would have to be enough. Taking a last look at the keep, he locked the image of it and of Kerem in his mind. He was unlikely to see either again.

A scream from inside pierced the night, startling him. It was a woman's voice, though not the umbusi's. Even so, Tau was out of time.

He ripped a strip of cloth from his tattered shirt and pressed it against the cut on his face, hissing at the pain. He couldn't leave a trail of blood to bring doubt to the story Ochieng would tell. His face feeling like a mask of fire, Tau slunk off, sticking to the shadows and heading for the spot where he'd hidden his travel sack and weapons. He'd retrieve them and make for the southern capital, Kigambe.

Nothing had gone as planned, but Lekan was dead and the Petty Noble had paid for his part in Aren's murder.

It didn't help.

It had happened too fast, too unintentionally, and Lekan hadn't had to face the evil he'd done, not fully.

As it stood, instead of seeing the scales tip back toward balance, all Tau could see was the Petty Noble's caved-in head, the image bringing bile up his throat. He swallowed, forcing it down, along with the guilt. Lekan deserved what he got, deserved it far more than the hedena Tau had killed in Daba.

And if Tau didn't feel better, it had to be because there was still so much to do. He needed to go to Kigambe and test to become an Ihashe. Then he'd have military status and the right to blood-duel anyone in the Chosen military. The old law was the only way a Lesser could kill a Noble with impunity.

Tau's mind raced, flitting from Zuri, his mother and sister, and Jabari to his life in Kerem, to all he'd lost, and then to Aren, his father. He felt hopeless, helpless, but that wouldn't do.

He breathed deep, taking the time to work his way back to calm, just like his father had always taught. That done, he took the first steps to Kigambe. He'd finish what he'd started.

"Kellan Okar, Dejen Olujimi, Abasi Odili," he said to himself.

There were three men left to kill.

CHAPTER FOUR

KIGAMBE

I t took Tau two days and most of the third to walk to Kigambe. He came down the mountains of Kerem and followed the Usebe path, paralleling the ocean. He watched the Roar as he traveled, letting the water's fury, its fight against itself, occupy him instead of his own thoughts.

But there were no distractions at night, and Tau's evenings were filled with dreams of the people he loved dying. The worst nightmare came on the second night. He had a dream of Daba and of driving his sword through the chest of the hedena warrior woman, but her face had turned into Zuri's. He'd woken in a fit, reaching for his sword, staring out into the darkness for signs of danger. It had taken him a full span to go back to sleep.

In the daytime, he saw few others, and those he did see kept their distance from the young man who carried two swords and had a weeping wound across his face. On the afternoon of the third day, he marveled at how flat everything was. Tau had been born and raised in Kerem. He'd never been to Kigambe, or Palm, or any of the larger cities that stood on the valley floor of the peninsula. He'd never been to the North. Tau had never been anywhere, and when he came upon Kigambe, it stole his breath.

The capital city of the southern half of the peninsula was the color of polished copper. Its adobe buildings stretched as far as the eye could see, and surrounding it all was a series of defensive walls that formed ever-smaller concentric rings. It reminded Tau of the toy mazes that Kwaku, the Mawasian toy maker, sold.

Smoke from the city, from the cook fires and furnaces of its several hundred thousand citizens, rose into the air above the urban sprawl. The smoke curled up, billowed, then merged with and disappeared into the sky, leaving the city under a sheet of haze and trapped heat.

Beyond the city's borders, Tau saw more people than he had believed existed in the whole world. Women and men from the Drudge, Common, Harvester, and Governor castes mingled on the paths leading to Kigambe, many of them crowding the countless market stalls stuck to its walls like ticks.

Kigambe was not on the water and the Roar was more than a three-span walk behind Tau, but the constant sound of so many voices made it seem like he was standing on a cliff overlooking the ocean. There were near on two million Chosen in the peninsula. Tau knew this, and to him it looked like all of them were in the city. Kigambe wasn't even the peninsula's largest city. Palm City was bigger, and Jirza, the North's capital, was said to hold almost as many.

In a daze, Tau walked up to Kigambe's outermost wall, the press of people and their stench growing as he got closer. He heard accents from the North and the Center, he saw styles of dress on women and men that must have been designed to shock, and he saw the cripples.

Everywhere had them, and Kerem had a few who had come back from the front lines or from other contested territories throughout the peninsula, but Tau had never seen so many in one place. He saw one-legged men hobble about on unknown errands, while men with stumps for arms carted heavy goods on their heads or strapped to their shoulders. The blind, they worked too, though with parchment and ink-dipped flaxen rods as they listened for calls from the market sellers before jotting down marks or counts.

Back home, men who had proven themselves in battle were given stipends and rations for their military service, and nothing more was expected. They had already given more than most, so the thinking went. The larger cities, it seemed, did not do it this way. Instead, they worked their Proven like they worked everyone else.

It seemed cruel. These men had already suffered.

"You're staring, village boy."

Tau started. The old man, who had just one arm and one eye, had spoken to him.

"It's impolite," the old Proven said. "B'sides, boy like you, looking like you, should be last to stare." The old man drew his finger over his nose and across his cheek, drawing the shape of the long gouge cut into Tau's face.

"I meant no offense," Tau said, touching the still scabbing wound and wincing when his finger brushed the flesh.

"First time in Kigambe? You're here for the testing."

Tau said nothing.

"You look of age and you've already taken a cut or two." The man laughed. "So don't let my scratches scare you!" He raised his stump of an arm. "There's no greater honor than to fight for the peninsula against the slough-skins."

"They...," Tau said, not knowing how to finish his question.

"They caught me after the Battle for Cata. They took the eye," he said, pointing to the ruined socket with his stump. "Burned it out and let the pain of that stew with me. Then they came for the arm."

Tau's mouth was dry. "They're savages," he said.

"They are," he replied. "No give in them, though. They fight hard and die harder."

Tau didn't know what to say to that.

"The Guardian Ceremony will be starting soon. You should see it before your testing. Inspirational to see the Indlovu Citadel's best. Better hurry if you want a decent spot."

"The ceremony where the queen speaks, that's today?" asked Tau.

"It is," said the maimed man, flicking a rough tongue over yellowed teeth. "I'll be there to watch. Always am. Find it heartening to see the next crop doing their duty. We must all do our part, neh?"

"We must," Tau murmured.

"Take Kibwe all the way to Ejiro, then left. You can't miss it, or everyone."

"What?"

"The ceremony. Take the Kibwe path all the way to Ejiro. Turn left and you'll see the crowd."

"Ah, my thanks," said Tau.

"Perhaps I'll see you."

"See me?"

"At the testing."

"Perhaps," said Tau, inclining his head and leaving for the nearest gate that would take him into Kigambe proper. He looked back and the Proven flashed his broken-toothed smile.

Inside the walls the sun's heat bounced off the cramped adobe buildings and turned the skinny paths of Kigambe into open-air ovens. The city stunk of damp clothes, dried sweat, urine, and rot, and no one seemed to notice. Tau had to stop himself from covering his nose, and he was jostled left and right by people who hurried from path to path. He mumbled apologies but received no response.

The Chosen of Kigambe seemed mute and stiff of neck. Most of them walked with their heads down, mouths shut, and eyes forward.

"Care, young warrior!" a voice yelled in his ear.

Tau jerked back. He was face-to-face with a Sah priest. The priest, in a sand-stained cassock, had his shoulder-length hair locked into a series of thick braids. He had a feverish look about him.

"Hear the Goddess's word!" the man singsonged to the people around him. "Hear Her word today!"

Tau moved to the side to let the man pass.

"Come, pray with us, fellow Chosen. The Goddess should hear all our voices raised in devotion."

"I have to go," Tau told the priest.

"All you have to do is the Goddess's will," the priest said, eyeing the jagged cut across Tau's face. "What else can matter?" He raised his voice then and began his singsong once more. "Hear the Goddess's word! Hear Her word today!"

Tau stepped back, letting the flow of foot traffic carry him from the priest and toward the place the old soldier had described. He walked until reaching the main circle of Kigambe, where the Guardian Ceremony was already underway.

The circle was filled with people, and a raised platform had been erected near its far side. Queen Tsiora, the KaEid, and members of the queen's retinue were on the platform. The queen stood front and center, her hands raised above her head, and in them she held a dagger.

Tau squinted, relying on his sharp eyes to tease out details. The dagger's blade was pure dragon scale, and its hilt was gold-veined bronze wrapped in leather. It was a work of art.

Queen Tsiora lowered the deadly weapon into the upturned hands of a kneeling graduate from the Southern Ihashe Isikolo. The single best warrior, from both the southern and northern Ihashe training schools, received a dagger to celebrate their achievement and graduation from the cycle-long training.

It was different for students of the Indlovu Citadel. The Nobles' training lasted three cycles and the top three students from each of the first two cycles received guardian daggers. Then the top three graduating warriors of the citadel were gifted with guardian swords.

The message was not subtle. Each cycle, Indlovu warriors received nine dragon-scale weapons to the Ihashe's one. An Ihashe's value could thus be calculated. They were worth one-tenth of a single Indlovu.

The cheering died down and the Ihashe initiate stepped back with his dagger. The first-cycle Indlovu initiates were next. Three men were awarded their daggers, and the second-cycle winners came to the stage.

It was the third man in that grouping who concerned Tau. That man had cut Tau's father's hand away. That man was Kellan Okar.

DAGGERS

Tau began pushing his way toward the platform. He'd been at the edge of the crowd, on the far side of the circle, but was determined to get closer. The women and men around him pushed back, not wanting to let him pass, but he paid them no mind.

Kellan Okar was on a knee in front of the queen. She held the guardian dagger aloft and placed the priceless weapon in his hands. She bid him rise, and Kellan Okar, murderer, accepted the honor the queen bestowed upon him. The crowd cheered.

Tau was nearing the stage, his sheathed swords banging into those around him. Kellan stepped back, Tau tracked him, and that was when he saw Abasi Odili. Kellan had gone to stand beside the guardian councillor, who smiled and clapped him on the shoulder.

The queen moved on, gifting guardian swords to the citadel's top graduates. The three men to whom she gave the weapons looked like violence molded into human form. Then she gave the stage to the woman who led the Gifted.

The KaEid stepped forward, raised her arms, and began to pray. Everyone grew still, muttering along to familiar words. Tau shimmied sideways, slipping past a group of Lessers, and bumped a woman to the ground. The man with her cursed him, then noticed Tau's swords, and his eyes went wide.

"You can't have weapons here," he said.

Tau pressed on, leaving the couple behind as the KaEid ended her prayer and began her speech.

"Chosen," the KaEid said to the crowd, "the Goddess, through her Guardians, guided our ancestors, guided Queen Taifa to this land."

Her voice was rich and full, the type that could calm or reassure. It did neither for Tau. His eyes were locked on Kellan and Odili, and it felt as if he had to get closer.

He wanted them to see him, knowing they wouldn't realize who he was. He wanted them to look at him and past him as if he didn't matter, when he was the one who mattered most. In little more than a cycle, he was going to end their lives.

"He's over there," a voice said.

Tau looked. It was the man who had commented on his swords. He was with two city guardsmen, and seeing Tau, they began pushing through the crowd to get to him.

Tau cursed himself for being a fool. He didn't know what rule or law he'd broken by having swords at the ceremony, but he couldn't risk the guards taking him. If the offense was a serious one, he might miss the testing.

Tau angled away, moving parallel to Kellan and Abasi as the KaEid gestured at the world around them.

"Our peninsula," she said, "is one of the Goddess's greatest gifts. It is a home where we are protected by ocean, mountains, the Curse, and Guardians."

Tau wondered if the KaEid had ever seen a raid. There was nothing about that day at Daba that had seemed safe. Hadn't the hedeni navigated the coastline of that protective ocean? Had they not climbed the peninsula's mountains? Had they not killed Chosen in their beds that night?

"Xidda is our proving ground. It exists to make us strong enough to end the world's greatest evil. We will pass the Goddess's test and defeat the hedeni. Then, triumphant, strong, we will return to our homeland. We will return to Osonte and end the Cull!"

Tau wasn't afraid of the Cull, of the mythical silver-skinned immortals. He'd never seen them. He knew no man, woman, or child who'd ever seen them. They were fairy tales to hide the real evil, the evil on the stage in front of him.

"There are challenging times ahead," the KaEid told them. "The hedeni have once again formed alliances among their savage tribes."

The crowd was unsettled by that admission, and the ripple of fear rooted many in place, making it difficult for Tau to push through and keep ahead of the two guardsmen following him.

"They are many! Ten to every one of us," the KaEid cried out. "But we stand firm against them. We are the unbroken cliff that cleaves the endless ocean." The KaEid had the crowd. They were quiet, listening. "What are countless hordes in the face of faith and righteousness? Nothing! What are spears and axes against the unyielding bronze of the greatest military the world has ever known? Nothing! What are savages...against the rage of dragons?"

The crowd roared and the honored warriors on the stage lifted their dragon-scale weapons in the air. The cheer was deafening, and in trying to evade the guardsmen, Tau was almost to the platform. Two more steps and he'd be close enough to see the individual beads of sweat on Kellan's forehead.

"I see him!"

The cry came from a guardsman ten strides ahead. The man's sword was clear of its scabbard and he was with two others. They were off to the right, between Tau and the platform, and were trying to coordinate with the guards behind him, trying to box him in.

"The Chosen must fight faithlessness," said the KaEid to the masses. "The Chosen must fight the hedeni. We do the Goddess's bidding and She blesses our valley, holding the curse that blights the rest of Xidda at bay."

One of the Lessers—he looked to be from the Governor caste— stood his ground against the guards coming for Tau, complaining about their rough treatment as they tried to muscle past. The closest guard bashed the man in the face. The Governor crumpled and was snatched up by the other two, who must have thought the mouthy Lesser to be part of the commotion.

Tau shot a look at the platform. The KaEid was still speaking, and most of the gathered were focused on her. Kellan, however, had noticed the disturbance. He hadn't seen Tau, but his eyes scanned the mass of people and Tau shrank back, feeling an instinctual need to hide.

"You, there!" the nearest guard shouted, pointing to Tau. "Hold!"

The crowd cheered the KaEid, the guard drew closer, and Tau took a step back. He needed time to think and had none with which to do it.

"Stop!" Time was up. The guard was within reach, shoved a Common out of the way, and stretched to grab at Tau.

Tau recoiled, slapped down the grasping arm, turned, and ran, forcing his way out of the crowd, away from the platform, and away from Kellan Okar and Abasi Odili.

He couldn't let himself be caught. He couldn't lose his chance at justice. He wanted Kellan to join his father, the coward Okar, in ignominy. He wanted Dejen's loss and death at a Lesser's hand to blight the Olujimi name for generations.

More than anything, he needed to face Abasi Odili and make him suffer. He already knew, with a seer's clarity, how it would end between them. He'd fight him in front of a crowd of Nobles and Lessers, he'd make it brutal, he'd make it last, and before it was over, he'd break the Royal Noble's spirit. Odili would beg for death.

As Tau ran, desperate to escape the city guards, the dream of it was all that mattered. He wasn't ready to destroy his foes, but he would be, and the first step on the path to vengeance lay before him. The testing began in the morning, and Tau would fight to win his place among the Ihashe or die in the attempt.

MATCH

He lost the city guards in the crowd. Tau had climbed a building, a store it looked like, and hidden on the roof to wait for them to pass. When it seemed safe, he'd climbed down, twisting his ankle on a loose rock. He was fine but had to limp his way through the city's poorer sections, looking for a place to rest.

That night he slept at the dead end of a short alley with his back pressed against its rearmost wall, watching the entrance. He placed his swords and pack behind him, hoping no one would risk a fight over his meagre possessions. Tau was hungry but too tired for an empty stomach to keep him awake, and he fell asleep sitting.

He woke before dawn, tired, and knew he should sleep more but couldn't. Instead, he waited until the sun's heat returned to the world, gathered his things, and went looking for the famed Heroes' Circle, where the Ihashe testing took place.

He found it by following the throng of armed young men, and walking alongside them, he tried to blend in. He drew looks anyway. The reactions made him worry he'd be turned away on appearance alone. He was dirty and smelled worse than he looked, and the scabbing wound, winding its way from nose to cheek, didn't help. True, every Lesser had the right, some would say duty, to test for the Ihashe, but Tau didn't relax until he saw others in equally rough shape.

In threadbare clothing, carrying rusting equipment and often barefoot, they were Low Commons from the smallest hamlets. They'd have had inadequate training, they'd be malnourished, and there was little chance of them passing the testing. Given Tau's condition, it was hard to think he'd fare better.

The Heroes' Circle was larger than the one in which the Guardian Ceremony had taken place, and it was filled with thousands of men. Traditionally, one in ten would pass the testing, allowing them to be trained at the Ihashe isikolo. The failures, especially if they were Low or High Commons, would have to become Ihagu or, refusing that, Drudge.

Ihagu were nothing more than guards, foot soldiers, and fodder, often first to die in battle, and most important, they did not receive official military status. Tau had to have military status, and that meant he had to be better than nine of every ten men in the circle.

"Test takers!" yelled a hard-faced Ihashe warrior in his middle years. "Line up." He was old enough to have been to the front lines and put in his time, and still had elected to serve another term. He was a full-blood Ihashe, a military man through and through. "You'll get a number and linen with which to wrap your practice sword. Wrap it well. If the linen falls loose or you draw blood because of an uncovered edge, you lose your match."

Tau and the men around him formed up as the Ihashe explained the rest.

"The rules are simple. The Proven who attends your fight will count each hit you make as a point, and they'll give your opponent a point for each hit you take. You win if your opponent begs for the Goddess's mercy or if you've more points when the match ends.

"Matches last two hundred breaths. The attending Proven counts the points and breaths. The match doesn't end if you yell 'no' or 'cek' or anything else. You say, 'Goddess's mercy,' and the hitting stops, neh?"

Tau and the others murmured their acceptance.

"Mind, there are no head strikes with weapons. You hit someone in the head, you lose. You step outside the ring, you lose. You lose on day one, you're out. You lose on day two, you're out. You make it to day three, you're in, but it's still a fight.

"The isikolo masters, that's 'umqondisi' to you, will be watching on day three. They're looking to claim talent for their scale. Trust me, you want to make it into a good scale."

There was more nodding.

"Last thing... You happen to be Tsiory reborn and win ten matches, then you're in, no matter what day you do it on." The full-blood smiled at that, all teeth, some mirth, none of it shared. "So make ten wins today," he said, walking away and calling over his shoulder. "Get your numbers, get to fighting."

The Ihashe knew their business, and the long lines of test takers were handled with speed as the busy circle hummed with hushed voices and nervous energy. It was the sound of thousands of men preparing, focusing, and wrapping dull practice swords in thick, protective linen.

Tau saw that those with gambesons donned them and those without wore many layers of their heaviest clothing. It made him thankful for his father's old gambeson. He knew the other men, the ones layering up, wouldn't last a two hundred count in the sun. They'd have to beat their opponents quickly or risk sun sickness.

"Five thousand forty! Five thousand forty!" a Proven called out near the set of five individual fighting circles to which Tau had been assigned.

"Ready," Tau shouted in response.

He was in the day's first round of fights. Other Proven called out other numbers and other men stepped forward. Tau took a deep breath, closed his eyes, and emptied his mind like his father had taught. He sought the calm, the peace, that would allow his muscles to relax and his training to take over. It didn't come.

"C'mon, then," said the Proven judging his match. "I've got a long day, neh."

Tau stepped forward, and the Proven, who was missing his right leg below the knee, handed him a battered helm and bronze shield. The shield's edges were rounded off, unlike the razor-sharp edges it'd have for war. Chosen fought with sword and shield, but Tau had always struggled with shields. He hadn't even taken one to the raid in Daba.

Tau hefted the round metal disk and slipped his left arm through the straps. It was heavier than the one his father let him use for practice. He raised and lowered his left arm to get a feel for it and plopped the ill-fitting helm on his head.

"Five thousand ninety-two!" the Proven said, calling for Tau's opponent. "Where are you, char it?"

"Here, here. I'm here."

Tau's opponent was Tau's height, and from the quality of cloth he wore and his proud strut, he had to be Governor caste. He was slim, he had squinty eyes, and the skin on his thin face was pockmarked badly enough to make him look like a hedena with curse scars.

The Proven gave the man his gear and pointed to the fighting circle. Tau's opponent ran onto it, choosing his spot first. Tau moved opposite him and learned why the Governor caste fighter had moved so quickly. Tau was facing into the sun.

"It's Tau," Tau said, introducing himself to his opponent.

The pockmarked Governor ignored him, warming up by firing his sword back and forth in a series of thrusts.

"Fight!" growled the Proven, and the Governor ran forward.

It took him no time to cross the distance, and he swung for Tau's head. Tau leapt back and brought his sword up to block the illegal blow. He was quick to realize his error, but it was still too late. His squinty-eyed opponent dropped the ruse, changed levels, and bashed Tau under the arm. Tau lurched backward, almost dropping his sword from the pain.

"Point!" yelled the Proven.

Tau was on the defensive and had to dance backward to avoid getting clobbered. The Governor was slender but fast. His follow-up attacks pushed Tau all the way to the edge of the ring, close to forcing him out. With no more than a step to spare, Tau skipped away from the edge and toward the fighting circle's center, taking a hit to the thigh and body as he did.

"Point! Point!" said the Proven.

Tau was panting, sucking air in heavy gulps. The match was in its earliest stages, but he'd spent all of it running. Getting desperate, he launched an attack of his own.

He thrust at his opponent and the Governor turned, avoiding the strike. Tau darted forward, jerking his blade into a sideswiping swing that would crash into the man's exposed back, but the Governor whirled, blocking the strike, and with his near arm he elbowed Tau in the temple.

Tau reeled, disengaged, and flashed a look at the Proven. The officiant shrugged. It seemed head strikes made without the use of weapons were allowed, though no points were awarded.

The Governor brought himself back to center, squinting worse than before. "Looks like your journey ends here, Drudge."

Tau swung and the Governor stepped out of reach.

"You're not bad," he said. "You're just not good."

"Half-match," the Proven shouted.

It had been a hundred count and Tau was three points down. He pushed forward, swinging at his opponent's shoulder, leg, and arm. The Governor blocked each attack while moving in circles.

"Why fight?" he asked Tau. "Commons shouldn't even be in the Ihashe."

Tau was tired, hungry, and hot. His underarm throbbed where he'd been hit, and his sweat was seeping into the wound on his face, making it burn. He was losing and it wasn't something he'd prepared for.

He'd trained his whole life for this, and though he had no love for fighting, he'd always believed himself strong enough to pass the testing. It seemed, however, he wasn't even good enough to beat his first opponent.

The Governor threw a mock thrust his way and Tau stumbled back. The Governor laughed and Tau grew angry. He refused to let a stunted pock-faced scapegrace stop him.

Yelling in anger and frustration, he went after the Governor, calling on fighting form after fighting form, intending to overwhelm the skinny cek, but the Governor pranced about, dodging this, blocking that, and counterattacking whenever Tau overextended.

"Point! Point!" the Proven called out two more times, Tau's barrage ending with him down five to nil.

"No matter, Tau," the Governor said, stretching out his name like it was a dirty word. "Your mother will still love you. Just tell her the truth. You lost to a better breed of man."

He was trying to make Tau angrier. He wanted him making mistakes, and it was working. Tau was furious, and even filled with fury, he couldn't deny it—the Governor was the stronger swordsman.

RULES

Tau wasn't going to beat him and tried telling himself justice did not depend on being military. He told himself he could go to Citadel City. He could find Kellan and put a knife in the man's back. He could learn where Dejen Olujimi lived and slit the Ingonyama's throat while he slept. He told himself Abasi Odili could die in a similar manner. He told himself it would serve, and he knew it wouldn't.

Tau could not give peace to Aren's soul by killing men in their sleep. No, he had to make it into the Ihashe. He had to win this match. He wanted revenge, needed revenge, and there was no price he wouldn't pay to get it. So Tau channeled Jabari at his teasing best. The Governor thought he knew taunts, but no one could make you lose your head like Jabari could.

"I'll tell my family," Tau said to the Governor. "I'll tell them I lost to a half-breed slough-skin whose real father, his hedena father, must have taken his mother in the dirt, on a raid."

"Nceku!" said the Governor, coming fast for Tau.

Tau tried to fend him off but lost another point. He was down too many and worried there wasn't enough time. He had to work faster.

"Did your mother like it, you think?" Tau said, disgusted with himself, his behavior, and his plan. "Rutting with a savage in the muck? How can the man who calls himself your father look at that marked-up face and not know you come from heretic stock?"

"You debased Low Common cek!" The Governor battered at Tau's sword and shield.

Tau did his best to defend, gave up another point, and lowered his shield and sword to cover the bottom half of his chest and waist. The Governor was in a fervor, and though Tau was taking a beating, he wanted to hurt him more.

"Yes, yes!" squealed Tau, doing his best, that time, to imitate his childhood bully Chibuzo, who had been three cycles older. "Give it to me! Put a pock-faced hedena in me!" Chibuzo, the bully, had made it into the Southern Ihashe Isikolo. Chibuzo had died there, in training.

The Governor screamed and swung wildly. It was the swing Tau had been waiting for. He stepped closer, avoiding the heaviest part of it, sent a prayer to the Goddess, and took the blow on the side of the head.

The world exploded in a dazzle of multicolored light. Then Tau was on the ground. His helm had come off and it rolled in lazy circles beside him. Dazed and expecting another attack, he raised his sword, but the attack didn't come.

"No! No!" the Governor said, pleading. "I didn't mean—"

"The match is over," the Proven told him. "We have a winner, by disqualification."

"You can't! He's not deserving! You can't—"

"What you can't do is strike an opponent in the head," the Proven told him. "The winner is five thousand forty."

Tau had won. He was still in the contest and needed to prepare for his next match. He tried to stand. The world turned green and his eyes crossed. He squeezed them shut and forced his way up. He could do this. He would do this.

He stepped out of the fighting circle, his head feeling altogether too large, as the sights and sounds of combat swirled round him. He heard bronze clanging on bronze, shouts, screams, and points being called as the young Lessers of the South battled for the chance to become killers.

The Governor was still arguing with the Proven who had judged their match. He had to be carried out of the fighting circle by two full-blood Ihashe. Tau felt no satisfaction. The Governor was right. Tau hadn't deserved the win.

In the nearest circle, a massive man, one of the biggest Lessers Tau had ever seen, was crushing his opponent, who quickly called for the Goddess's mercy. On Tau's other side, the match was more even. Two warriors hacked at each other like stonecutters. The fighting was all strength and bluster, no technique. Tau couldn't tell who would win, but at least the world no longer looked bright green.

"Five thousand forty!" a new Proven called out. The man was standing two fighting circles away and calling Tau's number. "Five thousand forty and five thousand three hundred ten!"

It was time to fight.

Tau walked over, swinging his sword and twisting his neck back and forth to loosen it. His opponent arrived at the circle as he did, and Tau tried to look like he wasn't on the cusp of throwing up. The Low Common across from Tau had a bulbous nose, wore several heavy shirts in place of a gambeson, and was barefoot. He nodded to Tau and Tau returned the gesture. They stepped in the ring and raised their swords.

"Goddess smile upon you," said the Low Common.

"Fight!" the Proven said.

Tau's opponent lurched into a looping attack. Tau blocked. His sword was inside the Low Common's blade and Tau lifted up and away, moving the man's weapon out of position, leaving him unable to defend as Tau brought his sword down on the Low Common's shoulder. The man cried out and darted back, but not before Tau swung again, smashing his blade into the Common's upper arm.

He yelped and dropped his sword, and Tau stabbed him in the gut. He doubled over, fell to the ground, and curled into a ball. Tau stepped back, waiting for the Proven to call the match.

"He has a twelve count," the Proven warned, encouraging Tau to batter the downed man.

Tau didn't move and the Low Common wheezed his way to his knees before crawling for his sword.

"He gets to his feet and the match continues to two hundred," the Proven said.

"Then it does," Tau said.

The Low Common got to his sword, put a hand round its hilt, and looked up at Tau. He must have seen something. He stayed in the dirt.

"The winner is five thousand forty," shouted the Proven.

The Low Common took his hand from the sword's hilt, watching Tau, shame writ large across his broad face. Ihagu or Drudge were his only options now, Tau knew, but he felt too empty to offer sympathy, so he left the circle, looking for water.

It was a sun span before Tau was called again. His opponent was a High Harvester in a gambeson. The pitiable bastard bleated for the Goddess's mercy after taking the first two hits.

Tau's fourth match was a war that lasted the entire two hundred count. Tau and his opponent were drenched in sweat by the time it was over, and Tau had lost count of the points long ago. He almost wept when the Proven lifted his arm in victory.

Fighting back tears and exhaustion, he tottered out of the fighting circle and collapsed. He knew if he was called for another match, he would lose. He lay and sat, in turns, waiting for and dreading to hear his number, and it wasn't until the sun was on its return journey to the earth that Tau heard someone beat the bronze gong that announced the end of the first day of testing.

He'd survived. He'd fought four matches and won them, though the first fight had been the most perilous. By all rights, the pockmarked Governor should be in his place.

Tau tried to take off his gambeson but couldn't raise his arms. He left the sweat-drenched padding on and shuffled away. He had to find something to eat, somewhere to sleep. The next day would be harder. Everyone would be a survivor of day one.

BRAWL

Day two was hotter. Tau hadn't slept much or eaten at all. His muscles ached, his head pounded from the blow he'd taken on the first day, and he was walking with a limp from a cramp that wouldn't loosen. The Heroes' Circle was just as crowded as it had been the day before, the failed competitors replaced with spectators come to see the "real" fighters. Umqondisi from both the Northern and Southern Isikolo had come too, scouting for talent. Tau spotted Jayyed, and thinking back to Jabari's words, he became determined to impress the man. He hoped the onetime Guardian Council adviser would see him fight.

"Five thousand forty!"

Tau stepped into his fighting circle and did not like what he saw. He was facing a stocky, bare-chested man with no shield. The man had raised welts over his chest, back, and arms from the day prior. He eyed Tau, looking him up and down, but said nothing. Tau tossed his shield outside the circle, though not in some misguided attempt at fairness. He hated fighting with the damned things anyway.

"Fight!" the Proven ordered, and they did.

The topless man held back, so Tau attacked, coming fast, looking to finish the fight early. The topless man was faster. He shrugged off Tau's first and second strikes with the edge of his blade and sent a jab for Tau's stomach. Tau parried and their swords tangled. The stocky man stepped in, grabbed the wrist of Tau's sword arm, and bent it. Tau mirrored the move and they grappled, tripping and falling in the dirt. There was a scramble, a dropped sword, a head butt, a curse, a retrieved sword, and a heavy kick, and then both were back up, circling.

Tau's left eye was swelling shut and the jagged cut Lekan had given him was bleeding through its scabs. The man's head had felt like a rock when he'd slammed it into Tau's face. At least the stocky fighter wouldn't be as fast. Tau had kicked him in the thigh as hard as he could and the bare-chested brawler was favoring the leg.

Tau lifted his sword, keeping it parallel to the ground and aimed at his opponent's chest. The brawler slapped at it with his blade, trying to keep Tau focused on the meaningless contact as he planned his next offensive. Tau didn't give him the chance.

He came forward, sword point leading and punching through the air like a needle through cloth. His opponent skipped backward and Tau harried him, taking him to the fighting circle's boundary. With no more room for retreat, the swordplay began in earnest.

The brawler yelled something unintelligible and attacked. Tau snarled and went for him. Blades connected; they repositioned, swung again: block, riposte, each looking for any advantage, any chance for a clean strike.

The brawler gave Tau a hard hit to the arm, Tau blasted him in the waist, and the man moved back, hunching over his injured core. Tau followed, smashing at him, the pressure forcing the brawler to his knees.

Tau had the advantage, but the match had taken a toll. He was wearied and could barely feel his arms or legs. He had to end this, and, roaring, he hammered at the kneeling man like an errant nail. Bang, bang, bang!

The sword fell from the brawler's hand. Bang, bang, bang! Tau didn't stop. He hit him on his arms and shoulders and clubbed him in the chest. The brawler fell over and Tau hit him and hit him until he heard the Proven's shouting over the blood booming in his ears.

"Victory! Victory! Match over! The match is over!" the officiant screamed.

Tau backed away. The brawler was mewling like a newborn. Five, Tau thought. Five more wins and he was guaranteed a place among the Ihashe.

He wanted to laugh and didn't have the energy. He had just gotten the joke, the one that had tickled the smiling Ihashe who had explained the rules the day before. Tau couldn't win ten of these fights. Tau didn't think he could win one more.

He made his way to the nearest bucket, cupped his hands, and drank, the cut on his face dripping blood into the water.

"Five thousand forty!" shouted a voice several fighting circles away. "Five thousand forty."

Tau looked toward the shouting and saw the Proven and the fighting circle. He could leave. He was so tired. He could leave.

"Five thousand forty!"

Tau left the blood-tainted bucket of water and walked over. He was joined by the huge Low Common he'd seen bludgeon a man on the first day.

"Uduak," the massive man said, pointing a thick finger at himself.

Tau looked up and into the muscular man's bland, heavy-browed face. "Tau," he told him.

The giant shook his head. "Nine," he said, pointing at Tau's chest. "Nine?"

"Ninth fight," he said, stepping into the same circle as Tau.

NINE

Uduak held a great sword almost as tall as Tau. On his other arm was a massive circular shield. He wore a full gambeson and was holding a bronze helm. The brute stuffed the helm onto his sweat-slicked shaven head. It covered him down to his neck and had a single piece of thick bronze down its center, protecting his nose.

"Shield, neh?" the attending Proven asked, as if he doubted anything would make the slightest difference to this match's outcome.

"Yes," Tau said. He didn't like fighting with one, but he couldn't imagine surviving a blow from Uduak's great sword, no matter how much linen was wrapped around it. A crowd was forming and Tau knew they weren't here to watch him.

"Fight!" the Proven shouted, and Uduak charged.

Tau tried to get out of the way, but Uduak's great sword was too long to dodge, so he blocked with his shield. The contact spun him around, putting him on his ass, and the pain was instant. It vibrated up Tau's blocking arm, into his shoulder, and down his back.

He jumped to his feet, scurrying away from Uduak, who came at him swinging. Tau blocked two thundering blows and could no longer lift his shield arm. He shrugged off the paltry protection, letting shield slip to hot sand. Behind him the onlookers gibbered, cheering and jeering in turns.

"He's done," one of them said.

"Burn him," another shrieked.

Uduak came on.

Trying to shake some feeling back into his arm, Tau danced out of the way of the oversized man's next swing but had to use his sword to block Uduak's follow-up. The collision of swords came close to tearing his weapon from his hand.

"Goddess!" chortled a faceless fool in the crowd, half-chewed food flying from his mouth.

Tau had to attack. He sucked air into his lungs, bellowed, and ran for Uduak. The crowd cheered and Uduak didn't move. He stood there, tall as a mountain, and swung that great sword.

Tau ducked beneath the linen-covered blade and thrust for the giant's gut. Uduak stepped off the line of the thrust and swiped at Tau with his shield. The shield belted Tau aside, lifting him off the ground and flinging him through the air. He hit the sand hard and the air was blasted from his lungs. Head spinning, chest burning, he rolled to his knees. Uduak was coming for him.

Tau couldn't win, not against this. He thought to call for mercy and end the foolishness before the brute killed him. Instead, he stood. The crowd went mad. They would get to see blood.

Uduak slowed, stretching the moment. He pointed at Tau. "Nine," he said.

Tau spat, tasting copper. "Cek your nine."

Uduak swung his great sword hard enough to disembowel, linen wrap or no. Tau dove to the dirt, letting the swing spin the big man half around, and then Tau came back up, slamming his sword in the weak space below Uduak's ribs. His blade hit the brute square, punched into the gambeson, and bit flesh.

With the linen around his sword intact, the superficial cut was legal, and Tau had blooded the beast. The crowd howled, their rapture rising to a frenzy when Uduak looked down to see where he'd been hit.

"Point!" said the Proven, flinging a hand in the air for emphasis.

Uduak's eyes thinned to slits and his fingers danced over the hilt of that horrible sword. He banged the blade on the edge of his shield, pushing the circle of bronze farther onto his arm, and he came for Tau.

Tau gripped his sword with both hands. It wasn't meant to be swung that way, but Uduak was angry and strong enough to kill him if Tau blocked wrong with one hand. Tau thought about playing keep-away. He was a point up, and if he could stay out of reach for the rest of the match...

Uduak must have understood Tau's thinking. He was angry but smart enough to move forward with care. He cut off all angles of escape, giving Tau no room to dance. Then he began to take Tau apart.

The first strike that Tau blocked rattled his teeth. The next almost knocked him out of the circle. The third he didn't time well enough, and Uduak's linen-covered blade slapped him in the shoulder, cutting him within the rules and flinging him to the dirt. The Proven called a point for Uduak and the match was tied.

Tau scrambled to his feet, but Uduak moved with speed, his sword already swinging. With no other choice but being chopped in two, Tau jumped toward Uduak and inside the deadliest part of the sword's arc. When he was hit, he wasn't sure he hadn't been hewn apart anyway.

The blow sent him flying and he crashed into the packed clay of the fighting circle, tumbling head over heels until his helm popped up and off his head like a startled locust. Tau groaned and found he couldn't draw a full breath.

"Point!" the Proven called out.

Tau was losing and the crowd chanted something guttural, ugly. "Uduak! Uduak! Uduak!"

On will alone, Tau got to his feet. The world was tilting, his chest was a maze of agony, and he still hadn't caught his breath, but he lifted his sword and pointed it at the man for whom the crowd cheered.

"Cek your nine," Tau said, sword arm quivering.

Uduak sneered and came on. Tau let him come and, at the last moment, he darted to the right, away from Uduak's sword. Gripping his blade, Tau spun in a circle, hoping the momentum-powered strike would smash into Uduak's side, break something, and finish the man.

Only, his sacrifice swing didn't hit flesh. It clanged against Uduak's blocking blade, jarring Tau to his seeds and making him stumble. Uduak jerked his weapon away, lifting his sword high but letting his shield drop. He meant to finish Tau with an overhead blow.

Tau stabbed out and over Uduak's lowered shield but was too close for power. His sword nudged Uduak in the stomach, soft as a first kiss.

"Point...," the Proven said, voice rising like it was a question.

Uduak shot the Proven a look, growled, grabbed Tau's sword, and tore it from his hands. He tossed the weapon across the circle, snatched a fistful of Tau's gambeson, and yanked him close, bringing them face-to-face.

Tau punched him. Uduak didn't seem to notice. Tau hit him again. Uduak smashed his forehead into Tau's face and let him drop to the ground, blood gushing from Tau's cut. Uduak's brick of a head had torn free all the scabbing.

Uduak kicked him in the side and Tau cried out. For some reason, he could no longer hear the crowd, though he could see them all around him, screaming, demanding more violence. And one person stood out. It was someone he recognized. Jayyed Ayim, ex-adviser to the Guardian Council and umqondisi to the Ihashe isikolo, was watching.

"He has a twelve count to rise," the Proven shouted over the crowd to Uduak. "Or...you can finish him."

"He is finished," the big man said.

Tau was weaponless and battered. He had no strength left and no chance to beat the man who stood over him. He was going to lose and wanted to lie there in the mix of blood, sand, and shame. He wanted to lie there and die.

Uduak leaned over him. "Nine," he snarled, spitting in Tau's face, before turning away and lifting his arms in victory.

The thick gob of phlegmy saliva clung to Tau's cheek and neck.

He left it there when he stood. He left it there when he ran at Uduak and tackled him.

The big man squawked as they went down. They rolled once, Tau got on top, and he rained down blows. Uduak still had his sword and shield, but from his back and in close combat, they were more hindrance than help.

"Nceku!" Tau swore in Uduak's face. "Nceku! Nceku!"

Uduak needed a free hand to deal with Tau but couldn't shake his shield free. He dropped his sword and used that hand to grab Tau by the head. He squeezed and tossed Tau aside like he was a child.

Tau landed beside the enormous sword, picked it up, and squared off with Uduak, who had only his shield. The crowd was silent.

Uduak stared at Tau like he was the only other being in existence. "I'm going to kill you."

Tau was having a hard enough time holding the huge sword and couldn't think of a response. So he attacked. Uduak opened his shield, offering up a perfect target, and Tau stabbed him full in the chest.

Uduak took the blow, took hold of Tau's right wrist, the one holding the sword, and pulled Tau to him. If the blades had been uncovered, if they had been razor sharp, Uduak would have died. The blade was not sharp. The blade was not uncovered. It did not kill Uduak. It dug into his gambeson, cutting into his flesh a finger-span, and he bashed it away, still holding Tau's wrist.

"Point!" screeched the Proven. "That was a point!"

Tau struggled and Uduak lifted his bronze shield into the air, aiming its edge. Tau's eyes went wide, fear coursing through him. He fought Uduak's grip but might as well have pulled on a mountain. Uduak brought the shield down and Tau was screaming before it smashed into his wrist. His screams grew louder when the bones there shattered.

Uduak released him and Tau went down, clutching his mangled arm. Uduak lifted the shield again, aiming for Tau's chest.

"Nine!" Uduak bellowed, but Tau didn't hear him over the pain.

"Two hundred! Two hundred! The match is over!" called the Proven, hobbling over as fast as he could on one leg and crutches.

Uduak turned to the Proven in disbelief and back to Tau. His lips were curled, teeth bared, and the muscles on his arms were flexed, tensed with the need to cave in Tau's chest.

"Kill him and you forfeit!" said the Proven.

Uduak screamed in frustration, tossed the shield aside, and sent a boot flying for Tau's head, knocking him senseless.

CHAPTER FIVE

SCALE

Tau woke on a raised straw pallet. It was night and he was in a large room with several other beds. His head throbbed and his wrist was splinted. He moaned and two shadows approached.

"Where am I?" Tau asked, throat dry as a dead man's eyes.

"The Ihashe barracks in Kigambe," answered the smaller of the two shadowed men. His accent reeked of High Governor caste. "We have been accepted as initiates, though the third day of trials is still to come."

"Accepted?" asked Tau.

"Yes, you're right to question it." The smaller man stepped into the light. He was a little taller than Tau, fit if wiry, and, unusual for Lessers, had green eyes. "My name is Hadith and I won ten matches. You already know him."

The second and much bigger man stepped into the light. It was Uduak. He looked like he wanted to finish the job he'd started in the fighting circle.

"Uduak beat the piss from you," Hadith said, "went on to win his next match and the match after that. He also has ten wins...plus a tie. Which makes you a strange case." Hadith tapped his lower lip with a finger. "I have ten wins. Uduak has ten wins. But you? You have five wins, a tie, and a broken arm. Yet, we three are Ihashe initiates together. The Goddess grows and reaps while mortals dream, does she not?"

"Water?" Tau asked, trying not to beg.

"We leave for the Southern Isikolo once the trials are over," Hadith told him. "Uduak isn't sure he's coming. The umqondisi said that if you died, Uduak would lose his place. He's been watching over you like a worried mother."

Uduak glared at Tau, flexing and unflexing his fists. Tau tried to glare back, but glaring hurt.

"Water?" he asked, begging this time.

"Ask Uduak," Hadith said. "He's the one who needs you alive."

Hadith left and Uduak growled, slipping back into the shadows. Apparently, Uduak believed Tau would live without the water. Tau closed his eyes and tried to lose consciousness, if only to hide from the pain in his wrist. He didn't think he'd be able to sleep, but when he opened his eyes again, it was morning.

Umqondisi Jayyed Ayim was there. He had food and water. Tau, mouth too dry to talk, and still in the clutches of sleep, reached for the water with his broken arm. The pain woke him the rest of the way.

"Takes longer than a day to heal," Jayyed said. "How are you, otherwise?"

"Thirsty," Tau said, looking over the middle-aged umqondisi as Jayyed helped him drink.

Jayyed was big for a Lesser, and well muscled, though nothing like Uduak. He had broad shoulders, sat straight-backed, and though his irises were dark, his eyes seemed to shine. He radiated strength, and, somehow, there was softness there too. Maybe it was his mouth, Tau thought. He looked like a man who preferred smiling.

"I've accepted you into the Ihashe isikolo," Jayyed told him. "It may be a mistake, but it's rare I'm surprised, and yesterday surprised me. We Omehi are warriors, and even among us, few have your... determination."

Jayyed helped Tau drink another sip. Tau sputtered and drank more, and Jayyed leaned in. "In a less cruel world, that determination would have made up for the gulf in skill between you and Uduak. This is not that world."

"Perhaps not," Tau tried, unsure how to respond.

"Trust me, it's not."

"Why take me, then?" Tau asked, pride pricking him.

"I know who you are, Tau Tafari," Jayyed said. "I remember you from the citadel testing. Though you didn't have that then." Jayyed waved a finger at Tau's face, near the fissure Lekan had carved across it. "It would have become infected, you know. I had the Sah priests attend to it, as well as your... more recent injuries. I can also guess why you're here, why you want to become Ihashe."

"My name is Tau Solarin," Tau said, offering nothing else. He'd made it farther than it was fair to hope.

"Solarin? Your father's name?" Jayyed guessed. "And Low Common instead of High?"

"My name is Tau Solarin."

Jayyed inclined his head, his eyes never leaving Tau's face. "So it is," he said. "Common Solarin, let me explain my interest, and you can tell me if it's warranted. Agreed?"

Tau nodded.

"I've been a military man for most my life, and throughout that time, I've chased the techniques, training, and men that make the perfect killer. The other teachers at the isikolo, given my prior posting as adviser to the Guardian Council, are willing to indulge me. They've given me a scale and will allow me to test my theories on the men in it. I'm interested in having you as one of them."

"My thanks," said Tau, not sure if thankful was a good description for how he felt.

"Maybe," Jayyed said, offering a cryptic smile. "I will push my initiates hard, taking them as close as I can to breaking, every single day. We will practice violence, we will hone it, and we will master it. I intend to turn the Lessers in my scale into warriors that are a near match for the Indlovu."

Tau's ears perked at that.

"I do it not for pride. I do it to prove that superior training methods exist that will produce superior fighters. I do it so these methods, once proven, can be adopted by all. I do it for our people's survival. Will you share my goal? Will you work toward it?"

Tau nodded, no hesitation this time. He thought of his father and he pictured Kellan, Dejen, and Odili. There was no limit to what he would do to face them as equals.

"I thought you might," said Jayyed. "I'm taking a chance with you, Common Solarin. You don't know how much of one and you may never know, but if you will put yourself through the crucible, live each day of training like you lived each moment of yesterday's fight, we'll find the man you were meant to be. And, alongside the other men in Scale Jayyed, we will show Lessers and Nobles just how far a man can go."

Jayyed stood. "Hopefully, we are the beginnings of a new Chosen military and, Goddess willing, that military will be enough to keep us all safe. We travel to the Southern Ihashe Isikolo tomorrow. Training begins when we arrive."

Tau hesitated, but his concern had to be voiced. "Umqondisi... he broke my sword arm."

Jayyed's face was not sympathetic. "Praise the Goddess, She gave you two."

ISIKOLO

The journey from Kigambe to the Southern Isikolo took most of the day. Tau was one of three and a half thousand new initiates, and though it was hard for him to admit, he was excited. Since he'd been a child, he'd dreamed of this day, and all the men around him had shared that same dream. They had done it. They were Ihashe initiates.

Tau stole glances at his new sword brothers. There was Uduak, of course, who was marching near the front of the scale, as close to Jayyed as he could get. Hadith was closer to the middle, chewing on a boiled root vegetable. The rest, the fifty-one other men Jayyed had selected, were Lessers, but that was where their similarities with Tau ended.

Physically, the fighters in Scale Jayyed were as close to Nobles as Lessers ever came. Every one of them looked like he had the strength to run to the horizon, hand-plow a field, fight a battle, and stay up drinking till dawn. Jayyed had been particular in the men he'd chosen, and Tau did not fit the mold.

The other scales were more in line with Tau's expectations. In them, he saw the kinds of men he knew, men like himself. They didn't care about that, though. They'd have nothing to do with him.

It was the first day and there was already a divide between Scale Jayyed and the others.

The isikolo leadership had allowed Jayyed to handpick his scale before the other umqondisi had a chance to make their choices. Many were annoyed at the breach in custom, and their frustration had passed through to their initiates. Jayyed's group was disliked, and given the looks he got from everyone within and without Scale Jayyed, none were as disliked as Tau, the initiate who hadn't won ten matches or made it to day three.

"Double-time!" came the call from the front, one umqondisi after another repeating the order. The column picked up the pace, running at half-speed over the tall and sun-browned grass that carpeted the valley floor.

Tau let his thoughts fade, focusing on the run. He was tired and injured and would have loved nothing more than to stop. He refused to do it, though. He told himself he could stop when he could no longer make the next step. He also told himself he could always make at least the next step.

He counted them that way, in ones. One step, one step, one step. It kept him going, to think of the task in its smallest pieces. One step, one step. When the call was made to return to a standard march, Tau was blowing hard, the slash across his face burned, and his broken wrist throbbed, but he hadn't stopped, and the run had taken them to their destination, with Scale Jayyed at the front of the column.

It was Jayyed who called the halt. Tau was beside him. Uduak and Hadith, too, stuck to the sword master's hip like twin scabbards.

Jayyed glowered at his scale, but Tau could see through that. Their umqondisi couldn't hide his pride.

"Welcome to the Southern Ihashe Isikolo," he said.

The military academy stood behind him. It was a soot-colored monolith that dwarfed the keep in Kerem. The isikolo was larger than the Onai's keep, pentagonal instead of circular, and its walls were higher. It was located a thousand strides from the ocean, built on the same ground where Champion Tsiory made his first advance camp, after he'd pushed the hedeni from the beach, or so the story went. Given its walls, twice as thick as keep Kerem, the heavy bronze gates, and the watchmen posted at every corner, the isikolo seemed impregnable. It would take a massive force to siege and take it.

"Inside," shouted Jayyed.

Inside the walls, the isikolo was filled with uniform one-story buildings. Tau thought he could identify the ones that were barracks, but that was it. Jayyed handed them off to a Proven attendant who would help the initiates learn their way around the compound.

"Name is Limbani," the sour-faced guide, missing an arm and eye, told Scale Jayyed. "I'll show you around, get you fed and bunked."

Other Proven were doing the same, acting as guides and introducing themselves to the incoming scales. Limbani began walking, prompting Tau and the others to follow.

"Over there, mess hall," he told his group, pointing with his one arm to the hundred-stride-long building near the center of the isikolo. "That's the armory; there is the umqondisi quarter; that way leads to the training grounds; latrines are there, there, and there. And, most important, over there is the infirmary." Limbani smirked. "You'll become well acquainted with the infirmary."

A few men muttered at that.

"On to your barracks. We'll settle you in, nice and comfortable, neh?"

Scale Jayyed's barracks, a long adobe hut with thin straw pallets running its length, was large enough for the fifty-four men in the scale. Uduak was first to claim a spot and took the cot closest to the door. After that, there was some jockeying for position, though Tau wasn't sure what made one spot better than another. He wound up with a cot near the rear of the building, next to a tall but slim-built man with a hacking cough that didn't stop.

"Tau," Tau said to him.

The man coughed, turned his back, and placed his pack on his cot. "Chinedu," he said.

"It's mealtime," Limbani told the initiates. "Better to be early rather'n late."

"Gonna...go...eat," coughed out Chinedu, and he left.

Most of the scale did likewise. Tau stowed his gear under the knee-high cot and sat on the bed that had become his.

He thought of his father, of Aren Solarin, who had deserved so much more from life than it had given. He lay back. Perhaps Aren had slept in this same spot, so many cycles ago, dreaming of what his life would bring.

. Tau tried to imagine his own life as it might have been. He couldn't. Only days had passed, and somehow, he was too far gone to ever go back.

He closed his eyes. Time to rest. In the morning he'd begin day one of his cycle of training. One cycle to learn how to kill men like the Indlovu, to become a military man, to take vengeance.

Tau frowned and poked at the raw skin on his face. This wasn't the life he wanted. He pictured Zuri, conjuring up a happy memory, trying to determine if there was a chance at something more as his fingernail caught and pulled on the edge of his wound.

He hissed at the pain and a drop of blood slid across his cheek and into the corner of his eye. He wiped away the red tear and the memory. One cycle.

TRAINING

He was up first. The sun hadn't risen, but the barracks were hot as a furnace and stunk of sweat. Tau, dressed in the same clothes he'd worn the day before, gathered his gear and made his way to the mess hall.

There were a few other initiates and a couple of umqondisi there, eating at one of the hundred trestle tables in the huge space. The food sat in large heated pots along the north and south sides of the building. Tau ladled the pot's steaming mush into an earthenware bowl and found a seat.

He couldn't tell what he ate, but it was better than anything he'd had to eat back home, and it boggled his mind to think he could finish his bowl, walk back to one of the pots, and refill. To prove it was possible, he did just that.

After eating, Tau left the mess hall to explore. It was getting busier. Drudge went about the work that kept the academy running, and he saw several umqondisi walking toward the initiate barracks.

"Tau!" a voice called. It was Jayyed. "If you're already up, follow me to the training grounds. Anan, my aqondise, is gathering the others."

Tau fell into step with Jayyed's long strides, walking fast to keep up with the much taller man. They were headed for gates on the opposite side of the isikolo.

"You've eaten? Good," Jayyed said.

Two guards opened the bronze gates. Once through, Tau got his first look at the isikolo's main training grounds.

For a thousand strides in each direction, the grasslands had been cleared and the ground was an enormous fighting circle, sur-faced with packed clay. Already, several scales were at work, doing warm-up exercises, sword forms, or sparring. Tau marveled at the scope of the training grounds, imagining what it would look like when the majority of the initiates were on it at the same time.

Marching over to Tau and Jayyed were Aqondise Anan and the just-woken, disheveled men of their scale.

"Form lines," shouted Anan.

Tau ran over and everyone fell to order. Jayyed faced them.

"You've already met Aqondise Anan," he said. "He will help me make men of you." Someone sniggered and Jayyed rounded on the man. "Perhaps, in your little farming village, you were special. A talent among the Lessers there, neh? You could hold a sword well enough and batter most men with it? Now you've gone through the trials and I've selected you. It's confirmation. Isn't it? You must be special. A real warrior."

Jayyed had their attention and, when he drew his sword, their curiosity as well. The weapon he held wasn't sharpened bronze or even a dulled practice sword. In his hand was a sword made of wood.

Jayyed waved Uduak forward. Walking over, Uduak eyed him. He indicated that Uduak should draw his blade. Uduak did so, his bronze practice sword reflecting sunlight. Jayyed attacked.

"I have been an Ihashe warrior; an umqondisi for the isikolo; an inkokeli, leading scales against the hedeni on the front lines of our war; and an adviser to the greatest military power in the known world—the Omehi Guardian Council."

Jayyed spun past Uduak's defense and cracked him across the tem-ple, sending the larger man to his knees. Uduak, a look of surprise on his face, stumbled back to his feet.

"The Goddess has seen fit to return me to the role of umqondisi, a role I left more than twenty cycles ago," Jayyed said, punctuating the last word by slamming the pommel of his sword-shaped stick into Uduak's chest, returning him to the ground.

Jayyed stepped away from him and waved the next initiate forward. It was Chinedu, Tau's coughing barracks neighbor. Chinedu glanced at Uduak, drew his practice sword, and went for Jayyed.

"All my life," Jayyed said, knocking aside Chinedu's attack and bashing a fist into his face, "I've believed that we do not train optimally."

Chinedu reeled, blood oozing from both nostrils. He rasped a hairy forearm across his face, dragging the blood away from his mouth and onto his chin. That done, he came forward, his sword up and knees bent for quick movement. It made no difference. Jayyed was on him and Chinedu was disarmed and put into the dirt.

Jayyed waved him and Uduak back to the line. "The Ihashe can be better," Jayyed said, calling Hadith forward.

Hadith already had his sword out and had found a shield. He smirked at Jayyed's wooden weapon, keeping the shield between him and the umqondisi. Jayyed jabbed and Hadith blocked.

"The testing exposed you to a faster pace of combat," Jayyed said, sending three strikes at Hadith. Hadith blocked the first two, but the third slipped between sword and shield, catching him in the guts, doubling him over. "That's why we cover the practice blades with linen."

Jayyed swung overhead and cracked Hadith over his exposed back. Hadith went down. "It makes you safer, so you can go harder, and that brings the fight closer to reality."

Without waiting to be called, the next man ran over, hoping to take Jayyed unaware. Jayyed sidestepped and struck the runner across the temple, knocking him out on his feet.

"You will all use wooden swords." Jayyed waved Tau over. "Our training will mimic real combat as closely as possible."

Tau drew his practice sword with his off hand. It was shaking. He had no practice fighting left-handed. Still, he refused to be embarrassed by someone twice his age. He stalked Jayyed, making sure to keep out of striking range.

"If you want to be a great fighter," Jayyed said, flicking his sword at Tau's broken wrist and causing Tau to jerk back, almost dropping his weapon without being touched, "you must practice fighting."

Jayyed closed the distance with Tau and they crossed swords, once, twice, three times. "Theoretical forms," Jayyed said, as Tau saw his chance, "and cautious sparring with bronze swords slows learning and advancement."

Tau changed levels, lunging for Jayyed's chest.

"We do not have time for slow."

Tau was midlunge when he felt his thrust being turned. Jayyed had his wooden sword whirling around Tau's blade, and with a flick of his wrist, Tau was disarmed.

"The Chosen do not have time for slow." Jayyed reached over Tau's lowered body, grabbed him by the scruff of the neck, and yanked him forward. Tau tripped, his lead foot hitting Jayyed's outstretched leg, and he went down.

"Too slow and you're dead." Jayyed was standing over Tau. "Too slow and we're all dead."

Jayyed paced, scanning the scale for his next victim. "We fight an enemy that outnumbers us many times over," he said, waving an initiate over. "Every one of us must be worth multiples of them." As he spoke, he ducked an energetic swing and shouldered his new opponent away.

Without finishing the initiate, he waved the next one forward. It was two on one. The men were smart; they spread out. Jayyed feinted at the first man, backing him off, and then he slapped the flat of his wooden sword into the groin of the second.

The first man bellowed and swung hard enough to break bones. Jayyed bent out of the way like windblown grass, and when the initiate's blade passed him by, he hammered his sword against the man's legs. Jayyed's sword snapped in half as it swept the initiate from his feet.

"The wood on Xidda is horrible," he said. "These weapons are expensive to make. But lives cost more. Great fighters are worth more than expensive wood."

Jayyed waved two others forward, so he would face three. He lifted his empty sword hand to Aqondise Anan and Anan drew his own wooden sword, tossing it. Jayyed snatched the stick out of the air and used it to club one of the newcomers. "You will not focus on forms or dance with each other while holding bronze."

There were two men left. Jayyed hit one on the upper arm, making the initiate drop his blade. The other man attacked and Jayyed darted in, dashing an elbow against the side of that one's head before disengaging and swatting him across the neck with the wooden sword. The attack would have killed the man, had the blades been real.

"You will learn to fight by fighting." Jayyed whirled and faced the man he had disarmed earlier. The initiate had been in the process of bending down to retrieve his weapon. Feeling Jayyed's blade resting on his forehead, he froze.

"You will be faster, more experienced, and more brutal than all who would oppose you." Jayyed sheathed the wooden sword and stepped back.

There were a few groans from the downed men, but they were drowned out by the cheers from the rest of the scale. Tau was surprised to find himself cheering with the rest.

"Enough, enough," said Jayyed. "Get water. I'll see you back here in half a sun's span. We begin in earnest."

Anan called for the men to form lines. Hadith had to wake the man Jayyed had knocked unconscious. The man was shaky on his feet and Uduak helped carry him back to the line.

"Take your leave," Jayyed told the scale, and the men made for the water buckets or mess hall, talking to one another in voices that were half-hushed but eager.

"Common Solarin, hold," Jayyed ordered.

MOMENTS

Y ou don't need water," Jayyed said.

"I don't, nkosi?" Tau asked.

"'Umqondisi' will do. I'm no Noble." Jayyed walked deeper onto the training ground and Tau followed. For a few breaths, they moved in silence. Tau watched the other scales go about their business, noticing how familiar they looked, practicing forms, skirmishing with dulled blades of bronze, swinging at a fraction of true combat speed, careful not to injure one another. Already, Tau was seeing training with fresh eyes.

"What do you want from the isikolo?" Jayyed asked.

"I want to defend the Omehi from the hedeni."

"Of course you do."

Tau considered what else he should... what else he was willing to tell Jayyed. "I need to be one of the greatest fighters alive. I'm willing to work. I will—"

Jayyed laughed. Tau stiffened.

"Easy," Jayyed told him. "I'm impressed is all. In fact, I remember wanting much the same thing. But what about Nobles?"

"What of them?"

"Nobles are bigger, stronger, and faster than Lessers."

"They're still men."

Jayyed smiled. "Men born with natural advantages for fighting."

Tau felt his blood go hot as he recalled the day of his father's death. "I was a match for Jabari Onai," he said.

Jayyed gave him a look, one eyebrow raised.

"I didn't say I was a good match," Tau said, backing off the point and missing his friend all at the same time. "But I did beat Kagiso Okafor."

"That nceku can barely call himself Noble."

"But he is one and I beat him. I need to be the greatest fighter of the Omehi," Tau said, fighting for calm, his fingernails digging into his palms. "Can you give me that?"

Jayyed grew serious. "I can't give you anything. It might be something you can take, if you're willing."

"I am."

"We'll see. The cost for greatness is high."

"I'll pay anything."

"Your life?" Jayyed asked, causing Tau to stop. "That's the price. Life is nothing more than moments in time. To achieve greatness, you have to give up those moments. You have to give your life to your goal."

"Easily paid," Tau told him.

Jayyed watched him. "Spoken like a young man, still new to the world." He continued walking. "We'll see if your actions match your mouth."

The rest of that morning and afternoon was spent sparring. Tau had to fight with his off hand and Jayyed warned the others that anyone targeting Tau's healing wrist would be punished. It didn't matter; Tau lost all his matches. He felt ashamed of his performance and worried that Jayyed would remove him from the scale.

At supper, he ate little, his hunger masked by worry over his fate. He spoke to no one and no one spoke to him. He felt miserable but promised himself he'd do better the next day.

Tau's second day was filled with practicing proper technique for swinging, performing a thrust, and lunging. The basics. Jayyed told them he would not teach traditional forms covering long sequences of attacking or defending. He argued that long forms made fighters too rigid. They did not allow for individual expression or the use of individual advantages.

"We are more alike than we are different," Jayyed said. "Two arms, two legs, one head." He had prodded the stocky and talkative Themba in the parts of the body he named, shutting the initiate up, for the moment.

"There are only so many good ways to attack or defend. I will teach those and no others. The rest you will learn by adapting the basics to your individual advantages and disadvantages." Jayyed had touched Tau's broken wrist with his wooden sword when he said that part. "We are more alike than we are different, but there are differences. I can't teach you yours. You'll discover them for yourself."

So they practiced the basics. Then they sparred, dueling the rest of the afternoon and the next two days away. The fifth day began as the others, with basic sword work.

"Thrust. Thrust. Thrust, damn you!" shouted Anan at the line of sweating men.

Tau was frustrated. Jayyed's impressive performance five days ago had begun to fade, and it was hard to imagine becoming a better swordsman by swinging a wooden sword. It didn't help that the other initiates made fun of Scale Jayyed for fighting one another with wood, and Tau was finding it difficult adjusting to life at the isikolo.

Many of the other men in his scale had formed small groups of friends. But they ignored Tau, and, reacting to their scorn, he'd decided he wouldn't bother with friendships. Tau was at the isikolo to learn, to get better, to become a brilliant fighter, and that was all. He was finding it a lonely path.

Worst of all was his performance. He lost far more duels than he won. Still, he never called for the Goddess's mercy, always fighting to the bitter end. Tau told himself he did it to push himself. At night, he wondered if it was because his pride couldn't survive both defeat and surrender.

"Form lines!" Anan hollered as Jayyed strode up to their practice area.

The scale ordered themselves for Jayyed's address. "Morning," he said, and they greeted him in chorus.

"Before we continue, I have something to tell you," Jayyed said. "I've asked Aqondise Anan to begin extra training for anyone who wants it, two sun spans earlier than regular training." Themba groaned, earning himself a sharp look from Anan.

"This is not mandatory," Jayyed said, "but time put in determines the value of what comes out."

Jayyed's eyes slid over the faces of the men before him. Tau felt as if the sword master's gaze slowed when it reached him. Whether that was true or not, Tau would be there early the next day. If Jayyed thought extra time would help, then Tau would take the help.

That afternoon, Tau sparred with Hadith, who crushed him.

"I'll see you at the early sessions, neh?" Hadith asked, forcing Tau back with a series of rapid-fire strikes.

Tau nodded, doing his best to hold the Governor at bay.

"Good," Hadith said. "You need it, and it'll be entertaining for Uduak and me to have more sparring time with you." Hadith stabbed Tau right where his heart was. "Kill hit and match," he said, resetting.

Tau rubbed at his sore chest. His gambeson didn't seem to do much to blunt blows anymore, and he couldn't be sure if it was because his body was bruised everywhere or because the padding in his armor had been beaten threadbare over the last five days of losses. He did know he was not looking forward to extra time with Hadith and Uduak.

TIME

The next morning, Tau made sure he was first to the early
practice. When he got to the training grounds it was still dark
and the day was warm, instead of furiously hot. He readied his body
with exercises, and as he did, five other men joined him. They were
Uduak, Hadith, Chinedu, Yaw, and Jengo.

Uduak was the first to the yard after Tau, and he stood as far from
him as was reasonable, swinging the massive chunk of wood he'd
asked the armorers to fashion as a sword for him.

Chinedu was next. Then came Yaw, smallest of them, which
meant he was only half a head taller than Tau. Still, he was vicious
and had a talent for sticking his sword right where it would hurt the
most. After Yaw came Jengo, strutting over like a Palm Royal Noble
and drawing his sword as if he was about to order a charge. Last to
the grounds was Hadith. He didn't warm up, opting instead to stand
off to one side, watching the rest.

When Anan arrived, he called for them to line up. He made them
run round the practice grounds, raising a sweat, before pairing them
off. Tau was with Jengo.

Anan had them spar, and he walked around correcting this and
adjusting that. Even fighting with his off hand, Tau was a fair match
for Jengo. Jengo's problem, Tau thought, was that he tried to get

through a match without taking a single hit. It made him too defensive, which gave Tau the opportunity to press him.

His unrelenting attacks wore Jengo down and stretched out the match. The others had finished their rounds and watched. They all cheered on a flagging Jengo.

"Bleed him!" bellowed Uduak.

"Char...and ashes!" said Chinedu, hacking out dubious encouragement. "Jengo...do something!"

Jengo pounced, shamed by his peers into attacking. Tau should have backed down, let Jengo's aggression break on a wall of defense. But, the one-sided comments had gotten under his skin and he did the opposite, going harder at Jengo.

They crossed blades, broke apart, and swung like drunks, each missing twice, until Tau clapped Jengo on the side of the helmet with his sword. Jengo wavered, and Tau hit him again, hard. Jengo dropped to a knee and Tau brought his sword down, going for a "killing" blow. Jengo got his wooden blade up in time to block then rolled away before lurching to his feet.

Tau gave him no space, and after trading blows, Jengo was too far out of position to defend. Tau hit him in the shoulder and then, as Jengo hopped back in pain, he cracked him in the neck. Jengo made a strange high-pitched sound and went down. Tau moved to finish him, forcing Anan to call the match.

Face hot and heart drumming, but victorious, Tau put his hands up and yelled, turning to face the onlookers, flush with his first real isikolo win. The other men were quiet. They wouldn't even give him the glory of this small obstacle overcome. Tau dropped his arms and sheathed his sword with force. To ash with them, he thought. He'd won with his off hand. He'd won.

Anan gave Tau a shallow nod. "Hadith, pair with Tau. Uduak, have at Yaw. Chinedu, you'll sit out with Jengo."

Tau grimaced and squared off against Hadith. His moment in the sun behind him and gone, without even time to wipe the sweat from his head.

"Fight!" Anan said, and he did, that day, the next, the next, and the next.

Hot mornings bled into torrid afternoons, and those spun away, becoming sweltering nights, and Tau's entire body became one contiguous injury. Some days he woke so stiff he had to roll off his cot and onto the floor, lying there until he was loose enough to rise. But he did begin to win.

It happened slowly, and every match was still a war, but Tau began to take wins from the rest of Scale Jayyed during the regular sessions. In the early mornings, during the extra training, Tau could beat Jengo with some reliability, but none of the others. Least of all Uduak, who, Tau had to admit, he loathed having to fight.

Then, one morning, Jengo did not come to the extra morning session. He was not there the following day either. The remaining four gave Tau sour looks, as if Jengo's leaving was his doing.

A moon cycle later, Jayyed came to see the progress. To date, he'd attended fewer than a third of the regular sessions and none of the early ones. Anan, when asked about this, told the men that it was important to break bad habits and accustom the initiates to a new life of combat. When that preliminary work was done, Jayyed would have initiates able to benefit from his focused attention. So it was a surprise to see him so soon.

"Scale ready!" Anan said. "Umqondisi present."

Tau lined up with the others and Jayyed walked the line, looking the men up and down.

"You are my five," he said. "You are the warriors who will be my proudest creation. You will become the Ihashe that are my legacy." No one said a word. "I've told many of you the cost for greatness is time. The rest of my scale puts in time. They put in work. You put in more and you work harder. You will be better. It is the natural order and the secret path to brilliance—put in more, get out more."

Jayyed stood at the center of the line of five men. He was in front of Tau, as if speaking only to him.

"Know you're not owed your spot," Jayyed said to them, said to Tau. "You can and will be replaced if you're outperformed. However, if you maintain your place, you will train and learn as much in a single cycle at the isikolo as the Indlovu learn in three at the citadel. You are Lessers, but you'll fight as hard as Nobles."

Tau took a breath he didn't know he'd been holding. This was what he needed. This was everything he wanted.

"Know this as well," Jayyed continued. "Improvement can only come through intentioned effort. Every day must be hard for you. The days without difficulty are the days you do not improve. The days you do not improve are the days the men behind you close the distance. It's then you give your enemies hope. Hope that, when they meet you in battle, they have done enough to finish you."

Jayyed drew his guardian dagger. Tau had not noticed him wearing it. The blade, dragon scale, was blacker than the darkest night. It looked like someone had torn away the fabric of the world and forgotten to replace it, leaving nothingness in its stead.

Jayyed held it high. "On the days you do not improve, you open yourself to the blade that will gut you, the knife that will enter your heart, and the hatchet or spear that will take your life.

"To defend against failure, every day must be hard. Every day must strengthen you. For it's in the crucible of hard days that potential becomes power."

Jayyed stepped closer, within arm's length of Tau. "The wars you'll wage aren't decided when you fight them. They're decided before that by the extent of your efforts and the substance of your sacrifices. They're decided by the choices you make every single day. So ask yourself: How powerful do I choose to be?"

A spell had been cast. None dared break it. They stood like statues.

Jayyed lowered the dagger and sheathed it. "Today, we do not train within our scale. Today, we put down our wooden swords and skirmish against the others.

"Go to the barracks and tell the rest of my men. Break your fast and gather your bronze, blade and shield. You'll fight as a unit and we'll see how powerful you've chosen to be."

On the way back to the barracks, Chinedu, in spite of his wretched cough, wouldn't shut up. "See the...dagger, did you? Dragon scale, neh?"

Uduak, head down, and voice tree-root deep said, "We saw."

The taciturn response didn't satisfy Chinedu. "Got to...fight the other...scales now."

"You're going to drive me insane with that coughing," said Hadith.

"To ash with...you, then," he coughed out. "Got a problem with...my throat, haven't I?"

"It's to be a skirmish," Yaw said, rubbing a sunburnt hand over his sunburnt head and flaking off dead flesh. Yaw was as light-skinned as an Omehi ever was and his coppery skin was never quite up to Xidda's sun. He was always blotchy and peeling, an inyoka shedding its skin.

Hadith spat in the dirt and turned to Yaw. "It's getting us ready for when we skirmish in the Crags against the Indlovu. They want us to start off against each other. Get a feel for scale on scale."

"Don't go...to the Crags for another moon cycle yet," said Chinedu.

"That's why it's called getting someone ready, you inkumbe," said Hadith.

Chinedu bristled but did nothing. Hadith was good with his sword; besides, he'd grown close with Uduak, who would pummel Chinedu, for his cough if nothing else.

"How does it work?" asked Tau, startling the rest.

"It speaks!" said Hadith.

"It shouldn't," growled Uduak.

Yaw took pity and explained. "When we go at the Indlovu, we'll outnumber them three to one. Sometimes they have Enervators, sometimes not. The numbers don't matter much. They always crush us. We're meant to mimic the odds the Indlovu face in the Wrist, when they go up against the hedeni, them being so numerous and all."

"He meant what's today supposed to be like," said Hadith.

"How you know that, then? What he meant, neh?" said Chinedu, perhaps coming to Yaw's defense, but more likely looking for any opportunity to take Hadith down a peg.

Hadith ignored him and lectured Tau. "Today they'll draw straws or pull names or some such. Our scale will be up against another scale. When we do it in the Crags, against the Indlovu, there are fighting grounds set up—"

"A mountain one, a desert one, even a city one, where they have pretend huts and longhouses and everything," said Yaw, interrupting Hadith.

"We face Indlovu soon. In a moon cycle," said Tau, thinking

about Kellan, wondering if he'd be there and if he'd get to fight him. His thoughts turned dark, then worrisome. Tau wondered how ready he'd be to kill again. He wondered if he was good enough and didn't like the answer that came back.

"We'll lose," Uduak said, breaking some self-imposed rule by speaking to Tau.

"Ihashe always lose to Indlovu. The Nobles like it that way," said Hadith. "Reminds us where we stand."

Yaw smiled. "It'll be different this time."

Hadith gave him a look. "What's that?"

"We're with Jayyed. He won a guardian dagger and knows how to get us good enough to give the Indlovu a real go."

"You think?" said Hadith. "You think we'll be anything against a scale of Nobles?"

"I'll fight," Uduak growled.

"Oh, I'll fight too," said Hadith. "Mostly 'cause we don't have a choice. Fighting isn't my worry. It's the winning I'm not convinced of."

"We'll kill them," Tau said.

The other men fell silent and Hadith gave him a look.

"Your mouth, Goddess's ears," Hadith said as the five men went into their barracks to tell the rest of their scale that it was time to fight.

BRONZE

It felt strange, holding bronze again. Tau had his practice sword in his off hand and a shield on his right, more to protect the broken wrist than anything else. It wasn't much and the shield felt awkward, but some protection was better than none.

He stood on one of the isikolo's several small battlefields. This one was square, extending a hundred strides in each direction, and the valley's water-starved grass rose to midcalf, making it somewhat difficult to run.

Tau was beside Yaw and Chinedu, near the front of their scale's formation but a row back from Uduak and Hadith. They were facing Scale Chisomo. It was a good first test, Jayyed's fifty-four against Chisomo's.

Chisomo, a newer umqondisi, was Jayyed's opposite. He was much younger and already a staunch traditionalist. His training focused on forms and he placed little stock in free sparring. And while Jayyed was tough on discipline, Chisomo exalted it as an art. His men polished their bronze swords and shields every evening and spent a substantial amount of time marching around the training grounds in perfect time.

Tau didn't know how well Scale Chisomo could fight. He was

pretty sure they would work well together, though, and that wasn't something he could say for his own scale.

Two aqondise stood between the scales, acting as skirmish judges. The rules were simple. A fighter was "alive" until a bone in his body broke, he touched the ground with anything but his feet or knees, he was rendered unconscious, or he called for the Goddess's mercy.

The aqondise watched for cheaters and the skirmish was won when one side was eliminated. Easy, like real war; all you had to do was survive long enough to slaughter your enemy.

"Scale Jayyed, weapons up! Scale Chisomo, weapons up!" called one of the aqondise.

The sound of bronze blades being unsheathed rang out across the field. Many of the other umqondisi, aqondise, initiates, Proven, and even a few Drudge had come to see the first day of skirmishes, and Tau was near enough to the battlefield's edge to hear men making bets. The odds were in Chisomo's favor. Scale Jayyed was filled with brutes, but, the thinking went, brutes were no match for disciplined men.

"Fight!" the same aqondise screamed.

The two judges ran for the sidelines and the men of Scale Jayyed charged, howling like bloodthirsty predators. Chisomo's men were not cowed. They split into three smaller but equal teams. Tau recognized the formation from his father's war stories. It was a standard Chosen military tactic, usually executed by an entire wing, but the principles were the same even with one-tenth the men.

The outer splits of the three-pronged attack aimed to flank Scale Jayyed, while the middle split joined shields and held fast. The middle would take the brunt of the charge, and if they held against the initial assault, the outer splits would be able to pick off half of Jayyed's men in short order. There was only one thing for it. Scale Jayyed had to smash through the middle and break free of the flanking maneuver.

Hadith saw the same thing. "Three-prong flank!" he shouted. "Break the middle!"

They crashed into their opponents and were among swords and

shields. Everywhere were snarling faces, flickering blades, and the metallic tang of oiled bronze and sweat-slicked gambesons. It was nothing like the training. It was more like Daba. Chaos.

Tau saw Uduak knock a man off the Chisomo defensive line and follow him into the middle of the enemy. Hadith tried to call him back, but Uduak either didn't hear or didn't care. Chinedu was bludgeoning one poor initiate, whose only defense was to hold his shield high enough to avoid being brained, and Yaw had already dropped a Chisomo man and was working on his second.

A lanky Chisomo fighter faced off against Tau and poked at him with a sword, like he was trying to prod a fire to life. Tau batted the attack off target and smashed his shield into the man's helmeted face, and he went down. Behind the felled swordsman was a tall Chisomo initiate with rheumy eyes. The initiate spared his defeated fellow a glance, snarled, came for Tau, and they crossed blades.

Tau was adjusting to the heavier weight of bronze after so long with wood, but the man he fought was having a worse time. Tau's opponent moved like he was wading in mud. He was slow, brutally slow, and trying to work his way through the intaka form, one of the first sword-fighting sequences Tau had learned as a boy.

Tau avoided the form's first and second sweeping attacks before crashing his sword into the man's side. He followed that with a cuff to the nose, then plowed into rheumy eyes with his shield, knocking the initiate to the ground and taking him out of the skirmish.

Two men came at Tau next, seeming more concerned with keeping out of each other's way than getting to him. Tau cut high, expecting a block from the first. None came, so he clubbed the man in the helmet, sending him sprawling. The second man squealed a war cry and swung. Tau caught the blow on his shield, wrist pinging with pain, then used the shield to force the man's sword low. With the shield out of the way, Tau came overhead with his sword. The blow connected and the squealer crumpled but didn't go down. Tau hit him again. He went down.

Tau looked up, watching for the next attacker. There was no one in front of him. He had, along with Uduak, Hadith, Yaw, and Chinedu, blasted through the Chisomo middle split. The fighting was behind them now. The left and right splits were heavily engaged with the rest of Scale Jayyed, and it was a mess. Scale Chisomo's discipline had melted in the furnace of first contact.

"Uduak, Tau, with me to the right split," said Hadith. "Yaw, Chinedu, help against the left."

"Why?" asked Chinedu. "Why should I . . . listen to you?"

"Let's just win," Tau told Chinedu, and he started toward the right.

"Other right!" Hadith shouted. "The right, from when we were first facing them."

Tau stopped, shrugged, not quite sure what difference it made, but changed direction.

"C'mon, then," Yaw told Chinedu, leading him the other way.

Fighting beside Uduak was a more pleasant experience than fighting against him. Tau knocked one more man out of the skirmish but saw Uduak bloody one, almost break the leg of another, and charge a third to the ground. Then, having adapted to the momentum of the skirmish and getting over his awe at Uduak's power, Tau sought his next opponent, only there wasn't one.

Scale Chisomo had been eliminated to a man. It took a moment, but, realizing they'd won, Scale Jayyed cheered, swords and shields raised high as bets were traded to the sounds of grumbling and curses all along the battlefield's sidelines.

Out of the fifty-four men they'd started with, Tau's scale had thirty-two still standing. Yaw was a few strides away, his face bright with an ear-to-ear smile as he patted Chinedu on the back. Uduak and Hadith had survived too. Hadith was standing close to the big man, talking to him and pointing at details on the battlefield. Tau imagined he was already going over where they'd done things right and where they could have done better.

Tau turned away, trying to remain grim, but couldn't hold back the smile. It started small, then crept across his face until he was grinning like he'd been in the sun too long. He pumped his fist, the wrong fist, and almost fell over from the pain. Eyes watering from the hurt, his mood still didn't sour. Jayyed's five had made it through the skirmish and the contest had been won. His scale had won!

Tau knew the rest of the day was his to do with as he saw fit. The surviving skirmishers of the winning scale were gifted that as a winner's bounty, but he wouldn't waste the time, not after Jayyed's speech.

"Well fought," Jayyed said, addressing the scale. "But we took too many losses and I own much of the blame for that. I've paid too much attention to individual sparring, thinking fifty-four men with better training could ensure victory. It's not so. If we are to be the best, we can't be just better-trained men, better fighters. We have to be the better scale.

"Chisomo had us on that front, though his initiates couldn't make use of their advantage. Truth? I'm thankful they exposed our weakness. Now we can see it for what it is and burn it away. We're going to learn how to work better together...tomorrow.

"Survivors, you have your day. The men who did not survive— you fought hard and well. You should be proud. Still, you have more to do and I leave you in Aqondise Anan's capable hands."

The men who fell in the skirmish couldn't have looked less happy.

"Think the mess hall serves masmas this early?" Hadith asked Tau and Uduak, drawing a smile from the big man.

"Do have a thirst," Uduak said.

"Let's gather Yaw and Chinedu, those slackards, and find out," Hadith offered.

"Going to spar with the rest for a bit," Tau said. Uduak tilted his head at Tau, staring at him like he was an oddity, or an idiot. Hadith looked like he was going to say something, thought better of it, and walked away instead.

"Uduak," he called, "let's ease that thirst."

Uduak waited a breath, still watching Tau. He grunted and strode off.

"Out of the dirt," Anan shouted to the men from Jayyed's scale who had gone down in the skirmish. "You thought that was a beating. You've seen nothing. Run twice round the grounds and then we do some real fighting!"

The men who didn't have to be carried to the infirmary looked wearied and defiant, but they got up and they ran, and Tau went with them. He could feel Jayyed's eyes on him.

Let him watch, Tau thought, as Jayyed's words came to mind: "The days without difficulty are the days you do not improve."

Tau ran harder. He was not the strongest, the quickest, or the most talented, not by any measure. He knew this and knew he could not control this. However, he could control his effort, the work he put in, and there he would not be beaten.

He made a pact with himself, a pact he swore on his father's soul. If he were asked to run a thousand strides, he would run two thousand. If he were told to spar three rounds, he would spar six. And if he fought a match to surrender, the man who surrendered would not be him. He would fight until he won or he died. There would be, he swore, no days without difficulty.

CHAPTER SIX

BATTLEGROUNDS

Jayyed was true to his word. The scale trained teamwork and tactics, which were new to Tau, who found the concept of coordinating battle efforts complicated. It worked, though.

Scale Jayyed fought two more skirmishes and won them. Tau survived both. So did Yaw, Chinedu, and Hadith. Uduak was "killed" in the second one, after men from Scale Thoko targeted him.

In that battle, several of Thoko's men swarmed Uduak, using the same strategy the hedeni did against an Enraged Ingonyama. Uduak made them pay. He fought like one of the mythical beasts from Osonte, dropping three of Scale Thoko's men before going down. One of them had a cracked skull.

Before Uduak fell, Tau tried to help. He forced his way to the big man's side, and for a time, they fought back to back. Thoko's men ignored Tau, thinking the scarred runt unworthy of their attention. Their minds changed after Tau battered two of them to the dirt. And they realized the full extent of their error when Yaw, Chinedu, and Hadith joined him, helping Scale Jayyed rampage through the Thoko ranks.

Tau spent the rest of that day training with the men from Scale Jayyed who had fallen. When they ran, Uduak ran beside Tau. When they sparred together, Uduak was less violent.

Tau noticed but didn't think on it. His training consumed him.

His dedication was absolute, and the hardest fights were not with the other men. They were with himself.

Every day a part of him whispered that he could rest, that he had done enough, that he could stop. Every day, the lies were whispered, and every day, Tau made himself relive the moment his father died. It was sick, masochistic. It was the only way he could keep himself going.

Time blurred, days cascaded one into another, the Omehi's endless war with the hedeni raged, and an initiate from Scale Idowu died in his bed. He was found in the morning. He'd bled from his eyes, nose, ears, and mouth, and his skin had ruptured like meat cooked too long on a spit.

Demon–death, the rumors went. It might even be true. Tau knew a family back in Kerem who had lost a child to a demon–death. Whatever the actual case, everyone paid more attention to their morning and evening prayers.

It was around this time that Tau's wrist healed enough to wield a blade. He didn't trust it and still fought with his off hand. It made sense; he'd become better with his left than he'd ever been with his right, and on the day they marched for the Crags to watch some of the other Ihashe scales fight the Indlovu, Tau was a difficult match for everyone at the isikolo.

The march to the Crags took from predawn to midmorning, and Jayyed counseled his scale on what they were going to see. "All of this prepares us for war. The skirmishes in the Crags allow Indlovu initiates to experience fighting against heavy odds. For us, and the Northern Ihashe Isikolo, it's a chance to hone our tactics."

"And get the bones kicked out of us," Themba mumbled as he marched beside Tau.

"The citadel fields men from all three cycles," Jayyed continued, "and some skirmishes have Enervators, so the battle can emulate true combat as much as possible." He waited a beat and asked, "Who here has felt enervation?"

Tau considered staying silent. "I have," he said when no one else answered.

"Indeed?" asked Jayyed.

"I fought with my . . . I fought at Daba."

"Daba? That's the largest raid the South has seen in a while. You were there?"

"I was."

"Got caught in an Enervator's wave, neh? Care to describe it for your sword brothers?"

Tau did not care to, but he cared to express that to Jayyed even less. "It drags you into Isihogo. Time slows and I saw . . ." He felt foolish.

"You saw . . . ," Jayyed urged.

"Demons."

The men muttered; one snorted.

"It's true," Tau said, voice harder.

"You did. Everyone does," Jayyed told the scale. "Enervation draws a man's soul to Isihogo and then the demons come."

Several men formed the dragon span with their hands, the winged sign to ward off evil.

"The demons from Isihogo cannot harm you, but they'll make you suffer," the sword master explained. "Once enervated and forced into the underworld, you will be attacked by the things that exist there." Jayyed had the men's attention, and even Chinedu held his coughs. "In war, a talented Enervator will hold your spirit in Isihogo until the demons have torn it to pieces, forcing it out of their realm and back to ours. This is worse than it sounds. The victim feels the agony of the demon attack as if it were real, and the experience is incapacitating. It renders men senseless on the battlefield, where they can actually be killed.

"A well-timed blast of enervation, just before our forces are entwined with our enemy's, can mean the difference between victory and defeat for the Chosen, between life and death. Our Enervators, Enragers, Edifiers, and Entreaters are critical to the defense of the peninsula."

"Umqondisi? They'll do it to us when we skirmish?" asked Oyibo, a muscled and talented fighter with boyish features. "They'll send us to the demons?"

Boyish features aside, Oyibo was steady. Tau had seen that in training. Oyibo did not look steady then.

"They will," Jayyed said. "But the Gifted at the Crags are initiates as well, learning how to control their powers. They won't hold you in Isihogo for long and they are asked not to try."

Themba whispered to Tau, "They used to try. My older brother went through Ihashe training already. He told me the stories the umqondisi told him. The citadel had to leash their Enervators a few dozen cycles ago 'cause no one would fight in skirmishes." Themba snorted. "Not fair, nor decent, letting a man's soul get ripped up by monsters."

"If enervated, you'll see Isihogo," Jayyed said. "You'll see the demons in its mists. They'll come for you. You'll be released before they have their way."

"Umqondisi?" asked Oyibo.

"Oyibo."

"Yesterday, I heard one of the Proven in the mess hall. He was telling stories to the initiates about his time at the isikolo. He wasn't old, a few cycles up on me. He said that, during one skirmish, a demon got him. He's had nightmares since, always the same. It's the one with that demon tearing at him."

Jayyed didn't answer right away. "The fast ones may get to you," the sword master conceded. "Time is different in Isihogo. A single breath taken on Uhmlaba will feel like fifty or even a hundred in the underworld. That makes it difficult for the Gifted initiates to time things."

Themba leaned over to Tau, his sour breath an assault. "Would rather the Ennies not send me at all." He hawked snot into his mouth and spat. "Still, we're better off'n what the hedeni get. Ennies hold them until the demons turn 'em inside out."

Tau and the rest of the men of Scale Jayyed marched in silence after that, and by midmorning the flatlands had given way to the rockier crumble that formed the base of the Fist. The men marched upward and the pace slowed.

As they climbed, Tau wondered how, when compared to the southern mountain range, where he was from, any reasonable person could call the Fist more than a big hill. Well, a hill that had been worked over by a giant with a sledgehammer.

The Fist was uneven, dry, and covered in thin, loose-rooted shrubbery. Still, the hill, or mountain, was well positioned. It divided the point of the Chosen's peninsula and, like the central mountain range, it separated North from South. The Fist was a natural barrier against heavy raiding from the ocean.

Tau had never been to Citadel City but knew it wasn't far. The training city for the Gifted and Indlovu had been placed at the eastern base of the mountain, an additional layer of protection against sea raids.

The hedeni would need to navigate the ocean, march over the Fist, conquer Citadel City, and march another day inland before reaching the capital and other settlements. To do it, they'd need a thousand ships filled with warriors, a full invasion force. They'd have to risk all those lives on the water and make it ashore with enough fighters to battle past Citadel City. It wasn't wise. It wasn't done.

Instead, the major fighting happened at the Wrist, the deadened lands separating the relative lushness of the Chosen's peninsula and the rest of Xidda. There, the hedeni came in endless waves. There, the majority of the Omehi military were stationed, lived, and fought. It was in the Wrist's wide-open spaces that the Guardians had the greatest effect, and its desert sands were said to be littered with the charred bones of a million hedeni dead.

Given the numbers of hedeni, the Omehi, even with their dragons, should have been wiped out long ago, but the peninsula was a natural fortress and the Omehi had held it for near on two hundred cycles. Upon reaching the fighting grounds of the Crags, Tau imagined they could hold for a hundred more.

The Crags, a massive plateau of rocky and dead earth, stood halfway up the mountain. It was sectioned off into several battlefields meant to simulate the conditions the Omehi military faced in their endless war. To the west, where the plateau gave way to more mountainous territory, the isikolo and citadels practiced tactics, defenses, and attacks suited to the highlands. On the plateau itself, there were a thousand strides of ground that had been churned over and over until the topsoil felt and shifted like desert sands. This battleground matched many of the conditions in the Wrist. There was also a field of sown grass, out of place at this elevation, that resembled the majority of the peninsula's flatlands.

Then there was the last battleground. Tau found it to be the most fascinating. It was a mock city that looked like the Goddess had scooped up a decent chunk of Kigambe and dropped it on the plateau. Tau stared in wonder at the city replica. He understood why it was the battleground used for the Queen's Melee, the end-of-cycle competition between the highest-ranked scales. The battleground's strategic and tactical possibilities were infinite, and it was tucked between two natural rises that had been cut into spectator seats. The city replica, surrounded by seating, was a war arena.

"Well, that's something," said Hadith.

"It's bigger than my village," added Yaw.

"Meant to be like if the hedeni got into one of our cities?" asked Themba. "Ask me, we lost already, if they ever get that far."

Tau had heard more than enough from Themba. "So, they get to our cities, you'd like to lie down and take what they give us?"

Themba was about to answer, but Hadith cut in. "He's not wrong. Once the hedeni are in our cities, we can't call the Guardians down on them in any good way. The dragons would burn everything and kill as many of us as they would them. If our enemies get into Palm, Kigambe, or Jirza, it would mean the end of us."

Themba smirked, vindicated. "Like I said, they get that far, we're already dead."

Anan strode over. "Too much talking. Stow your gear. We're for the desert battlefield to watch Scale Njere tackle a third of Scale Oban."

"Fifty-four Ihashe initiates against eighteen from the citadel?" Tau asked. He knew they let themselves be outnumbered, but a third of a scale wasn't enough men to do much and Tau couldn't see how the Nobles would come out on top against such odds.

"They'll have an Ennie," Anan said, as if that alone made up the gap in men.

"Happy to be watching and not fighting, then," chimed in Themba.

"Hurry over," Anan said. "We'll listen in on Umqondisi Njere's strategy. Maybe the plan will be simple enough for even you lot to learn something." Anan pointed to where Scale Njere was already gathered. He went that way himself, not bothering to see if they were following.

"Planning ain't gonna make much difference."

"Shut up, Themba." Hadith seemed to have had enough of him too.

Tau left them arguing and followed Anan. Lessers against Nobles. This he wanted to see.

ENERVATED

The plan, as best as Tau could judge, was a good one. Scale Njere would fight on the desert battlefield and that meant it would be a brawl. The desert had several man-made dunes, but there were few places to hide or maneuver. To take advantage of that, Umqondisi Njere opted for a brute-force approach, with one catch. He split the scale into four units.

The units would attack as one, but each unit was also given a direction on the compass. When the Enervator took aim, the units would run in the direction of their compass point. Tau had learned that a Gifted could make use of her gifts only once every quarter span or so, and given that limitation, the goal was to minimize her effect on the battle by minimizing the number of men she could hit.

The scale's inkokeli was Itembe. He was Governor caste from Kigambe and a strong fighter.

"Plan's good," said Uduak as the scale took the field.

"As good as it can be when you're fighting in a wide-open desert," Hadith agreed.

Themba picked his teeth. "Not gonna matter."

"Shut it," Yaw told him.

"You'll see," Themba said.

Most of the men had taken a seat on the ground just beyond the battlefield. Tau was standing. He scanned the Crags, hoping, praying, to find Kellan, and not knowing what he'd do if he did.

"Tau, you're making me nervous," Hadith said. "Sit."

Tau ignored him.

"Here they go!" said Themba as an aqondise blew a war horn, signaling the beginning of the contest.

Scale Njere's fifty-four Lessers and their opponents, the eighteen Nobles from the citadel along with their Enervator, ran onto the battlefield from opposite sides. The Indlovu broke into two teams, both making for dunes large enough to conceal their movements. The Enervator, dressed in the standard black robes, had been assigned two bodyguards.

It was forbidden and punishable by death to attack a Gifted, but coming within a blade's length of one during a skirmish counted as a kill. The "killed" Gifted had to leave the field, depriving her team of her power. The bodyguards were there to repel any who dared come close.

"Interesting," said Hadith. "Itembe has all four units going for the side with the Gifted."

Uduak grunted.

"It's clever," Hadith said. "If he can get there fast enough, he can take her out of play." Hadith leaned forward and Tau felt himself do the same as Scale Njere streamed up the near side of the dune, which hid just nine Indlovu and the one Gifted.

The twelve fastest runners in the scale made it to the top and were met by three Indlovu. This won't take long, thought Tau. Bronze flashed, and in two breaths, Tau saw four Ihashe dropped to the churned soil, one of them a bloody mess.

The three men from the citadel, all still standing, were joined by two more. The Nobles engaged the eight closest Ihashe as the rest of Scale Njere closed the distance. The Nobles smashed their way through the eight Lessers and closed ranks to take on the newcomers. Tau couldn't believe what he was seeing but thought the Nobles' luck had run its course; the Scale Njere fighters were together on the dune and attacking.

The other unit of Nobles, seeing their sword brothers facing all of Scale Njere, rushed to join the fight. They came for their opponents' rear side, likely intending to split the scale's attention in two. It was then that the Gifted, flanked by her two bodyguards, surfaced.

She waited until Scale Njere was committed to its attack, and her hands came up. The Indlovu guarding her stepped back, not wanting to be grazed by the energy she was preparing to blast.

Scale Njere saw her and scattered. It wasn't organized and it wasn't to predetermined compass points. The men just ran, clumping as they fled. They didn't get far before the Gifted fired.

To Tau it looked like heat pulsed from her fingers in a thick, unbroken, and shimmering wave that shot across the battlefield, dropping any man it touched. Itembe was one of them, falling to his knees, his face locked in terror. The Enervator lowered her arms, and less than a full breath had passed, but the affected men didn't rise.

A scattered few, wild-eyed and frantic, came back to themselves somewhat. They made as if to stand, weapons in hand, but were still useless as they threw their heads back and forth, eyes rolling, trapped in the afterimages of unseen horrors. The rest were worse. Some had gone prostrate, faces in the sand, as others rocked on their knees, whimpering or sobbing.

There was also Itembe, holding himself up on his hands, staring off at nothing. He was slack-jawed, the veins on his neck tensed to the point of bursting. Then, back hunched, Itembe craned his head to peer at the sky, stretched his mouth wide, and screamed.

The sound was raw, terrible, and it ripped from Itembe's throat like stitching torn from a wound. The howl chilled Tau. It chilled him to his marrow.

There wasn't much to the skirmish after that. As the men struck by the Gifted's powers struggled to recover, the Nobles tore through the rest of Scale Njere. By the time the afflicted Ihashe were on their feet, it was a simple thing for the Nobles to send them back to the dirt. Just two Indlovu had been "killed" in the skirmish, and every last man from Scale Njere had been eliminated.

"Hmm," said Themba. "They did better than I thought. Got two Nobles."

"Nceku," said Hadith, no force behind the curse. He looked crestfallen.

Tau glanced at Uduak. The big man was shaken.

"Not good," Uduak rumbled. "Not good."

"Let's go," Anan said. "We'll help the injured off the field."

Tau didn't know why he did it, but he went straight to Itembe. He helped the initiate to his feet and saw the large lump on the side of his head where a Noble had struck him. Itembe didn't seem to notice the injury.

As Tau walked him over to the Sah priests, Itembe spoke, his words tripping over each other. "Is it over?"

"It is."

"The demons, they're real."

"I know," Tau said.

"They got me. I couldn't stop them. They fell on me with claws and teeth, ripped my skin, tore the eyes from my head, and I could still see them! I watched them cut my stomach open, pulling the ropes of my guts from my body. I could see them, and the pain..." Itembe snatched at Tau's tunic, bunching the worn material in frantic fingers. "Help me!"

"It's over."

"Then why can I still see them?"

Tau jerked free of Itembe's grasp. "What?"

"Easy, Itembe." Umqondisi Njere had come himself for his student. "Easy."

Tau watched until Njere got Itembe into the priests' healing tent.

"Itembe got it bad," Hadith said, stepping up beside him.

"Demons had enough time to tear into him."

Hadith rubbed a hand across the back of his neck. "It breaks people."

"They almost got me," Tau said.

"Neh?"

"The ones at Daba," Tau told him. "They came for me. I've never been so scared. My father pulled me out of the Gifted's wave right before they got me."

"Lucky. That was war. The Gifted would have held the hedeni, and you, in Isihogo for as long as possible."

"He pulled me back..."

Hadith clapped Tau on the shoulder. "Your father's a good man."

"He's dead," said Tau, walking back to the rest of the scale.

They watched another skirmish, this one without Enervators. The Indlovu adjusted for the lack of Gifted by fielding half a scale against a full scale from the Northern Isikolo. Tau had met only a few northerners and, on the march over, had looked forward to seeing them fight.

After watching the Indlovu crush his brothers, he no longer felt eager. Tau understood the point of the games. The Nobles were bigger, stronger, and faster than the Lessers. True, the skirmishes between them were meant to train the Omehi for war, but they were also meant to remind the Lessers of their place.

The scale from the north fought the Nobles, who numbered half their men, on the grasslands battleground. Without the aid of a Gifted, the Indlovu lost a third of their fighters before the final Lesser fell. The initiates around Tau acted like it was a triumph, cheering their northern brethren's efforts. Tau didn't see anything worth cheering. A loss was a loss, and managing to beat one-third of your enemy when you doubled their number was pitiful.

Jayyed, Tau thought, had raised them up with well-spoken words about effort, superior training, and winning, but the reality was in front of him, and it was undeniable. The Nobles had natural-born advantages, and Tau wasn't sure those advantages could be overcome.

He'd hoped to see Kellan, hoped to deliver swift justice to the citadel initiate. And Tau had spent night after night picturing his eventual duel with Dejen, how he'd kill the Ingonyama and then demand that Abasi face him. The path had seemed clear until Tau saw Nobles fighting Lessers.

Jayyed approached. "Tastes rotten, doesn't it?"

Tau thought it did. "You didn't tell us the truth."

"Didn't I?"

"We can't beat them."

"Not yet. They use men from all three cycles in each third or half scale they field. We need to get better first."

"They'll snap our scale like dry firewood."

"I wanted all of you to see this before you fought in your first skirmish. Most umqondisi disagree. They prefer their initiates to come in blind. Every Lesser knows Indlovu are incredible fighters, but, the thinking goes, our new initiates have the best chance to perform well if they don't know how outclassed they are."

Jayyed shook his head. "I won't have my men ignorant. When you fight for me, you'll do it with eyes open. You'll know the odds and understand the challenges. I'll point you to victory, but it's you who has to get there."

Tau wasn't interested in Jayyed's easy words. "It's a farce," he said. "They use this to keep us in our place. They know we won't win, that we can't. They hold skirmishes, they have the Queen's Melee, and we're told Ihashe and Indlovu rise on talent. Noble, Lesser, they say it doesn't matter on the fields of war." Tau waved a hand across the grasslands, where men from the North were still being helped away. "It matters. It matters in war as much as it does everywhere else, and everything they do is to remind us of that."

"So your eyes are open. You see the world for what it is. Is it enough? The world as it is?"

Tau was frustrated and had been bold with his umqondisi. He tempered his answer and lowered his eyes, out of respect. "You know it isn't," he said, wanting to say much more.

"And perhaps it never will be. But, while we breathe, the best of us never stop trying to make it better, even if just by a little." Jayyed turned away, shouting to the rest of the scale. "The skirmishes are done. The rest of the day is yours. I will go to Citadel City to visit friends I have not seen in too long. As you've likely heard, there are drinking houses and markets where you can waste your stipend. There are the citadels, the Guardian Keep, and, yes. Yes, yes, yes. There are comfort lodges. Be smart, be safe; we march home at nightfall."

The men cheered, excited to see the famed city, drink, couple with the women of its renowned comfort lodges, and stand in front of the Guardian Keep, the locus of military power, where the Guardian Council decided where and when it would spend their lives. Tau wanted nothing to do with any of it.

"Come." Uduak wrapped a heavy arm over Tau, pulling him forward. "The thirst has me again."

Themba sauntered close. "For what? Drink or women?" he said, making a lewd motion.

"I have no interest in that," Uduak told the much smaller man.

"Looking as you do, they'd have none in you either." Themba laughed, sprinting away as Uduak lunged for him.

"Tiny man, big mouth," Uduak said.

"He's taller than me," Tau muttered.

"You are tiny too," Uduak told him, returning his arm to Tau's shoulders and pulling him down the Crags, toward Citadel City, a place that turned Nobles into gods of war and women into weapons.

REUNION

Citadel City was not what Tau expected. It was small, less than a tenth the size of Kigambe, and looked like a cross between a military base and a religious mission. On the Crags-facing side, it was protected by a thick wall that stood as tall as the average Noble. On the side facing toward the Wrist, with its days-distant but ever-present war, the wall was three times a Noble's height. The city itself, underpopulated given its footprint, was spacious, its skyline dominated by four towering domes, each rising high enough to be seen from three thousand strides.

"That one must be the Indlovu Citadel," said Hadith, pointing to the closest dome, flying a black-on-black flag. "The one beside it will be the Gifted Citadel; beyond them both, that's the Guardian Keep; and furthest back, that'll be the Sah Citadel, house of the Goddess."

Tau stared at the Gifted Citadel. Its domes were black and gold, and what he could see from outside the walls was both impressive and beautiful. It made him think of Zuri. He wondered if she'd run from her fate. He missed her, and with his mind going to painful places, he pushed the past from his thoughts, making sure to pray for her safety first.

"The first city of the Chosen," Yaw said, voice hushed.

"First on Xidda," Hadith said. "We had an empire on Osonte. We numbered in the millions and millions."

"You really...believe that?" coughed Chinedu.

"Believe it? It's our history."

"That'd make the Cull history too," Yaw said, leaving Hadith with no good answer.

The five men, along with the rest of Scale Jayyed, entered the city. There were locals bustling to and fro, but the paths could not be called crowded. Tau saw some Nobles, more Lessers, and a few Proven, but no Drudge. The last made sense; the only Drudge allowed into the holy city were the ones assigned to the comfort lodges.

Also unusual, the city's buildings were all single story. Well, not all. The citadels stretched for the sky and the tallest of them was the bloodred Guardian Keep. It was not just domed; it had pointed spires that reminded Tau of blades.

"The four pillars that keep us, Chosen of the Goddess, protected and safe against all who would do us harm," intoned Hadith. "The Sah, Indlovu, Gifted, and Guardian Citadels."

"Four? What are we, then?" asked Yaw.

Hadith smiled. "Us? You mean Lessers? We're the fodder that feeds the Chosen military's insatiable appetite."

Themba had sidled up during Hadith's preaching. "We distract the hedeni with our dying, so the Indlovu and Gifted can kill 'em back," he explained.

"You again?" Yaw said.

Themba showed teeth, shrugged, and sauntered away.

"Where first?" asked Chinedu, managing to get through both words without hacking.

Uduak pointed at one of the long buildings that sat just inside the city's gates. "Drink."

Hadith was already on his way. "I won't argue."

The drinking house was rough adobe, with more of its interior open to the street than walled in. It was smoky and had a dirt floor covered with scattered straw. It reeked of sweat, the tang of over-cooked vegetables, and the unmistakable stink of brewed masmas.

Jayyed's five, accompanied by Themba, who clung to them like a flea, and Oyibo, who stared at everything with moon eyes, found an empty table and sat. The houseman came over in short order with seven jugs of masmas. He laid them on the table and was about to walk away when Hadith stopped him.

"You have Jirza gaum?"

The houseman, skin so dark he could be half-dragon, looked Hadith up and down, then nodded.

"I'll take that," Hadith told him. The houseman sniffed, scooped up one of the jugs, and went to get Hadith his drink.

"Gaum?" Tau asked. After his last experience with it, he couldn't imagine drinking the stuff for pleasure.

"He's trying to be fancy," said Themba. "In Jirza, they don't drink gaum at the manhood ceremony only. They mix a couple drops of the scorpion's poison with heated water. It makes it weak enough to sip, like you're a proper Noble."

Tau screwed up his face.

"It's better than rotted cactus milk," said Hadith, peering at the yellowish white brew in Tau's jug.

"Lies." Uduak said, lifting his freshly emptied jug into the air, signaling the houseman to bring another.

"To Goddess and queen," said Themba, raising his jug.

"To Goddess and queen," they all said, guzzling back the thick and lukewarm liquor.

Tau swallowed some wrong, coughed, and burped. The others laughed. He glared and burped again, and Yaw guffawed, spitting a mouthful of masmas on the table as the houseman returned with Hadith's watered-down gaum and Uduak's second jug. The houseman gave Yaw a look for dirtying up his table and Hadith tried to smooth it by thanking him graciously. The houseman pursed his lips but left, saying nothing. He wasn't five strides distant when the initiates burst out laughing. Tau too. He couldn't help it, and it felt good.

"Empty," said Uduak, glaring into his jug like it had offended him.

Tau stole a look at the small purse on his belt. He had enough of his stipend to carry the circle. "On me," he said, turning toward the houseman and raising a hand.

"A blue Noble, this one!" said Hadith, grinning.

That annoyed Tau, and he was going to make his annoyance clear, when he saw her. She was walking down the street. His hand dropped, his mouth fell open, and it felt like he couldn't move. He had to be dreaming...but she was real. Zuri was here, in Citadel City, and in the black robes of the Gifted.

"Ordering?" asked Uduak.

Tau dropped his coin purse on the table and walked out of the drinking house.

Chinedu called after him. "Tau?"

Themba must have seen her first. "Leave him. He saw a girl. Anyway, he left his money, and like the man said, the circle is on him."

As Tau got to the street, he heard Hadith's reply. "That's not a girl. That's a Gifted."

It was her. Tau was several strides back, but there was no mistaking her figure or her gait. It was Zuri.

He called to her, still feeling like he was in a dream. She turned at her name and his knees went weak. Memories, history, the life he had wanted to live and lead with her, it came flooding back in a torrent that threatened to knock him flat.

"Tau?"

"It's me," he said, going to her, reaching out for her, praying she wouldn't reject him. She let him take her hands, and the soft, warm skin of her palms and fingers soothed him, calmed the rage in him faster and more completely than the drink and the jokes could ever have done.

"It's you," she said. "It's really you." And then she brought him pain. "Did you...did you kill him? Are you trying to kill them?" There was fear in her voice. "Is that why you're here?"

Tau stiffened, letting her hands go. "It's not," he said. The admission stung, but he forced himself through all of it. "I'm not here to find them. I...I'm not ready."

She nodded as if she understood, as if she was trying to understand. "Lekan, though?"

Tau didn't know what to say, and he could feel her eyes tracing his scar.

"Ekon told me what Lekan did to Anya and her family," Zuri said, her voice little more than a hush.

He'd almost forgotten his scar. He'd almost forgotten Lekan. "Lekan..." He trailed off. What could he say?

Zuri seemed to take her answer from his hesitation. "Thank you," she said. "Thank you...for that."

Tau didn't want to talk about Lekan. "You're here?" he asked. "A Gifted? I thought—"

"I was afraid to become this. I guess I was more afraid of running away on my own."

He couldn't tell if her tone held an accusation. "I had nothing—"

"Of course," she said too quickly, brushing his unfinished excuse away.

"I don't know this place. Is there somewhere...I would like to talk."

"Of course," she said again. She began to reach for his hand, to hold it, and to lead him. She stopped herself, paused, and said, "Follow me."

Tau followed. They didn't go far. There was a circle just a couple of paths away from the drinking house. At the circle's center was a small fountain that was so dry it looked like it had never seen water. Along the periphery, near the adobe buildings that formed the circle's walls, were stone benches. Other than an old Proven sleeping on the bench with the most shade, the circle was empty.

Zuri led him to the bench farthest from the man. She sat and he joined her.

"It doesn't feel real," she said.

"It doesn't," Tau told her. "Zuri"—it was good to say her name— "how long have you been in Citadel City?"

"Two moon cycles. They took me...I left not long after you did." She looked at his sword and clothes. He was wearing the slate-gray uniform the isikolo provided for all initiates. "You're an Ihashe?"

"I'm an initiate," Tau said, unable to ignore the question in her voice. "As an Ihashe, I can duel Kellan Okar."

"Kellan Okar?" she asked, before realization came. "One of the men who—"

"He's a third-cycle Indlovu initiate. I can duel him within the law. Then, when I graduate and become a military man, I can demand a blood-duel of Abasi Odili."

Zuri's eyes widened. "The guardian councillor? He'll have a Body, an Ingonyama. Did you know that?"

Her question made his plan seem mad, impossible. He refused to let her see his doubt. "I do."

"Tau…" Zuri shook her head, and her eyes slipped to his scar again. It was too close to pity.

"They murdered my father!"

"And will your death, to the same man's blade, bring him back?"

"I have to do this."

"I see," she said, and Tau knew she didn't.

"How are you?" he asked, changing the topic. "How are you, here?"

She offered him a tight smile. "I'm well. It's both better and worse than I expected."

Tau tried to lift her spirits. "You outrank Umbusi Onai."

Her smile grew. "I am looking forward to seeing her again and asking her to wash my underthings, for once."

Tau laughed. It was forced, but the tension between them eased.

"Did you hear about Jabari?" she asked.

Tau didn't think the name would affect him as much as it did. "Jabari? What happened? Is he well?"

"Yes, sorry. I didn't mean to startle you. He tested in the North. He passed."

"He's in the city?"

"Somewhere."

Two of the most important people in his life had, somehow, found their way to this strange city of domes, gifts, and violence. "Have you seen him?" Tau asked.

"No. Not yet."

"If you do, will you tell him…" Tau had no idea what he could possibly say to Jabari. "Never mind." Zuri eyes softened and she gave him a little smile. More pity he didn't want. "Do they have you doing witchcraft already?" he asked, hoping to lift some of the dark around them.

Zuri guffawed and covered her mouth, eyes gleaming. "You heathen! Not witchcraft. Gifts!"

"Ah yes, gifts. Of course."

Her smile was large and real. "And yes, they do. I'm still learning, but I'm doing well. Very well." Her chin lifted with pride. "I'm one of the strongest in my cycle. Can you believe it? Me?"

"I believe it," Tau told her.

The compliment made her look away, pleased and shy in her pleasure. "I've hoped for this day," she said.

Tau hadn't dared hope, but he nodded. Zuri reached for his hand. He met her halfway and their fingers touched. She looked up at him, a new question on her face. He tried to read it but heard footsteps and laughter. Zuri snatched her hand away as three Indlovu, first cycles by the look of them, came into the circle. They were drunk. Tau tensed.

The first Indlovu, two heads taller than Tau and half again as heavy, noticed them first. Zuri's black robes stood out, identifying her as Gifted. The Noble thumped a fist into his chest, saluting her. That was when he got a good look at Tau.

"Lady Gifted," he said, "you are well?"

"Thank you, Initiate, I am."

There was an uncomfortable silence. The Indlovu wanted to do more, say more, but wasn't certain enough of protocol to push the issue. He tried another tact. "May we escort you home, my lady? Are we worthy?"

"Ever worthy, as are all men of the Indlovu Citadel. However, I am not on my way home, but I thank you again. Good evening and may the Goddess smile upon you."

The other Indlovu were watching Tau, their hands close to their swords. Tau fought the instinct to reach for his weapon.

"And may She smile on you as well," the lead Indlovu said, turning his attention to Tau. "The sun is setting, little Lesser. Time to run home."

Tau's hands itched. He pictured drawing his bronze and attacking but knew he'd die before bleeding the first one. He held himself as still as he could and nodded his assent. It wasn't enough, and the man waited, his huge hand sliding along his belt toward his sword.

There was nothing else for it. Tau stood. "It is late, nkosi. Thank you." He bowed to Zuri. "Lady Gifted, your advice and time have been more than I deserve."

Zuri was tense too, but she had a part to play if violence was to be avoided. "It is our duty to serve in what ways we can."

Tau bowed again and walked away from her. He heard the Indlovu walking closer, believed they planned to attack him as soon as he was out of Zuri's sight, but they stopped and Tau heard the Indlovu talking about the pleasant coolness of the evening. The man meant to stay with her, to be sure Tau wouldn't come back.

Tau had few reasonable choices, and so he returned to the drinking house, grinding his teeth hard enough to make his jaw ache. He saw the others as they were leaving.

"Tau!" Yaw called.

Hadith smiled when he saw Tau and threw something across the distance. Tau snatched it out of the air. It was his purse, empty.

"Two circles!" Hadith said. "Had enough for two circles."

"On us, next time," Uduak said.

Themba wobbled into view. "I'm drunk."

"A nice long march will sort that out," Hadith told him, making Themba grimace.

"Tau? You well?" Yaw asked, while Oyibo blinked at him, his eyes bleary and round as a spice mortar.

Tau wasn't. He nodded anyway. "Fine." He moved alongside the men and they left the city, heading for the meeting place.

Halfway through the march, Hadith drew apace with Tau. He'd been waiting for a moment alone. Tau didn't want to hear what he had to say.

"You knew her from home." Hadith wasn't asking. "Maybe she was someone special, but she is Gifted now." Tau marched on as if he wasn't listening. It didn't deter Hadith. "She must marry one of them, a Royal Noble, eventually. Do her part in producing more

Gifted." Tau shot a dangerous look at him, confirming the things Hadith had been saying. "You knew her," Hadith said, "but you don't anymore."

Tau picked up the pace, walking away from Hadith and marching to the head of the scale, alongside Anan. Anan glanced at him, saw his face, nodded, and kept marching.

Tau ground his teeth until his jaw locked from pain. He hadn't wanted to hear that. What he wanted was to beat one of those feckless Indlovu into the dirt.

He swore to train harder in the upcoming days. Scale Jayyed would fight in the next skirmish, and his eyes were open now. Jayyed had made sure of that. He had shown Tau the odds, and there was no hiding from them, but Tau didn't want to hide. He wanted to destroy.

SYMMETRY

In the days that followed, Tau trained as one of Jayyed's five in the morning, with the rest of the scale in the afternoons, and at night with the men being punished for misconduct. Many evenings, Yaw joined him. Shadowing Tau seemed to amuse Yaw, and the extra sparring sessions gave the slippery fighter plenty of opportunity to poke, jab, and injure other initiates. Even so, the evenings took their toll and Yaw dropped out of the sessions, but that didn't stop him from telling everyone just how hard Tau trained.

The stories, Tau decided, weren't a bad thing. They gained him a measure of respect, and that meant the other initiates treated him like less of a pariah. He began to feel like he might belong, wanted everyone to keep believing it too, and decided that, since his martial progress had led them down this path, the way to truly convince them was to become the best among them.

As soon as his wrist healed, he increased his efforts. He was determined to take advantage of having the full use of both arms.

He tried sparring with shields, but they slowed him. He used smaller ones and found they brought little in the way of defense and nothing to offense. So he abandoned them, trying bigger swords that needed both hands to wield. That was a disaster. He didn't have the strength or stamina for it and went back to one sword, choosing to focus on speed and a fighting style that was wholly aggressive. The intent was to overwhelm his opponents. It worked with weaker fighters but lost him winnable matches against the isikolo's strongest, leaving Tau frustrated and confused about how to improve.

He did know one thing. He was no longer right-handed. One season at the isikolo had improved his swordsmanship more than the lifetime of work that had come before, and against the isikolo's strongest—Hadith; Itembe; Yaw; Runako, who moved faster than a striking scorpion; and Uduak, the last man among the initiates who still won more fights than he lost to Tau—Tau could win with his left, but almost never with his right.

It drove him mad. He stood among the isikolo's best but could get no better, his progress halted. Worst of all, he hadn't sparred Uduak in several days, and that meant Jayyed or Anan would make the match soon.

Their fights had become events that the other scales watched. When they sparred, the betting was fierce, even the umqondisi participated, and it was common for an entire moon cycle of stipends to trade hands when a winner was declared. Their next fight could come any day, and Tau wanted to win. He had to work harder.

"Another round," said Tau. He was in the practice yard with Oyibo, and if not for the full moon, they'd be fighting in the dark.

"It's late," said Oyibo, avoiding Tau's eyes. Tau had conscripted his help after Yaw stopped showing up.

"One," Tau said. "Only one more."

"It's just... it's just you keep saying that..."

Tau didn't want to drive Oyibo away and tried to keep the disappointment from his face.

"Just one?" Oyibo asked.

Tau nodded his thanks. "Only one," he said, coming forward.

Oyibo wasted no time. He readied his sword, feinted with it, then swung his shield horizontally at Tau's chest. Tau quickstepped out of reach, avoiding the attack, and countered with a straight thrust. Oyibo threw himself backward and Tau's wooden blade sliced air, a handspan from hitting.

Following up, Tau closed the distance, and Oyibo, having lost all night by fighting cautiously, attacked in earnest. Tau blocked every swing, and though he was ratcheting up the pace, he did it slowly. If this was going to be the evening's final round, he wanted it to last. He used no true attacks but blocked and countered with precision.

Tau wanted to work his parries, ripostes, and endurance. He wanted a long match and planned to force Oyibo to call for the Goddess's mercy from exhaustion. He'd take Oyibo to his limit, then break him, without landing a single killing blow.

The plan, however, wasn't working. Oyibo was flagging but must have realized Tau's attacks weren't committed. The boyish-faced initiate had switched from heavy attacks to probing ones, meant to do little more than keep Tau at bay. He was slowing the fight down and giving himself time to rest.

Catching on to the strategy, Tau came at his sword brother fast, causing Oyibo, eyes widened with worry, to yank his shield up. Tau went at him, bashing the shield this way and that, knocking Oyibo's arm one way and then the other, drawing rare curses from him.

Still, Tau meant to stick to his plan. He wouldn't hit Oyibo directly, but the man he faced held a shield and Tau had no qualms about hitting it.

"I should have gone to bed," Oyibo said, grunting between words.

Tau laughed, enjoying the contest. It wasn't something he'd expected, but he couldn't deny it; every fight was a rush.

It was the purity of it, the honesty. When Tau sparred, it was just him and his opponent. All that mattered was experience, skill, determination, and will. The rest of the world slipped away, leaving only the next move, the next counter, the next attack, the next victory.

Tau blasted his sword against the top side of Oyibo's shield, hoping to knock it down so he could close the distance and shoulder him to the ground. But when his wooden blade hit the shield, edge to edge, half his sword exploded, showering them both in kindling.

For the barest breath, the two men were stunned to stillness. Tau reacted first. He shouldered Oyibo away; Oyibo fell, rolled, and was back up. Tau ran to the edge of the fighting circle, grabbed a spare weapon with his right hand, and turned to see his sword brother charging.

Oyibo swung hard, an overhead strike, and Tau was out of time. He was wearing a helm and Oyibo's sword was made of wood, but there was weight behind the blow. If it hit, Tau's head would pound for the night and ache the next day.

Desperate and moving as fast as he was able, Tau raised both swords and crossed them. Oyibo's attack thundered down and into the intersection of Tau's blades, coming to a bone-jarring stop when it hit. Tau had enough time to see Oyibo's jaw drop, before using both swords to pull his opponent's blade sharply to the left, throwing him off-balance and giving Tau a chance to reset.

Oyibo didn't want to give Tau that chance. Although off-balance, he lunged, stabbing at him like he held a spear. Tau slashed his broken blade onto the incoming weapon and whipped his other sword at Oyibo's helm.

Tau's severed sword pushed the attack wide, and as they were taught, Oyibo kept his eyes on his opponent's dominant hand, his opponent's weapon hand. The problem was that Tau had two weapon hands, and the sword in the one Oyibo wasn't watching was coming for his head.

Tau hit him cleanly, ringing his bronze helm like a bell and staggering Oyibo, who swung about wildly. Dodging the first drunken swing and halting the second with the half sword in his left, Tau used his other blade to continue battering Oyibo's shield.

Oyibo stumbled back, trying to get his bearings, but Tau was there, clubbing him in the thigh with one sword and clipping him in the ribs with the other. With twin hisses of pain, Oyibo backpedaled at speed, intent on getting out of striking distance.

The two men had reset and Tau knew it was win the match then or never. If he let Oyibo steal the fight's momentum, he'd also be letting him take advantage of Tau's deficiencies. Given time, Oyibo was good enough to use Tau's broken sword and inexperience fighting with two blades against him.

Thinking fast, impulsively, Tau launched into the choreographed sequence of attacks most trainers used to drill basic sword swings into new fighters. It was a sequence taught to children, meant to encourage comfort and confidence around weapons. As such, it started slowly but rapidly increased in speed and power. Still, it wasn't meant for two swords, and to avoid blocking his own attacks, Tau began the sequence with his left. Then, after the first swing, began it again with his right.

Oyibo's eyebrows shot up when he saw that Tau was still attacking with both swords. His surprise slowed him enough that he misjudged the first strike and was hit. He did catch the second attack in time, predicting it. He had to have recognized the sequence and knew Tau's right hand would do the mirror-same thing his left hand had just done. He was using his memory of the sequence to predict Tau's swings, but he'd never had to do this against two swords, and the whole point of the sword form, the reason Tau chose it, was that, though it began slowly, it ended in a whirlwind.

Oyibo stopped the third strike, but the fourth and fifth hit him. The sixth and seventh did as well, eliciting a grunt and then a much louder yowl, the eighth dropped him to a knee, the ninth disarmed him, and the tenth Tau pulled short, the blade in his right hand quivering a fingerspan from the crown of Oyibo's head.

"Goddess's mercy," Oyibo whispered, eyes crossed as he stared at the sword's too-close point. "Did you just fight with . . ."

"I think so," said Tau.

Oyibo swore using words that made even Tau cringe.

"One more round?" Tau asked, trying not to beg.

BLOWS

It was a few days later when Anan called on Tau and Uduak. The sun burned high overhead, its heat near enough to smelt metal. The rest of the scale, already having a sluggish day, put down their weapons and got comfortable, happy to cool off and ready to bet on the fight's outcome. The word went out and initiates from the other scales wandered closer. Most of the umqondisi followed their men, putting on a show of casual disinterest.

Anan was set to officiate the match and Jayyed stood off to the side, chewing a blade of dried grass. Uduak stepped in the fighting circle, warming up with his oversized wooden sword and shield. Tau, holding his wooden sword, followed him into the ring and the betting began in earnest.

Anan raised his hand to start the match and Tau asked for a moment. He stepped out of the circle, with Anan and Uduak watching him like he'd lost his mind and then looking certain of it when he walked back with a second wooden sword. Tau swung his two swords in circles, flowing the blades in opposite directions.

Uduak cocked his head. "Two?"

Tau stilled his swords, ready.

Uduak shrugged as if to say, one or two, he'd break the man who held them. Tau watched Anan, waiting for the call.

"Fight!" Anan shouted.

Tau attacked and Uduak stepped into the fray. Tau wanted to distract him with the second sword. The plan he'd developed, over nights of secret training with Oyibo, was to use it to keep Uduak's shield busy while he found openings with his left blade, his strong side. In the beginning it worked, and he scored two quick hits.

Uduak adjusted and came on harder. This put Tau on the defensive, and the extra attention needed to dual-wield was taxing. Tau realized that if he played this match according to plan—distract and engage—he would lose. So he let go, allowing the instincts bred into his right hand over cycle after cycle of training with his father to take hold. This allowed his stronger left side to reap the full benefits of training in the isikolo.

He attacked full on and full out, each blow capable of maiming or killing if it had been dealt with bronze. The effect was instant, and Uduak began to buckle under the pressure of Tau's twin blades as they whipped against his sword, shield, and body. The men who had gathered to watch stood without words, and the only sounds in the broiling air were the clashing of wooden weapons and the painful grunts from Uduak as Tau hit him over and over.

But Uduak refused to fall. He bellowed, his temper lost to Tau's flurry, and struck out as hard and as fast as he was able. Tau's blades met his anger with equal rage, greater speed, and finer skill. Uduak's shield arm was bludgeoned, his helmet crunched in on its right side, and the big man could not get past the stinging swords.

Uduak began to retreat, no other option left, and Tau came forward, blades whirling. Tau beat him to his knees, forcing Uduak to drop his sword and use both hands behind his chipped and cracking wooden shield. He would not surrender, though, and, caught in the rush, the violence of combat, the shouts of the other men, and his own instincts, Tau no longer saw an initiate of the isikolo. He no longer saw a sword brother. He no longer saw Uduak.

In his place was Kellan Okar, then Dejen Olujimi, and, at the last, Abasi Odili, and Tau let his anger spill out in a storm of blows that rained down on Uduak's shield and body, but Uduak still would not surrender. Tau, screaming his rage at an opponent that refused to be vanquished and seeing the world through a haze of red the same shade as his father's lifeblood, smashed Uduak's shield in two, clubbed the helmet from his head, and went to cave his skull in, when Jayyed called the match in a stunned Anan's place.

"It's done," Jayyed yelled, moving to stand between Tau and Uduak.

"Move," Tau snarled, swords held to strike.

"It's done, Tau."

"Uduak has not called for the Goddess's mercy," Umqondisi Thoko said.

"And that is why the match is declared a draw," Jayyed told the circle of men, causing an outcry. "This is sparring, not a blood-duel. I'm not keen to see good Ihashe injured. I congratulate the efforts of both men, and Uduak is an example to you all. Think on his bravery the next time you face an Indlovu in the Crags."

Thoko snorted, snatching back a handful of coins from Umqondisi Njere. "Next time they face an Indlovu? There's no example here. Tau is no Indlovu."

"Thoko, you can't even be thankful?" Njere asked. "Jayyed just saved you your drinking money."

That drew stifled laughter from many of the initiates.

"The match is over," Njere continued, "and Umqondisi Jayyed has called it a draw. Enough gawking and back to training. You can be sure the hedeni are sharpening their spears while we sit in the heat like sun-dazed lizards." The initiates dawdled. "Go!" ordered Njere.

The circle of men wandered off as Jayyed moved close to Tau, speaking to him alone. "Your swords are raised but the battle is over."

Tau lowered his weapons, trying to come back to himself. He'd been ready to kill. The thought frightened him, and he looked past Jayyed and down at Uduak. The big man was still on his knees, breathing with difficulty. He was cut all over and blood flowed from his head.

"Uduak," Tau said.

"There's a demon in you," the big man said, without the strength to lift his head.

"That's enough for now," Jayyed told them both. He turned to the men of his scale. "Yaw! Hadith! Help me get Uduak to the infirmary."

"I'll help," said Tau, leaning down to take one of Uduak's arms. Uduak flinched, grimacing in pain. "No."

Tau didn't know how to make things better. "I'm sorry. I'm—"

"Give it time, Tau," Jayyed told him as Yaw and Hadith ran over.

They put Uduak's arms over their shoulders and hoisted him off his knees. He groaned and fell against Hadith, almost bowling the smaller Lesser over. Hadith found his balance, then glared at Tau, and the trio stumbled off toward the nearest infirmary.

Jayyed's eyes followed the three men as he spoke to Tau. "You should continue with two blades. If you train with as much dedication as you have done, there will come a day when no Lesser in all the peninsula can stand against you." Jayyed paused and stepped closer, so no one else could hear. "But Uduak is your sword brother, Tau. Would you have killed him, if I had not stopped you?"

CHAPTER SEVEN

DRAW

The next morning, Hadith stopped Tau on their way to the practice fields. "You need to see Uduak," he said.

Tau hadn't slept. He'd lain awake thinking about what he'd done. Still, Hadith's urging felt like chastisement and Tau brushed past him, resenting the request.

Hadith took hold of Tau's arm. "You need to do it before it's too late. I'm here as a friend."

"Are we friends?" Tau asked, looking to Hadith's hand.

Hadith released him. "I had thought we were becoming so," he said, walking away.

The practice was even more rigorous than normal, and Jayyed was there, pacing the whole time. "We fight in the Crags! We fight Indlovu! We fight Enervators! Are you ready? Is this what ready looks like? Feels like?"

Tau had never seen Jayyed this anxious, and perhaps the umqondisi's anxiety was justified. His scale would be put to the test and his methods would be under scrutiny. Jayyed had taken liberties, and the other umqondisi and their Indlovu counterparts would be quick to use a poor performance to pull him down.

Despite Jayyed's prodding, when it came time to spar, Tau held back. He was still shaken up, but Jayyed wouldn't accept a half-hearted performance.

"You think to move behind the Goddess's back?" he shouted at Tau, his voiced raised loud enough to be heard by everyone. "Don't dishonor yourself or our efforts with self-pity and guilt. You're afraid you'll lose control again? Good, you should be. You must have control, but this is not the way. You'll watch brothers die and see your life wasted if you leash yourself to mediocrity's post. Fight, damn you!"

Tau increased his effort and pace against a concerned-looking Chinedu.

"Not enough!"

Tau pushed harder, forcing Chinedu back.

"I want all of it," Jayyed shouted, looking around at the rest of the scale. "Anything less is an affront to the time we're given. Anything less and you're waiting to die instead of fighting to live. Fight, burn you!"

Tau fired a look at Jayyed, and Chinedu took the opening. He leapt forward, shooting his sword at Tau. Tau reacted at full speed. He swatted the thrust aside, slapped his second sword against Chinedu's neck, and twisted the blade of his blocking sword free, blasting it into Chinedu's side.

Chinedu, taking near simultaneous hits on either side of his body, contorted as if he didn't know which way to fall.

"Ack! Mka!" Chinedu dropped his sword and shield, grabbing for his neck to see if the sting meant he was bleeding. "Goddess's mercy. Goddess's mercy! Char to ashes!" he said, too fast to cough.

Jayyed nodded at Tau. "It's never acceptable to be less than you are. Chinedu!"

"Umqondisi," Chinedu said, nursing ribs with one hand and neck with the other.

"You tried to stab Tau when he wasn't looking... a truly honorable and valiant effort, but you lowered your shield as you went in. Don't treat combat like you do women. Keep it up next time."

Yaw and Hadith were sparring nearby and both snickered.

"To Isihogo with both of you," Chinedu hissed. "You fight him, then."

"Why not?" asked Hadith, tapping Yaw with his sword. "Ready?" The two men came for Tau.

"Two on one?" Tau asked.

"I see two swords in those soft hands," said Hadith, pushing Yaw to one side of Tau while he moved to the other.

Tau was about to protest, until he saw Jayyed nod, allowing the match to proceed. He went for Yaw first. Hadith was the better fighter, but Yaw had a precision with his sword that a man would regret ignoring. Yaw saw Tau coming and shimmied back, blocking Tau's first strike and second but taking the third and hardest swing full on the thigh.

"Goddess!" he yelped.

Tau spun, crossing his two swords in time to catch Hadith's downcut, the same move he'd first used on Oyibo. He turned Hadith's sword and forced him off-balance, then disengaged, elbowing Hadith in the chest.

Tau pushed away, squared up, and came at him with his swords whirling, attacking from two angles. Learning from Chinedu's example, Hadith raised his shield high, but he couldn't bring his sword to bear. He took a punishing hit on his sword arm, then helmet, and when he got his sword in position, Tau avoided it, hammering his blade flat into Hadith's armpit.

Bent double, Hadith stumbled away. Swords still whirling, Tau swung for Yaw, who had been slinking over. Yaw's eyes widened when he saw he was expected. He swung for Tau's face, a well-aimed thrust, but Tau was faster. He leaned out of the way, spun in a tight circle, and pounded both swords into Yaw's side.

Yaw went down gasping and Tau returned his attention to Hadith, who ran forward, yelling at the top of his lungs. Their blades danced a few steps until Tau increased the pace beyond Hadith's ability to match.

His loss inevitable, Hadith risked a sacrifice swing that Tau blocked, turned, and used to disarm him, sending Hadith's wooden sword flying through the air. Hadith lifted his shield again, but Tau went low, knocking Hadith's legs out from under him, putting him in the dirt. Tau stood over him, sword at Hadith's throat stone.

"Cede," Tau told him.

"Thank you, I'll wait for the draw."

"What?"

"Any breath now."

Smiling, Jayyed came over. "This match is a draw."

"What!" said Tau, and Jayyed couldn't hold it in. He laughed, a full and infectious sound. The rest of the scale joined in. Tau looked from face to face, stopping on Hadith's. Hadith was smiling broadly.

"If it worked for Uduak..." Hadith extended his arm. Tau grabbed him, wrist to wrist, and pulled his sword brother to his feet.

Jayyed was still chuckling. "A draw. Char to ashes, a draw. Well fought, all three of you. Well fought."

Jayyed called the men back to sparring. "A draw," he muttered to himself, and then guffawed, startling the nearest initiate.

"When will you see Uduak?" Hadith asked Tau.

"I don't know that he wants to see me."

"Only one way to find out," Hadith said.

Tau breathed deep and nodded. He walked over to where Jayyed was watching Mshindi and Kuende, the two twins, spar. "Umqondisi Jayyed, permission to step off the fields."

"Where to, Common Solarin?"

"The infirmary."

"Eh, granted. We'll be here when you're back."

Tau saluted and left the training grounds. It was past time to see the big man.

BROTHERS

Uduak's face and body were a rash of welts. His shield arm was in a splint and his left eye was swollen shut.

"Uduak..." Tau had no idea what to say.

"Tau."

"I'm sorry."

"Nceku."

Tau bristled.

"Nceku."

"Should I leave?"

"No, I want to insult you. Nceku!" Uduak said.

Tau glanced around the infirmary. Most of the other cots were empty, and he didn't see any of the Sah priests, but three beds over, a thin initiate with a broken leg was watching.

"Would you stop?"

"Nceku!" Uduak said with vigor, like he was singing a fireside song.

"You've lost your mind."

"Doing less than when you lost yours, neh?"

Tau softened at that. "You are my sword brother and deserved better from me."

Uduak laughed and winced. "Might not survive better'n what

you already gave." Uduak watched Tau from the eye he could open. "Never happened."

"What?"

"Not since I was small. Not since I grew and whupped that Petty Noble for being a wretch to my cousin."

It was the longest sentence Tau had heard Uduak speak. "You whupped a Noble?"

"Whupped him. Whupped him good." Uduak's eye twinkled. "Could have had me hanged. Guess he didn't want anyone to know a Low Common blooded him."

"You beat a Noble . . . ," Tau said.

"Went on whupping everyone. Got good at it. Got to like it. Then you come along in the testing and I whupped you too, except you kept getting up. Thought it then, think it now, you've a demon in you." Uduak went silent for a beat. He seemed hesitant. "Won't let you stop, will it?"

"I've more to do," answered Tau.

"Can see that." Uduak shifted on the cot. "It's in me too. Think mine's smaller than yours, but it pushed me until I could stop that mka of a Noble."

"It left you then?"

Uduak held Tau's eyes with his own. The twinkle was gone. "No. There's always more to do." The mood had darkened and both men seemed uncomfortable. "Never been beat," he said. "Not like that."

"Two swords. Few people are used to it."

"Wasn't two swords that beat me. And when I knew I was beat, couldn't surrender."

"Your demon?"

"No. You would have killed me."

That startled Tau. "I'll be better," he said, unable to deny Uduak's words outright.

"You'll try."

"I'll be better."

Uduak grunted. "Strange not to be the strongest," he said, changing the topic. "Been it for so long."

Tau tried a smile. He meant it to be comforting as he issued a gentle challenge. "A bit more work and maybe you'll be it again."

Uduak stared at him for several breaths. "Not as long as you live, I won't."

Tau's smile faded.

"It's fine. Maybe now the thing inside me will quiet a bit." Uduak rolled over, turning his massive back to Tau. "Thanks for coming."

The conversation had been unsettling, but Tau was glad his sword brother would be fine, that they would be fine. He nodded and realized Uduak couldn't see it with his back turned.

"Don't let that demon go too quiet," Tau said. "We're for the Crags. It's time to introduce the Nobles to Scale Jayyed."

PAIN

Scale Jayyed arrived at the Crags without Uduak. The big man had tried to join his brothers, but Jayyed had forbidden it, telling him to take the proper time to heal. Uduak's absence was felt, and Hadith did what he could to lift the spirits of the men.

It was for that, as well as for his mind for military strategy, that Jayyed made Hadith the scale's inkokeli, and Hadith took the responsibility seriously. During the march, he'd gone over and over his battle plans with Tau, Yaw, Chinedu, Oyibo, Runako, Themba, and Mkiwa.

Tau wasn't sure why he was being involved. He had little interest in tactics or strategies and had told Hadith, "Point me in the direction you want me to fight and I'll fight." He didn't need more than that.

Hadith had called him an ass and demanded he listen so he would understand. Tau had listened. He wasn't sure how much he understood.

Besides, how much could they plan for something that had not happened yet? Their actions would depend on what the Indlovu did and on whom the Enervator hit. Itembe had gone into his skirmish with a detailed plan. Tau had seen how that went.

"Remember, Oyana is a brawler," Jayyed told them as they formed up at the edge of the battlefield. "His Indlovu initiates will be too. We're on the urban battleground and they'll try to use that to their advantage. They'll come out hard, fast, looking for quick kills and immediate victory. Hold off their initial push and you'll make them doubt themselves."

Tau eyed the battleground in front of him. In the spaces between the tightly packed adobe buildings he caught glimpses of the Indlovu lined up at its other end. All of them had their dulled practice swords out and ready. All of them wore shields.

He also saw their Enervator. She looked scared. Funny, she was the only person who would come out of this without a scratch, and she was unsettled. Chances were that it was her first skirmish. Though that was true for Tau as well.

Tau glanced at the men beside him. Hadith was there, ready to run in and take point as they wound their way through the pretend paths of a pretend city. Hadith wanted them to push deep into the battleground. He wanted them to make it to one of the two circles, built to reflect the much larger circles all Omehi cities had.

Hadith wanted enough fighting space for his superior numbers to have an effect. The circle he was targeting had three entrances, two that were on opposite sides and a thin path that was closer to the direction from which the Indlovu would come. Hadith wanted Tau, Yaw, Chinedu, and Oyibo to hold the thin path against any Indlovu who tried to splinter off from the main group to flank Scale Jayyed.

It would be difficult for more than two Indlovu to stand abreast in the narrow path, which was bordered by single-story buildings. This, Hadith hoped, would give the advantage to Tau's group.

"When the war horn sounds, we make for the circle," Hadith told the men. "Keep close. Fight as a scale. No heroics. We're here to win and we'll do that by taking the bastards down together!"

The men cheered.

"Watch out for the Ennie. You see that inyoka so much as twitch in our direction and you call it out."

The men passed the message back, and Tau saw fear flicker across their faces. No one liked the idea of being hit by enervation.

"Make ready, he's going to blow it," said Yaw, a breath before Tau heard the war horn's call. The Indlovu roared a call of their own and sped onto the battlefield, making Hadith curse.

"Go, go, go!" he yelled at his men, urging them on.

Tau ran with the others, racing into the winding maze of the false city. The paths twisted and crisscrossed and Tau was thankful Hadith had made him listen. It would have been an easy thing to make a wrong turn. Yaw, small and quick, kept pace with Tau, and they sped along, shoulder to shoulder, Chinedu and Oyibo just behind them. Tau could hear Chinedu coughing as they ran. Strange how much of a comfort that was.

It was one more turn and they emerged in the circle. They'd arrived first. Tau looked up to the building rooftops. Two aqondise, one from the isikolo and the other from the Indlovu Citadel, were up there. They would make sure the defeated men stayed out of the contest and would call fouls where they saw them.

Moving his eyes lower, Tau spotted three Indlovu thundering down the main path just a hundred strides from the circle. From the path nearest Tau, Hadith emerged with a dozen men.

"Tau, hold the side path. We have the circle!"

In the time it took for Hadith to speak, ten more of his sword brothers had reinforced the circle. Tau hoped they would be enough, as the two dozen Lessers engaged the three Indlovu, who had backed up into the path, where they could not be surrounded.

No time to waste, Tau ran for the side path with his men, getting there at the same time as four Indlovu and the Enervator.

Yaw skidded to a stop. "Mka!"

"At them!" screamed Tau, charging.

"Really?" said Yaw, running after him.

"Touch the Enervator! Take her out of the skirmish!" Tau yelled, launching himself at the first Indlovu.

Their swords smashed together. The Indlovu, bigger than Uduak, had on a thick leather gambeson that would have cost Tau's stipend for his entire cycle at the isikolo. The Noble's face was flat, nose broad and flared, and he snarled at Tau, teeth out.

They exchanged a flurry of attacks, the Indlovu battering at Tau with all his might, seeking to bury him under the weight of his much greater strength. Tau deflected each strike, shifting the force of them down and away. The Noble growled in frustration, coming at Tau again, but Tau danced back and Yaw was there, ramming the point of his dulled bronze sword as hard as he could into the Noble's side.

"Gah!" the Indlovu roared, a rib broken. He swung at the much smaller Yaw, who skipped out of reach.

Tau gave the injured man no second chance. He thundered his two swords into his helmet, chest, side, and arm. The Indlovu seemed to weather the first hits, then collapsed when Tau delivered a more violent blow to his head.

A woman screamed. It was the Enervator. She had her hands over her mouth. She looked horrified by the violence, as if she wasn't there with the intent to yank their souls from their bodies.

Tau moved his head on a swivel, saw that Oyibo and Chinedu were losing their fight. Oyibo's shield was on the ground, his shield arm limp, his sword wavering. Chinedu was giving all he could, but the Indlovu he faced shrugged off his attacks.

"Help Chinedu," Tau told Yaw.

"There's two more Indlovu coming."

"They're mine," Tau said.

Yaw looked at Tau like he'd lost his mind, and then, with little better to do, he followed his orders, dashing to Chinedu and Oyibo's defense.

The two remaining Indlovu came on, and Tau smiled at them. "I will give you pain."

The leading Indlovu, a head taller than Tau, stopped, shook his head, and laughed. "Let's see if I can knock your brains back in place, Lesser."

He charged, and Tau grinned like he was sun sick. The Indlovu, in his eagerness, had left his partner behind.

The first touch went to Tau, who ducked under the Noble's head strike, blasting him in the shin with the edge of his strong-side sword. The Noble fell and Tau spun, whipping his blades in a shining arc that ended in dual hammer strikes across the falling man's back.

The citadel fighter hit the ground in a clamor of bronze and expelled breath. Tau kicked him in the face and smashed the pommel of his weak-side sword into the man's temple. That done, he rose to face the next Indlovu.

"I will give you pain," he told the man, and this time, his words were given weight.

The Indlovu tightened his grip on his sword and his eyes thinned to slits. Tau rushed forward and the Indlovu jerked back, surprised by the suddenness of Tau's movement. Tau was on him then, and so were his swords. He swung them with hatred, smashing the dulled blades into the Noble's body and shield. Every time the Indlovu sought to bring his weapon to bear, Tau slapped it aside and hurt him.

That was when he heard the woman scream again.

I'll be with you shortly, he thought, but then the whole world went dark as she engulfed him and everyone else in the narrow path in a torrent of enervation.

Tau was still in the path, in the fake city in the Crags, and yet he was not. It was as dark as night, but he could see, though what he saw made him wish he couldn't. The Enervator was there, but she was cloaked in shadows as dark as dragon scale. She was hidden. The others, though, shone bright with the golden energy of their souls, and this had attracted demons.

The closest one was a mass of shard-like bones that pierced the shell it had in place of skin. Its eyes were bulbous and red and its razor teeth were as long as Tau's fingers. It shambled toward him and he scrambled back. It gave him no thought, choosing to fall on the Indlovu Tau had been fighting. The young Noble opened his mouth to scream, but the beast had already clamped its jaws around his face and ripped the man's nose, lips, and tongue away. The Noble fell, what was left of his mouth open but voiceless, eyes darting in terror.

Tau took another step back, desperate to hide, desperate to get away. He could feel the Enervator's hold on his soul, locking it to this evil place. He sought her out but had lost sight of her among the swirling mist.

"Tau!" It was Yaw, his voice a thin and distant thing, like a deadened echo. Tau looked over. Yaw was only a dozen strides away, suffused with a golden glow. Tau looked down at himself; he was lit too. He moved to go to Yaw and held. A demon had found his sword brother.

The thing shared nothing with the one still feeding on the Indlovu. It was squat, not quite reaching Yaw's shoulder, but it bristled with muscles, like a perverse rendering of an Enraged Ingonyama. It snarled at Yaw, its thick lips dripping ichor and revealing blunt, crushing teeth. Yaw fell backward, calling for help with his underworld-muted voice, and the demon went for him.

Tau resisted every impulse he had and ran away from his fear and into combat. He raised his strong-side sword, surprised to realize he still had it, and swung it onto the neck of the demon attacking Yaw. The blade struck true, biting into the meat of the thing. It howled, reared, ripped the sword from Tau's grip, and clawed at him, catching his forearm and tearing away the skin there like it was paper.

The pain was instant and furious. Tau drew his arm back, near to blacking out from agony, and lashed out with his remaining sword, slicing the demon across its chest. It reared, roared, dropped to all fours, and charged him. Tau braced himself, thrust hard for the place he imagined the creature's heart to be, and was bowled over as the demon crashed into him, sending them both tumbling along the swampy muck of Isihogo.

Tau lost his weapon and his sense of up or down. He tried to kick the demon away but was like a child in its grip. He prayed he'd killed it with his last sword thrust, but its eyes centered on him and it dove for his neck.

Tau raised a blocking arm to stop it. It clamped its jaws around his elbow and bit down, crushing through skin and bone. He screamed as the pain, horrifying in its intensity, hit. Then the agony threatened sanity itself when the beast swung its head back and forth, jerking his whole body about and tearing his destroyed limb to shreds as the light came back to the world.

"Tau! Tau!" Yaw was standing over him.

Tau scrambled away, his back banging into the wall behind him.

"Run! It's on me." Tau shouted, looking at his arm and expecting to see a ruin. It was whole. He searched himself for the pain that had tormented him. There was nothing.

"Tau, listen to me, we're out," said Yaw. "You...you saved me from it."

Tau took a steadying breath and, wide-eyed, looked around the path. The Enervator was on her knees, crying. The last Indlovu Tau had fought was scrubbing his hands across his face and gibbering on the ground in front of her. The one Oyibo and Chinedu had faced was lying in a fetal position, his body wracked with tremors.

"What in the Goddess's name," Tau said, his voice shaking.

"She held us too long," said Yaw.

Tau stood on weak legs and took a step toward the Gifted, ready to risk the wrath of the citadel, Nobles, and isikolo. He would give this incompetent wretch a piece of his mind. She heard him coming and looked up from her knees. She was young, more child than woman, and she looked small, lost, scared. She was a…she had been a Low Common, and the curses Tau had been ready to sling slipped away.

"What did you do?" he asked, but she just wept.

Yaw came over. Through her tears, the Gifted saw him and raised an arm as if to ward him off or maybe cast another wave of enervating energy. It was too soon. Her powers wouldn't be back, but Tau couldn't help it and backed away in fear.

"None of that, Lady Gifted," Yaw said as his fingers brushed the top of her shoulder. "I've touched you. You're out of the contest, neh?"

She didn't speak, but she did nod.

"Brothers," Yaw said, "let's get back to the circle. We'll help the others and tell them the Enervator is down."

"I can't," said Oyibo.

"What?" asked Yaw.

"Oyibo took the Goddess's mercy before…before the rest happened," Chinedu explained. "This one"—he indicated the quaking Indlovu—"he was…a thing got him and it…"

Tau had trouble finding his voice. "All right, us three, then, let's go," he said, gathering up his fallen swords.

"Lady Gifted," Yaw asked, "you'll see to the Indlovu here? You'll call for the aqondise when we go?"

She didn't answer and her eyes were shut tight.

"I'll call out," Oyibo assured them.

"Let's go," Tau said a second time, and the three men trotted down the path, back the way they had come and toward more fighting.

SKIRMISH

When Tau emerged from the path and into the harsh light of the wide-open circle, he counted seven Indlovu fighting just eleven of his sword brothers. The fighting was fierce and not going well for Scale Jayyed. The skirmish had broken down into smaller contests, and six Indlovu fought in pairs. The seventh was backed into a corner, swinging at the three Lessers harrying him. Hadith was on his feet, but the scale's inkokeli had taken cuts and had an angry welt on his forehead.

"The Enervator is ash!" Tau shouted into the circle, trying to give his scale hope. Turning to the sword brothers with him, he gave orders. "Help where you can. We finish this!" he said, before running to Hadith's aid.

"For…the Goddess!" Chinedu cried out.

Hadith was with two other Ihashe, and the three of them were fighting two Indlovu.

"I have left," Tau told the three men as he joined the fight.

The Indlovu on the left was granite thick and had a neck like a barrel. His dark skin shone with sweat and his face was the type that looked like it always smelled of offal.

"He's their inkokeli," Hadith warned. "I'll stay."

"Go!" Tau told him. "Finish the other. He's mine."

Hadith held position.

"Hadith!" Tau urged.

Hadith shook his head at Tau but did as he was bid, moving to engage the other Indlovu with his two sword brothers.

The inkokeli used the reprieve to catch his breath. "You're a fool, Lesser, to try me alone." He raised his sword. "I am Zesiro Opio, Greater Noble of the Opio family in Palm, a second-cycle Indlovu of the citadel and inkokeli of Scale Oyana."

Tau pointed the ends of his dual swords at the man's broad chest. "I am a Common of Kerem and you will beg me for mercy."

"Nceku!" Zesiro said, attacking.

Tau did not back down. He gave no ground. He met Zesiro Opio in the circle of the Crag's fake city and went to war. Their blades flashed and flickered, faster and faster, as the men wielding them lunged, spun, deflected, and parried.

Zesiro, Tau realized, was a brilliant fighter. Zesiro was good enough to beat him, if he had not already fought under the hot sun on a long morning against overwhelming numbers and the well-trained men of Scale Jayyed.

In training, Tau had taken himself to the breaking point every day. Every day he pushed further than the day before, making himself a little stronger, a little harder, a little faster. The sword was his religion and, a devout disciple, he sacrificed to it without end.

So, amid a melody of metal, Tau Solarin and Zesiro Opio burned across the circle grounds like wildfire, each man reaching deeper than he had ever done before. One man fought, ready to die. The other battled, thinking it impossible to lose. But thinking a thing has never been enough to make it so, and Tau could see fear set in when Zesiro Opio realized he wasn't winning.

The Noble couldn't keep up and Tau's blades kept getting through. Desperate and in pain, Zesiro raised his shield, hiding behind it, unable to slow the onslaught as Tau's blades bashed the bronze disc from every angle. Zesiro yelled for help as Tau, merciless, came up and under the bronze disc, cracking the hand there and breaking noble fingers.

Zesiro howled, his sword flying from his ruined hand, and Tau did not stop. He increased his pace, refusing to let the Goddess's mercy take this man's beating from him.

"Zesiro Opio! Greater Noble!" Tau roared, smashing his blade against the cheek plates of the Greater Noble's helmet, breaking the bones beneath and cracking the Indlovu on his temple. "A name? A caste? That won't shield you from me!"

Zesiro Opio did not cry out in pain and he did not beg. Instead, he slumped forward and flopped to the ground, unconscious. Tau, trembling, shouted his victory at him, seeking satisfaction, finding none. He licked his lips, no spit to wet them, and looked for the next fight.

Hadith and the two men with him had downed their lone Indlovu. The man was on his knees and had a gash on his head. He gawped at Tau, flinching when Tau stepped in his direction. Tau ignored him. The man had surrendered. He was nothing.

There were two pockets of fighting left, three Indlovu and nine Scale Jayyed men. The odds were in their favor and Hadith pointed to two Scale Jayyed initiates fighting a single Indlovu. The four of them rushed over, and the Noble, seeing the count at six to one, surrendered. The six sword brothers joined Chinedu, Yaw, and Runako, who had been losing to the last two men of Scale Oyana.

They surrounded the holdouts, forcing the two Indlovu to go back to back. Tau, too tired to be effective but refusing to give in to his exhaustion, pushed forward.

"It's done," Hadith called out to the Nobles before Tau could engage the men. "We're nine, you're two. The Enervator is out of the contest and your inkokeli is down." Hadith pointed to Zesiro Opio in the dirt. Seeing Opio broke the smaller of the two Nobles. He looked ready to drop his sword.

"We don't lose to you!" the older and bigger of the two Nobles said.

"Not usually," said Hadith. "Today is different." He waved his nine men forward and they came on, swords bristling.

"I'll take mercy from no Lesser," the larger Indlovu told Hadith.

"Nor should you," Hadith said. "Only the Goddess grants mercy. It's Her I'd like you to ask."

"Lutalo . . . ," cautioned the younger Indlovu.

"Shut it," Lutalo told the man at his back.

"Goddess's mercy," Lutalo's sword brother said, lowering his sword.

"To ash with you," Lutalo swore at his fellow. "Rot in Isihogo, all of you!" He raised his sword to fight, and the circle of men, swords ready, pushed closer. Lutalo eyed the men, grimaced, and threw his sword down.

"Say the words," Hadith told him.

Swordless or not, Lutalo looked like he was about to take a run at Hadith. "Goddess's mercy," he growled, and the circle of Lessers erupted in cheers.

LEGEND

Tau and the rest of the scale stayed to watch the next skirmish. Emboldened by the efforts of their southern brothers, the Northern Isikolo fought hard. At times it looked like they might force a draw, but the citadel Enervator waited, holding back her powers until the northern scale was crowded together.

She caught sixteen men in her blast, and the Indlovu ripped through the rest of the scale, punishing the Ihashe for daring to believe they had a chance. The match ended with more serious injuries than was typical for a skirmish.

Tau and his sword brothers attended to the northerners. They carried men to the nearby infirmary and helped those who had been sent to Isihogo to recover as best they could.

The loss, and the Indlovu's brutality, cooled the heat the men felt from their win. But as Tau and Hadith carried a northern Ihashe, his leg broken by an Indlovu blade, the fires burned again.

"I saw you fight," he said to Tau and Hadith. "By the Goddess, I've never felt so proud to be a Lesser."

Hadith smiled so large, Tau thought his face might split.

"I wanted to win. I fought to win," the northerner said, "because you showed us we can."

Tau grunted, which the man took as encouragement. The

northerner raised his voice, calling out to the men on the battlefield and beyond. "Victory! No enemy stands before the rage of dragons! Where we fight—"

Tau wondered if the man had taken a blow to the head, when the rest of the Ihashe, to a man, shouted the response to the ancient Omehi battle cry. "The world burns!"

The Indlovu, stowing their gear as they readied to leave for Citadel City, watched the shouting Lessers, a strange look on their Noble faces.

"The world burns! The world burns! The world burns!"

As the chanting broke down to general cheering and hooting, the man with the broken leg clapped Tau on the back. "They'll splint this and then I'm celebrating with you!"

"Celebrating?" Tau asked.

"In Citadel City, we'll drain the drinking houses dry!"

Hadith had that grin on his face again. "Yes, we must. What is Uduak always saying? I have a thirst!"

They dropped the northerner off at the infirmary, promising not to leave without him. Hadith gathered up the rest of the scale and even wrangled Anan and a visibly proud Jayyed into the group. Together, the combined forces of the Southern and Northern Isikolo invaded Citadel City, heading for the largest drinking house they could find.

Good to his word, Hadith bought Tau's rounds and Yaw told the story of "Tau's Path."

"We're in the path, thinking to hold it against an Indlovu, maybe two, and bearing down on us are four of the bastards and the Enervator!" Yaw paused, giving his audience time to be impressed by the odds. "I'm a fighter, no doubt about it, but I was near to soiling my breeches. No shame in it, not when facing those odds."

Yaw pointed a finger in Tau's face, a handspan from touching his nose. "Then, Tau here, he turns to us and says, 'Charge them.'"

Tau didn't remember it like that but stayed quiet.

"He gets onto the first Indlovu and does his thing." Yaw waved both hands around in the air like they were swords. "And, like that, he beats the Noble to pulp. I'm over there with Chinedu and Oyibo and we're giving the second Indlovu a good go. He's a giant of a thing, bigger than Uduak by two or three heads."

Tau didn't think the man had been that large. Yaw had the audience, though, and even Jayyed, who had stayed to drink with them, was leaning in.

"So, we're busy fighting this tree of a man, which leaves Tau with two Indlovu and the Enervator. She's standing there, nose in the air, knowing her Noble protectors are going to break Tau's head in two. Only thing is, someone forgot to tell that to Tau."

Yaw raised an eyebrow and looked round the room, catching the eye of every man, making the story feel told for their benefit alone. Other than Yaw's voice and Chinedu's occasional cough, the place was silent.

"The Indlovu go for Tau and, I swear to the Goddess and my mother, Tau tells them, I swear it, he tells them, 'I will give you pain!'"

For a breath, the room was silent, until, as one, the men went wild, roaring their approval and stamping their feet. Yaw let the cheers go, nodding like nothing less was expected or deserved. Then, patting the air for silence, he continued. "'I will give you pain,' Tau told the Noble bastards, and in sight of the Goddess and within Her will, as all things are . . . he did!"

The room exploded again and jugs were slammed on tabletops, backs were slapped, and masmas was spilled.

"He dropped two Indlovu while me, Chinedu, and Oyibo are doing all we can to avoid getting run through by one."

Tau felt their eyes on him and tried to look stoic or something. He wasn't sure what was expected. He wanted to explain that he didn't fight the two Indlovu at the same time and that he only said what he had to make them angry enough to come at him one on one, but someone distracted him by shoving an overflowing jug of masmas into his hand. He had a jug in each.

"Was it after she saw her Indlovu go down that she enervated you?" asked a man from the North.

Yaw's mood changed with the question. He'd been a playful and buoyant storyteller but turned somber. "Tau lured a demon away from me," he said.

The room was quiet again, even Chinedu.

"It was going to kill me and there was nothing I could do. I know it can't actually...but it's so real....It..." He trailed off.

"It shouldn't have happened," interjected Aqondise Anan, his words slurring. "The Enervator held you under for too long. I made a formal complaint to the citadel and her preceptor. It was improper of them to place someone who wasn't ready into a skirmish."

Jayyed spoke. "She made a mistake."

"Eh, but what if she had turned one of our men demon-haunted? Last skirmish, Itembe damn near broke. Some nights he...All I'm saying is that I'm proud of you lot. It's been a while since we've had a victory like that, and"—Anan glanced at Jayyed—"it makes this old soldier's dream of seeing Ihashe in the Queen's Melee again seem a little less idle."

Jayyed inclined his head, acknowledging Anan's words and the respect he was paying to the umqondisi's own history and legend. "A long while since we've had a victory when an Enervator was present," Jayyed said before raising his jug. "To the Ihashe, to the Omehi, to the Goddess, and our dreams."

They drank, laughed, celebrated, but Tau couldn't focus, and as soon as he could, he spoke with Jayyed.

"Maybe this cycle will see Ihashe in the Queen's Melee again," Tau said, trying to be patient, trying to hold back the thing he really wanted to ask.

Jayyed smiled. "Maybe."

"Is it often the same scales from the citadel that make it to the melee? Or is every cycle different?"

"Like most things," Jayyed said, "a few become dominant, some maintain a measure of power, and most remain powerless. The citadel is no different and the majority of the sixteen scales that qualify for the Queen's Melee are there time and again."

"So, though new initiates come in, the same crop of umqondisi seem to train and produce the best?"

Jayyed chuckled. "Yes. And they'd swear to the Goddess their results were entirely due to their brilliance. Closer to the truth, early success eases the way for more success, often leads to better resources, more say in matters that contribute to success, and even the power to hamper the progress of those behind you."

Taking a long drink, Jayyed drained his cup and placed it at the table's edge, balancing it. "The same crop of umqondisi do tend to train and produce the best, but it's not just because they're the best teachers. Remember, my reputation allowed me to bend rules. I chose all the initiates I wanted in my scale before any of the other umqondisi had a chance."

Tau's patience had seen the seeds he'd planted grow. It was time to harvest. "Which scales do you expect to see in the melee?" he asked.

Jayyed looked off, thinking. "Hmm... I'd wager a good sum we'll see Scales Ojuolape, Onyekachi, and Otobong, but I'd face down dragon fire if Scales Osa and Omondi didn't qualify."

Tau nodded at the names, memorizing them. "They're the best?"

"They are."

"We'll be better," Tau said, not really meaning it, but looking to end the conversation.

Jayyed laughed. Tau smiled and pretended he had to make water so he could slip away. He left the drinking house and wandered a while, not wanting it to look like he traveled with purpose. A quarter span of that and he made for the circle where Zuri had taken him on his first trip to Citadel City. It wasn't hard to find it, though he felt foolish doing so.

How could he think she'd be there? As if she had nothing more to do than wait for him. Would she even know his scale had been in the skirmish today? Tau shook his head, told himself to turn back and enjoy the rest of his time in the city with his sword brothers, but he didn't want to go back, not without looking.

So, Tau strode into the circle, ready to find disappointment. He found Zuri instead.

GIFTS

She was sitting on the same bench. She was the only one in the circle.

"I didn't think you'd come," she said, standing.

Tau went to her and didn't know quite what to do when he got there.

"You could hold me," she told him.

He wrapped her up in his arms. She melted into him and he sighed at the feel of her.

"I think of you almost as much as my training," Tau said.

"That much? You shouldn't," she said, her voice edging toward laughter.

"I . . . I think of training all the time. It's a lot, really."

"I'm sure." She laughed that time and drew back slightly, so they could look at each other.

Seeing her calmed him.

"I heard you won," she said.

"We did." Tau couldn't take the pride from his voice. "We beat the Indlovu and their Enervator."

"It caused a stir. Preceptor Inti has been removed from teaching duties. They're sending her to the front, to fight, and the initiate,

Namisa, she'll be doing newcomer lessons for the next four moon cycles."

Tau hadn't thought of that, how the ones on the other side, the losing side, would suffer for being part of such a dramatic failure. "I'm not happy to hear that, but we deserved to win. The odds are heavily weighted against us and we beat them."

"You had three times the men."

"They're Nobles, and the citadel fields initiates from all three cycles of training. They had an Enervator," Tau said, to drive the point home.

"Namisa is barely that."

"She knew her work well enough to cause me to lose an arm to a demon." His words shocked Zuri, and none of this was going the way he wanted.

"She held you long enough for a demon to attack?"

"I saw one eat the face off an Indlovu."

"She sent a Noble to Isihogo?"

"She sent the lot of us, Ihashe and Indlovu. Is that not acceptable, if the Gifted can save herself in the bargain?"

Zuri's voice went hard. "Not in a skirmish."

"Ah." Tau was beginning to understand why Namisa and her preceptor's punishments had been so harsh.

"My first skirmish was a few days ago," Zuri offered.

"You could have faced us?"

"It was a scale from the Northern Isikolo."

"You won?"

"Of course."

"Of course," Tau repeated, rolling the words in his mouth like they were rotten.

"You know what I mean," Zuri said.

"What it's like? Fighting on their side?"

"Whose side? The Omehi?"

"You know what I mean," Tau said.

"I don't. We all train to defend our people against the hedeni."

"Then, why are the skirmishes set up so Lessers lose?"

"They're not. Lessers can rise up the scale ranks as the citadels do. Lessers can win the Queen's Melee."

"When did that happen last?"

Zuri was no longer in Tau's arms. "What do you want me to say?" she asked.

"This isn't how I wanted this to go."

"Should I leave?"

"No," he said. "Can I start over?"

"How does that work?"

"How are you? How is the Gifted Citadel?" Tau asked.

Zuri sat on the bench, leaving room for him. He sat.

"It's incredible. It's horrible," she said. "Discovering what I can do, how far I can go, it gets so I can barely sleep. I'm scared to waste even a moment of learning. But that makes me complicit. If I take the power and ignore the cost, I'm not so different from the worst of them."

"The worst of them?"

"I don't want to talk about it."

"You can tell me," Tau said, thinking it very much sounded like she wanted to talk about it.

She took his hand but said nothing. He slipped his fingers out of hers so he could put his arm around her shoulders. He gave her his far hand to hold instead. She leaned against him and they sat like that for a time, letting the day turn from dusk to evening.

"I'll have to go," he said.

"I know."

"I'll come back."

"Next skirmish."

"Will you—"

"Of course. I'll wait."

Tau nodded, didn't want to spoil the evening, but had more he needed from Zuri. "Can I . . . may I ask two questions?"

She raised an eyebrow. "That's formal."

"Ah . . ."

"Of course, go ahead."

Tau hesitated, unsure if he wanted to know. "What scale is Kellan Okar in?"

She was staring at him, and for a moment, he didn't think she'd answer. "Scale Osa," she said.

Tau let out the breath he'd been holding, his mind going over and over Jayyed's words, "I'd face down dragon fire if Scales Osa and Omondi didn't qualify." That's what he'd said.

"Do you still want to ask your second question?"

"Neh?"

"You said you had two questions."

The second question mattered more, now that he knew Kellan was part of Scale Osa. "The Gifted…"

"What about us?" Zuri asked, emphasizing the last word.

"How does enervation work?"

Zuri sighed and lifted her head from his shoulder. "How did you get the scar? Was it…Lekan?"

"Lekan."

She turned to him and really looked at it. Tau didn't think of himself as vain, but it was uncomfortable, having her study the mark that marred him. Zuri lifted a hand to his face and let her fingers rest below the puckered flesh on his right cheek.

She let her hand fall, lowering her head. "The first part you know. Enervation pulls a man's soul out of this realm and into another. To understand the Gifted, our abilities, and enervation, you need to understand the realm to which your soul is sent. You need to understand Isihogo."

"I see," said Tau.

"No, you don't. Isihogo is the realm of Ukufa and his demons. It is the prison the Goddess made to hold them."

Tau performed his daily prayers but would never have called himself religious. Still, at mention of Ukufa he made the symbol of the dragon span, warding away evil.

Zuri noticed his quick hand movement and the corner of her mouth twitched upward. "Yes, well, everything began with Ananthi when She spun the universe out of Her desire for more. She created the sun, stars, Uhmlaba, and all that is between them."

"I remember hearing this when I was a child."

"You're the one who asked," she said.

"About enervation."

"This is about enervation."

Tau kept silent.

"Ananthi created everything. She created life. She made all the creatures and She made all the races of man, each of them unique in the way they commune with Her."

"Gifts."

"Gifts. Every race has unique capabilities," Zuri said. "And Ananthi continued to create, seeking perfection in what She had begun. The races of man, however, were combative, destructive. Ananthi needed to create order among them. To do this, She set the races of man tests. These were tests of service, honor, will, passion, empathy, and intelligence. It took a thousand cycles for the tests to be complete, and when they were done, Ananthi created order."

"The castes."

"More than that. She made the Omehi Her Chosen and placed all others below us. We are Ananthi's voice on Uhmlaba, and that did not sit well with Ukufa.

"Ukufa was a man and, like all the first women and men, he was immortal. He held his jealousy in check for a time, but as the eons slipped by, his hate for being less than his betters did not subside.

"He gathered a following, women and men from many of the races, and corrupted them with lies. He told them Ananthi had decided to end their immortality, that She would let them die. He told them that if they used their gifts together, they could drain Ananthi, pass Her power into him, and he could prevent Her from damning them with death.

"The corrupted women and men did as Ukufa bid and attacked Ananthi. We, the Omehi, saw Ananthi's need and led the faithful races of man to Her aid. We did not come soon enough.

"Ukufa had gained power beyond the abilities of other men, and the fight that followed was so devastating it split the earth into masses of land divided by rivers that became seas, seas that became oceans. The sky, once pure and whole, smoked and burned. The fields, flat and bountiful, dried and cracked, until all the races of man grew fearful that Uhmlaba would turn too desolate a place to sustain life.

"The Omehi, determined to prevent an apocalypse, gathered their might and attacked, forcing Ukufa and the ones he had corrupted back, but we could not finish them. We were going to lose. Ananthi was weak, too weak, but it fell to Her to end the war. She was the only one who could. So, She did.

"Using all She was, Ananthi wrapped herself around Ukufa and his corrupted, trapping them. She used the energy of Her being to form a prison, an impenetrable new realm.

"Ukufa, already trapped and seeing his defeat was inevitable, could still use his powers. He reached beyond the prison before Ananthi could seal it and drew the natural energy from Uhmlaba, pulling as much of it as he could into Ananthi's prison. It was in that final attack that the races of man lost their immortality. Ukufa's evil actions made his lies true, and worse.

"Fear of death broke the weakest among us and these weakest called out to Ukufa. The prison was breaths away from closing forever, but in those breaths, Ukufa made his offer. He promised immortality to those calling to him, immortality in exchange for their souls and service.

"The cowards accepted, swearing to kill us all. They swore they would eliminate Ananthi's Chosen and, in so doing, destroy Ananthi, allowing Ukufa to escape the prison. In this way, the weakest among us became the strongest, for though they can be killed, they do not die from age or sickness."

"You're describing the Cull," said Tau.

"I am."

BREATHE

T he Cull are a tale, meant to frighten children into doing their prayers," Tau said.

"I am telling you what we are taught at the citadel."

"They teach make-believe?"

"Shall I finish?"

"Is the rest a child's tale too?"

"Fine," said Zuri, turning away.

Tau grimaced. "Go on. Please."

Zuri sighed but turned back. "Ukufa stole the energy Ananthi left for our realm and pulled it into his prison. There is nothing left of Ananthi in Uhmlaba, which means our powers must come from Isihogo. This is because Ananthi is Isihogo. Her essence forms both the realm and the barrier that Ukufa and his corrupted may never pass. So, if we are to use Her gifts, we must enter the underworld and use them from there. All the races can do this, and every man, woman, and child can enter Isihogo."

"All? It's forbidden for any but Gifted to let themselves slip to the underworld."

"Yes, and you are warned away for good reason. The demon took your arm, you said?"

"I . . . I fought but couldn't beat it."

"No, you couldn't. Thankfully, the harm they do cannot transfer to Uhmlaba, unless—"

Tau's eyes widened. "Unless?"

"Unless you draw power from Isihogo."

"Only Gifted can do that."

"No, anyone can do it."

"Everyone is Gifted?"

"I didn't say that," Zuri said.

"You're losing me on this path."

"Everyone can enter Isihogo, but the corrupted, the demons, attack all living souls, seeking vengeance for their imprisonment. They can do no physical harm, so long as the soul they seek to destroy does not draw energy from Isihogo. Drawing energy from the underworld makes you corporeal there."

"The entire purpose of being Gifted is to draw energy from Isihogo. Why don't demons kill Gifted?"

"They . . ." Zuri stopped herself. "You are asking what makes someone Gifted. The answer is that Ananthi gave us the ability to hide from the demons."

"Hide? . . . Ah, I think I saw that. The Enervator—"

"Namisa."

"Yes! In Isihogo, my body and the bodies of the other fighters were cloaked in golden light—"

"The light is your soul. It draws the demons."

"Namisa had no soul light. She was all darkness."

"That's half-right," Zuri said. "Namisa has a soul, and it must shine in Isihogo, but she can shroud it. That is the definition of being Gifted. It is not being able to enter and draw energy from Isihogo. Everyone can do that. It is the ability to shroud your soul's light for long enough to draw, then use the energy."

"How long?" asked Tau.

"How long what? Can we shroud? It's individual and depends on the strength of your gift."

"How do you strengthen your gift?"

"You can't . . . You're born with your gift. It's always the same."

"You can't improve it? Train it? Why are you at the citadel? For the stories?"

Zuri did not look amused. "We are here to learn how to use the strength we are given."

Tau frowned, trying to place this in terms that would make sense as a fighter. "You can't train your gift?"

"It is a gift."

"So is my body. I can train that, make it stronger, faster."

"That's not how it works."

"Perhaps," Tau responded, earning himself a cold look. "Either way, what happens if you take energy from Isihogo and are found by the demons?"

"We are killed."

"Like in Daba . . ."

"What?"

"During the raid on Daba, there were several Gifted with the Entreater who called the dragon."

Zuri's face changed. "Yes . . . ," she said.

"A demon must have found one of the Gifted. She died without any cause that I could see, but . . . she wasn't using power. The Entreater was, but the one who died, she was just standing there."

Zuri said nothing. It gave Tau pause. He could tell she was hiding something. He thought to press her but still didn't have what he needed. It was enervation that interested him. "If I don't take power from Isihogo, is there anything the demons can do to me?"

Zuri relaxed, a little. "No, nothing real, but the demon-haunted—"

"The crazy ones who see things?"

"They're not crazy. It's just . . . some people break after a demon attack."

"It feels real. The pain, the fear, all of it feels real." Tau clicked his tongue against the roof of his mouth. "Can one learn to hide?" he asked.

"Have you listened at all? The ability to shroud is what it means to be Gifted. You are either born with it or without. That, like the strength of the gift, does not and cannot change. Also, among the Chosen, only women are ever Gifted. It's why the citadel tests every

Omehi girl when she becomes a woman. The testers teach us how to shift to Isihogo and how to leave it. They show us how to shroud ourselves. We flee the underworld before the demons attack, and the test is repeated as many times as needed to confirm each new woman's gift, or lack of it."

"Every Omehi woman has faced a demon?" Tau shook his head, trying to picture his mother doing it. "No one talks about that."

"It's not something you talk about."

"No," said Tau, recalling his own experience. "It's not."

"So, other than shroud yourself," Zuri said, "you can do everything in Isihogo that I can."

Tau tried to see if Zuri was teasing him. "I can enervate?"

Zuri tilted her head from side to side, weighing the question. "You can learn the technique, you can take yourself to Isihogo, you can even take energy from the underworld, but you'd die before you had the chance to use it."

"The demons," Tau said.

"In part. Time works differently in the underworld. A single breath on Uhmlaba is more than fifty in Isihogo. Also, souls shine brighter when they take on Isihogo's energy. Without being able to shroud, the demons would find you and tear you apart before you could use what you had taken. Tau, if you are ever in Isihogo, never take energy into yourself. Never."

"Show it to me."

Zuri started. "Show you what?"

"I need to know how to resist the enervation." Tau could tell Zuri was beginning to regret the discussion, but he pressed on. "I got lucky today. We were isolated from the bigger fight and Namisa hit her Indlovu as well as my sword brothers. I won't be able to keep winning if an Enervator can just point her hands and drop me."

"Resist enervation?" Zuri shook her head. "If a Gifted hits you with it, you can't stop your soul from being shifted to the underworld. Anyway, in the skirmishes, we're not supposed to hold you there."

"I know, but that's not the point," Tau said. "Even if I'm not held long enough for the demons to attack me, I'm still dazed when I come back."

"Your soul was taken from one place to another. It's not the kind of thing you shake off."

"How do you do it, then?" he asked.

"I . . . That's different."

"Maybe . . . or, maybe having experienced it so often, you're able to better manage it." She looked far from convinced by that, but Tau pressed on. "Zuri, I can't allow myself to be made useless on the battlefield. I need more experience with enervation. I need to know how it affects me, so I can learn to recover faster."

"I don't think it works that way, and I'm not going to enervate you."

"I have to try."

"Then go to Isihogo yourself," Zuri said, flicking a hand at him, dismissing the request.

"How?"

Zuri eyes widened.

"No, you're right," Tau said. "You said everyone can do it. Teach me how to go to Isihogo?"

"I wasn't serious when I said that."

"But you could teach it?"

Zuri licked her lips and looked around at the still empty circle. "You already know how. It's why we pray, to anchor our souls to this realm. Some of us still drift to Isihogo when we sleep and our defenses are down."

Tau considered this. "The ones who die bleeding in their beds. The ones who wake and have lost their minds. That's why we pray? To prevent that?"

"It's not the only reason. We pray to show faith. To worship Ananthi. She protects us."

"Of course She does," Tau said, trying not to sound brusque. "Help me, Zuri. I almost couldn't keep fighting after the enervation."

"If you were attacked by a demon you shouldn't have been able to fight at all."

"Help me."

"You want this? To learn how to travel to the underworld?" Zuri asked. "You'll have no power there. You'll be hunted the instant you enter."

"But they can't hurt me?"

Zuri laughed without mirth. "What do you mean? You've already experienced it. They'll hurt you. They'll rip you to pieces and you'll feel everything. Your physical body won't be harmed, but who knows what it'll do to your mind."

Tau was insistent. "But they can't kill me."

Zuri pursed her lips. "Not unless you draw energy from Isihogo."

"Then I just won't do that."

"As you wish," Zuri said, standing.

Tau jumped to his feet, nervous, and wondering just how much of a damned fool he was being. "Now?"

"Isn't this what you want?"

"Eh . . . yes, of course."

"You're sure?" She arched an eyebrow and Tau caught up to her game. She had thought to scare him off the path by putting his feet to it.

Tau refused to be scared away. "I am."

Zuri's eyebrow dropped and she looked tired, like the day had been a bit too much. "Fine. Fine. Close your eyes."

"Here?"

"If I can teach you how to enter Isihogo, here is as good a place as any. Fifty breaths there are less than a single one here. You won't be gone any time at all."

"As you say." Tau closed his eyes.

"You need to know how to return. There are two ways."

Tau saw spots of light behind his closed eyelids.

"Our souls conceive of Isihogo in terms of our experiences in Uhmlaba. You will think of yourself as having one head, two arms, two legs, everything. You will even think and behave as if you are breathing there."

"Yes," Tau said.

"The first way to return is to expel all the breath in your body. Breathe it out until you are empty. Let your body, if you want to call it that, remain empty. You will feel as if you are dying, as if you must breathe. Leave your lungs empty, let this false death take you, Isihogo will fade, and you will leave the underworld."

"That's it?"

"We are meant for the world of the living, not the world of the demons. Exiting Isihogo should not be hard."

"And the second way?"

"Let the demons kill you."

"Ah," Tau said.

"Ah," Zuri echoed. "When the demons destroy your soul's conception of its body, you'll be forced from Isihogo." Zuri took a step closer to Tau and put a cool hand on his arm. "You don't have to do this."

"I do. I have to get into the Queen's Melee. I can't risk letting an Enervator disable me. I can't risk being taken out of the fight."

There, he'd said it out loud and it was true. He had to get into the melee. He had to take Scale Jayyed deep enough into its rounds to face Scale Osa... to face Kellan. Men died in the melee every single cycle. Men died there.

"The melee?" Zuri asked. "It's all on your shoulders, then, your scale's chances? You know an Ihashe scale hasn't qualified in over a generation?"

He nodded. "It's different now."

Zuri smiled. It didn't reach her eyes. "As you say," she said, taking her hand from his arm. "Then, with eyes closed, I want you to think about a wave of calm rising up through the earth and into you."

Tau closed his eyes and attended to her words.

"Relax your feet and let the tension flow out of them. Let the muscles go loose and limp and allow this calming wave to rise into your calves, slowly, into your thighs, slowly. Let them go loose, limp, feel that wave continue higher, as you allow this world to slip away."

Tau was swaying.

"I want you to take deep breaths in and out, in and out.... Yes, like that.... Every breath in lifts the calming wave higher, every breath out moves our world further and further away.... Let go and it's there... our other home—"

DEMON

The noise accosted him first, the eerie gusting of wind that blew grit into his face and exposed skin. Tau felt it, heard it, and, snapping his eyes open, he saw the permanent twilight of Isihogo.

He was still in the circle in Citadel City, but it was a twisted version of the place. The colors were muted, the sky colorless, the ground soft, like loose mulch, and the underworld's mists swirled around him.

"You did it." Zuri's voice was quiet, like she spoke to him from a hundred strides away, though she was next to him. Tau could hear the surprise in her voice. He looked at her. She was veiled in a darkness so deep he had trouble making out her features.

"You're shrouded," he said, having trouble hearing his own voice.

"They come," she said.

Tau had the impression of her turning her head, though it was hard to tell where her face was. He looked in the same direction he thought she might be facing and saw them. His heart seemed to stop and fear had him in its white-hot grasp.

Two demons were running for him. One was twice his size, had a mouth full of teeth and a tongue that hung down past its neck. It came for him on two legs. The other thing ran on all fours. It had pointed ears, eyes on either side of its head, and skin like an inyoka.

Tau sought to calm himself. It didn't work. He looked down at his body, saw the blinding light he was giving off, and he reached into himself, working to dim it, to hide as Zuri was.

"What are you doing?" Zuri asked. "It's time. Exhale."

Tau did not. He focused his mind on the task of dimming his soul's light. He tried to understand how such a thing could work, and he felt something. It was an oppressive and enormous wall of energy that existed all around him, and the temptation to grab hold of it, pull a portion of it into himself, was intense.

Without knowing how he knew, Tau realized that this was the prison that kept the demons in Isihogo. It was also the field of Ananthi's energy from which the Gifted drew power. He resisted the impulse to draw in the energy. That was death. Instead, he did all he could to mask his light, to hide the glow of his spirit.

"Tau?" Zuri shouted.

He looked down at himself and saw, to his astonishment, that he glowed bright as ever. He looked up. The demons, snarling and slavering, were almost on him. His bladder felt overfull and fear thickened his blood.

He hated that they made him feel this way. He hated that the underworld, these creatures, and the fear of it all could disable him in his world. It could not continue.

Tau inhaled, drawing in as much of the underworld's fetid air as he could. He had come to learn how to defeat enervation. He would not leave until he had done so.

He snarled at the products of Ukufa's evil and placed his hands on the hilts of his swords, which had come with him. He drew them and faced the beasts.

"What are you doing?" Zuri screamed.

"They can't hurt me!" he told her. "You can't hurt me!" he roared at the demons. Zuri fled and Tau fought.

The thing on all fours got to him first, and Tau brought his strong-side sword down on its snout with as much force as he could. The creature was dashed to the ground, tripping over its feet and rolling. There was no time to appreciate the small victory. The other demon, a thing twice the height of a Lesser, loomed over him and swiped for his guts with a black claw–tipped hand. Tau threw himself back, but he'd underestimated the demon's reach. Its claws raked across his stomach, tearing him almost in two.

Tau fell to the murky ground and felt his insides spilling out. He looked down and cried out in pain and horror. His intestines were exposed to the air, ropes upon ropes of them. He reached down to try to push them back. The pain was indescribable, and then the demon was on him.

He tried to swing his swords but had lost them when he fell. He tried to beat the beast back, but it ignored him as it feasted. The thing on all fours, recovered from the sword strike, joined the feasting, and Tau lost his mind to pain. He tried to exhale, as Zuri had taught him, but it was too late for that and he suffered more than he'd believed possible as the two demons tore him apart.

"You hateful cek!" Zuri slapped him across the face. "What is the matter with you?"

She had tears running down her face and was crouched next to Tau on the dirt of the circle in Citadel City.

"By the Goddess, that was worse than I imagined," Tau whispered. "So much worse. How can a place like that exist?"

"Are you well?" Zuri asked, before recoiling. "I shouldn't even ask. You are undeserving of concern. How could you do that? Why would you do it?"

"I can't be afraid of them. I can't let the Gifted stop me when I fight. I can't be afraid."

"Are you trying to become demon-haunted?"

"I'm well."

Zuri stood up and Tau thought she might kick him. "What if you had died?" she asked.

Tau made himself sit up, and though he was uninjured, he cradled his stomach. "You told me the demons couldn't harm me."

"What if I was wrong?"

"You weren't. Zuri, I felt the energy there. I could have taken it. I didn't."

"Obviously."

"I tried to hide myself." Tau forced a smile. "It didn't work."

"Omehi men cannot be Gifted!" she hissed, leaning in as if proximity would make the point more clear.

"Doesn't seem fair, does it?"

Zuri threw up her hands. "Why do I bother with you?"

"Help me up?"

"I'm done helping. Get yourself up."

Tau struggled to his feet and shuffled over to the bench. "I can't fight like this."

"Fight?"

"I thought, maybe, if I faced the demons, I could come out of Isihogo and still be ready to fight. It doesn't . . . That won't work. I still feel the claws." Tau brushed his fingertips against his stomach and the muscles there spasmed, anticipating the pain from wounds that did not exist.

"You had to fight demons to learn that?"

"I thought I could win."

Zuri shook her fists at him. "You're an idiot."

Tau tried to stand and fell back onto the bench. He was exhausted and his body was shaking. His plan, in retrospect, seemed foolhardy, the act of an impulsive child. There were large forces at work in the universe and he did not understand them.

"Zuri, it's dark out. I have to leave the city. Will you help me?" Tau felt weak; that was true. It wasn't the only reason he asked, though. He didn't want to go alone.

Zuri's face softened. She'd seen through him. "Lean on me. I'll walk with you until you feel more yourself."

"Thank you," Tau said.

"Don't say another word. If I didn't feel . . ."

Tau very much wanted to hear what she'd been about to say. "What's that?"

"Nothing. Here." She slipped his arm over her shoulders and helped him stand. "You're bigger than you were in Kerem."

"They feed us more than in Kerem."

"It's muscle."

"I swing swords all day."

"Mhmm," she said, grunting under his weight.

Tau tried not to lean on her, but he was shaky and might have fallen over otherwise.

"Thank you," he told her again.

"Don't talk," she said, but she watched him with worry. She didn't hate him, and for that Tau was grateful.

Zuri walked him within a hundred strides of the city gates.

"We shouldn't be seen together," she said, stopping.

"I know."

"You can make it?"

"I have a lot farther to go than the gates," he reminded her.

"Yes." Zuri kissed him.

Her movement had been sudden and the demon's attack had not left him. He almost jerked away from her. Her lips calmed him, eased his mind. "Your kiss. It's healing."

"Mmmm," she murmured, biting her lower lip. "Is it?"

"Another one would make me stronger, for the journey."

"No, you should remain weak. It'll remind you that we must all live with the consequences of idiocy."

The edges of his mouth drifted upward. "One more? To help me sleep?"

"Do your prayers, that will help you sleep," she said, slipping into his arms and kissing him again. "You have to go," she told him, stepping away. "Come back to me."

"Always," he told her, watching as she left the way they'd come.

When she was lost to sight, he walked through the gates of Citadel City to join his sword brothers. He was late, but after an afternoon of celebration, he was not the only one. It took another span before every man could be accounted for and the marching could begin. Men stumbled, a few couldn't hold their drink and, when the mood hit, they sang marching songs.

Hadith, Yaw, Chinedu, and Oyibo found Tau. They marched with him. He was glad for the company, but it worried him that, even surrounded by his sword brothers, he kept seeing strange shadows in the tall grasses.

CHAPTER EIGHT

GAMES

Tau was on the practice field before the sun rose. The rest of Jayyed's five found him there, lathered in sweat. He'd been running and had not slept.

He'd tried. He'd performed the evening prayers three times, steeling his will and mind against Isihogo, but he did not know whether his nightmares were dreams or something else. Whatever the case, he'd come to the practice fields. He was too afraid to sleep.

Along with Hadith, Yaw, and Chinedu, Tau saw Oyibo. The boyish-faced warrior spoke to Tau, unable to meet his gaze. "During last night's march, Jayyed told me to join you."

He said it as if he needed Tau's permission, and, not knowing what else to say or do, Tau clapped Oyibo on the shoulder, as he imagined Hadith would have done. "Welcome, brother," he said. "I wondered what was taking Jayyed so long."

Oyibo's face brightened and he raised his head. "I won't let you down."

Tau wasn't sure why Oyibo needed to worry about letting him down, but he was glad his words had bolstered his sword brother's confidence. Hadith nodded at Tau. He approved as well. Good, thought Tau. With that out of the way they could begin.

Tau paired with Oyibo and trounced him ten touches to none.

It was odd, Tau thought. Oyibo managed to look both pleased and frustrated.

"It's an honor," Oyibo said when their match was over. Tau clapped Oyibo on the shoulder again, since the gesture had worked the first time. Oyibo went off to find water, looking happy.

Tau wasn't tired and paired up with Hadith. "What's going on with him?" he asked as they crossed blades.

"Worship," Hadith grunted between breaths, retreating under Tau's offense.

"Seriously," Tau said. He disarmed Hadith, stabbing him in the chest.

Hadith rubbed at the spot, working out the bruise. He picked up his sword and squared up. "I am serious. The whole scale thinks you're Tsiory born again."

Hadith shoved his shield at Tau's face and swung his blade at his waist. Tau used one sword to clear the shield, his other blocked Hadith's swing, and he used a front kick to push Hadith back, making space.

"Because of one skirmish?" Tau said.

Hadith lunged; Tau stepped aside, dodging, and smacked Hadith across the back. Hadith went sprawling into the dirt.

Sitting up and spitting out loose soil, he said, "Do you know how good I am?"

"What?"

"I can beat almost every man in Scale Jayyed, and Scale Jayyed is the best in the Southern Ihashe Isikolo, likely the best in both academies."

Tau shrugged. They should be among the top initiates. They trained harder than the others.

"Tau," Hadith said, "you could kill me with one hand strapped to your back."

"I have to be this way."

"As you say, but did you not see Oyibo's face when he sparred with you?" Hadith asked.

Tau waited, thinking Hadith didn't truly expect him to answer.

"He fought you like you were an Enraged Ingonyama, like he'd do what he could but knew he had no hope."

"He doesn't commit to his attacks as much as he should and needs to work on his speed."

"After Runako, Oyibo is our fastest blade. By the Goddess, why do you think Jayyed offered him a spot with us? Why do you think I sent him with you to hold the path in the skirmish against the Indlovu?"

Tau considered this.

"Oyibo is an incredible fighter," Hadith said, "and he spars you like a child hoping to learn from his father."

Tau remembered what it had been like to spar Aren. His father had seemed like a god, able to dodge, predict, and counter, with a patient smile and ready words of encouragement.

"You don't know what it's like." Hadith stood, brushing dirt from his gambeson. "We all work hard, but you get here earlier than the rest of us and stay later. All of us want to be better, but there needs to be balance. I find the time to laugh, play, drink. I find the time to . . . Tau, it's like you live for this and nothing else."

Tau grimaced. "The mistake is in thinking you have time for the rest."

"We don't? We don't have the time to live? Only for war?"

"The sword, the learning, the improvement, it's a means to an end."

"You want to kill hedeni so badly?"

Tau didn't answer.

"Or someone else? You train like you want to become an Ingonyama."

"We can't," Tau said. "Our blood is too weak."

"Then the Goddess gives our enemy hope. I'm on your side and shudder to think of you as an Ingonyama."

"I'll fight an Ingonyama," a voice behind Tau said. "I'll fight anyone."

Tau turned and was smiling before even laying eyes on Uduak. "Big man."

"Little demon," Uduak returned, making Tau wince. "I am here for a rematch."

Behind Uduak were Jayyed and Anan. They were smiling too, though Anan looked gray and bleary-eyed. The jugs of masmas from the night before still had their claws in him.

"Whenever you want," Tau told Uduak, moving to hug the over-sized Common.

Uduak seemed surprised at Tau's embrace. Tau was surprised at himself. Uduak clapped him painfully on the back and, both a little embarrassed, they stood apart.

"Well met," Tau said.

"Well met, Tau Solarin," Uduak said.

"If you two require privacy..." Hadith whispered loud enough for everyone to hear, making Chinedu do his coughing laugh. Yaw chuckled and Oyibo looked lost.

"Yes, yes, well met, all," Jayyed said, traces of his smile playing along the edges of his mouth. "Let's begin."

Jayyed's five were once again Jayyed's six, and they worked until the rest of the scale joined them and then trained with them until the sun set.

They ate and Tau came out to continue training. Oyibo, Yaw, and Uduak came too. Hadith stayed behind with the rest of the scale, doing as Hadith did, talking with the men, making jokes, being a friend they could trust.

It made him a good leader, the way he dealt with his sword brothers. Tau admired it and thought Hadith might be right. Life was about balance. Tau decided he'd work on it.

By the next morning he'd forgotten his decision to live a balanced life. Over the next moon cycle he spent every waking span in the practice yards and every night tossing in his bed. He tried to feel guilty about how distant he was with the rest of the men. He tried to get the demons out of his head so he could sleep. He failed both ways and chose to fixate on what was ahead, to keep himself sane.

The scale had to win their next skirmish. A victory gave them a chance at the Queen's Melee. A spot in the melee gave them a chance to skirmish against Scale Osa, Kellan's scale, and Tau wanted that more than anything.

If Tau could fight Kellan, he could kill him on the battlefield and claim it as an accident. The Omehi would think it a tragic and shameful end to such a promising Noble, dying at the hands of a

Lesser. But there could be no punishment. Every cycle men died in the melee. Every cycle.

Tau told himself this was why he trained so hard. It was for revenge. He told himself that he didn't love every span of it, because his path should not involve pleasure, satisfaction, or joy. It was about hate and pain and rage. But he did love it, the training, the sparring, the sword.

Hadith thought differently. He wanted time to live life, to play games, but their world was at war and that meant the sword was life. It meant fighting was the only game. And, in the upcoming skirmish, Tau intended to prove how good a player he was.

MERCY

It was the hottest day of the cycle and things were not going well. The skirmish had already lasted longer than most, and more than half of Scale Jayyed was still in play, as well as two-thirds of the citadel warriors. They were fighting on the mountain battleground, which favored the Indlovu, who could use the rocky terrain to avoid taking fights with odds worse than three to one.

Jayyed's six had been reduced to four—Hadith, Uduak, Oyibo, and Tau. Yaw had been disabled by the Enervator's first blast and knocked unconscious by the Indlovu follow-up. Chinedu had gone down a few moments later, trying to rally near a choke point where several Indlovu had sheltered. The skirmish had become hit-and-run among the diminutive cliffs of the battleground, and Hadith was loath to commit his men to a full assault.

Tau knew he was worried about the Enervator. They hadn't isolated her position and it had been more than half a sun span since she'd fired off a blast. She'd be ready to use her gift again.

"We can't stay out here all day," Tau told Hadith as he slicked a river of sweat from his brow. They were crouched behind an outcropping of rock, looking up. Twenty strides away, several Indlovu were entrenched in an improvised stronghold of boulders. Tau couldn't be sure how many others were there, or if the Enervator was with them.

"I know," muttered Hadith.

"We have to do something."

"Like what? Call dragons out my ass?"

"Calm," rumbled Uduak.

"She has to be up there," Hadith said. "She has to be."

"But if she's not, and we go in...," said Runako with his paper-thin voice.

Hadith shook his head. "She's there. I can feel it. Get ready, everyone. Three prongs. I'll lead middle, Tau takes left, Uduak right."

It was dangerous. If the assault didn't work, they'd lose too many men to win the skirmish.

"Goddess go with you," Hadith said.

"If She's not already with them," Themba whispered, as the three prongs arranged themselves.

Oyibo glared at Themba, cowing the talkative initiate, and glanced at Tau for approval. Tau nodded. Oyibo's idolization was a little awkward, but he was a good fighter and Tau would exchange any amount of awkwardness for that.

Tau saw Hadith check the position of the three prongs. They were in place. Tau would stream up the left side of the hill with eight other men, Hadith would charge the center, and Uduak the right. It was a simple plan. Tau hoped that would count for something.

Hadith raised an eyebrow at Tau. Tau pointed a finger toward the Indlovu. He wanted to go.

"Where we fight!" Hadith shouted.

"The world burns!" bellowed the twenty-seven remaining Lessers of Scale Jayyed as they rose from their redoubt and streamed up the hill. They were spread out far enough that the Enervator could not get them all, if she was there.

She was. Tau saw her stand from behind one of the larger rocks and raise her arms in his direction.

"Cek!" yelled Tau as the wave of enervation struck him, hurling his spirit into Isihogo.

The wind's howl was deafening, the sky dark, and Tau's blood ran cold as he imagined all the horrible things that could be hiding behind the rocks. He looked back at his men. The collective glow from the other eight fighters was blinding, and they had been noticed.

Demons, misshapen and terrible, emerged from the mists. They keened and bayed, predators on the hunt. Tau heard men wail in fear, their voices muted by whatever forces controlled this place. Many cowered and some broke, running for their lives, as if there was anywhere to run. Tau gritted his teeth, thinking, If you're already in the underworld, don't stop there. He pulled his swords and charged, heart hammering and filled with blinding fear.

"The world burns!" he roared as he ran into and right through the lead demons, emerging into the bitter heat, harsh sunlight, and divine blessing that was Uhmlaba. He stumbled, almost fell, and tried to right himself, but the world spun in a dizzying wobble as he spotted and struggled to hold his eyes on the stunned Enervator standing just a few steps ahead.

She had lowered her arms and was staring at Tau in disbelief. He looked back at the way he'd come. His prong was a shambles, not a single man up. Oyibo was closest, but on his knees, head bowed, chest heaving.

The Enervator's blast had been particularly brief. It was her duty to release them before the demons attacked, but she'd gone too far the other way and Tau's lesson with Zuri, learning how to let his soul slip to the underworld, had made the Enervator's forced transition less stupefying. She'd weakened but not broken him.

He shook his head, hoping to tear loose the last hooks the journey to Isihogo had on him. His mind was a muddle, but he knew enough to run for the Enervator, making it her turn to cower. He managed several strides and was almost on her when two Indlovu, the Nobles assigned to guard her, rose from behind the boulders, greeting him with bronze.

Tau slashed at the nearest man, his attack premature, clumsy, a result of his time in Isihogo. The Indlovu blocked and the second Noble swung for Tau's head. His instincts saved him. Tau dropped to his knees and the sword his body told him was coming whistled overhead.

Tau smacked his weak-side blade into his attacker's calf and was rewarded when the man yelped. Tau stabbed up and forward, aiming for the groin of the first man in a move that would disembowel had his practice blade possessed anything resembling a true point. The Indlovu blocked the strike and Tau sprang to his feet, pressing him further.

The Indlovu's eyes, deep set beneath a heavy brow, shone, and the man was grinning. He's enjoying this, Tau thought, noticing that the Enervator was scrambling away. He needed to get to her, fast.

No time to waste, he sent his blades spinning in attack after attack, showering himself and the grinning Noble with sparks. The man's smile slipped as he struggled to weather Tau's storm. Then it returned.

Tau leapt to the side. He wasn't fast enough. The other Indlovu, the one behind him, cracked him in the shoulder. The blow had been aimed for his neck. Not that it mattered, much.

The strike fired a wave of pain down Tau's arm, sent his strong-side sword flying down the hill, and knocked him to the ground. Certain they weren't done with him yet, Tau rolled and avoided getting his face stomped by a boot. He darted to his feet and both men were on him.

He tried to keep them away. He tried to regain his momentum. He was down a sword, Isihogo sick, and defending against two citadel-trained men. He was losing.

The grinning Noble was beaming now, sweat dripping down his thick brow and tongue flicking out to catch it. The other Noble, even limping, was quick. He looked like a lizard with his wide-spread eyes and thick, long nose.

Tau swore he would not lose to the sweat licker and lizard face, and the fighting began in earnest. He took a glancing but painful hit to the side, when he had to choose between accepting that and risk taking a blow that might break his arm. Soon after, he was doubled over when he chose a thrust over a riposte that threatened to disarm him.

Short on breath, he sprang back and straightened. Both Ind-lovu were swinging, and he blocked the blade coming for his chest, accepting, in trade, the sloppy backswing aimed for his helmet. The last was a mistake.

The blow to the head stunned Tau, and he stumbled away, trip-ping over loose rocks. He was in pain. His breathing was ragged. He could not last much longer.

Common sense told him to run. He'd already lost sight of the Enervator, and she was his reason for facing the two Indlovu. But Tau stayed. He would not run from Nobles.

They came at him together, swinging hard enough to cripple. Tau defended as best he could, yelling with frustration and anger. He could not turn the fight around. He took two more heavy hits and came close to going down.

The attackers moved to his sides, making it impossible for him to defend against both. They'd be able to circle him and beat him to the ground. Tau hissed at them, striking out this way and that. The sweat licker smirked like he knew the world's best joke, and, as one, they pounced.

Tau was hit twice, his sword almost taken out of his hand, and he took a shield to the face. His nose didn't break, but blood gushed from it anyway.

He'd let them kill him before he'd beg for the Goddess's mercy.

"Where we fight!" a voice screamed, startling the sweat-drinking Indlovu as he was tackled. It was Oyibo.

Tau had a chance. "The world burns!" he shouted, remounting his offense against lizard face, who squawked in dismay at having to deal with Tau one-on-one.

Lizard face was quick, precise. He reminded Tau of a larger Yaw, but Tau treated him with far less love than he would have his sword brother.

He slashed a bright cut across the Indlovu's face, darted back, giving himself enough room for a powerful cross-body swing, and pounded his blade into the man's helmet. Lizard face went down like the bones had gone out of him.

Tau spun, found his second sword, and snatched it, running to help Oyibo. Oyibo was on the ground, the sweat licker standing over him, sword up. Oyibo smiled at Tau; he'd saved him and made the upcoming fight an even one.

"Goddess's mercy," Oyibo said, no shame in his voice. Tau would finish this one off.

The sweat licker saw Tau coming and looked down at Oyibo.

Oyibo's smile vanished. "Mercy!" he said again, as the Indlovu brought his blade down, smashing Oyibo's helmet and skull to pieces, killing him.

Tau stopped dead. It didn't make sense. The Indlovu pulled his gore-soaked blade from the mess that had been Oyibo's face and raised the weapon at Tau.

"He asked for mercy," Tau said, trying to piece the world back together. "He asked for mercy."

The Indlovu, still standing over the body, grinned, and that made Tau attack. He knocked him to the ground, landing on top, and was on his feet first, firing strike after strike. The Noble tried to defend, but this was not a fight; it was an obliteration.

Within the first few sword crosses, the smiling Noble lost his grin, his nostrils flaring like an animal driven to slaughter, his eyes rolling, desperate. "Goddess's mercy! Goddess's mercy! Stop, damn you! Stop!"

Tau's next swing broke the Noble's arm, and the follow-up crashed into his head, knocking his helmet off and rendering him near senseless. Tau backhanded him with his sword's pommel, tearing the man's bottom lip to bits and bashing teeth from his mouth. The Noble staggered and Tau hammered a blade into his leg, fracturing his femur and dropping him to his knees.

Tau raised his sword and the Noble tried to speak, blood flowing from his ruined mouth.

"Merthy! Gawdeth merthy," he managed to spit.

MURDERER

"Here's my mercy!" Tau said, bringing his sword down and hitting bronze on bronze, hard enough to shake his bones. Uduak stood beside him, his oversized blade holding Tau's killing blow aloft, a handspan above the Indlovu's head.

"Move!" Tau screamed at Uduak, the rage in him enough to make the big man take a step back.

"No," Uduak said. "They will kill you."

"He murdered Oyibo!" Tau told him, eyes blurring with tears. He hadn't cried since Aren and didn't want to now, but watching Oyibo die had made old wounds new again.

"They will kill you," Uduak repeated, using his blade to turn Tau's aside.

"Yeth. Merthy!"

Uduak clubbed the kneeling Noble in the side of the head, knocking him unconscious, and Tau stumbled back, away from his beaten foe. He let his swords fall to the dirt and went to Oyibo, knelt beside the body of his sword brother, and cried.

All around him was chaos. He heard the tumult, but it seemed a thing apart, a thing across a distance he could not traverse. He heard they had won. Uduak's prong had bored through the Indlovu's defenses with ease. Hadith's prong had struggled until Uduak's men joined them, helping them finish off the rest of the defenders.

They'd found the Enervator. Not enough time had passed for her to manage a third attack. She'd surrendered and they had come to sweep up these last two Indlovu, her bodyguards. That was when they saw the skirmish's true cost.

The rest of the morning went by in a blur. Oyibo's body was taken from the battlefield and prepped for burning as the umqondisi from the citadel suggested punishing Tau with death, or at least whipping. In skirmishes, men were injured and sometimes killed, but the citadel umqondisi argued that Tau had forfeited his right to protection under skirmish rules when he ignored the Noble's calls for mercy.

Jayyed and several other umqondisi protested this, begged even. They claimed Tau had become emotional at the death of a sword brother. They claimed he had not heard or, at least, had not understood the calls for mercy from the Noble's mangled mouth.

The citadel had not liked that but stopped short of calling the claims lies. Instead, they focused on the Indlovu's condition—a mangled face, a broken arm and leg!

Things that happen in a skirmish, Jayyed told them. He asked, who among them had not broken limbs or received a lump or two? They were warriors, not farmers. Besides, was it not an Ihashe initiate they had to burn this day?

A Lesser, a Common, the citadel umqondisi had replied, as if they spoke of grains of sand on a beach, all the same and easily replaced.

A man who would have fought for the Goddess and the Omehi against the hedeni, Jayyed told them, his anger beginning to show. It all flowed over and beyond Tau, as he tried to understand Oyibo's death.

Tau had begun to treat the world of the isikolo and citadels as a game. Fighting with dull swords, playing at battle. He had let himself forget that everything they did, they did to be better at real war, at actual killing. Oyibo had looked up to him, and Tau, forgetting the nature of their world, had let Oyibo down, just as he had let his father down.

Jayyed suggested they cancel the second skirmish. The citadel umqondisi refused. Had they not given enough by agreeing to spare the Common from a whipping, from a hanging? So, a second Ihashe scale took the field and lost.

Anan proposed they leave. The other aqondise and umqondisi disagreed. They shouldn't break with tradition, not on a day like this.

They wanted the men to be able to go into the city, drink some of their sorrows away, if they must. Maybe they would also remember a victory had been won today. Though the price, set at a man's life, had been too dear.

Tau remained numb. Scale Jayyed intended to stay with him in the Crags, but he remembered Zuri would be waiting, and feeling more than ever that he needed to see her, Tau said they should go to the city. They should drink to Oyibo's life and memory. So, Jayyed's six, once again Jayyed's five, went with the rest of the scale and the two isikolo to celebrate a victory and mourn a brother.

Tau drank one jug and left. His sword brothers let him go. They knew him to be solitary. He walked to the circle, not expecting to see Zuri there. It was too early, and that was fine. He'd take the time to sit and think. Maybe offer a prayer for Oyibo's soul.

But Zuri was waiting; rather, she was pacing. When she saw him, she let out a cry and ran into his arms. "I heard someone was killed. I thought...By the Goddess, I was so frightened."

"I'm well," Tau mumbled.

Zuri knew he wasn't. "You knew him?"

"My sword brother. He fought beside me. I didn't save him."

"It's not your fault."

"You said the same thing when my father died, and here we are again. Me, alive, and the man who came to my aid, dead."

Zuri opened her mouth to try a response, then closed it.

"How did you hear?" Tau asked.

"A friend, a small and bold Gifted initiate who always seems to know more than she should. You'd like her. I wish you could meet..." Zuri looked down and Tau was reminded of the great distance their world sought to keep between men like him and women like her.

"She knows about you and came running to tell me that there was..." Zuri didn't seem to want to say the rest. "That there was an accident in the morning's first skirmish. A man went to the Goddess."

"Went? Oyibo was murdered. He asked for mercy. The Noble killed him anyway."

"Tau," Zuri said, reaching for him. He felt her delicate fingers tracing the hardened calluses on his palms. She looked around. They were alone in the circle, but it was early enough that others could come by at any moment. She wanted to hold him. He could see that. Propriety held her back.

Tau rejected propriety. He wrapped her up in his arms. She didn't hesitate then. She put her arms around him, pulling him tight to her body.

Tau's eyes grew damp. He hated himself for being so weak. He squeezed them shut to quell the tears and leaned against Zuri, drawing comfort from her presence.

"Lesser!" a man yelled. "What in the Goddess's name!"

Zuri jerked back. Tau opened his eyes. Three Indlovu, first cycles, by the look of them, were striding over.

"Get away from her, you disgusting nceku! What do you think you're—"

The Indlovu did not finish his sentence. In a single, unbroken motion, Tau drew one of his two practice swords and struck the man on the temple. He was unconscious before his body hit the floor.

"Ukufa's tongue!" yelped the second Indlovu, drawing his blade, its sharp edge hissing on the scabbard as it was pulled free.

"Stop this! Stop it now!" Zuri ordered.

The third Indlovu looked at her, and Tau drew his second practice sword. That ended the man's internal argument and, seeing little else for it, he drew his very real sword, readying himself.

"Put them away. My name is Gifted Zuri and I order it."

Both Indlovu looked uncertain. By rights they should accept Zuri's authority. Tau decided the case for them. He attacked. "Tau!" Zuri called, but he'd already bled and dropped the second Indlovu and was working on the third, whom, he could tell, he'd overwhelm in moments.

"Stand down!" called another Indlovu from across the circle. Tau slapped the man he was fighting across the face with the flat of his blade, sending the Noble reeling. That one dispatched, he turned, eyes blazing and heart on fire, seeking out the speaker.

Tau recognized him immediately. How could he not? Barely a dozen strides distant stood a third-cycle Indlovu of the citadel, guardian dagger recipient, and murderer. Barely a dozen strides distant stood Kellan Okar.

DUEL

Somewhere in another realm, it seemed to Tau, he saw more men run into the circle. He heard Hadith shout something, turned, and saw that he was with Uduak.

As he moved his gaze back to Kellan, a small part of Tau wondered why his sword brothers had come, but that part was drowned out. He was reliving the day his father died.

Tau remembered Kellan standing over his father, watching Aren, hand cut from his body, scream and writhe in helpless pain, and every fiber in Tau's being roared at him. His hate burned hot enough to immolate, his body shook with rage, and his thoughts were loud enough to be the voices of those around him.

Rip Kellan apart, they said. Wipe his evil from the world, they urged, and Tau listened.

"Who started this?" Kellan asked. He was with two Indlovu, and, bolstered by their presence, the Noble whom Tau had slapped with his sword answered the question by pointing.

Tau paid no attention to him or the two other Indlovu. They were nothing more than ghosts. The only thing of substance was Okar.

"Your name, Initiate?" Kellan asked him.

"Death," said Tau, moving to kill the man who helped murder his father.

Kellan was surprised, Tau could see that, and it made the next breath even more astonishing. Kellan drew his sword and blocked Tau's first and second strike in less time than it took to blink. Tau pressed on, heard more swords come free of their scabbards, and heard one of the Indlovu saying, "Hold. Let Kellan have him. It'll be over soon."

Tau let the full force of his fury loose, raging against Kellan, his dual blades whipping in and out like the skin-slicing sands of a desert whirlwind. He moved faster than the eye could track, every attack meant to wound, maim, or kill, but every attack met Kellan's sword.

From the corner of his eye, Tau saw Zuri, hand over her mouth, run from the circle, and then he had no time to see more. Kellan had dashed forward, engaging him.

Okar had no shield. It didn't matter. His sword played offense and defense both.

Tau took a cut to the arm that bled furiously. Kellan was not using a practice sword, and his blade slit flesh like it had kissed a whetstone that same day. Tau increased his pace, eyes focused, teeth clenched, and Kellan met him, matched him, surpassed him, until, in awe, Tau realized that Kellan was better. Much better.

Tau tried to stay in each moment, living alongside the ebb and flow of the fight, but his doubts grew, pulling at him, dragging his mind out of the swordplay, worrying at him. The voices of hate had gone quiet and he was left with the thought that he would die here and that his father's murderers would live. His worries whispered that justice would not be done and it was because he was not strong enough to take it.

Tau yelled in frustration. Kellan looked calm, fresh, as if he could fight at this impossible pace for an entire sun span. Tau was already near his limit, past it, in fact. His arms were heavy, his footwork clumsy, and he could no longer keep track of Kellan's darting blade.

Tau skipped back, desperate for room and a moment to breathe. He glanced around. The circle was filling up. There were Indlovu, the ones who had come with Kellan and others.

There were also the men from his scale. Hadith had a sword in hand; so did Uduak. They looked like they wanted to help, but the Indlovu accompanying Kellan had their blades out as well, and the two groups were at a standoff. More to the point, all eyes were on the battle between him and Okar, and Tau saw his doubts reflected in the sorrowed faces of his brothers.

Tau blocked three, then four and five more attacks. He was a full step behind Kellan's pace now and had no chance for offense. It wouldn't be long until Kellan pierced his lackluster defense and killed him. Tau made space again, thought of calling for help, and rejected it. If he had to die, he'd do it like a man.

Then he saw Zuri running back into the circle. She had Jayyed with her. Tau felt shame, deep shame, because he was so grateful Zuri had found and brought him. Maybe Jayyed could stop this before Kellan killed him.

It wasn't Jayyed who saved him, though.

"I said stop!" Zuri yelled, her hands aimed at Kellan. Tau saw her and leapt back as she doused Okar with enervation. Kellan had enough time to see Zuri and gawped at her. He had that much time, and then he was on his knees, caught in Isihogo and defenseless.

This was not how Tau had wanted it, but he'd take it. He ran for Kellan and lifted his blade for a blow that would, dull or no, take Okar's head from his shoulders.

"No!" It was Zuri. She cut her enervating blast, Tau swung down, and, impossibly, Kellan had his sword up, blocking Tau's cut. The Indlovu in the circle erupted in outrage.

"He's trying to kill him!"

"The Lesser is insane!"

"Hang him!"

The surrounding Indlovu closed in. Scale Jayyed came to Tau's defense, and Jayyed was there too. He got to Tau first, took him by the neck, and yanked him back and off his feet.

"Enough!" he roared. "Enough, damn you all. Enough!"

The Indlovu were howling for blood, their outrage mixed with disbelief. It shattered their worldview to think a Lesser would try to kill one of their own.

Tau struggled to get back to his feet but Jayyed had him.

"I said enough." Jayyed squeezed Tau's neck. "Was this a challenge? Blood-duels are not permitted between initiates."

Kellan, still on his knees, was trying to shake off the vestiges of Isihogo. "Of course not," he said. "I don't even know this Lesser."

Tau growled at that and Jayyed squeezed his neck tighter.

"Do you wish to press charges for the attack?" Jayyed asked Kellan.

Zuri gasped, and the Nobles who were close enough to hear raised their voices in a chorus of assent.

"What?" asked Kellan.

"Will you lay charges, nkosi?" Jayyed said again.

"Don't. Don't do this." Zuri was facing Kellan.

Kellan looked at her like she was mad, but he schooled his features. "Are you ordering me to forfeit justice, Lady Gifted? How have I given such great offense that you would attack me and deprive me of my natural rights to restitution? Whatever it is I have done, tell me how I may make amends."

"Don't do this," Zuri said, imploring Kellan more than instructing him.

"Remind me, Umqondisi," Kellan said to Jayyed. "What is justice in this case?"

Jayyed answered in perfect monotone. "The offending Lesser will be hung, nkosi."

"I see," said Kellan to Jayyed, but looking at Zuri the whole time. "Then, you deal with him in whatever way you see fit. I've had enough madness for one day." The Indlovu with Kellan protested, but he raised a hand, silencing them. "Are we done here?" Kellan asked.

Jayyed bobbed his head. "I believe we are, nkosi."

Kellan gave Tau a strange look, turned, and sketched an unsteady bow to Zuri, his head still spinning from the underworld. "I beg forgiveness for any offense I have given you, Lady Gifted." That done and with his back straight, he left the circle with all but one of his Indlovu entourage following.

The one who stayed behind spat in the dirt beside Tau. "Death? Death?" the Noble said, throwing Tau's words back at him. "Nceku, stay in the dirt where your kind belong."

Tau tried to go for him, but Jayyed wrenched him back in place.

"If you please, nkosi." Jayyed said to the man by way of dismissal, his words respectful, his tone anything but.

The Indlovu smirked and left.

Jayyed turned to Zuri. "My thanks, Lady Gifted. We all thank you." He dragged Tau to his feet and pulled him from the circle, shouting for the rest of the scale to follow. When they turned the first corner, Jayyed picked up the pace, almost running. "Scale Jayyed, we are leaving, now!"

JAYYED AYIM

"Don't look back, don't slow down," Jayyed told his men. He didn't want to admit it, even to himself, but he was scared. He forced his voice to sound neutral, like he was mentioning the heat. "Tau, if the citadel umqondisi hear about the duel before we get out of the city, I won't be able to save you."

"I don't need saving," the scarred young man said, trying to be tough but sounding petulant.

Jayyed clamped tighter on his neck. It had to hurt, but the initiate bore it, walking tall. Jayyed wanted to squeeze harder, force Tau to bend. "You're a fool," he told him. "A damned fool!"

Jayyed had rushed to the circle when word came that a fight had broken out between Lessers and Nobles. On his way, he'd almost run over a Gifted initiate. She'd come looking for Lessers and, finding Jayyed, had told him to follow her.

He'd known that tensions were high after Oyibo's death, but he hadn't expected things to go so far. He'd come into the city with his men, ignoring common sense because he was also burning for a fight, and that was stupid.

"You have no idea how close to death you came," Jayyed told Tau, struggling to keep his voice calm, a man commenting on the heat. "Dueling an Indlovu? Attacking a Greater Noble!"

And the Gifted had blasted Kellan Okar with enervation. Jayyed hadn't believed his eyes, and that was before Tau tried to kill the man.

"If it had been anyone but him, you'd already be strung up," Jayyed said.

"I will kill that man."

"That man? Do you know—"

"You don't know—"

"I do!" he screamed at Tau, losing patience and having to wrestle it back. "I know exactly what Okar did, and I know what he didn't." Jayyed could feel the vein in his neck throbbing and Tau shook himself free from his pinching fingers.

"My father—"

"Kellan Okar didn't kill you father!"

"He attacked—"

"Under orders! Under direct orders by the chairman of the Guardian Council and perfectly in his right to kill him. Can't you see? Okar did everything he could to follow orders and still spare him."

"You think I'll accept that?"

"You fought Okar today. Don't you think that, if he'd wanted to kill your father, your father would have died by his hand?"

Tau was silent. Jayyed knew why. He might not want to face the truth about Kellan, but Tau couldn't pretend he wasn't already a better swordsman than his father had ever been.

Tau's efforts, without benefit of birth or natural talent, had allowed him to surpass the skills of his peers and many of his betters. Still, there were limits. Tau could not have held Okar for much longer, and his father could not have held Okar at all.

The brash initiate simmered like a pot ready to boil over, and the roil of emotions on his face reminded Jayyed of the moment he'd recognized him at the testing. At the time, it had been only a few days since he'd watched Dejen Olujimi ram a blade through Tau's father's chest. Only a few days, and Tau had changed.

The boy, with his angry and weeping wound, had looked like a savage in the fighting circle against Uduak. Jayyed had wondered how Tau managed to get cut so badly. He remembered thinking the wound would fester. It could kill the boy, and as the match began, he remembered thinking that when Uduak was through with him, the scratch wouldn't matter at all.

Jayyed had heard about Uduak half a cycle before the testing. He'd had him watched, and, as expected, Uduak was exactly what Jayyed was looking for. Jayyed found more like him, but Uduak was the first choice for his new scale, and at the testing, the brute did not disappoint. He'd smashed his way through everyone he faced, and then he faced Tau.

The boy was small, even for a Lesser, and it should have been a slaughter, but Tau fought Uduak for the full two hundred count. It seemed impossible. It wasn't, and that challenged Jayyed's thinking in ways that worried him.

In the first moments of the fight's aftermath, Tau's feat felt threatening and Jayyed had wanted to dismiss or deny the accomplishment, but denying a thing just because he'd rather it not be true would make him no better than the Royal Nobles of the Guardian Council. So, he chose to do the opposite. He chose to see Tau as a beacon of hope.

Jayyed had gone to the other umqondisi. He'd argued for Tau. He'd burned important favors to have the match declared a tie, to get Tau into the isikolo. And, when it was all done, wondering if he was playing himself for a fool, Jayyed went to see the boy.

He'd spoken with him, sensing the young man's doubts. They echoed his own. Hiding those reservations, Jayyed had chosen to be encouraging. He wanted Tau, the boy who had achieved the impossible because he could not see how impossible it was, to continue to believe in himself, to know that Jayyed believed in him.

He wanted to see if Tau could continue to defy the odds, because if what Jayyed had learned was true, the Chosen needed to see that almost as much as they needed a better breed of fighter. They needed to believe that odds could be defied.

He'd given Tau a chance and, bolstered by superior training, but more through inhuman effort, the boy had become the thing Jayyed had both hoped and feared to create. Like dragons, like Gifted, like Ingonyama, Tau, a Lesser, had become a living weapon.

"You stubborn intulo!" Jayyed railed at him as they rushed for the city gates, fleeing like criminals. "Think! Think for a breath. Kellan didn't even remember you from the day of your father's death. You were nothing more than a crazed Lesser and he still didn't want you to die. Can't you see? He's not the bloodthirsty villain you'd like him to be. If he were, he would have killed you long before I arrived."

Tau said nothing.

"Yes," Jayyed said, hammering the point home. "You're not too stupid to see that." Jayyed aimed for a nerve. "I've watched Kellan Okar fight for the last two cycles. Almost without doubt, he'll win a guardian sword when he graduates. He will, without doubt, become an Ingonyama. He's the best Indlovu the citadel has seen in twenty or thirty cycles!"

Tau turned his scarred face away. "You told us training would outdo talent," the boy said. "You worked us half to death with promises that we could be like them."

"What?" Jayyed countered. "You think Kellan Okar doesn't train? You think he wakes at midday, gorges himself, poles Noble women in the ass, and then, when occasion merits, happens to fight like that?"

Themba, marching behind them, spluttered, trying to hold back a laugh.

"Move off!" Jayyed hollered.

Themba ducked his head, the chastisement chasing him and the other men away.

"I do nothing but train," said Tau. "I give my life to the sword. That's what you asked. It's what I've done. You told me I would be their equal. You told me—"

"Tau," Jayyed said, afraid to admit what he must. "Kellan is... There aren't enough spans in the day for you to out-train that one. He's a Greater Noble, but for much of his life, the other Nobles treated him like a pariah. He lives his life in defiance of that, as if to prove that he is more than 'the coward Okar's' son. He's in the citadel practice yards for as long as you are in ours. You have to understand, he lives his life as a rebuke to his father's legacy. That, coupled with the fact that he's..." Jayyed trailed off.

"Bigger, stronger, faster," Tau said, finishing Jayyed's unspoken thought. "He's Noble and that makes him too much to overcome."

Jayyed hesitated. Sometimes too much hope leads men to bad ends. "He's too much to overcome," he conceded.

"That's it, then? I'm a Lesser and the best I can do, after giving my life to the sword, is to match their weak?"

"They think we can't even do that," Jayyed told him. "And, if you want the truth, I wasn't sure we could either."

"How can you tell me that, when you led a scale of Lessers to the Queen's Melee, to fight against the Nobles' best? How can you tell me there are heights to which I cannot climb, when you were the one who forged the paths?"

"I am not like you," Jayyed said, the words frightening him as he spoke them.

"You work harder than I do? Smarter?"

There was no one close enough to hear their conversation, and Tau needed to know some of the truth. Telling him was the right thing to do, but it didn't make the words easier. "My father was a Greater Noble," he said.

Tau jerked as if he'd been whipped. "What?"

"Before I was born, my village was attacked in a raid. The Indlovu came but the hedeni had already razed most of it. They were retreating and my mother's parents were murdered. They were among the last to die and my mother was next. Three savages came for her. A Greater Noble got there first. He killed them. He saved her. He felt he was owed. My mother was not yet a woman. He thought it safe to use her."

Tau shook his head as if the words made no sense. "No...Lesser-Noble crosses are not permitted....The babies are stillborn."

"Not all," Jayyed said. "When my mother learned she was pregnant, she told the other villagers that she'd lain with one of the Lessers who died in the raid. I was born later that cycle, alive."

Tau didn't say a word. He was staring at Jayyed and taking quick, shallow breaths.

"I've spent my life fighting and killing, doing all in my power to help my people survive," Jayyed said. He paused then, unready to tell Tau everything and deciding to explain only as much as he needed to know. "A few cycles ago, I found something that could help. I'd learned how to spot many of the characteristics of a Lesser-Noble cross."

"What? Why?"

"Because we're losing the war," Jayyed said. "We'll never match the hedeni's numbers, and the only way we avoid annihilation is with Gifted and better fighters. But we have too few Gifted and too few Nobles. Our Lessers are better trained than the hedeni, but the difference between a well-trained Lesser and a hedeni warrior is too slight. We're losing."

"We're losing? Who knows this?" Tau asked.

"Not many, and some who should know refuse to believe."

"But you believe it? So why send us to fight and die in a war we can't win?"

"Because I think I've found a way to stave off our end," Jayyed said, thinking carefully about how to word the next part. He wasn't ready to invoke the queen's name or reveal the endgame, and he didn't think Tau was ready for that either. "I have to hope that, if we can last several cycles more, we can find a way to finish this war, without our people being wiped out."

"Scale Jayyed? Are we to play a part in seeing that hope realized?"

"The rest of them are," Jayyed said. "You were never part of the plan."

"My sword brothers . . . they're of Lesser-Noble blood?"

"They are," he said. "Once I learned that cross-caste children survive in much larger numbers than we're led to believe, I realized that, in them, there's a chance." The unburdening was cathartic. Jayyed had held this for too long. "I filled my scale with as many crosses as I could find. If I was going to challenge our ideas and laws on crossing the castes, I needed to prove that the offspring of these unions make better fighters than the standard Lesser."

He knew he should ease Tau into this, but he also wanted him to understand. "I need proof that we can create a new and necessary caste, between Nobles and Lessers. The Guardian Council won't heed my warnings about the war, but maybe they'll take my help.

If they see the strength and possibilities of cross-caste warriors, the council might allow us to find and train them separately. If we can do this in the open, future generations will be stronger with this new caste. This is my goal, and in pursuing it, I found you, a pure-blood Lesser with a Noble's determination."

He offered Tau a small smile. "You gave me more hope. You see, maybe we can help more Lessers reach the limit of their potential. Those Lessers, alongside Nobles, Gifted, and cross-castes, can help us hold the peninsula until, one day, this war ends."

Tau was not looking at Jayyed when he spoke. "You want to create a new caste, something between Lessers and Nobles? You'll make a new training school for them, something between the isikolo and citadel?"

Tau was too quiet, but at least he understood. "Yes," Jayyed said. "That's right."

Tau looked at him then. "Hadith, Yaw, Chinedu, Themba, Uduak, they're cross-castes?"

Jayyed nodded. "Yes. And, when all this began, I was so very certain Uduak would be my greatest find, but it seems I've discovered something more." He willed his words to do more than be heard. Jayyed wanted his aspirations understood.

"I'll tell no one," Tau said, and Jayyed knew the boy was not convinced.

They walked in silence, the weight of the confession heavy between them, until, as they marched out of the city's gates, Tau spoke, his tone sharp. "You raised me up with bold words and ideals that you don't believe. You don't think Lessers can be great. All you think is that those of us who share Noble blood can be more."

"You say that, yet I took you into my scale."

"Tell me why," Tau said.

"I wanted my men to see that with enough determination our natural limits can be pushed."

"I think you wanted to shame them into working hard enough to never lose to someone like me."

"What you're calling shame I think of as pride. I wanted them to share the determination and pride that you have in yourself.

Granted, I had no idea you'd become good enough to match a few Nobles. That's not something I thought possible."

"You're content to be less than," Tau said.

Jayyed shook off the comment. "I'm telling you that you can be proud and that your achievements prove that all Lessers can do more." Jayyed smiled. "We all have our place, but perhaps the gap between Noble and Lesser is not as wide as most think. Perhaps—"

"No. After all you've done and all you've seen, you still believe they're better than us. You still think blood determines destiny."

"You want to know what I think?" Jayyed asked, his frustration slipping free. "I think that, especially after today, a Lesser should know better than to believe he can match a Greater Noble."

Tau reeled as if slapped, then rounded on Jayyed. "They tell me that we're winning the war. It's not true. They tell me that the off-spring of Nobles and Lessers die in childbirth. It's not true. They tell me that we are Lessers, but I'm starting to think that's also not true."

"You won't help your people if you don't know your place."

"I don't think I like the place they've set for me."

"It's based on what you are."

"They don't know what I am," Tau said, "but I can show you."

Jayyed knew what was coming and he stopped marching. He faced Tau, looking down at him, letting the boy have his moment.

"Fight me, tomorrow," Tau said. "Come to the practice yards before dawn."

And, like that, the time for words and soft persuasion was over. Jayyed failed Tau that night, but he would try to help the boy see the truth, because, if he did, Tau could light the path to greatness for other Lessers. He just needed to be put in his place.

"I'll meet you, Tau Solarin," Jayyed said, "and, together, we'll see what you are."

PYRRHIC

Tau was drilling in the practice yards when Jayyed found him the next day. The sun had yet to rise.

There were bags under the older man's eyes. "Morning, Tau. Care to spar?"

There was no heat in Jayyed's voice. He could have been asking about the weather. Tau paced, letting his muscles loosen. He nodded at his umqondisi.

Jayyed stripped off his tunic and stretched, his body a mass of scars and corded muscle. He picked up his sword and shield and stood, ready. Jayyed was the taller, stronger, and more experienced man. Even the blood in his veins claimed superiority.

Tau put down his swords and pulled his tunic free. Retrieving his weapons, he twirled them through the warm air. Without a word, Jayyed attacked.

In the beginning they flowed with each other, letting their swords dance. Then flow gave way to force and, with dulled swords that could not manage the task, they fought as if to kill. Circling, attacking, defending only when they must, they pushed each other, both men seeking to send the other past the limits of his prowess.

Tau fought with the fervor of a zealot. He would prove he was more than Jayyed believed his birth allowed, and to do it he would maintain the pace until he won or his heart burst. It was what made him the fighter he was.

His edge didn't come from his body or blood. It didn't come from gifts. It was that he desired mastery more than he desired breath. It was that he wanted revenge more than he wanted to live. It was that his father's life had mattered every bit as much as the lives of Nobles, and though they didn't believe that yet, they would.

Already Jayyed was flagging and had taken to pushing off and away from Tau, using the gaps in battle to catch his breath. Then he began using the gaps to waste it.

"We are a people besieged," he told Tau, his voice thin with the strain of speaking and defending. "We have all lost something, someone."

Jayyed threw a feint at Tau's face. Tau slapped it away and sent his umqondisi stumbling back.

"My mother lost her parents to a raid and I lost my wife to one," Jayyed said.

Tau was not interested in Jayyed's losses and fired his blades at the man's shield and sword.

"My daughter lost her mother and never forgave me for not being there. I was in the Wrist, fighting. She hated me for that. For protecting others and not being there to protect them."

Soft stories, Tau thought, clenching his jaw and switching from sword form to form, mutating and enhancing each as he went. He darted in, Jayyed reached up to block, and Tau's weak-side blade cracked him in the ribs.

"Ack!" Jayyed wheezed, pain evident on his face as he backed away and continued to prattle. "My daughter is Gifted. I found out from my neighbor. Jamilah was already gone when I returned. Our hut empty. No goodbye."

Tau hit him again, forcing out another cry of pain.

"She excelled at the Gifted Citadel." Jayyed was retreating, unable to string together a consistent defense. "She fights now. Calls down dragons on hedeni. Relishes—Ah! Cek!" Tau had taken him in the thigh with the edge of a blade. "She ... she relishes her role in their deaths."

Tau saw a killing blow and took it. Jayyed blocked and Tau sent in another kill strike, this time with his strong side. Jayyed darted left, moving away from Tau's swing, swaying with weariness. Tau, tasting blood from his overworked lungs, dashed forward, reengaging.

"Horrible," Jayyed said. "To think her...like that. Anger, hate... burning her alive."

Tau stabbed out, hitting Jayyed in the shield arm.

Jayyed yelped, grimaced, but kept talking. "This war...it's made monsters of us. I don't want to die a monster. I don't want it for Jamilah...I don't want our people exterminated and remembered that way."

Tau growled, swords whirling for Jayyed's head.

Jayyed blocked one sword, ducked the other, and ran backward in an unsteady lurch.

"Can't keep going this way," Jayyed said. "Guardian Council is too blind to see that. I tried to show them....I analyzed attacks, numbers, tribes...each raid. Know what I found?" Jayyed punctuated the question with a thrust of his shield, meant to smash Tau in the face.

Tau jumped back, braced himself, and slammed the points of both swords into the shield's center. Jayyed grunted. He'd have a bruise from that.

"More hedeni than we thought," he said, "beyond peninsula. Far more."

Tau attacked, working in a pattern that would require his opponent to raise his shield. When he did, Tau would deliver a killing blow. Jayyed would not last another three crosses. He was already dead.

"We can't beat them!" Jayyed raised his shield and Tau smashed its underside, sending it higher, exposing the umqondisi's core.

Jayyed didn't even try to block, and Tau stabbed the point of his weapon into his chest. If they had been fighting with sharpened blades Jayyed would have been skewered. Tau's sword would have pierced his chest, his heart, and come out his back like...like Aren.

It was over, but all Tau felt was pain. He looked down. The point of Jayyed's sword was dug deep into his side, drawing blood. Had they fought with sharpened blades, Jayyed would have gutted him.

"Can't win." Jayyed coughed. "Not as we are. Cross-caste fighters, if we can even find and train enough of them, only prolong the inevitable.... There's only one way we survive...just one.... Peace."

Tau dropped his blades and batted Jayyed's sword away from his side. "This is your answer? After all your talk of great Lessers, cross-castes, warriors, and Nobles, you stand in front of me begging for peace?"

Jayyed went to his knees, holding himself up on shaking arms. "Our real war is with the Cull." Jayyed retched, nothing coming up. "But the Royal Nobles and old queens have forgotten that. We have a new queen now and it's time for new leaders who remember what actually matters."

Tau was furious. Jayyed had turned his victory into a draw and it burned. "You think the child queen, the same one who did nothing when you were thrown off the Guardian Council, will get rid of the current crop of Royal Nobles? You think she'll do this so she can surrender us to the hedeni, because our real fight is with fairy-tale monsters?"

Tau turned his back on Jayyed and spat in the dirt. "I am one man, mourning one man, and will never have peace as long as the Nobles who murdered my father are alive. How can the Omehi or hedeni do what I cannot, when our history holds almost two hundred cycles of killing? You ask too much and I see why the Royals got rid of you!"

"The Royal Nobles of the Guardian Council can't see anything but war and the lives they've built for themselves from it. The queen is different and strong in her faith. The Goddess did not send us here to die on the bone spears and axes of people who are not our true enemy."

Tau scoffed.

"The queen couldn't stop my dismissal. She was too new to her power and throne, but I'm loyal to her, as loyal as she is to the Goddess. I'm telling you this because you can be part of the new world. Tau, the old Royals have lost their way and the Omehi too, but their time is coming."

"Old Royals? New world?" Tau asked. "You're not even talking about a revolution. You just want to replace one master for another." The whole thing made him sick. He gathered his swords and walked off, clutching his injured side, leaving his kneeling umqondisi in the dirt.

"Tau," Jayyed called after him. "Watch for sacrifice counters. Your enemy doesn't have to win for you to lose."

Tau ignored him. He was thinking about the Jayyed he'd known on the first day of training. The Jayyed who had told a scale of Lessers that, though men had their differences, they were nothing compared to their similarities.

Two hands, two legs, one heart, one mind. Nobles shared more with Lessers than they didn't. They were more akin to Tau than they weren't, and to say different was to speak lies.

Tau's limits were not decided by his birth or nature but by the bounds of his determination and the extent of his efforts. That was what Tau believed, and he was going to prove it. He was going to show them all.

CHAPTER NINE

LESSER

The day after he fought Jayyed and the day after that and the day after that, Tau slept no more than three spans a night. His life was offered like a sacrifice to the sword. Yet, when the moon had cycled, he was forbidden to attend the scale's next skirmish.

He railed against the decision, demanding to speak with Jayyed, who had not come to tell him this himself. Aqondise Anan was stoic in the face of Tau's anger, saying nothing could change the order. Word of the duel had reached the citadel umqondisi, and though Kellan Okar had relinquished his right to justice, Jayyed believed it best for Tau to remain beyond easy reach.

When his scale prepared to leave, Tau went to confront Jayyed. He was met by the men of Scale Njere. They were polite but insisted that Tau remain in the barracks.

Tau's sword brothers returned before dawn on the next day. The skirmish had been close, but they'd lost. Tau threw over his cot and yelled in Hadith's face; shadowed by a brooding Uduak, Hadith took a lesson from Anan and accepted Tau's anger.

That day and the next and the next, Tau beat, battered, and embarrassed his sword brothers, as if doing so would make them better or soothe his disquiet. The lack of sleep, the overwork, the stress, and the tempers caught up to him, and he woke with a chill. He stumbled his way to the practice yards, made it through the morning run, and collapsed. No one could make him leave until Jayyed came.

Tau, feverish, threatened to fight his umqondisi. He demanded they finish what they had started. Jayyed and Anan dragged him to the infirmary. He spent two days burning off the sickness.

On the third day, Jayyed visited. He asked Tau if he was trying to kill himself. Tau, the fever gone, spoke as if he were still in its grasp. He told Jayyed he needed more time, that the days were too short for all he had to do.

"Every woman, man, child, Lesser and Noble, is given the same time in a day, and no more," Jayyed had said.

The next morning, Tau was first on the practice yards and last to leave them. He battered the flaxen practice dummy, hitting it so hard its dented helmet spun in circles on its thin head. He sparred without relent, and even weakened from the fever's aftereffects, he pushed himself harder than anyone else in the scale.

When his sword brothers left the yards, he fought mock battles with himself, replaying every sparring session. Then, when his body's exhaustion could no longer be denied, he sat in the yards, eyes closed, reenacting every skirmish in his mind, mentally correcting the errors in his sword work. Still, it would not be enough.

Jayyed's theory of training had been meant to turn cross-castes into the fighting equivalent of Petty Nobles, not Lessers into Nobles. Even so, Tau found no fault in Jayyed's methods. They produced superior results, and those results did not depend on lineage.

The best way to become a better swordsman was through intelligent effort spent on swordplay. The more effort put in, the faster the fighter would become better. Jayyed had the right of it and Tau was trying. He was giving everything he had, but he could not match the citadel's three cycles in the isikolo's one.

The time remaining before Tau's cycle of training ended was not enough for him to overcome a disciplined and trained Greater Noble's natural advantages. A man like Kellan Okar would still be his better.

Startling the guard on top of the isikolo's nearest wall, Tau threw his swords to the ground and yelled into the night. He went to his knees, sitting on his legs in prayer position, but had nothing to say to Ananthi.

What could he say to the Goddess, who had allowed his father to be murdered and who had made Tau a Lesser, so justice would be impossible everywhere but in his dreams? How could he treat with a creator who had given him the will but not the way?

A burst of lightning caught his attention, illuminating the black sky, forking a dozen times, and striking the distant water like a spear. That was rare. Storms and rain did not come often to Xidda. Tau waited for thunder. It came, booming across the distance, its sound reaching him in the same breath as the thought that promised to change the course of his life.

Tau rocked on his heels. He saw a way, a path waiting to be walked, and it frightened him beyond measure, because he no longer knew if he had the will. He thought to forget it, ignore it, reject it. He could go to bed, join his fellows in sleep, wake in the morning, and do as they did, training, laughing, drinking, and fighting in a war without end, against an enemy that Jayyed believed could not be defeated. He could let the memory of his father fade and become a great Lesser, a man with the skill to stand mere steps behind the Nobles on the Omehi's march into history's pages.

Or he could be more.

Tau, on his knees, closed his eyes, took slow breaths, and let Isihogo take him.

ISIHOGO

He was in the practice yards, but the training grounds and grasslands were covered in mist. He saw no guard on the indistinct walls of the isikolo, and the sky rolled, as unsettled as the Roar. Tau looked down at himself. He was glowing and knew it wouldn't be long. He stood, feeling relief that his swords had come with him, and he drew them, hands shaking, bile rising. He resisted the urge to expel his breath and flee this evil place. He stayed and the demons came.

The one that saw him first was monstrous. It stood half again as tall as Tau, was covered in mottled chitin, and had two long limbs tipped with pincers. It scuttled toward him on six spiny legs while chittering from a circular maw that opened and shut reflexively, displaying rings of teeth that went back into its throat.

Tau twirled his swords with a bravado he did not feel. "Come on!" he shouted, charging.

The creature skittered to a stop, pincers frozen aloft. Tau used its confusion to land the first blow. His blade slammed into the monster's right arm and claw. It shrieked at him, withdrew the arm, and with its other pincer snapped for his neck. Tau blocked with his weak-side sword, but the creature shoved his blade back, clamping down as it did, almost catching his head. Tau drew back and pulled his sword from its grasp, using both blades to attack the monster everyplace he imagined it could be weak. He broke small pieces from its shell but managed little else.

In the distance, hidden by mist, Tau could hear an ululating call that made the hairs on his neck stand. He didn't dare look. His courage was failing. He focused on the fight he had, frantic to get around the monster in front of him so he could face both it and the incoming other, but the pincered monster could not be beaten.

His fear grew, threatening to overcome him. He would not be able to face the demons one-on-one and it was too late to leave Isihogo by expelling his breath. The demons would tear him to pieces before he could escape that way. There was only one possible end. But he'd known that when he came.

He was going to die horribly, though knowing it and facing it were different, and in that moment, Isihogo became truly dangerous for Tau. As the demon behind him closed in and the one he faced lashed out, Tau could no longer ignore the underworld's immense power.

He felt it all around him, and it would be a simple thing to draw it into himself. He could use it to stop them, to fight them. He could use it to blast them to pieces, to escape, to save himself. The power was there, offering itself as the pincered demon caught his strong arm and snapped the bone in two.

The pain and shock hit Tau at the same time, and without thought, he reached for Isihogo's offering. The second demon got him before he could take it. The creature closed its jaws on the back of his neck, cracking his spine and dragging him to the ground. He fell, powerless and crippled, his body broken, his mind not far behind.

The unseen demon bit him again while the pincered monster scuttled over, one of its carapaced legs stabbing through the skin and bone of his right hip as it hurried to feed. With his spine severed, Tau could not feel the leg or his rib cage being torn open by the two demons. He could hear them, though, as they slopped up his innards and shook his body with their jostling.

When a third demon got to him, there was only room for it by his head. It bit into his cheek and jaw, its teeth slicing into him and tearing the ruined flesh from his face. That he felt, and the pain shattered him, splitting his consciousness into a thousand slivers, each one a suffering, a scourging without end. Tau's tongue, mouth, and jaw had been torn to shreds, but as he died he found a way to scream.

He came back to the world in sections. He sensed a leg, his mouth, the beating of his heart, his eyes. His own body was disjointed, a thing apart, hard to reconcile and impossible, in those early breaths, to control. Moving from Uhmlaba to Isihogo was always hard. It incapacitated men inexperienced with it. Dying to demons was infinitely worse.

Tau opened his eyes. He was on the ground at the edge of the practice yards, moaning, rocking. No time had passed, but he had been to the underworld, fought there, almost taken its power into himself and come close to a true death. His nerves were on fire, his limbs trembled, and his mind was misery.

He tried to sit, couldn't, and lay still, waiting for the shock to pass, the loamy ground warm against his cheek and lips. He'd soiled himself.

It was in this state of suffering and degradation that Tau knew he'd been given everything he wanted. The Goddess had answered his prayers. She'd shown him how to make one span worth a hundred, one cycle worth a lifetime.

Her gift was a generous one. If accepted, it would make him the greatest warrior in Omehi history, and all he had to do was fight and die to Isihogo's demons over and over and over again.

COUNT

"What sme... Whassat smell?" Chinedu coughed out. "Tau, that you?"

"It's not me," Tau said, rolling out of his cot, eyes heavy, head heavier. "Is that you, still in bed," Chinedu clarified.

Tau thought he'd been able to wash himself well enough the night before. He'd been so tired, though.

"Surprised is all," Chinedu said. "First time I'm up before you, neh?"

"It was a long night in the yards."

"Not sure how much... how much value is in it." Chinedu raised his hands, empty palms facing Tau. "Don't mean anything by that. Way you fight is... is evidence enough. Just hard to see how swinging a sword at shadows helps, is all."

"I think you're right. I won't stay out as late. Not if it means I'm sleeping in."

Chinedu chuckled. "Sleeping in? Sun ain't even up yet." He buckled on his sword belt. "I'm... off."

"I'll be along in a moment," Tau said, looking around the room filled with sleeping men. Hadith, Uduak, and Yaw were already gone. Tau rushed to catch up, trying to sort out what parts of the night had been normal nightmares and what parts were the nightmares he'd lived through. He touched his jaw and cheek. They were there and they were whole, though memory of the attack made the skin tingle.

Tau snatched up his practice swords, belt, and gambeson, which did smell like dung. He'd have to rush through the early practice, make an excuse, and wash it again. He'd have to go through the afternoon without it.

Tau strode for the barracks door, spotting the demon a breath before it could take him. With no time to yell a warning, he threw himself to the floor and rolled back to his feet, swords drawn, facing the shadows and nothing more.

"Cek! What're you done?" asked Mavuto, still half-asleep and sitting up. "Tau?"

"Nothing," Tau told his lanky sword brother. The demon was gone. It had never been. "It's nothing."

"What's that smell?"

"What? Go back to sleep, Mavuto."

The man grumbled, lay down, and pulled his rough blanket over his head. Tau left and went straight to the bathhouses. Practice would have to wait until he'd scrubbed his body and gambeson. He also needed a quarter span to center himself. He'd thought he'd seen a demon in the barracks.

The rest of the day fell in line with Tau's routine. He trained hard, sparred well, ate supper at twilight, and went back to the yards alone. He was shaking when he went, because what he meant to do scared him. He wasn't ashamed to admit that, and as the night deepened, he saw things beyond the yard, in the grasslands, crawling things, things with too many arms and legs. The hairs on his arms rose and his skin went rough, like on those Harvest nights when the air ran cool.

He cautioned himself not to overdo it. He thought to go back to bed to get proper rest. Isihogo would be there for him on the next night, or the one after that, if he needed two days to recover.

Tau wanted to believe his rationalizations more than anything, because the only other thing he could think to do was to sit at the far edge of the practice yard, farthest from the protective walls of the isikolo, where the grasslands began. The only other thing he could think to do was to sit there, slow his breathing, close his eyes, and allow his soul to slip from the world of his birth and into the world of death.

The demons came. Tau fought. They slaughtered him. Back in Uhmlaba he threw up his dinner and crouched in the grasses, heaving until he believed his seeds would come out his mouth. Throat burning from bile, he stood and took a step toward the barracks, but the night was young and would remain that way. Time was different in Isihogo.

Whimpering, cursing himself a coward, Tau sat in the grass, a step away from his spew, and let his soul fly to the prison Ananthi had wrought for Ukufa. He tasted blood. In his fear he'd bitten through his lip.

They came. He drew swords and battled them until a misstep allowed a demon to slice his leg off below the knee. He dropped to the ground and that was it. They had him and he was brutalized.

He went back. A pack of them found him and, losing his nerve, Tau dropped his swords and fled. They ran him down, the fastest of them ending Tau's flight when it caught and tore the tendons in his calf with its hand's-length claws. He went down and they had him. He begged and he pled. "Mercy," he said, "Goddess's mercy." If they or She heard, it made no difference. He was eviscerated.

He went back. Only one found him. It was a war between them, like the stories old men told children around blistering fires meant to keep the darkness at bay.

The demon had two arms and walked on two legs. It behaved like a human, and this Tau understood. This he could fight. They roared at each other and fought bitterly, two demigods, their battle holding the fate of creation in its balance. Then the demon caught Tau across the throat, slicing him from ear to ear.

He collapsed, gulping for air and tasting copper. The demon stood over him, eyes glowing red as it watched his lifeblood pump through the trench it had carved in his neck.

Tau's head lolled. He was dying. It hurt. It hurt so much and it hurt every time. The skin around the wound burned and he could feel his heart pounding in his chest, desperate to keep him alive. Just let me die, he thought.

He rolled his eyes to the demon's face. It had tusks and where its nose should have been there was a slitted hole. Tau couldn't speak but tried to goad it, tried to make it put him out of his misery. It made no move, letting him suffer, watching him bleed to death.

Tau went two more times that night but could manage no more and stumbled back to the barracks. As best he could discern, he'd been out in the practice yards for less than two spans. He had to do better, he thought. He was wasting too much time between deaths. He could fight many more battles if, after he died, he went straight back in.

The next night Tau went back and fought more often than the night before. He began keeping a count of each evening's battles. He forced more out of each night, and his work was not done until he'd bested his previous number. He told no one what he did, but the scale noticed.

BORDERS

Yaw, Chinedu, Hadith, you'll spar Tau," Jayyed ordered. It was early afternoon and the scale was in the practice yards.

"Give us Uduak," Hadith said.

"There's three of you. Get on."

"Three against Tau, we'll take Uduak," Hadith said.

"Uduak, stay where you are," Jayyed said. "Fight!"

Hadith sucked his teeth, pulled his sword, and waved Yaw and Chinedu forward. The two men did as they were bid but were slow about it.

Tau waited until they were three strides out of sword range to attack. He feinted at Yaw with his weak side and caught him on the temple with the strong. Yaw crumpled, his helmet tumbling across the yard. Chinedu swung hard, but Tau's sword caught the blow and, with the pommel of his other blade, he smacked Chinedu in the back, near his spine. Chinedu fell, cursing, and Tau was already chasing a backpedaling Hadith. Tau disarmed him, tripped him, and stood over him, sword point grazing Hadith's throat stone.

"Mercy," Hadith grumbled.

Tau stepped back. It had gone better this time. His sword brothers had not taken on the faces of demons. That had been happening more often of late. He thought to take time away from Isihogo, to settle his mind, but brushed the unworthy idea away. It was his cowardice speaking.

"Uduak," Jayyed said, "join Hadith, Yaw, and Chinedu. Try not to embarrass yourselves."

Uduak stood beside Hadith, who had regained his feet. Yaw picked up his helmet, shook the dust from it, stretched his neck, and returned it to his head. Chinedu coughed.

"Fight!" Jayyed yelled.

Hadith went down first, Chinedu was next, Tau knocked Yaw unconscious, unintentionally, and then there was Uduak. He was big and he was a demon, horns on his head. Tau had to blink away the vision as they crossed blades. It happened fast. Thrust, swing, block, riposte, move, strike, strike, strike, and Uduak was down.

The big man eyed Tau. "Mercy."

Tau sheathed his swords and stepped back. The rest of the scale was watching.

"Impossible," muttered Anan.

Jayyed did not speak. Tau could feel the older man's eyes on him, though. They held a question he would not ask and one Tau would not have answered. Their relationship had been strained since they'd fought.

"A circuit around the yards. Go!" Jayyed told the scale and, with some groaning, the men began to run. Tau went with the rest but saw Anan sidle over to Jayyed to speak to him.

"I know you work hard, very hard," said Hadith, running beside Tau, "but how are you doing this?"

"Demon," said Uduak, the word making Tau stumble.

Hadith noticed. "Tau is a demon?"

"Inside," Uduak answered.

"That makes no sense," said Hadith. "But I'll be happy to see you try some of your newfound gift on the Indlovu. If we win the next skirmish, we qualify for the Queen's Melee."

"Another circuit!" Anan told them, receiving more groans.

"This is it. Everything!" Themba said, running up. "An Ihashe scale hasn't placed in the Queen's Melee since before our fathers squirted us into our mothers."

"Too much," grumbled Uduak.

"He's not wrong. We can make history," said Hadith.

"We will," Tau said.

"One more time round," Anan called, this time to audible curses. The aqondise glared at everyone and Tau sprinted ahead of Hadith, Uduak, and Themba. He was done talking. The next skirmish was ten days out. He would have to train harder, he thought, blinking away the demon he saw standing in the shadow of the isikolo's closest wall.

The days that followed blurred. Tau woke, he fought, he ate, he fought, he slept, he fought, he ate, he fought, he died, he died, he died. He'd never been talkative but spoke less. He stopped shaving, growing stubble on his face and head, like a Drudge or, worse, a hedeni. His bathing habits slipped until Chinedu complained and Jayyed's five dragged him to the baths. Tau thought that memory real, the bath, though he couldn't swear to it.

He also saw visions with increasing frequency and worried he might be losing his mind. He couldn't give in to that thinking. It was an excuse to avoid Isihogo. It was fear and he would not let it rule him.

The time for the next skirmish came and went. The match was postponed as initiates from both the Indlovu Citadel and Northern Ihashe Isikolo were sent to the Northern Mountains on patrol. It was beyond unusual to use initiates in actual combat against the hedeni, but they were unusual times. The hedeni were attacking with frequency and in force. It was all anyone could speak of during the evening meals. Tau let the conversations about the expanding war flow over him, the only salient detail being the postponed skirmish.

Still, he was not deaf and could not help but hear the constant chatter about the military's recent defeats. In the Wrist, almost five hundred men lost their lives to a hedeni assault. That was an entire military wing gone, and the hedeni had, in that single push, moved the front lines of the century-and-a-half-long war deep into territory traditionally held by the Omehi.

They had attempted to push farther but General Tiwa, a commanding officer of the Bisi Rage, had split his force, sending two military dragons, almost three thousand men, to hold the line as he continued to fight in the southern passes of the Wrist.

The gossip in the mess hall was that the hedeni were starving, that they had to push into the semi-arable lands of the Wrist or die. That did not sound right to Tau. He would have asked Jayyed about it, maybe, but Jayyed was not there.

The sword master had been called away by the Guardian Council. The rest of the scale were proud of this. Their umqondisi was needed by the highest military powers of the Omehi. Perhaps, the rumors went, the Guardian Council would reinstate him as one of its permanent advisers.

Tau did not know. These things meant nothing when pitted against his need to win the next skirmish. They marched to the Crags on the morrow, and the fight would either qualify or disqualify Scale Jayyed from the Queen's Melee. Tau had to win.

BLOOD

Scale Jayyed had the highest ranking in both the Southern and Northern Isikolo, and they were about to fight Umqondisi Osinachi's Indlovu. Scale Osinachi had done well all cycle but had taken a couple of brutal losses to other Indlovu. As it stood, the winner of the skirmish would enter the Queen's Melee, eliminating their opponent's chances to do the same.

Tau was lined up with the rest of his scale on the edge of the desert battleground in the Crags. An aqondise from the Northern Isikolo had the war horn to his lips. He blew it and the battle began. Tau ran with his scale for the nearest dune that could offer cover. If they beat the Nobles, they were in the Queen's Melee. The Queen's Melee was where he would face Kellan again.

Hadith, crouched beside him, swore as he peeked over the dune. "Char to ashes!"

"What?" asked Yaw.

"They have their Enervator near the center of the battleground. She's standing on top of the tallest dune with four Indlovu. The rest of the scale is hidden."

"Then we send men to take her out?" asked Yaw.

"Yes," drawled Hadith. "That's exactly what they hope we'll do."

"Well," said Themba, "we remove her or she blasts half of us out of the game when the fighting starts."

Tau ground a handful of the dune's sand through his fingers. "They murdered Oyibo in a skirmish."

Themba shot Tau a look. "What?"

"This is no game."

Hadith nodded. "We remember Oyibo, Tau. But, for now, we need to know where the rest of Scale Osinachi are, before we do anything."

"No, we don't," Tau told Hadith. "Give me a team. We'll crawl around, get behind the Enervator, and attack. If we hit hard enough, she'll have to waste her enervation on the six of us."

"Weren't you listening?" Themba said. "There's four Indlovu with her. She won't need to hit you with anything. The Indlovu will do the hitting."

Tau glared at Themba. "You think they'll stop me?"

"You think no one can?" Themba countered.

Hadith eyed Tau, clicking his tongue. "Right. Do it. Take Uduak, Yaw, Muvato, Duma, and Themba."

Themba started. "Why me?"

"Because I want to see you fight four Indlovu."

"Not interested in dying today," Themba said, but he moved closer to Tau, along with the other men Hadith had assigned to the team.

Hadith outlined the plan. "We hold until Tau's team launches the attack. If we stay hidden the Indlovu will do the same. When they see Tau's six men against four of theirs, they'll think the fight over before it begins. They won't reinforce and risk revealing their positions." Hadith spoke faster, becoming excited. "Tau, for this to work, we need the Enervator to hit your team. We can't attack until her powers are spent."

Tau nodded to Hadith. He wanted the scale to feel confident. He wanted his words to be bold. "Be ready. It'll happen fast," he said as he began crawling toward the battlefield's center.

"Always does," Tau heard Themba grumble.

It took a quarter span, crawling to the battleground's center, but they'd done it and Tau's team was next to the dune on which the

Enervator stood. Tau pointed, indicating they should go farther, the men nodded, and the six slunk to the opposite side of the man–made knoll.

The plan was to attack from the rear, from the side closer to the Indlovu's starting point. The Indlovu wouldn't expect an attack from that angle, and the surprise might gain them a few steps. Those few steps could mean the difference between getting to the Enervator and getting blasted.

Tau signaled his men to be ready. They'd round the last bend and charge the dune, engaging the Indlovu and beating them, forcing the Enervator to hit them with her powers or surrender. Whatever she chose to do, it would keep her out of the skirmish for its most critical phase. Hadith and the rest of the scale would attack and it would be fighters versus fighters, no gifts. It was as even as a group of Lessers could make combat against Nobles. A simple plan, a good plan, and it burned to ash.

Tau crawled forward into three Indlovu, also on their stomachs, who looked as surprised as he was. They must have had a similar plan, initiate a small attack and force the other side's hand. Given how little progress they'd made in their crawl, they'd come up with the plan long after Hadith.

The Indlovu closest to Tau leapt to his feet. "Blood will show!" he yelled, pulling his sword free of its scabbard.

Tau did the same, thinking it strange Nobles had their own war cry and that, even when the Omehi fought as one military, the Nobles still sought to make themselves more.

Blood will show. The words tumbled in Tau's mind as he spun his dual practice blades. The words were a promise to the enemy. More, he thought, it was a reminder to Lessers that Nobles were different, that the purity of their blood would reveal itself through their deeds as well as their caste.

Blood will show? Blood, Tau wanted to say, will flow deep and heavy like a flooding river, but there was no time. His swords had crossed with the Indlovu's.

The Noble was taller and much thicker than Tau, which put him in line with a small demon. He, with his shining helm, ornate practice

sword, and sand-spattered shield, attacked hard, meaning to sweep
Tau aside like a blade of grass in a breeze. Tau slipped past the man's
crescent swing and brought both his swords against the Indlovu's
helm. It sounded like a thunderclap and the Noble stiffened and fell.

Tau engaged the next citadel warrior before the first had hit the
sand. The second was cautious. As Tau came within range, he raised his
shield. Tau swung with both blades, his double strike clanging on the
circle of beaten metal. The Indlovu stabbed out below his shield, aiming to ram his dulled blade into Tau's gut. Expecting it, Tau turned the
bronze away with his weak-side sword while swinging with the other,
hard enough to break the Noble's leg. The citadel fighter dropped with
a yell and Tau launched himself at the third man, who turned and ran.

Tau gave chase.

"No!" shouted Uduak.

Blood will show. The words banged around in Tau's head as he
ran down the Indlovu. Blood will show. Like dried sticks, he would
break their pride on the blade of his sword, he would... Tau skidded
to a halt. Including the running man, who had stopped running,
eight Indlovu faced Tau. They had come around the dune, and by
the time he'd seen them, it was too late.

Tau shot a look up the sandy hill. The Enervator and her four
were gone. He looked behind. Uduak, Yaw, Themba, and Muvato
were fighting three Indlovu.

Tau counted. Two down, three behind, eight in front. It meant
five Indlovu, and the Enervator, were unaccounted for. They would
go for Hadith. It had been Tau's job to stop her. He'd failed and
she'd be free to unleash her gift on the rest of his scale.

Tau lowered his swords and heard laughter. It was the Indlovu
who had run from him.

"We've heard of you, Common," he said. "We heard you played
swords with Kellan Okar. How did that go?" He laughed again.
"Probably better than this will."

The eight men closed in, the laughing Indlovu smirking, and
from the looks on their Noble faces, Tau knew the Goddess's mercy
would mean nothing. Their war cry tossed around in his head,
"Blood will show." The words held more than one meaning. Tau

raised his swords, bared his teeth, and told the eight Indlovu the truth. "I have come for you, and I bring Isihogo with me."

He charged. The laughing man was closest. He was also the most prepared. Tau closed the distance between them, the laugher swung, and Tau darted outside the arc of his blade, crossing his swords in an X and leaping on the Indlovu behind the laugher.

The collision knocked the second man back, and Tau's blades fell on either side of his neck, beneath the protection of his helm and above his leather armor. Tau sliced as hard as he could, the dulled edges of his swords drawing cuts just above the man's collarbones. The Indlovu's neck spurted blood and he screamed, dropping his weapons and grabbing for his throat.

Tau spun into the next man, hoping to take him down before the seven remaining Indlovu could encircle him. This Indlovu was staring, slack-jawed, at the blood pulsing from his sword brother's neck. Tau stabbed him as hard as he could. His practice sword could not pierce the Indlovu's thick leather armor, but the strike was vicious and Tau felt the man's ribs break. The Indlovu stumbled and Tau, sensing danger, spun again, whipping his sword around. He missed the laugher, who had come from behind, but Tau carried through with his spin's momentum, catching the one with the broken ribs in the side of the head and sending him flying into the dirt.

The laugher traded his smile for heavy attacks that came with surprising speed. Tau blocked three of the man's cuts, saw him pause, knew he was being baited, and ducked. A sword whizzed over Tau's head and he backpedaled, slamming his elbows into his unseen attacker's chest. The attacker wheezed and Tau stood to his full height as fast as he could, smashing the top of his head into the man's chin. He heard the Indlovu's teeth click together and Tau's head was spattered with sticky wetness. Tau broke away from the man and faced him, ready to continue the fight.

The Indlovu had bitten off the tip of his tongue and his mouth was a soup of blood. Tau went for him, punching the pommel of his sword into the man's throat stone. He gurgled, reeled back, and collapsed, as Tau was struck from behind.

Tau spun. It was the laugher. Tau caught the man's follow-up, but his back burned from the cut he'd taken. The laugher struck again; Tau blocked and was hit on the helmet by one of the other Indlovu. He staggered, then threw a shoulder at the nearest man, trying to break free of the circle in which they'd trapped him. The Indlovu he ran into was as solid as a mountain, and he pushed Tau back.

With no choice but a bad one, Tau moved to the center of the five men surrounding him. The laugher pointed to someone behind Tau and waved the rest forward. Tau spun, blocking the jab aimed for his spine, spun again to stop a head strike, and barely blocked a third blade, arcing for his neck, with the tip of his weak-side sword.

He leapt forward, engaging the laugher, slicing the bastard across the cheek before the Noble could totter out of reach. He whirled to engage the next man and was hit from behind and cut on the calf as the five Indlovu took turns harrying him or fighting defensively, avoiding injury while keeping him trapped between them.

He roared, spinning this way and that, crossing swords with any who came close, taking cuts on his arms and legs and bleeding from everywhere. They couldn't get a clean hit, but they had him penned in and it was only a matter of time.

The laugher, blood and sweat streaming down the side of his face, smiled. "Kill him," he said and all five attacked.

HISTORY

With no chance to beat them all, Tau went for the laugher. The Noble tried to block but wasn't fast enough, and Tau's sword smashed into the wrist on his shield arm, breaking it, twisting the man's smile into a wide-mouthed scream.

Tau pushed on, his other sword lashing out, taking the laugher in the same cheek he'd cut earlier, this time splitting it like a tent's flaps. The Noble fell back and Tau had his escape. He took a step, was hit on the back of the head, saw stars, and found himself on his knees. He tried to stand but was kicked to the ground. He rolled, was kicked again, and a dull blade hammered into his side.

Pain blossoming, Tau tried to scrabble away. He'd lost one of his swords. Could see it. It was a few strides distant. His head was pounding, making it hard to think. He needed his sword, crawled for it, and was kicked back to the dirt.

Nothing left and tasting copper on his tongue, he rolled to his back, looking up at a cloudless sky. The hot sand burned him through the worn patches in his gambeson, and he lay there panting, somehow finding the energy to turn his head and spit blood as the silhouettes of four Indlovu moved to stand over him.

He squinted, trying to see their features past the brightness of the day. He reached for his remaining sword. It was gone.

He'd done well, though, he thought. There had been eight at the start, eight Indlovu in leather armor. And the one with a missing tongue tip, he'd never speak properly again.

"Kill him!" shrieked the laugher from somewhere beyond the four Indlovu. "Kill him!"

"To the Cull with you," Tau said, his words coming out slurred, making him think the hit to the head had been worse than it felt. He saw a sword rise into the air and kept his eyes open, watching it. He'd died before, he thought, trying to convince himself that doing it one last time wasn't special.

"The world burns!" came a shouted mishmash of voices, and the sword, raised above him, came down and into a defensive position.

The four silhouettes closed in around Tau, and he tried to sit, to see what was happening. He couldn't move, though, not with his skull throbbing itself to pieces. He turned his head, seeing stuttering afterimages as he did, seeing the shuffling of Indlovu feet, seeing their heels. They had turned their backs to him.

He heard the clang of swords, and one of the Indlovu tripped, falling on him. The Noble's weight made it difficult to breathe and Tau tried to push the man away. He couldn't. He had no strength left. Another Indlovu fell beside him. This one's eyes were glazed, unseeing.

"Goddess's mercy! Mercy!" called out a Noble, his voice tight. Tau was facing the man's heels, which, as Tau blinked, turned into the soles of leather shoes. The Noble had gone to his knees and dropped his sword. Another blink and the man was pushed into the dirt, facedown, beside Tau.

"I'll have your heads!" That was the laugher, no mistaking his voice.

Tau twisted his head in that direction, lights flashing behind his eyes in time with the throbbing in his head. The laugher was fighting Uduak, Hadith, Kuende, and Mshindi.

He was focusing on Kuende and Mshindi. Not surprising. The two men had shared a womb, they fought like they could read each other's minds, and their preferred weapons were absurdly long swords that always caught an opponent's attention. Still, Tau thought, the laugher was making a mistake, focusing on the twins instead of Uduak or Hadith.

Hadith smashed his shield into the laugher's back, pushing him toward Uduak, who clubbed him, putting him down hard.

"Blood…will show," Tau slurred, the words striking him as funny. They'd won, somehow. They'd beaten the Indlovu, made it into the Queen's Melee, and it had been Hadith's doing. Tau had, as far as he could tell from his position in the dirt, mostly taken a beating. He wanted to laugh, started to, and then the darkness took him.

"Never seen the like," Tau heard a voice say. "There were eight of them. Eight! I wasn't so close, but I was close enough to see him holding them off." It was Anan speaking.

Tau forced his eyes open and had to squint. It was day and bright, but there was no sky. No, that wasn't right. There was a sky. Tau was in a tent.

"I didn't see it. I was positioned to see Hadith tackle the group with the Gifted." That was Jayyed.

The only tents in the Crags this big, thought Tau, were the infirmaries. There were a couple for Lessers and one extra-large and well-equipped one for the Nobles.

"Foolish of them," said Anan, "to send five Indlovu against forty-nine of us."

The tents were open on the sides. Tau hadn't turned his head, but he knew that. Still, it was bloody hot. Bloody bleeding hot.

"Truth? I thought it was clever," Jayyed told Anan. "It would have worked on any other Ihashe scale. How many men would you use to assault a Gifted's position, if you saw she had four Indlovu with her?"

Tau let his eyes close. His head still hurt and it felt like it was twice its normal size.

Anan grunted. "You think they expected more men to splinter off?"

"You would have sent more men," Jayyed said. "I would have sent more men. Hadith, though, Hadith sent Tau, Uduak, and four others."

Anan chuckled. "Goddess take me, but I swear I'd let a Sah priest snip away one of my seeds to have seen the faces of those five Indlovu when they dashed round the dune and charged into forty-nine Ihashe!"

"The entire crawl over they must have been thinking how easy it would be," Jayyed said. "They'd show up, their Gifted would blast as many fighters as she could, and the five Indlovu would take care of the few she couldn't hit. Then they'd go back to help the men they left as ambush."

"Eight Indlovu," said Anan, awe in his voice. "He ran after their inkokeli and into seven others. Then he fought them!"

Jayyed chuckled. "You say it like he won."

"You didn't see it, Jayyed. I know we've watched him in the practice yards. What he does... What he... It was eight Indlovu, though, eight... and he had me believing he could do it. A Noble lost most of his tongue. The other still hasn't woken from the knock Tau gave him... and their inkokeli? Goddess wept, you can see into the fool's mouth through the hole in his cheek."

"Tau is exceptional, I'll grant that. He's no Ingonyama, though, and, being foolish enough to fight eight men, he's lucky to have come out of it with little more than scrapes, cuts, and a demon of a headache. He'll be fine, this time, but if the Indlovu had three more breaths alone with him we'd be attending a burning tonight instead of a celebration."

"Ack, an inyoka has warmer blood," Anan said, "but I know you, and I've never seen you as proud."

There was a pause. It was long enough that Tau thought it might be a good time to let them know he was awake.

"I'm not sure I have been," Jayyed said.

Maybe it wasn't the best time. Tau heard footsteps and then shuffling feet as Jayyed and Anan turned to face whoever was approaching.

"Umqondisi. Aqondise." That was Hadith.

"Hadith, Uduak, Chinedu, Yaw, well met," said Jayyed.

"Awake?" Uduak asked.

"Not yet."

"Why is his head wrapped?" said Yaw. "Was his skull cracked?"

That was, Tau realized, why his head felt so damned heavy. It was bandaged.

"Nothing broken," said Anan. "The bandages are to hold down

swelling and to stop the bleeding. Scalp cuts bleed like a woman on her moon."

Tau had had enough of people talking about him. He turned his head toward the voices. "I'm awake," he rasped. "Can't sleep with Uduak's booming voice in my ear."

"Not near an ear," rumbled Uduak.

"Tau!" said Chinedu, coughing. "We...did it!"

Tau knew, wanted to hear it anyway. "What?"

"The Queen's Melee!" answered Yaw, throwing a fist in the air. "The Queen's Melee! We're in!"

"First time in...," started Hadith. "How long has it been?" Tau was sure Hadith knew how long it had been to the day.

"First time for Lessers in twenty-three cycles," Jayyed told them. "And the Ihashe have never placed at the melee. Never."

"Time for new traditions," Hadith said.

"The world burns," said Yaw.

"It will," Tau promised, receiving broad smiles from everyone but Jayyed, who looked away.

"Goddess's eyes, Tau," Yaw said, "why'd you charge into eight Indlovu?"

"I was chasing one," Tau told him. "Didn't know he had friends."

His sword brothers laughed.

"Good to know you're not completely mad," said Hadith.

Yaw wore a large grin. "I'm telling it the other way. In my story you see all eight of them and you charge! I was there, wasn't I? Who can say it went different?"

Hadith shook his head. "You and your stories." He turned to the big man. "Uduak?"

The big man nodded. "Thirsty."

Hadith stroked his chin. "Thought you might be."

"Only one thing...for it," said Chinedu, coughing and grinning.

"Only one thing," echoed Yaw.

Hadith looked to Tau. "Drinking houses and celebration. We achieved something that may not earn us a page in the history books, but it merits a footnote and a hangover, at least. Tau, if you can stand, you can drink."

"You're not at risk of punishment for the duel," said Jayyed. "Kellan Okar did not seek restitution and the time allowed for him to do so has passed. Make no mistake, if you go to the city, and I'm not sure I should allow it, you need to be careful."

Tau considered going. He needed to see Zuri, but Jayyed's mention of Kellan Okar took him to darker places. He thought about the beating the laugher and his seven Indlovu had given him. They'd intended to kill him and he'd been unable to stop them. He needed more time in Isihogo.

"Not sure I can handle enough liquor to split costs with you drunks," Tau told his brothers.

They looked disappointed, and Hadith wasn't ready to surrender. He tried another angle. "Tau, take the day to yourself. It's earned. We have time. It's two moon cycles to the melee."

"Yes," Anan added. "Today you lot secured our place. Means we don't skirmish again until the melee. That's good for us. We can focus on training hard and careful. No injuries and a well-rested scale, ready for the real show."

"Both the Northern and Southern Isikolo as well as the citadels will attend the melee," Jayyed told them. "It's the largest gathering of initiates in each cycle. The Guardian Council will be in attendance and even the queen will come to observe. It'll be a difficult contest but I can't say I'm not excited to be participating instead of watching."

That settled it. "Aqondise Anan, are any of the other scales returning to the isikolo?" Tau asked.

Anan hesitated, probably thinking Tau should celebrate with the others. "Some of the scales that came to watch will leave soon. The second skirmish is under way and I imagine they'll march once it's over."

"May I return with them? I hope to rest and return to training as soon as possible."

It was Jayyed who nodded assent, and Hadith, his opportunity to sway Tau gone, sucked his teeth. Tau appreciated that his sword brothers wanted him with them. He had to go back, though. He had to be ready if he was going to kill Kellan Okar in the Queen's Melee.

CHAPTER TEN

PRISONERS

It had been a moon cycle since Scale Jayyed's win over Scale Osinachi, and, bolstered by their brethren's accomplishment, Scale Chisomo left the Southern Isikolo to compete for one of the final spots in the Queen's Melee. The isikolo saw them off and several scales accompanied them to the Crags, thinking to see history made again.

Scale Jayyed, their position secured, remained behind to train. Jayyed and Anan agreed the men could not afford to attend. Tau was glad. Time was too short to let any go to waste, even if the past moon cycle had taken a toll.

Every night Isihogo and its demons tempted Tau, offering him his greatest wish in exchange for agony. Every night he accepted their offer and they brutalized him. The horrors of countless deaths lingered and, during the day, he fought to hold on to his sanity. But when the sun fell beneath the earth, Tau embraced the madness. He needed it to fight the monsters.

The Queen's Melee was almost upon them and Tau Solarin, a Common of the Omehi, man of average height, strength, and aptitude, and born without any particular gift for combat, had suffered the underworld and its demons in preparation. The path had its costs, but he had traveled it, coming out the other side with an intuition for fighting that was more like instinct. Tau had gone to the demons as a man, but under their ministrations he'd been transfigured.

On difficult nights, when the underworld came close to breaking him, he tried to remember that. And on that night, a moon cycle from the melee, he had to tell it to himself over and over again.

The evening had been grueling. The demons were hunting in packs and his deaths had been harrowing. Tau was shaken up, but the day's torture was done and he was near the barracks, ready to fall into his cot, hoping for a dreamless sleep. It was his weariness that allowed the thing in the isikolo's main courtyard to get as close as it did.

Tau saw it late but with enough time to snap his hands around the hilts of his swords, ready to draw. It spoke with a human voice.

"Tau? I've been looking for you," said Aqondise Fanaka. "You've been summoned to the umqondisi quarter."

The words made no sense, and before speaking, Tau shut his eyes, hiding the demonic face he saw in place of Fanaka's plain features. "Summoned?"

"You're needed in the dignitary rooms."

Tau didn't know they had dignitary rooms, and though he knew where the umqondisi quarter was, he had never been there. It was where the isikolo's masters had their beds, baths, and meal halls.

Tau forced himself to look at Fanaka's glowing yellow eyes, snout, and dagger-long teeth. "I don't know the way," Tau told him, working hard to keep the distaste from his voice.

"Go into the quarter. The dignitary rooms are the third building on the right."

"Thank you, Aqondise."

"Tau?" the man said, stepping closer, and causing Tau to draw a fingerspan of bronze. Fanaka, eyes wide, retreated, raising empty hands. "Are you well?"

Since Scale Jayyed's last skirmish Tau's reputation had taken on a life of its own. Yaw's stories played some part in that, and it seemed even the aqondise were unsettled around Tau. He let his sword fall back into its scabbard. "Apologies, Aqondise. Apologies. It has been a . . . a trying night."

"Of course," Fanaka said. "You train hard. I understand."

Tau inclined his head. "It's late. Am I expected tonight?"

"You are," Fanaka said, eyes flickering to Tau's scabbarded sword.

"Thank you, Aqondise, for the message and advice." Tau pressed his palms together and touched his fingers to his forehead, saluting. It wasn't necessary, but he hoped the extra respect might repair any damage his odd behavior had caused. Fanaka did a slow blink, recognizing the salute, and he left. It was getting harder, Tau thought, to hold himself...together.

The umqondisi quarter was hidden from plain view behind walls and a gate. The gate was open and there were no guards. They weren't needed. Initiates would not go in uninvited.

The inside of the quarter was well kept, if cramped. The buildings were scrunched together to provide enough living spaces for all the umqondisi and aqondise. Tau counted the buildings as he walked past them. The third on the right was less cramped than the others and it had a bronze door that an artisan had worked over with a map of the peninsula. It showed the peninsula, widest at the door's base and coming to a point near its top.

The metalwork illustrated how the Northern and Southern Mountains separated the land from the Roar. The door also had raised areas, representing the Central Mountains and the Fist. Its knocker was where Palm City would have been.

The whole thing was meant to be impressive, but it reminded Tau of his conversation with Jayyed, who believed the numbers of hedeni to be far greater than estimated. It reminded Tau that, after almost two hundred cycles, the Omehi still had no idea what lay beyond their peninsula. The door depicted their home. It also outlined the borders of their prison.

Tau knocked. He heard footsteps. Light ones. The door's bolts were pulled and it opened without a sound. It must be well oiled, was Tau's last thought before seeing Zuri.

UNMOORED

Zuri looked more beautiful than ever and Tau felt his heart soar. "Why are you here?"

She tensed and her hand whipped out, coming fast for his face or neck. There could be a weapon, he thought, slipping inside the blow, rejecting his swords. There was too little space to wield them. He pulled free the dagger he kept on his belt. Zuri's attack, her open-handed slap, connected with empty air. Tau realized she had no weapon but was already shoving her into the room against the closest wall, his dagger pressed against the soft skin of her neck.

She looked like she might scream. Tau whisked the dagger away, back into his belt.

"Zuri," he said, horrified, retreating. "I'm sorry! I thought…" She was trembling, her lips pursed, her eyes locked on his face. "Zuri?"

Her hands flew up. Tau could have closed the distance, could have knocked her unconscious. He stood there, letting her blast him with enervating energy that sent his soul spinning into Isihogo. On arrival, his swords were out, dual blades reflecting his spirit's golden glow.

He could see Zuri, two strides off, shrouded in darkness. He heard a demon roar to his left, adjusted his stance, fight ready; then Zuri vanished, and he went with her, returned to Uhmlaba.

"Zuri, please," he said, adjusting to the realm switch. She stared at him like he'd returned from the dead. Her reaction confused him. Then he understood. She expected him to be incapacitated by being pushed and pulled into and out of Isihogo.

Her voice was pinched. "Tau, what have you done?"

"What I had to," he said.

She put a hand over her mouth. "What have you done?"

He'd already answered that. "Why did you attack me?"

"Attack you? Attack you? You put a knife to my neck! Have you gone mad?"

Tau could not understand any part of this. She had attempted the first strike and he'd defended himself. Then she'd used her gift against him. She was the aggressor. He was about to tell her that, but some small part of him warned against it. He held his tongue.

Zuri did not. "You abandoned me! Abandoned me after attacking a Greater Noble in the streets of Citadel City. You do something like that and then slither away like…like an inyoka in the grass!" She looked him up and down, as if she saw the inyoka there, wrapped around him. "I thought Okar would kill you. I thought the Indlovu would hang you. You avoid both those fates and I'm foolish enough to feel relief." She poked him in the chest. "I prayed to the Goddess that night, thankful for the mercy She showed to the man that I…that…" She clenched her fists, hit his chest, and made a strange sound in her throat. She glared at him. "Then you avoid me!"

"That's not how—"

"I needed you. I looked for you after the next skirmish, waited in that circle all night, like a fool. Then, not learning my lesson, I was back the next skirmish. I heard you won? They talk about it as if you did. They talk about Tau, who could be Tsiory reborn. Uduak, the Indlovu breaker. Hadith, the military mind to rival a guardian councillor. They talk like you won. I'm not sure, though. I did not see you, to hear it from your lips."

"I have reasons," he said. "The first skirmish, after the duel, I was not allowed—"

"I needed you." Zuri pushed off the wall, bumped him on purpose as she walked past and sat in a chair. It was a nicer chair than Tau had seen anywhere else in the entire isikolo.

She switched topics. "The things I'm learning, the things they have me doing...I worry I can no longer tell right from wrong." She switched again. "I thought I meant something to you. I thought we'd help each other find a path through this. I held on to that thought, but it turns out I don't matter and that makes everything so much worse."

Tau believed it was meant to be his turn to speak. He was unsure what to say. He was sorry he'd hurt her. That had been furthest from his mind. He could say that, but he didn't think it'd come out right, telling her she'd been far from his mind.

Zuri raised her head, speaking as Tau was opening his mouth. He'd missed his chance. "I can't believe I keep thinking about you," she told him. "I want you to know that I'm permitted to journey home twice in my three cycles of Gifted training and that I used one of those trips so I could pass this Goddess-forsaken isikolo. So I could come here, see you, and tell you that I hate you."

That hurt, and Tau dropped to his knees in front of her. "Zuri—"

"I hate you for making me feel this way," she said, eyes brimming with tears.

Tau had no clue how to deal with this. He wanted to reach out for her but didn't want to upset her further. He moved closer, keeping his hands to himself. "Zuri...," he said again, deeming her name safe enough.

"Damn you, Tau. I'm crying. You could at least hold me, you coldhearted bastard."

Even more confused, Tau leaned in and held her, wrapping his arms around her.

She nuzzled into him. "By the Goddess, I hate you," she said, putting her arms around his neck and pulling him closer.

"You have it wrong—"

"What?" Her voice, though muffled, was sharp.

"Eh...you do matter. Very much. More than..." He'd been about to say "almost anything," changed his mind, and finished with, "You matter more than anything."

She nuzzled deeper into his tunic. "That's all you're going to say?"

"Yes? Eh...no," Tau stammered. "I didn't want things to be this way." He wasn't prepared for this. "I wanted a different life...for us."

Zuri looked at him then. "Us?"

"I could have worked in the Onai's keep. Our lives could have been different." Pain flooded him. "You deserve so much more than I am."

"No. You don't get to decide that for me. You can't tell me who is worth my...I feel the way I feel, and that's that."

"It's too late, isn't it?" he said. "We're both wed to war."

"You're a poet now? Why would anyone wed a war?"

"Because that's all life is....Because the most any of us can do is fight to make things a little better, a little more just or safe."

Zuri returned her head to his shoulder. "Just? Safe? I'm not sure that's why we fight, and if it were, I'm not sure we deserve it."

"Why not?" Tau asked, talking more about the two of them.

"Because of the things we do."

It felt like she knew and was talking about what he'd been doing in Isihogo. "We are what we must be," he said, "if we want to make this world even a little better."

"Can a better world be found at the end of a dark path?"

Tau thought his time in Isihogo threatened his sanity, but he'd been with Zuri less than a quarter span and had already lost his moorings.

"I continue to the south in the morning," she said, the sudden switch in topics making his head spin. "My escort is already billeted in the building next to this one."

"Oh," said Tau, sorry to hear her visit would only last the night, but grateful the discussion had settled on firmer ground.

"Why did you grow the scruff?"

"What?"

"The beard. The patches of one anyway."

"Eh...I've been training. There's not been time."

"I see. Too busy to shave...or bathe."

That was unfair. Tau had washed the day before...perhaps two days before.

She laughed. It sounded like music. "Let's go."

"Where?"

"These rooms have a bath. You need one and you need a shave. I'll help."

And, like that, the firm ground was gone, swallowed by a sink-hole. "A bath? Shave? I don't need—"

"Tau, far be it from me to tell others what they do or do not need, but in this case I'll make an exception. Come."

"To the bath?" Tau's voice cracked. He cleared his throat and lowered his voice. "To the bath?"

She took his hand and led him to the next room.

FORBIDDEN

He followed Zuri. It was like he was floating, and he couldn't help but wonder if she was using some strange gift to make him feel this way.

The next room was opulent. It had plush furniture, a raised bed larger than anything Tau had seen before, and the floor was carpeted. A show of this much wealth would have been gross in Umbusi Onai's bedroom, and Tau was reminded of Zuri's new standing.

Zuri seemed to be enjoying his reaction to the space. "An advantage to being Gifted," she said, gracing him with her smile, the one that could turn night to day.

She led him to the next room. It held a personal bath and Tau found the very thought alien. Who on Uhmlaba needed such a thing?

"A personal bath...," Tau mumbled, staring at the bronze tub that had been built into the ground.

"We have them in the Gifted Citadel and so do most Royal Nobles in Palm."

"There's more than one of these?"

"See here," Zuri said, turning a knob near the head, or foot, of the tub; he wasn't sure which was which. The knob turned and water flowed from the attached spout. "It's drawn from the isikolo's well."

Tau walked over in wonder. He put his hand beneath the water and felt it pass over his fingers. It was cool.

"Get in."

"I'm dressed."

Zuri pursed her lips. "Yes, that is a problem."

Tau's eyebrows shot up. "Lady Gifted!"

"Exactly, Lady Gifted! That's an order, Initiate. We will not permit the unwashed in our presence. And you do happen to be both particularly unwashed and particularly in our presence." Zuri waved her arms at his clothes and Tau looked down to make sure she hadn't gifted them away somehow.

"Off," she said, stepping closer to help with the process.

Seeing she wouldn't be deterred, Tau stripped as fast as possible and stepped into tub's cool waters, sitting down to hide as much as he could. He caught Zuri looking him over.

"That's good," she said. "I'll get soap."

"Soap?"

Zuri took a rust-colored brick from a shelf near the bath. She knelt beside the tub and dipped it in the water near Tau's thigh, lingering there, her fingers brushing the flesh of his leg. Tau's face burned as he felt his body reacting. Zuri must have seen it as well but didn't comment and began rubbing the damp brick over his body. It wasn't a brick, though, and, as she stroked it over his skin, it created a lather that smelled of sun-dried grass.

The soap wasn't as large as Zuri's hands, so where she cleaned, she touched, her fingers caressing his body. Tau shifted his hands, placing them over his lower stomach and upper thighs, trying to hide his body's betrayal.

Zuri moved the soap in slow circles over his chest. "So many bruises. So many cuts." She placed the soap in a bowl beside the bath and walked to another shelf. She came back with a tiny bronze dagger. "Face first," she told him, going for his neck.

Tau caught her by the wrist, holding her fast.

"Tau . . ."

He tried to make his fingers relax, but they wouldn't. He was lost in memories of the demon, the one with hand's-length claws that had slit his throat. It morphed into the one with the barbed tail that had ripped his chest open with its teeth. Then that one shifted, becoming the four-armed nightmare that had strangled him, snorting foul breath in his face as he died.

"Tau?"

Hands shaking and mind still in the fog of memory, he managed, somehow, to let go. Zuri moved with deliberateness, letting him see every movement as she brought the dagger to his face. He jerked at the blade's first touch.

"Care! I don't want to cut you."

He closed his eyes, breathing too fast and flinching when the blade kissed his flesh again. Zuri was gentle and fast. She used water to wet his skin and scraped away the scruff he'd grown. To keep her balance as she leaned out and over the tub's edge, she placed a hand on his shoulder.

His eyes were still closed—they had to be for him to ignore a knife so close to his face—but her touch had him reacting again. She finished his face and neck, worked on shaving the stubble from his head, and her hand moved to his chest. As she shaved him, her fingers drew lazy circles and his body's need shifted from arousal to desire to insistence. He groaned in discomfort, shifting in the tub, hoping to find a position that would offer relief, and didn't even realize when Zuri was done.

She moved to the side of the tub and reached for him, the fingers of her right hand touching, then holding his manhood. Her caress made him jump, sloshing water out of the tub as his eyes flew open.

"Tau...," Zuri said, her face determined, the same look she'd worn the first time they'd kissed. Her eyes were large but hooded, lips apart and full. Tau thought to say something, but her hand was gliding up and down, reducing his world to her fingers.

Zuri kicked off her slippers and eased into the waters, her black Gifted robes still on. She came near, sitting over his legs, her clothes floating around them. He could feel the bare skin of her thighs on his, and her left hand was around his neck, her right still stroking. She leaned toward him, closing her eyes, and she kissed him.

Her lips, her body, they brushed against him. And, where once the fingers of her hand, rising and falling, had been enough, they became too little. Tau's own hands drifted to Zuri's hips, and she rose onto her knees, using the hold she had to guide him to her.

"We can't," Tau said, knowing she would have to be the one to stop, because he couldn't. "It's forbidden."

She kissed his forehead, his cheek, his lips, and, fumbling at first, she drew him inside her.

"Goddess...by the Goddess...," Tau said, feeling her sheathe him.

"Is this so wrong?" Her voice was breathy. "Why would this... Ah!" She closed her eyes, let her head fall back. "Why would this be..."

They found a rhythm and all the demons in Isihogo could have assaulted the bathing room and Tau would not have stopped. They moved together, kissing, caressed by the cool waters, suspended in ecstasy. Then Tau found there was more.

It was as if he was caught in an avalanche, picking up speed and force. Zuri kept pace. No, she was the one making the pace.

"Yes," she whispered, her lips near his ear. "Yes, Tau. Yes!"

Her voice, the need in it, did something to him. The avalanche became a flood and, eyes squeezed shut, he felt pressure, pleasure, and pain. His ardor coalesced, crowned. It drew him into her, overcoming him until, like a drowning man piercing the surface to take a breath, the tension burst, granting release.

"Goddess wept," Tau groaned as he looked into Zuri's fire-bright eyes. He was drained of... everything, but felt whole. "Zuri..." Her name, it meant something new, something he wanted to understand. He lifted a hand from the waters and touched her face, wishing everything and everyone gone, wishing life could be the two of them and nothing more.

"Tau," Zuri said. "Tau, you can't stop." Zuri was still moving.

"Neh?"

"Tau, I need—" She grabbed him by the chin, making him look at her. "Don't stop!"

His need was vanishing with astonishing speed.

"Tau? Tau!" Zuri said.

He moved his hand back into the waters, took hold of her hips, and moved, syncing up with her again.

"Yes!" she said. "Like that! Like that! Like . . . Oh! Oh, Tau!"

Her nails dug into his neck; she arched her back and pressed her knees into his sides. He felt her body around him, almost forcing him from her, and she threw her head back, crying out so loudly he had to stop himself from putting a silencing finger to her lips. Then, with one last spasm, she collapsed on him, shaking. Tau was about to check that she was well, when she kissed his chest.

"Can you go again?" she asked, lips tickling his collarbone.

"I . . . Give me a few breaths?"

"Yes, a few breaths. This time in the bed."

"The bed?"

"Yes, I want to try there."

Tau nodded and Zuri shifted, unsheathing him. She stood in the tub and wriggled out of her robes, letting them fall into the bath. Her dark skin was smooth, her breasts round, firm, and as perfect as the rest of her. Ananthi couldn't be more beautiful.

"I'm ready . . . for the bed," Tau said.

Zuri got out of the tub and walked to the bedroom. "Come, then," she said, and he did.

SURVIVAL

Some spans later, hot, sweaty, and more at peace than he'd been in recent memory, Tau held Zuri close in the oversized bed. "Why can't these moments make up the whole of life?"

She laughed. "Wait another span or two. You'll be hungry and all you'll want will be your next meal."

"You're all I need to survive," he told her.

She rolled her eyes and punched him in the arm. "Silly man."

He pulled her close, kissed her, then kissed her again, enjoying her nearness. "I feel happy."

"Why do you make it sound like a question?"

Tau rubbed his shaven head. "Can it last?"

"Nothing lasts. We have these breaths, though." Her eyes roamed his face. "You take yourself to Isihogo?"

He nodded, confirming her guess.

"Tau, do you have any idea how dangerous that is? If the demons find you they'll attack and won't stop until your soul thinks itself dead."

"I fight them."

"You can't, they're immortal. They—"

"No, I didn't say I could. I do. I go to Isihogo to fight them."

Zuri shot up into a sitting position. "What?"

He sat up as well. "Time is different there—"

"Yes, thank you, I taught you—"

"I needed more time to—"

"To what, Tau? To what?"

"To train, to fight, to become more than the time in my life can make me."

"You fight the demons? Can . . . can they be killed?"

"No. I don't know if they're immortal or immune to attack or . . . I can hold them back, but . . ." He trailed off.

"They get you in the end," she said. "Each time you go?"

He nodded.

"And you keep going?"

He nodded.

"How many times?"

He shook his head.

"You don't know? You've lost count? By the Goddess." She reached out, touching him on the shoulder. "Tau, if you have sense left, you have to stop. It's dangerous."

"I can handle it."

"No, you can't."

"I'm fine," he lied.

"The shaving knife in the tub . . ."

"I'm fine," he said again.

"For how much longer?"

"For as long as it takes!" he said, his tone making her draw back.

She stared at him, eyes flitting about his face. "The Omehi don't deserve the sacrifices you're making."

"You think too much of me."

"It's for vengeance, then? You'd see your soul burn for it? If so, you're adding to the same evil you think your vengeance will lessen."

"It's for justice, and for that I'll face any suffering."

"Tau—"

"You think the world we live in is good enough? This same world where we can never be together? They will take you to a Royal Noble. He'll force himself on . . ." Tau wrestled for control. "He'll try for a pure bloodline, for future Gifted."

"Please—"

"What am I to do when that happens? Should I bring tributes for the children you'll bear?"

She watched him.

"We're worth more than that," he said.

Zuri put her hands on either side of his face. "I'm here with you now, aren't I?" she said.

"Are you allowed to be?"

"I'm here."

"For how long?"

"For these breaths."

Tau shook his head. "They aren't enough! I want more. I want to marry the woman I love, to have children with her, to watch them grow... with my father beside me."

"Tau..."

"If I can be better than them, then any of us can be. The Nobles? They are great because we are on our knees. No more. I choose to stand."

She lowered her head, eyes closed. "And what if all we're owed, Lesser and Noble, are these breaths? What if the Cull happened for a reason and Xidda isn't a test we're meant to pass?"

"How can you say that?"

Zuri opened her eyes. "Because I've been at the citadel."

Tau waited, letting silence prompt her.

"Gifted...," she said. "Gifted are born with differences in their ability to shroud themselves in Isihogo. The weakest among us can enervate, grabbing power and releasing it quickly. The stronger of us can enrage, taking energy from Ananthi's prison and using it to greatly empower a man, so long as the blood of a Greater or Royal Noble runs through his veins. Others can edify, delivering messages across distances in the mists of Isihogo that would take days in Uhmlaba.

"But the most powerful of us can entreat, calling out to any living creature that can reason. It's why the hedeni bring no beasts to war with us, and it is why, in the early days, they burned our valley to ash. They sought to kill as many of us and as many animals as possible."

"The hedeni burned the peninsula?"

"Down to the dirt. It's why we have little else but insects, reptiles, and the few horses and other mammals that the Royal Nobles saved and now breed."

"Can you entreat a man?" Tau asked, focusing on the thing she'd said that worried him most. Even speaking the words felt wrong, as if he might give the citadel a new and twisted thing to try.

"It can be done," Zuri said. "But it is not. Entreating is an opening up of souls. It connects the Entreater and the entreated. Creatures of high reasoning, like women and even men, can fight the connection or hold it."

"Fight it? Hold it?"

"If I were to entreat you, I would be half here and half in Isihogo. I would have to draw power from the underworld for as long as I wished to hold sway over you."

"This is why you have to be powerful? You need to hide from the demons the entire time."

"Yes, but it's more dangerous than that. If I entreated you, then you could hold me in Isihogo just as I hold you. You could keep me there after I'd exhausted my ability to hide."

"Until the demons found you?"

"Yes," Zuri said. "Yes. And ... it's why one of us dies every time a dragon is called."

Tau started. "What?"

Zuri licked her lips, never looking away from his face. "The Gifted hold an immature dragon captive under the Guardian Keep."

"They do what!?"

"The youngling is chained, masked, and kept enervated by a group of Gifted called a coterie. There are tunnels connecting the Guardian Keep and the Gifted Citadel. The tunnels give us constant access to the youngling. They allow us to rotate out wearied Gifted and bring in fresh ones. In this way, we keep the youngling enervated indefinitely."

Tau could barely speak. "Why?"

"To control the Guardians. We think they may originally have come into our world through Isihogo."

"They're demons?" asked Tau.

"Don't we believe they were created by Ananthi?"

"I . . . I also believed they helped us willingly and not because we held one of their children captive."

Zuri grimaced, unable to argue the point. "An Entreater can enter Isihogo and mimic the cry of a Guardian youngling. All Entreaters are taught this. When the Guardians hear the cry they come looking for their missing child. Once the dragons are close, we entreat them and they, being caught, latch onto us in turn."

"Us?"

"We cannot allow our most powerful to die every time we need the Guardians. Entreaters work with five other Gifted and together they are called a Hex. Each member of the Hex is powerful enough to be an Entreater in their own right, and when a Guardian is called, they entreat one another."

"They link souls?"

"In a way. It's done so that, when the Guardian pierces the shroud of the actual Gifted entreating it, the rest of the Hex can step in."

"To fight?"

"No. Guardians, like demons, cannot be defeated in Isihogo. The Hex steps in to save the Entreater and the Guardian takes one of the five remaining members of the Hex instead. We call it a backlash."

"And the Gifted, the one being backlashed? If she's entreating the other members of the Hex, she'll be holding energy from Isihogo."

"She will."

"Then, when she's killed in Isihogo . . . ," Tau said.

Zuri nodded.

"That's why . . . That's why the Gifted in Daba died in blood? It was a demon-death."

Zuri nodded.

"How does the dragon decide which member of the Hex to hold in Isihogo? Why doesn't it kill you all?"

"The five remaining members of the Hex are linked. They look like a single soul to the Guardian and they fight among themselves, twisting energy from Isihogo, using it against each other until someone's shroud collapses. When the first shroud fails, the other Gifted force all the energy they hold into the failure's soul."

"You make the defeated Gifted brighter."

"As bright as the sun."

"And the demons attack."

"Every time a dragon is called, someone dies."

"Goddess wept," Tau said, his voice little more than a whisper. "And we hold one of their young to compel them to come when called?"

"We do."

"That means we've held their child captive for near on two hundred cycles?"

"We have."

"This is a horror story."

"This is the story of our survival," Zuri said. "Tau, the Gifted Citadel sits half-empty. We cannot replace the women we lose to the never-ending fighting and the backlashes. Every cycle we find fewer Gifted at the testings, and every cycle the hedeni attack more frequently and in greater force. These days, even raids can require a Guardian defense."

"Tell me you can't..."

"I'm powerful."

"Tell me—"

"I'm slated to become an Entreater when my education is complete. My training for it has already begun."

"No."

"My first military assignment will be as an Enrager. It is difficult to master entreating. I have time. "

"Until what? Until they bind you to a Hex? So you can fight the women you trained with to feed a dragon's wrath?"

"I'm powerful."

"How powerful are the rest?"

Zuri's melancholy smile was her only answer. They sat for a while. They held each other. In time, Zuri slept. Tau did not.

He was awake to see the sun, its shadows creeping across the room's carpeted floor like skulking demons. His sword brothers would be in the practice yards. They would wonder where he was. He needed to leave and wanted nothing less. He kissed Zuri.

"Already?" she said.

"Already."

"We leave for Kerem after breaking our fast," she told him, "but I'll be in the Crags for the melee, along with the rest of the Gifted initiates and preceptors. Be safe. Find me in the city after."

"I will," he promised. He kissed her, readied himself to leave, and at the door to the bedroom, he tried to bind her image to his mind. She was so much more than he deserved. He walked through the door.

"Tau." The worry in her voice stopped him. "Be careful. Something's coming, a reckoning for the things we've done."

CHAPTER ELEVEN

COUNSEL

Zuri had been gone for days, but her look, her feel, the smell of her skin, they stayed with Tau. He was walking with his sword brothers to the mess hall after the morning's training and she kept coming to mind, distracting him, making it difficult to pay attention.

Hadith was talking over strategies for the Queen's Melee. He was worrying over their chances, trying to determine the optimal tactics for a contest whose rules were as different from standard skirmishes as those skirmishes were from actual war.

The melee was the ultimate test for the Omehi's best fighting men and, as a consequence, Gifted did not participate. That should have tilted the competition in favor of the Lessers, but it was not the only significant rule change.

Every qualifying team began the melee with a full scale. Tau and his sword brothers would face no Gifted, but they would fight fifty-four Lessers against fifty-four Nobles. The last time Lessers had participated in the melee was twenty-three cycles ago. Jayyed had been that scale's inkokeli and they'd been crushed. Seven of Jayyed's men died and thirteen were injured badly enough that they did not serve a single day of active military duty. They placed sixteenth out of sixteen.

Tau had no idea how his scale would perform. He did not know if men would die, though he imagined some would, and it would be ridiculous to expect them to rank, coming at least third out of sixteen. What Tau did know was that he would keep Scale Jayyed in the melee until he had the opportunity to meet Kellan Okar in battle. After he'd taken care of Kellan, after the Queen's Melee, the initiates of Scale Jayyed would be confirmed as men of the Omehi military. That was when Tau would challenge Abasi Odili. He was ready.

These were Tau's thoughts as he walked past the central courtyard in the Southern Ihashe Isikolo. These were his thoughts when the academy's primary gates opened and in marched eighteen full-blooded Indlovu, led by Dejen Olujimi, protector and escort for the man he accompanied, protector and escort for chairman of the Guardian Council, Abasi Odili.

Odili was as Tau remembered, handsome, regal, a man with the discipline to control himself and his surroundings. He had not changed at all. He was perfectly preserved, a golden idol of Noble malevolence.

Tau saw him and wanted nothing more than to kill him. His hands slipped to the hilts of his practice blades.

"Tau!" Uduak's voice sounded distant.

"What's he doing?" he heard Hadith say.

A thick hand grabbed his wrist. Tau turned, barely able to register that it was Uduak beside him.

Uduak's face changed when he saw the look in Tau's eyes. "No," he said, his grip tightening.

Tau's jaw clenched, the bones creaking. A hand fell on his shoulder. His head swung. It was Hadith.

"Come away now," Hadith said. "Come."

"Those . . . men," Tau said, seeing demons in Abasi and Dejen's places.

"Come away," Hadith said.

"Food," Uduak said, pulling Tau along.

Tau let his sword brothers pull him to the mess hall, his mind a jumble, seeing demons everywhere, as if Isihogo and Uhmlaba had become one. They sat him at a long table. They brought him food. They watched him eat.

"What was that, outside?" Hadith asked. "You looked like you were about to kill every last one of those Nobles."

"Just two."

Hadith fumbled his spoon. "Wait! You were actually thinking of attacking them?"

"Leave it," Tau said.

"I don't think I can," Hadith said. "I think you need to explain."

"He killed my father."

"Neh? Who did?" asked Hadith.

"The guardian councillor, Abasi Odili. He had his Body stab my father through the heart at a citadel testing."

"Why?" asked Uduak.

"I sparred with and beat a Noble."

Uduak tilted his head, no doubt trying to recall conversations about Tau's old life. "Jabari?"

"No. Jabari was…Jabari is my friend. It was an incompetent named Kagiso Okafor. He was a terrible swordsman. He tried to injure me and I stopped him."

"The Nobles took offense?" asked Hadith.

"Odili put me in a blood-duel against Kellan Okar. The councillor wanted me to die for knocking a useless nceku on his ass."

"Your father took your place," Hadith concluded.

Tau was having trouble breathing and closed his eyes. "Okar cut away my father's hand. Odili's Body put bronze through his chest."

"And now?" Uduak asked. "Revenge? You'll be killed. Your family too."

"The melee," Hadith told Uduak. "Then graduation. Then a blood-duel."

Hadith had pieced it together. Uduak, still thinking it through, shot him a questioning look.

"Kellan Okar fights in the melee," said Hadith. "He can die in it. Nobles do every cycle. After the melee, we become full-bloods. Full-bloods can blood-duel anyone in the military, even the chairman of the Guardian Council."

Uduak made a strangled sound.

Tau kept his eyes on his plate. "They killed my father."

"They did," Hadith said, tone neutral.

"I'm going to kill them."

"Listen," said Hadith, "you have to retreat a few paces, but here's what we can do—"

"We?" said Tau.

"Yes, we," said Hadith. "We're brothers. And, we're going to do nothing, for now. Leave the guardian councillor to his business. You get caught and everyone sharing your blood dies. Tau, I'll promise you something. Let us take care of Okar as a scale. If we face him in the melee, we'll punish him for his part in your father's death."

"I don't need your help."

"Really? 'Cause from where I'm sitting, it looks like you do." Hadith put a hand on Tau's shoulder. "You can't actually think that the rules the Nobles made up to protect themselves will protect you. What do you think happens if you gut Okar in the melee? What do you think will actually happen if, as a full-blood, you challenge the chairman of the Guardian Council to a fight to the death?"

Hadith had gotten louder, Uduak shushed him, and he took a breath. "Let us help. I'll think of something. We can punish Kellan, at least."

"At least?" said Tau.

"Be at peace, just for now. Let me think. Agreed?"

Tau was wound tight as rope, his posture and the set of his mouth as clear and instinctual a warning as any man could give.

Hadith would not be cowed. "Swear it, Tau," he said. "You risk us in this too. Swear it on your father and know that I have my own reasons to hate Nobles."

Hadith Buhari, specifically chosen to be in Scale Jayyed; Tau could guess his reasons. Like the rest, he was a cross-caste, his mother likely taken by force. Hadith would consider it a dark secret, a shameful beginning, thought Tau. It made Hadith think he hated the ones whose blood he shared, but he did not know what hate really was. Tau would help with that. He'd become Hadith's shining example.

"I'll do nothing while Odili is in the isikolo walls," he said.

"On your father," Hadith reminded him.

Tau nodded, stood, and left. A chair scraped behind him and he heard Uduak's heavy footfalls as the big man shadowed him. Avoiding the central courtyard and the Indlovu, Tau returned to the training grounds.

Uduak didn't need to play escort. Tau would keep his word. No harm would come to Odili while he was in the isikolo's walls because Tau knew a Royal Noble like him wouldn't spend a night among Lessers. He'd leave that same day, and Tau would follow.

STONES

J ayyed had not been at practice all day, and in the mess hall that evening, rumors spread, branching like a tree's roots. It was said the chairman of the Guardian Council had spoken with Jayyed. It was said Jayyed was to accompany him when he left the isikolo.

Many in the scale were proud of this, glad to see their mentor respected enough to be called upon by their military's leadership. Tau was not pleased. If the rumors were true, Jayyed would be with Odili when Tau followed him.

At dusk, the Indlovu prepared to march. Jayyed was with them. The initiates, their training day over, returned to the barracks. Tau went too, then gathered his swords and left the barracks, as Hadith joked and drank with the men. This was usual. Tau always trained in the evenings.

On his way to the barracks door, Tau noticed Uduak watching him. Uduak had seen Tau sheath his real swords in the scabbards he was wearing. Tau had his father's razor-edged blade on one hip and his grandfather's sword on the other. Uduak's gaze lingered on the weapons and their eyes met. Uduak said nothing, but Tau could feel the big man's stare on his back as he walked out of the barracks and into the hot night.

Tau waited in the grasslands beyond the practice yards until he

heard the convoy of Indlovu. Their armor, gear, and weapons clat-
tered as they marched from the isikolo, and, seeing demons that
weren't there, Tau followed.

The men marched north. Tau gave them a good lead. The grasslands did not offer cover and he could not risk being seen. After
a couple of spans, he realized they were closing in on the Crags
and Citadel City. The rumors were right. Odili had come to bring
Jayyed back to the Guardian Council.

That made things difficult. Tau would have to sneak into the city
and was already having trouble keeping his head straight. He itched.
It was the first night he'd not gone to Isihogo, and lost in worry over
how much he wanted to go and suffer, he was almost seen.

They'd arrived at the base of the Crags and the Indlovu had
stopped marching. Tau was too close and one of them turned in his
direction. He dropped to a crouch in the tall grass, hiding and praying to the Goddess that he'd not been seen.

A breath passed and Tau feared he was discovered, but the man
turned away, peering out in the dark at something else. That was when
Tau heard the newcomers, the sounds of their approach resounding
off the rocky ground. Tau crawled closer and did not like what he saw.

The Indlovu had been joined by another unit, and this unit was
guarding two on horses. Tau peered into the twilight, surprised that
he recognized the riders. The horses carried the queen's champion
and the KaEid of the Gifted Citadel. Behind them walked three
hooded Gifted and two men wearing the blackened leather armor of
the Ingonyama.

Tau considered slipping away. Something far beyond him was
taking place and it made him uneasy to think that the Chosen he
was stalking, once joined by the Gifted, had enough power to take
on four scales of Ihashe.

The champion's horse made a noise with its nose and Tau almost
leapt from his hiding spot. He worried the beast could tell he was
there, but none of the others seemed alarmed. Tau calmed his nerves
and stayed put, watching the champion for any signs that the animal
had alerted him to Tau's presence.

The champion was as Tau remembered, tall and strong. His

shaven scalp was edged with gray stubble that seemed to shimmer in the dim moonlight, and he had his guardian sword at his hip. The KaEid, of an age with Champion Abshir Okar, was graceful and attractive, though stern. He could not see the faces of the hooded Gifted, worried Zuri could be one of them, and rejected the notion. She should still be in Kerem, and these were some of the most important people in the peninsula. The Gifted with the KaEid would be full-blooded, not initiates, not Zuri.

Then, after a brief discussion that Tau could not hear, the eighteen Indlovu were left to guard the horses and gear as Jayyed, Odili, the queen's champion, and KaEid began to climb the Crags with the three Gifted and three Ingonyama. The group had split, and the horses, whose capabilities Tau did not understand, had been left behind. Tau considered going home but rejected the notion. He had to be careful, exceedingly so, but he'd see the night through.

Odili and his group took the easiest and widest path up the Crags. Tau could not follow that way. The horse-guarding Indlovu would see him. He had to sidle back and around the Crags until he found a section he could climb, unseen. It wasn't a path, but climbing the Crags was no challenge to a man born and bred in the Southern Mountains.

Odili's group went up, past the battlegrounds and into the Fist itself. It was well past the middle of the night and Tau couldn't shake the feeling that something was wrong. The feeling increased when he saw movement higher up the climb. It was a person, weaving between the larger rocks.

At first, Tau thought the group he was following must have a scout up there. That made no sense, though. How had the scout gotten so far ahead? And the scout seemed to be watching down the climb, toward Odili's group, instead of watching up and guarding against others.

Tau picked up the pace, getting ahead of Odili's group and closer to where he'd last seen the scout. He did his best to be quiet. He could climb well enough but was no ranger, and if discovered, he was dead.

He clambered over a large rock and was about to work his way over its even bigger brother when he heard his quarry send a loose stone skittering. She cursed to herself and Tau froze. He'd not been able to understand her words.

He swung his head in the direction of her voice and, unable to believe his eyes, slid behind a large rock, hiding. He heard more voices, these ones on their way up the mountain. These he could understand, since they were speaking Empiric.

Odili's group had arrived and were walking into the clearing below the rock behind which Tau hid. The clearing rose to a crest and the group were entering it from its lowest point. Unlike Tau, they couldn't see over the rise. Unlike Tau, they couldn't see the hedeni scout and the rest of her raiding party.

ABOMINATION

Tau's heart hammered. He had to warn Jayyed. By the Goddess, he'd have to warn Odili. He swore under his breath. Even if he saved all their lives, they'd hang him for being there. Time was short, the hedeni were a few steps from view, and their party was larger than Odili's. Odili had Gifted and Ingonyama. That made some difference, though not enough if the group was ambushed. Tau made his decision and began to draw bronze; he'd take out the scout first.

"We are here," shouted Abshir Okar, the queen's champion, as Tau's swords were halfway from their scabbards.

"You are here," came the response from the man at the front of the hedeni raiding party, in broken Empiric.

Tau held, hoping the scout had not heard his bronze whisper against his scabbards. All was quiet beyond the large rock where she hid. A good sign. Tau checked the clearing. Kellan's uncle had stepped into its center.

"We have come in good faith," Champion Okar said.

It seemed the hedeni were expected.

"We shall see," the hedeni man replied, stepping into the clearing as well.

Tau started. It was the burned man who had led the raid at Daba.

"Warlord Achak," Champion Okar said.

"I see you, champion of the Fire-Demon Queen," Achak said, as a few members of his party crested the rise.

Warlord Achak, as Abshir named the burned man, had more than sixty warriors that Tau could see. The fighters were mixed, women and men. Most carried cruel-looking spears, their shafts tipped with jagged bronze.

Abshir stopped a few strides from the clearing's center. Achak did the same on his side. The hedeni warlord wore leathers, but unlike the Indlovu's, it held no bronze plate for protection. He had no helmet and held his spear well, a fighter.

"My queen accepts the terms, the timeline," said Abshir loud enough for the warlord, his party, the Ingonyama, and the Gifted to hear. "She will gather our military leadership to arrange for a drawing down of our forces. We will have peace with the Xiddeen."

Tau had been swallowing and almost choked on his spit.

The champion cleared his throat and continued. "As agreed, upon peace, Queen Tsiora will proclaim Kana, son of Warlord Achak, to be the regent of the Xiddan Peninsula. He will share power with Queen Tsiora during the merging of the Omehi and Xiddeen." The warlord nodded at this. "Once done, Queen Tsiora will swear fealty to the shul, who will counterswear, in the presence of his entire Conclave, to protect and care for all Chosen, all Omehi."

There was a pause, the warlord waiting for more.

"With peace secured and Chosen safety promised," Champion Abshir said, "the Guardians will leave Xidda."

Tau sat back on his haunches, leaning against the rock behind him for support.

The warlord spoke, his accent and warped Empiric difficult to understand. "The greatest Conclave in memory has gathered. All Xiddeen stand together to see peace done or enemies destroyed. You, in small valley, cannot count the people, more than the sands that touch the endless water, who stand against you."

Abshir did not react. Tau imagined he'd expected a speech of this sort.

"Heed," the warlord continued, his voice rumbling like falling stones, "the fire demons must leave. There can be no peace without this."

It took Tau a breath to understand that the burned man was using the Empiric word for demons to describe the dragons.

Abshir Okar had something else on his mind. "The queen requires proof of your claims."

The warlord signaled behind him and, on cue, a skinny hedeni came forward. The skinny man was with a warrior. The warrior was male, well built, and just a head shorter than an Omehi Noble. He looked familiar, resembling the warlord, but with no burns, fewer curse scars, and much younger.

It was Kana, the warlord's son, and Tau had seen him at Daba too, when he'd captured the Gifted there. The same Gifted he now led, bound and blindfolded, into the clearing.

Tau's stomach turned when he saw her, and he had to stop himself from rushing the clearing. The Gifted had been tortured. She was missing a hand, she dragged one leg behind her, and when the blindfold was removed, Tau saw that one of her eyes had been burned away. Her hair was dirty, knotted, and she was hunched in a way that told him it was more than fear that kept her back bowed. Tau thought back over the past cycle since he'd seen her at Daba. He thought over all that had happened to him, in the many days, and realized that her days had been worse. He had suffered in Isihogo, but when he was cast out, so was the pain. She lived with hers, constantly.

"You filthy hedeni nceku," cursed the KaEid at the warlord, coming forward into the clearing as she did. "The Goddess's curse is too little!"

Achak's back stiffened, the burned side of his face quivering. "Leash the demon whore," he said to Abshir.

The KaEid took another step. "You believe any man could hold me? You believe yourself safe?" Abshir placed a hand, palm out, toward the KaEid, asking for calm. She took no notice, closing in on the warlord, about to cross the clearing's center.

Kana, the warlord's son, had a spear in his hand, and several of the Xiddeen warriors moved forward. Achak himself showed no signs of worry. He was waiting. Waiting, Tau knew from experience, for an excuse to do violence.

"Taia," Guardian Councillor Abasi Odili said to the KaEid, "this is not the place or time."

Abasi was chairman of the Guardian Council, and Tau had limited knowledge of military politics, but he knew Odili could not command the KaEid. And yet, she heeded his call for calm. She stopped advancing and turned her gaze to the tortured Gifted, her face softening. In reaction, the warlord's son lowered his spear, and the other fighters who had come into the clearing slipped back to their places.

"Champion," said the warlord, "I have your proof. You will bear witness and take word to your young queen, telling the tale with a tongue cold with fear. And I would have your demon whores prove their worth as well." The warlord flicked a hand at the tortured woman behind him. "This one has no more to give."

Then, his body still square to Abshir, still ready to draw down and fight, Tau noted, the warlord turned his head to his son and the skinny cursed man. He nodded at them.

The skinny man, bare chested, with a body thin as a whip, jangled as he raised his hands, the large golden bangles on his wrists clattering. He pointed to the warlord's son, Kana, and began chanting in the savage tongue. It took a breath, no more, and Kana began to change. His muscles multiplied and grew. The bones on his face thickened, hardening and protruding, stretching the skin that covered them to its limits. The skinny one began chanting louder, and Kana groaned as the enraging worked its twisting gift on his body. His spine went rod straight and Tau could swear he heard it creak as it stretched out, increasing his height by two or three handspans.

The Omehi in the clearing shuffled back, but not from Kana. Omehi understood the nature of an enraged man. They moved away from the skinny savage who wielded the gift. He was the abomination.

Abshir couldn't contain his horror. It was writ large on the stoic Greater Noble's face. The KaEid was in worse shape. She stared in disbelief, a child whose nightmares had stepped into the world.

"The Goddess wept," said one of the Ingonyama, intertwining his thumbs, fingers outstretched, making the dragon's span. If the religious warding symbol had any power, it was not in evidence in the clearing. Kana's transformation completed and he'd become monstrous. He towered over everyone else, his muscles bunching and rippling.

Tau heard crying. It was the tortured Gifted.

Achak spoke. "You see. We found a way back to nyumba ya mizimu. The Xiddeen can touch the spirit world again!"

TERMS

The KaEid could barely speak. "How many can—"

"We can end you. You see that now," the warlord said, speaking to Champion Abshir and over the KaEid. "Send us the one who will teach the magic that makes warriors kneel."

"What you have done violates natural law," KaEid Oro said. Achak ignored her and the KaEid seethed. "Are you ready, hedeni?" she asked. "Are you prepared for what we bring?"

The KaEid signaled one of her Gifted. The Gifted dropped her hood and entered the clearing, and Tau found himself looking at a familiar face. The woman, a little older than he was, resembled Jayyed. It was his daughter, Jamilah. It had to be.

Tau looked away from her, finding Jayyed at the edge of the clearing. The sword master looked like he was being strangled, like he was close to running into the clearing after her. Jamilah's hood had been up. He must not have known she was with the KaEid, and Jamilah had said nothing to the father she hadn't seen in so many cycles.

Jamilah, dressed in the black robes of the Gifted, stood next to the KaEid, and without ceremony or announcement, she raised her hands and blasted every hedeni that Tau could see in a tidal wave of enervation. All of them but the skinny Gifted man dropped like they'd been cut down.

Then, in less time than it took to blink, Jamilah cut the wave. The skinny Gifted man, already half in Isihogo, was the only savage still on his feet. Even Kana, fully enraged, had gone down. The warlord, one knee in the mud, fought to get himself under control. He was furious.

"We should kill you all," he hissed.

The KaEid readied herself. She wanted to fight as much as he did. Abshir stepped forward, throwing a hard look her way, before sinking to the earth in front of the warlord. They were both on the ground, both on their knees.

"Peace is what has been asked of us. Peace," Abshir said.

The warlord, swaying, regained his feet. He looked like he might strike the champion. Abshir did not move away. He waited a breath, ceding power and dignity by staying down.

"Queen's Champion," the warlord said, voice shaking. "Were I the shul, did I lead my people, I would feed this valley's soil with the blood of every invader I could find."

The venom in the warlord's words unsettled Abshir and he stood. "Will you honor the peace?"

Tau saw it then. The warlord did not want it. He wanted to exterminate the Omehi. The meeting was not his idea.

"The Xiddeen," Warlord Achak told Abshir, "will uphold the terms." He looked to the KaEid and Jayyed's daughter. "We offer this because we are not evil." He rolled his shoulders, shrugging away the last of Isihogo. "The shul wishes an end to the war. He wishes the fire demons, who poison our earth and throw the spirit world into turmoil, gone. He wishes for Xidda to be as it was."

Abshir inclined his head. "Let us do our leaders' will, then."

Achak waved a hand at his shaman, who released the tortured Gifted and gave her a push. She stumbled and looked back at him, unsure if she could trust his intent.

"Come, Nsia," said the KaEid, her face filled with worry. "Come home." Nsia didn't move. "Come home, my child."

Nsia glanced once more at her captors and, as if she feared being stopped, limped as fast as she was able to the KaEid. She cried as she went, the sounds almost inhuman.

When she got to the KaEid, she fell into her arms and Taia Oro held her. Her face was hidden by Nsia's soiled hair, but Tau saw the powerful woman's shoulders shaking. The KaEid was crying.

Fixated on the Gifted women, Tau did not notice that Kana had crossed the clearing with Nsia.

"The shul honors me," Warlord Achak said, his tone sounding anything but. "He chose Kana to finalize terms with your queen. He chose my son to rule with her, over your people." Achak spoke as if reciting an unpleasant but memorized lesson. "Sanctified by the gods, the shul has declared the peaceful joining of our people to be my firstborn son's xanduva, his lifelong duty. My son joins your people in deed and blood. He will marry your queen." Achak was breathing like he'd run a race. "May the gods bless their union."

The same Ingonyama as before made the dragon's span at Achak's blasphemous mention of gods. Champion Abshir Okar, face impassive, nodded at the warlord's words. Jayyed looked aghast. He was focused on Jamilah and nothing else. The KaEid, holding Nsia as if to shield her from the world, eyed the hedeni with hate.

Tau took it all in and couldn't help but think that Hadith would have admired the Xiddeen shul. From the warlord's words, it was clear that the shul's power was not absolute. To make peace work, the hedeni ruler needed Achak on his side, but Achak wanted to eradicate the Chosen. To have his peace, the shul had made Achak need it too, and in so doing, he had turned an opponent into an ally.

By arranging a marriage between Kana and Queen Tsiora, the shul had, in a single move, found a way to honor his warlord's son, shame the Omehi by polluting their royal bloodline, and neuter Achak's ability to oppose peace by committing Kana to its success.

Abshir, certainly seeing this and more, was gracious. "All that has been offered has been accepted," he said to Achak. "The shul will have his marriage and today you will have one of our most powerful Gifted. She will teach everything she can."

Hearing his words, Jayyed's daughter made her way to the Xiddeen side of the clearing. Jayyed came after her.

"Be still!" ordered Abshir, and the nearest Ingonyama grabbed Jayyed, stopping him.

"We make peace, Jayyed," Guardian Councillor Abasi Odili said, his lips curled, showing teeth. "Is this not what you wanted?"

Jayyed, restrained by the Ingonyama and unable to go to his daughter, ran his eyes from person to person, seeking hope from any corner. Finding none, he turned to the source of his distress, calling to her. "Jamilah!"

Jamilah kept walking.

The warlord kept an eye on Jayyed but continued to play his part. "Hear me," he said. "Your queen chooses to delay peace until the moon is full again. She says she must close these terms with her councils. The time will not come without cost."

Tau counted the days. Peace would come a quarter moon after the conclusion of the melee.

"Understand that the attacks on your people, your villages, your warriors, will not end until peace is made," the warlord said. "Peace waits on your queen, and every person who dies from this moment dies because of her delay."

"Jamilah!" Jayyed begged. "Jamilah!"

Abasi Odili sneered. Jayyed was too distressed to notice. Jamilah had crossed the clearing. She stood next to the skinny Gifted man, who still had Nsia's leash and other bonds in hand.

"If we break your defenses, there will be no peace and surrender will be rejected," Achak said.

Here was, Tau saw, Warlord Achak's unhidden hope. Queen Tsiora's need to deal with her Ruling Council, and the delay that caused, was one final opportunity for the warlord to kill them all. It had to be why the hedeni had been attacking in such strength for the past few moons.

This was the shul's concession to a powerful political opponent. For as long as peace was not confirmed, Achak could wage war, and if he conquered the Omehi, the Omehi would die.

"Know this," Achak said. "If harm comes to my son, there will be no peace, no surrender. We will drown you in blood for what you, your demon whores, and your fire demons have done to Xidda. We will—"

"Jamilah!" shouted Jayyed.

"Shut him up," Councillor Abasi Odili said to the Ingonyama holding Jayyed.

The Ingonyama raised a fist.

"Leave him," commanded Abshir.

The Ingonyama withheld his blow but pushed Jayyed to his knees and kept him there.

"KaEid Oro," said Champion Abshir Okar.

The KaEid raised her voice, addressing the warlord and the Gifted hedeni man. "Our Gifted, like Kana, is not to be harmed. She will cooperate."

"The demon whore will be well treated. So long as she will teach."

"She'll teach you the full extent of our power," the KaEid told Achak. "We'll see what the hedeni learn."

The warlord smiled without mirth. "You still don't understand what we are." He turned away and walked out of the clearing. The skinny man blindfolded Jamilah, leashed her arms and neck, threw a sack over her head, and led her away. The rest of the Xiddeen vanished over the rise. Jayyed, still on his knees, moaned, putting his head in his hands.

"Be still, Jayyed," the champion told him. "This is done for peace."

"And you thought I wasn't a friend," Councillor Odili said, "when I did so much to help you achieve your dream."

Jayyed lurched to his feet, hand going for his sword. Dejen Olujimi, Odili's Body, had his sword out and pressed into Jayyed's neck before Jayyed could pull free more than a fingerspan of bronze.

"Odili!" cautioned the champion.

Councillor Abasi Odili was focused on Jayyed. "Something you need, Common Jayyed Ayim?"

Jayyed let his hand fall from his sword hilt.

"Put it away, Dejen," the queen's champion ordered and, fast as thought, Dejen's blade disappeared into his scabbard.

"Remember, you wanted this," Odili told Jayyed as he walked away. Dejen followed.

Jayyed turned in the direction the Xiddeen had gone. He began to walk up the rise, across the clearing.

"No," said Abshir. "If they see you they'll cut her throat and you'll have made peace impossible. Jamilah chose this duty."

Jayyed shook his head, unable to accept it.

"It was offered and she chose it," Abshir said. "She was not forced. She was not ordered. She risks herself for peace."

"No . . . Not like this."

The champion laid a hand on Jayyed's shoulder. "She does this for all of us," he said, guiding his anguished brother-in-arms away from the clearing and back to the Crags.

Tau waited for everyone to leave, trying to process all he'd witnessed and finding himself unable to reconcile the idea of peace as possible. The Omehi and Xiddeen were enemies and had been so for generations. The bloodshed, on both sides, was—

One stone clicked against another as someone behind him moved closer. Tau swayed to his left, desperate to avoid any incoming spear thrusts, and, swords ready, he swung round to face the Xiddeen scout.

BLESSED

Neither Tau nor the Xiddeen scout moved. She was taller than him, slimmer, would have been pretty if not for the weeping sore that ate away at the skin on the right side of her neck. Her eyes were wide and her spear was point down, its shaft held in loose fingers. She had not expected him.

Tau could kill her, but not before she could call out. Hearing her shout, the Xiddeen and Chosen would return to the clearing. What would it mean for peace if he killed this woman? Whatever happened, the Nobles would hang him.

Tau wished he was as smart as Hadith, who could have figured all sides to this puzzle, solved it, and acted already. He thought to speak to the woman but had no clue if she'd understand him.

He was troubling through this when she took a tentative step back, and waited. Understanding her motive, Tau took a step back as well. She took another step. He did too. They had moved beyond striking distance of each other. She nodded to him. He returned the gesture. She left.

Tau remained where he was, swords out and ready, ears pricked for any sounds of alarm. There were none. In time, he relaxed, put his blades away, and began the journey back to the isikolo, wondering at the strangeness of the night, which had ended without him needing to kill or be killed by his enemy. It troubled him, considering that, had he been discovered by his own people, his life would have been forfeit.

Tau arrived at the Southern Isikolo with the sun. The long march had done nothing to calm his mind. The Omehi were finalizing peace with the Xiddeen, peace that came with a regent who would marry and share power with Queen Tsiora.

Peace, Tau thought. It sounded more like surrender, and he could not understand how the Nobles, royal family, or queen could accept this.

Jayyed must have been right. The Xiddeen could not be overcome, and continued war would result in the annihilation of the Chosen. Tau turned the thought over in his head but kept coming back to the notion that assimilation was a different path to the same destination. In two generations, maybe three, would the sons and daughters of those who had been the Omehi pray to the many deities the Xiddeen worshipped? Would their gifts, unique among Uhmlaba's races, be wiped out through improper mixing?

And what would happen to the Omehi military? When you counted the Ihagu, Ihashe, and Indlovu, one in six Chosen men were soldiers. Chosen society was built around the military, around defense, survival. With peace, what would his people become?

What would the Nobles become? As far as Tau knew, the hedeni did not have castes. Under peace, would Royal Nobles be subject to the same rules, opportunities, and failures as a Low Common?

Peace, Tau thought, would destroy the Omehi.

"That you, Tau?" called Chuks, the sharp-eyed Proven sentry at the top of the isikolo's walls.

"It's me."

"What are you doing outside?"

"I was exercising. Can you open the gates?"

"Exercise?" Chuks tossed the word around in his mouth like it was unfamiliar food.

"Chuks," Tau said, thinking gate guards the entire world over must be trained to be as annoying as possible, "can you open the gates?"

Chuks grumbled, scanned the dry grasslands, and, seeing no one else about, shouted to the men below. The bronze gates creaked and swung open wide enough for Tau to enter. Tau nodded to the gate men, walked past Drudge, the other initiates, Proven, aqondise, and umqondisi. He walked to the practice yards, where his scale was already practicing for the melee. He saw Hadith eye him. Tau ignored him.

"Where were you?" Hadith asked when Tau drew within speaking distance.

"My head was clouded. I took a walk."

"What did you do? Do I need to be concerned?"

Uduak was near. He said nothing but was listening. Tau shook his head, giving Hadith little to use.

"Does that mean I have nothing to worry about because nothing was done? Or, there's nothing to worry about because, naively, you believe you will not be caught?"

"I was not able to do as I wished last night."

"I see," Hadith said, watching him.

Tau, still unsteady over the night's events and seeing Themba sauntering over, changed the subject. "Jayyed is not here. What is the plan for our training?"

"Anan wants us working as a scale," Hadith said, seeing Themba as well. "He's recruited help from Chisomo, Tabansi, and Hodari. Their scales will spar versus ours and the masters have agreed to allow us to use the umqondisi quarter as a mock urban battleground."

"Letting us use their quarter as a battleground?" said Themba, smiling. "They really want to give us every chance to do well."

"We're the only Lessers in the melee," said Uduak.

"Shame Scale Chisomo lost out," Themba said, before grinning. "Eh, wonder what the Nobles will do if one of us claims a spot as one of the top six."

"Guardian sword," said Uduak.

"You would focus on the sword," Themba said

"Top six kills and you're an Ingonyama," said Uduak.

"Ingonyama have to be Greater Nobles," Tau said, doing his best to sound normal, to be normal.

"No," said Hadith. "There's no rule saying that. Eight cycles ago, a Petty Noble defeated fourteen men in the melee. That made him top six and he became an Ingonyama. He couldn't be enraged but was accepted.

"Ingonyama are selected by the citadel umqondisi or by ranking top six in the melee. The umqondisi only select Greater Nobles, but they have no control over who gets into the melee and who secures the most kills there." Hadith looked at Tau, with meaning.

"I have no interest in a fancy sword or ceremonial duty," Tau said.

"Best fighters," said Uduak.

"Uduak's right," Hadith told Tau. "Ingonyama are to the average Indlovu as the Indlovu are to the average Ihashe, and they're led by the queen's champion."

"Abshir," said Tau.

"You and Champion Okar close friends?" asked Themba. Tau ignored him, but that never stopped Themba. "Might try for the most kills myself. Wouldn't mind being an Ingonyama. Could mean I become the next champion. Queen Tsiora needs a new one. Can't very well bed old Abshir, can she?"

Themba's grin grew wide enough to show crooked teeth. "Or could be you," he said pointing to Uduak. "Champion Uduak," Themba made his voice a sultry falsetto, "would you help your liege undress? The lacing over my bosom is so difficult to reach."

Uduak's eyebrows flew up.

"Tau, dear, I have an itch, right down here...," Themba whispered, pointing a finger to his nethers.

"Are you sun sick?" asked Tau. "Our queen, Queen Tsiora Omehi, with a Lesser? The nobility would tear the peninsula apart." They'd see her with a hedeni princeling first, he thought.

Themba snorted. "Think what you will, I'm going to do my best to get those kills in the melee. Imagine it, Themba Chikelu, queen's champion. Themba Chikelu, queen's lover."

Uduak waved Themba off, shook his head, and walked away, too scandalized to hear or be any part of Themba's fantasy.

"Don't run, Uduak. You know you'll be wondering how soft her skin must be for the rest of the day . . . and night!"

"I think not," Hadith said. "We're not all like you. Leave him be."

"Men like him need a little teasing. He's too serious. Besides, it's only him and Tau who have any chance of doing what needs done to make the top six."

"I don't want it," Tau said.

Themba grinned. "Just murder and mayhem."

"Care," Tau said.

"Or you'll do me first, neh?"

"Enough, Themba." Hadith turned away from him and raised his voice, shouting for the scale to hear. "Aqondise Anan will be here any breath now. Form up. I don't know which scale will come with him this morning, expecting to fight and lose against us, but I know I don't want to disappoint them."

Some of the men laughed and all of them snapped to attention, forming up. Tau went with them.

The first scale they fought was Hodari's. It was a slaughter. They ate after the skirmish and fought Tabansi's men in the umqondisi quarter. Tau took out fifteen men and had to hold back to avoid injuring anyone.

"You're Goddess blessed," Umqondisi Tabansi told him when the fighting was finished. "I do not think I have ever seen a man so skilled with the blade. It is a gift of a new kind."

Themba had been close enough to hear Tabansi's praise. He'd winked at Tau. Tau ignored Themba and did not think himself Gifted. He wasn't sure Tabansi would either, if he knew what Tau had done, and continued to do, to acquire and increase his skills.

After their third and final skirmish, another slaughter, the men ate and took to their rest. Tau went to the practice yards. He worked until it was dark, pushing himself as hard as he could, training until most in the isikolo were asleep.

He looked up at the cloudless sky. There were many stars, countless and shining bright across the breadth of the Goddess's creation. It was at nighttime, alone, when he missed his father most, missed him so much it felt like all of Uhmlaba should stop and take note.

Instead, the world moved faster, promising change, and the time for Tau to use its old rules to make things right was running short.

He knelt and closed his eyes. He went to Isihogo, to its demons, where spans meant less and suffering could be an ablution of sorts. It was time to fight in the Queen's Melee. Peace could follow, but three men had to die first. It was time to kill.

CHAPTER TWELVE

MELEE

The first skirmish of the Queen's Melee was chaotic. Scale Jayyed was matched against the Nobles of Scale Ozioma. They fought on the mountain battleground and, though the other competing scales were sequestered so they could not observe their opponents' strategies, Tau had never seen the Crags so crowded.

The queen's brother, Prince Xolani Omehia, opened the melee, both citadels were in attendance, and the Northern and Southern Isikolo stood empty, their initiates crammed into the area of the Crags reserved for Lessers. Full-blooded Indlovu and Ihashe as well as many private citizens had come to watch, and an endless horde of Drudge waited on them all. When it was confirmed that Queen Tsiora was traveling to see the games, the Crags crackled with tension and energy.

The queen would watch the final day of the melee and, thought Tau with bitterness, she'd use the occasion to meet with the gathered Guardian Council without raising suspicion. She'd leave Palm City, having explained peace to the Ruling Council, and she'd come to Citadel City to finalize it with the military's leaders. She'd come to begin the end of the Omehi.

Over the past moon cycle, these thoughts had plagued Tau with as much ferocity as his demon visions, and the only thing that calmed him was fighting. When Tau fought he did not have time to think.

"Uduak, I need your unit to break that team of Indlovu on the ridge before they flank us!" Hadith yelled, receiving a grunt from the big man, who set off with his men. "Tau, they'll come at us again. They need to break through."

Tau didn't need a strategic mind to know Hadith was right. Scale Jayyed had their collective backs against an unclimbable section of the battleground. The Indlovu had herded them here like the brainless harvest animals from the old stories. Hadith had ordered several pitched fights, but they'd not gone well. Scale Jayyed was unused to fighting against an equal number of Nobles. This, combined with the stress of the day, the massive crowds, and the skill of Ozioma's scale, was overwhelming them.

Hadith had minimized their failures with cleverness. He refused to stick to unfavorable battles and was careful to lose as few men as possible, a critical tactic in the Queen's Melee, where each winning scale entered the next round with the number of men left standing at the end of their previous skirmish.

Melee competitors began the tournament with fifty-four men. If a scale lost ten men in round one, they began round two with forty-four. If that same scale lost eighteen in the second round, they went into round three with twenty-six fighters.

Jayyed, who had returned to the scale but remained distant, Anan, and Hadith had devised several strategies to take advantage of the melee's rule set. The main strategy was to "sacrifice" Uduak, the scale's second-strongest fighter, and his unit to bolster any faltering line. Uduak's unit was a reserve defense that would crash into a losing battle to save the scale. They could do this because it did not matter which man was "killed" in each skirmish. All that mattered were the numbers. Uduak could "die" in round one and still fight in round two, as long as the number of fighters they fielded balanced against the number they had lost.

This was why Tau needed to win. If he could get far enough into the tournament, he was sure to face Kellan. Kellan Okar was Scale Osa's strongest fighter, and his umqondisi would field him in every skirmish.

"No, Tau! Stay back!" Hadith hollered. "Retreat!"

Tau wanted to hit something, someone, maybe Hadith. "We are running out of room to run!"

"This is not where we fight. The ground favors the Nobles."

"You've said that for the past span," Tau argued.

"You want to win? We have to fight smarter. We cannot match them man for man, and the moment we go into a skirmish under-manned, we're done."

"We've already lost men and taken none of theirs!"

"Four down in a span? That's a victory, Tau."

"The only victory is putting all of them down," Tau said, as the time to stand and fight blindsided them.

"Indlovu!" screamed Utibe. He'd run into a unit of Indlovu that had circled around Scale Jayyed, and Utibe was backpedaling fast, trying to avoid being cut down by the men chasing him.

Hadith shouted orders. "This is it! They've split three ways but their timing is wrong. The main unit is still a hundred strides away and Uduak has the rest of them engaged on the ridge." Hadith pointed at the Nobles chasing Utibe and called to his scale. "Stop running! We outnumber them. Full force, kill!"

Words Tau had waited to hear. He raised his swords and ran at his enemy. He rushed past a backpedaling Utibe and charged the closest Noble.

Tau heard his scale's war cry as he leapt into the air and brought his dulled skirmishing blades together, clapping either side of the Noble's helmet. The Indlovu's momentum kept his no longer con-scious body running a few steps before he collapsed, and by then, Tau was in the fray.

These Indlovu had never fought Scale Jayyed. They might have heard of Tau; most in the citadel had. They might have laughed off the stories, mocking their Noble brothers who had fallen to him.

They might have told one another it would be different when they faced such Common scum. They might have laughed then, in the comfort and safety of the Indlovu Citadel, but they were in the melee, Tau was among them, and there was only pain.

Tau slipped through them like the wind. Where he went, bones broke, the courageous became cowards, and always, always, there were the screams of men in torment, of prey who had forgotten what it was like to be hunted. In a small way, the world changed that day, when the Nobles of Scale Ozioma broke and ran, scattered by a new and horrible creature, born in Uhmlaba but bred in Isihogo.

When the rest of Scale Ozioma caught up, expecting to trap a few Lessers in a vise comprised of their betters, they found no such thing. The main unit of Ozioma's Nobles fought hard, bravely. The Omehi rarely did less, but in losing an entire unit, the Indlovu had taken heavy losses, and they did not understand Tau's nature.

"Follow him! Protect him! Follow, you spineless inyoka!" Hadith pointed, shouted, ran after Tau, pulled men along with him, fought an Indlovu, was almost brained and would have been if not for Yaw, and Tau was still three or four strides ahead. "Fight! Fight, damn you!" he roared at his men.

Tau's world was a haze of violence. He did not see men around him. Not men, demons, but these demons could fall and that was a glory given by the Goddess. He lashed at them, swords used like bronze whips. The blades were blunt, but his brutality made him a butcher. He carved through the meat in his way with the ease of cutting through a carcass long dead.

"Mercy! By the Goddess, man. Mercy!" This demon had a new trick. It could speak with the voice of men. Tau raised his swords, face twisted. He would not be fooled.

"Tau!" Hadith called. "Tau!"

The fog thinned and Tau saw the Noble in front of him. He was on his knees, shield and sword abandoned. "Mercy! Goddess's mercy!" His hands were up, palms out; his head was turned to one side, eyes shut. He expected to be struck down, killed in the same way one of them had murdered Oyibo.

Tau lowered his swords, breathing heavy, eyes wide, trying to see the real instead of the illusion. He saw Hadith and heard the groans of the injured. He stood in a circle of suffering, and the Indlovu were down, to a man.

"It's done, Tau. We won," said Hadith.

"Won?"

"Yes."

Tau blinked, sheathed his swords, and stalked off the battle-ground, head down. He hadn't defeated the demons. That couldn't be done, and as if to mock his foolishness, he saw one among the tents. It was shadowed but loomed tall above the crowds, its red eyes boring holes into his skull. Tau blinked, wishing it away, and, too frightened to know if it had gone, he turned his head so it would be beyond his sight.

He wound his way to the tent made up for Scale Jayyed. The rest of the men would join him when they could. He knew he should be out there, on the battleground, helping his injured sword brothers to the infirmary. He knew it, but he couldn't. He was so tired.

The crowds beyond the battleground were thick, but they melted away in front of him. On this side of the Crags, the east side, the people were Lessers. He felt their eyes on him. It was odd that so many were so quiet.

One of them, a Low Common Proven with a gaunt face and miss-ing both an eye and a leg, hobbled forward. He didn't speak, elect-ing instead to tuck his crutch under his armpit so he could bring his hands together, palms touching, fingers outstretched. He moved his hands to his forehead and held them there, saluting Tau with the reverence reserved for a wing or even dragon inkokeli. The behav-ior unnerved Tau, who thought to return the salute, changed his mind, and nodded.

Then it happened again. This time it was a full-blooded Ihashe, who, from his look, must have been either a Harvester or Governor before joining the military. He saluted Tau and held the salute. Tau acknowledged the man and increased his pace, anxious to get to the privacy of his scale's tents.

As he went, more and more people in the crowd saluted. It all happened in silence, not one of them said a thing, but when Tau stood in front of the flaps of his scale's tent, it seemed as if everyone was saluting.

He wasn't sure he wanted to look back. He told himself to continue on inside, to forget the whole thing, but he couldn't help it. He looked.

The crowd, all of them, were saluting. Tau froze, unsure what to do and feeling relief when he saw Hadith emerging from the mass of people. The relief was short-lived.

Hadith stood beside but a step back from Tau and whispered, "Where we fight."

"What?" Tau hissed back.

"Say it."

"No."

"They're waiting."

"For that?" Tau asked.

"Yes. They just don't know it."

"No."

"You do them an injustice, stealing the moment from them."

"What moment?"

"Give them the day."

"Curse you...," Tau whispered, lips tight, as he raised his head, lifted his voice, and shouted, "Where we fight!"

The crowd came back in a single voice that echoed through the Crags. "The world burns! The world burns! The world burns!" On and on and on.

Tau, nostrils flared and pulse racing, spoke so only Hadith could hear. "Now what? They won't stop."

"Give it four breaths. I'll go in the tent first. When the breaths are done, follow me in."

"I should strangle you."

"Do it after you've waited the full count."

Hadith disappeared behind the tent's flaps. Tau breathed four times, heart hammering, as the crowd's chant crested. He nodded to them and followed Hadith into the tent as the Lessers shook the Crags with the power in their voices. "The world burns!"

LISTEN

Tau marched to the nearest cot and collapsed on it, closing his eyes.

"Tau." It was Hadith.

Tau grunted, wanting to be left alone.

"Well done."

"And what did I do?"

"You reminded them they are valuable. That they can achieve incredible things. That they are not just fodder for this eternal war."

"We've always been more than the Nobles make us out to be."

"Perhaps, but most have never seen proof, until today."

Tau grunted again.

"The rest of the scale will be here soon," Hadith said. "Jayyed and Anan as well. At least wash your face."

Tau let his eyes slide open. Hadith was standing over him. "Why?" Tau asked.

"You have blood all over it."

"Not mine."

"I know. We all know."

"How did Uduak's unit do?"

"They did well. They held against the Indlovu unit on the ridge but lost men doing it. All in all, we're down seventeen fighters.

Eight to surrender, the others to injury. Thankfully, Uduak had the sense to surrender before getting hurt. He can fight in tomorrow's skirmish, in place of another."

"Give him Utibe's spot," Tau said.

"Utibe?"

"He ran."

"He was facing an entire unit of Indlovu."

"He ran."

"Most would consider his actions prudent," Hadith said.

Tau rolled over, giving his back to Hadith. No point arguing.

"You're leading the Queen's Melee in number of men dispatched," Hadith told him.

Tau looked over his shoulder. "It's the first day."

"They maintain a running tally. Keep it up and you'll be the first Lesser Ingonyama, ever." Hadith smiled like he didn't mean it. "Don't push in so far among the enemy next time. We can't protect you if you do."

The words were said kindly, sword brother to sword brother. Tau was in no mood for it. "You can't protect me."

Hadith lost the smile. "Maybe not, but do as I say, because it's an order. Fighting so far ahead of your brothers endangers them as well as you."

"Yes, Inkokeli," Tau told him, looking away. He was so tired.

That afternoon, Proven from the Northern Isikolo stood guard outside their tent. The men of Scale Jayyed were sequestered until the day's skirmishing was done. They could not observe the tactics, strengths, and weaknesses of the other competing scales, but they could hear the crowd roaring approval and, on occasion, disappointment. Jayyed and Anan spent time with the scale, briefly celebrating their historic victory and going over plans for whomever they might face in tomorrow's skirmish.

As the day turned to dusk, a Proven came into the tent to tell Jayyed and Anan they had drawn Scale Ojuolape for tomorrow's match. Tau swore. It wasn't Scale Osa. It wasn't Kellan. He swore louder when Jayyed told them the rest.

Scale Ojuolape had lost just ten men and would outnumber them. The skirmish was set for the first thing in the morning and they would battle on the grasslands.

Tau exhaled, whistling air through clenched teeth. The grasslands simulated a losing proposition for the Omehi, who could never match the hedeni's numbers. Skirmishing there was done to teach future inkokeli that taking a fight on open ground, when outnumbered, was not something to be done.

"The grasslands?" asked Hadith, speaking so everyone could hear. "Good," he said. "There won't be anywhere for the bastards to hide."

The men stamped their feet, approving of their inkokeli's brave words, but their faces told another story. They were being sent to slaughter. Only a fool couldn't see that.

"The sequester is over," said Jayyed. "You may leave the tent, stretch your legs, and breathe air not fouled by your sword brothers' stink. Go, but don't dally. We're up before dawn to discuss our strategy for Ojuolape's men."

Tau stood. He would walk for a bit, let night fall, and he would go to Isihogo.

"Tau." It was Jayyed.

Tau forced his face to be neutral. He did not want to speak to the man who had helped plan his people's surrender. "Umqondisi."

"A moment, if you please." Jayyed motioned Tau over to a corner of the tent where they would not be overheard.

Tau didn't think he had a reason to worry, but he did so. Had Jayyed noticed him at the meeting between the Omehi and the Xiddeen? Nothing the umqondisi had done since that day indicated it, but he'd been so distant since seeing his daughter go with the hedeni that it was hard to say.

"I'd tell you that you did well today," Jayyed started, "but that falls so far beneath the truth it mocks it. In my highest estimations for the scale I did not expect to be here, in a competitor's tent at the Queen's Melee."

"We have your leadership and training to thank," Tau said.

Jayyed smiled. "I have done what I could to bring out the best in each of you. But what you're doing...what you are...How?"

The question, coming from Jayyed, made Tau angry. "Desire and sacrifice. I desire the ability to protect what I love and I will sacrifice everything to do so. My thinking comes from your teachings, your methods. You taught us that to achieve greater results we must outlay greater effort."

Tau leaned in, not to share secrets but to strike Jayyed with the force of his words. "You ask me how? I'll tell you. By refusing to surrender, no matter how bad the chances, because as long as we fight, the outcome is not set. As long as we fight, there is a chance."

Tau had gotten very close, but Jayyed did not back away. He stood toe-to-toe with Tau. "I've been a soldier for most of my life and I've learned hard lessons. Fight for too long and you lose sight of the things you started the fight for. Fight for too long and you lose anyway."

Tau sneered. "What then? Surrender? That's your answer? Surrender, when the fight becomes hard?"

"No. Fight for what's right, but never forget that fighting can also be done without violence. It can be done as it is now, with words, ideals, people seeking a better path, together." Jayyed put his hands on Tau's shoulders. "You can't imagine a world where we work as hard at peace as we do at war?"

Tau stepped back, letting Jayyed's hands fall free. "I can't imagine a world where the man holding a sword does not have the last say over the man without one. If you're not prepared to fight, you place yourself and everything you love beneath the blades of others, praying they choose not to cut. I have felt the mercy of armed men and they will never find me helpless again."

Jayyed sighed. "Then you'll stand in a world of char and ash."

"But I'll stand."

"So you say." Jayyed raised his hand to the bridge of his nose and pinched it, closing his eyes. "Hadith has a plan for the skirmish. He came to me with it because it is too risky to do without my blessing. If it works, the scale gets through the grasslands against superior Indlovu numbers and, for the first time, Lessers will fight in the semifinals of the Queen's Melee. Hadith's plan hinges on you, Tau Solarin."

Jayyed took his hand from his face, looking into Tau's eyes, as if he could see past them and into his soul. "Will you listen?"

PRIDE

The sun battered the land, its heat reflecting from the earth in shimmering waves that warped the light. It was a cruel day, but the crowds had come. They'd come for the sport and, in some small way, to be part of the making of new legends. They'd come to watch Jayyed's scale of Lessers do battle against Ojuolape's scale of Nobles.

It was day two of the Queen's Melee, the quarter finals, and eight of the original sixteen scales remained in competition. Tau, his scale first to fight, stood on the edge of the grasslands with thirty-six of his sword brothers. Five hundred strides in front of them were forty-four citadel initiates, Ojuolape's Noble warriors.

The grasslands were a crowd favorite. There was nowhere to hide, no obstacles to leverage, few tactics to employ. They were a killing field. Men rushed each other. Men fought. Men fell. It spelled doom for the outnumbered Ihashe.

"Hadith," said Yaw, "not to be cowardly, but I really hope your plan works."

Hadith smiled. Tau could see his mouth twitching, though. He knew his inkokeli well enough to know when he was nervous. "It'll work," Hadith said. "Nobles are so proud they'll walk themselves into this ocean."

The war horns blew; the Nobles, certain of their win, raised their swords. The crowds cheered and both sides advanced. There was no point in a charge. The distance between them was too great. Instead, the two scales marched, ratcheting up the morning's bitter tension with every stride.

When there were two hundred strides separating the eighty men, the crowds fell silent. Another hundred strides and the Crags were quiet enough to hear lizards skittering across the cracked stones that gave the plateau its name.

Chinedu coughed, a loud, whooping sound that broke the spell, startling many in the crowd. A woman fainted, whether from emotion or sun, Tau did not know. Then Hadith raised a fist and it was time.

Scale Jayyed stopped and Hadith stepped forward, setting himself apart from the rest. He called out across the distance, loud enough for the crowds to hear. "Inkokeli Mayumbu Opeyemi of Scale Ojuolape, I have heard you are a Greater Noble slated to be an Ingonyama. I have heard your intelligence and deeds honor the blood of Nobles everywhere, but I would see it proved."

Mayumbu Opeyemi called a halt and, matching Hadith, he came forward. He was short for a Greater Noble, which meant he was only half a head taller than Uduak, but he was also broader in the shoulders and chest, and his neck was as thick as Tau's forearms.

Mayumbu's bald head glistened with sweat and his skin was dark as lightning-charred wood. He cracked his neck and addressed Hadith, his voice a scorpion's sting. "Before the morning's done, you'll have your proof, Lesser."

"Indeed, and yet, I have an offer you may find interesting."

"There are no interests between dragons and inyoka."

"Truly? When what I offer is the Queen's Melee itself?"

Mayumbu blinked. "I'll waste no more words on you."

"I mean what I say, Inkokeli. I offer you the melee today. Will you take it?"

"It is not yours to offer, and if it were, I'd tear it from you."

"Maybe you will, Inkokeli. I've seen the betting and heard the odds. Mayumbu and his men, favored to come second, behind the greatest Noble initiate to have ever entered the citadel, Inkokeli Kellan Okar of Scale Osa."

"Little man, I will kill you and crush Okar."

"And how many men will today cost? How many did you bring to this field? Forty-four? I'm Governor caste. One thing we do very well is count. And, at last count, Okar lost five men in yesterday's skirmish. Today he faces Scale Ongani under Inkokeli Mukuka Olumide..."

Even from a hundred strides away, Tau could see Mayumbu's disgust. Scale Ongani was the weakest group of men that had made the melee and, somehow, they had survived day one. After losing forty-two men in the first skirmish, Mukuka would lead no more than twelve against Scale Osa. Kellan would obliterate them.

"We'll be sequestered. We won't have the chance to see the glorious battle between Ongani and Osa," Hadith said, causing laughter to ripple through the crowds, "but I feel confident in its outcome."

"Make your point," said Mayumbu.

"Osa will go through to the semifinals and, as we stand now, there is a twenty-five percent chance that one of us will face them—"

"A twenty-five percent chance I will face them!"

"That's...that's what I said. Regardless," Hadith continued, "do you think to battle us here, lose more men, and prevail against Okar? No, Mayumbu. Your journey ends here, on this battleground. Tomorrow is nothing more than a formality—"

"We shall see!"

"Unless..." Hadith smiled his best grin.

Mayumbu licked his lips, ready to order the attack. "Unless what?"

"Unless we find another way."

"What way, fool?"

"Why risk all our men? Why risk our chance to make it to the semifinals? Why risk anything at all? Here's my offer, Inkokeli Opeyemi—we, as leaders of our scale, swear before the umqondisi, Gifted, and crowd, to duel for the win. To a man, the loser's scale will call out for Goddess's mercy, leaving the winning scale to go through to tomorrow's combat with the most men possible. With a duel, we give ourselves a real chance at victory, before queen and country."

Mayumbu inhaled. It was his first breath since comprehending the offer's gist. The man was caught on Hadith's hook and Tau knew that Mayumbu was already picturing himself before Queen Tsiora on the melee's final day.

"I fight you for the win?" Mayumbu asked, eyes closed down to slits.

Hadith chuckled. "No. I may as well beg mercy now, were that the game. We present our best and you present yours."

Mayumbu snorted. "You mean to test that two-sworded freak against me."

"I may. I pick one man, you do the same. Doesn't have to be you, Inkokeli. If you don't believe you can win, put up another." Hadith spread his arms wide. "That's the offer."

Mayumbu pointed to Tau. "You think your kudliwe can beat me?" He laughed. "Give him three swords, I'll kill him just the same."

There it was. Hadith had done it. Tau watched him turn to the crowd. "You've heard my offer. You've heard the Greater Noble and inkokeli, Mayumbu of Scale Ojuolape, declare that he can best our man in single combat. This duel is to mercy, or death, with the remainder of the loser's scale to accept the result and surrender the skirmish. Women and men of the peninsula, do we have your blessing?"

The crowd screamed their blessings with the thunder of ten thousand voices that threatened to bring the mountain quaking down on all their heads.

Tau had to respect Mayumbu's self-control. He could tell the inkokeli saw the trap into which he'd stepped. The impressive thing was how fast the man adjusted to the new reality, accepting that a new path had emerged where there had not been one before.

Mayumbu took a careful step on the path, testing its possibilities. "Can this be done?" he shouted to the group of umqondisi officiating the skirmish. The group huddled, conferred, and the lead officiant, a muscled but wiry umqondisi, nodded to Mayumbu.

The night prior, when Jayyed outlined Hadith's plan, he'd explained that the melee's rules did not forbid this. So long as Mayumbu accepted, it could be done. Of course, Jayyed also explained, losing the duel did nothing to bind the rest of the scale to its result.

Scale Ojuolape could still attack, wipe out the Ihashe, and move on in the tournament. It was likely they did not know that. It was even more likely that, if their inkokeli lost, their honor would force them to do as promised and they'd forfeit.

It was a good plan, a simple plan. Hadith had played his part. It was Tau's turn.

"Scale Jayyed calls Tau Solarin, Common of Kerem, Lesser of the Chosen, to fight," Hadith announced, both hands raised as if he were a priest delivering a holy proclamation. Tau unsheathed his swords and stepped up beside Hadith. The Crags were quiet.

A hundred strides away, Mayumbu's unit leaders tried to have a word, perhaps to put up another man, perhaps to offer advice. Whatever it was, Tau could not hear and Mayumbu would not listen. He was furious. Again, Hadith's plan in action.

By naming Tau as both a Common and Lesser, he was goading Mayumbu, telling the crowds that here was a match where the outcome should be as certain as the sun's rising. A Greater Noble and a Common dueling? What a farce. What a show.

Mayumbu had been burdened with the weight of everyone's honor. He fought in the name of his scale, the citadel, the Nobles. If he did anything less than demolish Tau, the duel would feel a failure.

"Come, then, Common of Kerem," said Mayumbu, sword drawn, shield mounted, and advancing. "Let's get this done and chase the stench of your Lesser stock from the melee."

Tau said nothing. He twirled his swords, loosening his wrists, and broke into a loping jog. Mayumbu bared his teeth, joined Tau in a run, and bellowed the Noble war cry. "Blood. Will. Show!"

COMMON

The Crags lost their quiet and the bloodthirsty calls of women and men echoed across the mountainside. Tau imagined how confused the sequestered scales would be, hearing the tumult. He centered himself. It was time to work.

Mayumbu, bigger, holding a longer sword, came in range first and sent a thundering blow for Tau's neck. His sword, moving faster than an untrained eye could track, ripped through the air, keening as it went. Tau swept beneath it, came up, and smashed the hilt of his strong-side sword into Mayumbu's wrist, snapping it. Using both their momentum, he thrust the dulled point of his other blade into the leather armor covering Mayumbu's guts. Tau's aim was true and he hit the gap between two protective bronze plates, piercing the expensive animal hide, the undershirt beneath, and Mayumbu's stomach.

Mayumbu was a massive man. Tau braced. The collision pushed him back a stride and, though less time had passed than it took to draw breath, the men were entangled.

Mayumbu, standing over Tau, grabbed him by the neck and crashed his sword arm across Tau's back. Tau was looking into his face. He wanted to see the moment when Mayumbu realized it was over.

It wasn't until Mayumbu's broken wrist and empty fingers slapped across Tau's shoulder blades. It wasn't until he tried to draw a breath and the pain hit, from two handspans' worth of bronze buried in his core, that Mayumbu realized he was undone. He screamed then, the pain catching up with the moment and taking him somewhere else.

Tau ripped the Noble's weakened grip away from his neck and stepped back. His blade came with him, sliding out of Mayumbu with the sound of a stick pulled too quick from mud. Mayumbu fell to his knees, gasping and gawping.

He was scared. Tau could see it in his eyes and, though it was not mercy, Tau took away the fear. He flew his sword's dulled edge into Mayumbu's head, smashing a dent in the man's helmet over his temple and felling him, sending him to the grass in a heap.

Tau remained over the body, glaring at the rest of the Indlovu, daring them to do anything other than what they'd promised. The Crags had gone quiet again, even the few wispy clouds in the sky holding their place.

"Goddess's mercy," said the first Indlovu, going to one knee.

"Goddess's mercy," said the next and the next and the next, their calls for mercy flowing fast, like water from the bathtub tap in the umqondisi quarter.

"The skirmish is won by Scale Jayyed," came the voice of the wiry citadel officiant. He sounded shaken. "Scale Jayyed advances to the semifinals."

The tap opened further and the crowd became part of its flow, drowning the plateau in the deluge of their shouts, cheers, triumph, and loss.

Scale Jayyed rushed to Tau's side and they surrounded him, celebrating him and their victory, but he neither heard nor felt them. He was looking down at Mayumbu's blood as it ran through the grass and into the dirt. It was dark, arterial, and nothing about it looked noble at all.

Tau had never seen men so exuberant without masmas or gaum. If he hadn't known better, he would have sworn the Goddess had turned their cups of water to olu. They were in the scale's tent and men were dancing, hooting. Azima had his drums, which he took everywhere, between his legs and he beat them ferociously, if not rhythmically. Anan was soaked; the men of the scale had doused him with water from the drinking pails.

"Semifinals!" crowed Yaw, pulling Tau around in a tight circle as if they were dancers at a Harvest festival. "Semifinals!" he said, spinning off to find a new partner.

Uduak caught Tau's eye, raised his water cup, and drank from it. Tau returned the gesture.

"You shouldn't have agreed, Tau!" said Hadith, weaving through the men as if he were drunk. "The plan only let you dispatch one man. You've fallen from the list of greats slated to become Ingonyama."

"There's tomorrow," Tau said.

"That there is!" said Hadith. "To tomorrow!" he shouted, thrusting his cup of water high in the air and spilling its contents over Tau and several others.

"To tomorrow!" came the voices of close to sixty sword brothers as the tent flaps were whisked aside and Jayyed strode in, his appearance hushing the men.

"We have a match," Jayyed told them. "In the semifinals, we fight on the urban battleground. Our opponents lost no men today, and tomorrow we face them at dusk. Tomorrow, we fight Scale Osa."

The men murmured, unsure how to react. Tau's eyes were bright. "Kellan."

CHAPTER THIRTEEN

OSA

Everything had gone wrong. Uduak and his men had fallen, Yaw's unit hadn't been seen for half a span, and Tau was trapped in a crumbling building, surrounded by twenty-seven Indlovu.

The skirmish had started slow. Both sides had been cautious, taking ground in the cluttered urban battleground with care. To goad Scale Osa and fulfill his promise to Tau, Hadith gave Tau three men to use as a roving group of assassins.

Tau, with Runako and the twins, Kuende and Mshinde, had been like a reaper at harvest. Whenever the Indlovu were otherwise engaged, separated, or distracted, Tau and his half team found and dispatched them. It had worked well, until Kellan adjusted. After losing too many, he kept his men together.

In spite of this, Hadith wanted Scale Jayyed divided into the Chosen's standard three units. He felt its flexibility gave them more options than Kellan's unified scale. Perhaps that would have been the case, if Uduak's unit had not gotten cut off. Or if Yaw's unit had not been blocked by buildings, unable to join the fight.

At the time, Kellan had thirty-one Indlovu to Uduak's nine Ihashe. Tau demanded they go in. Hadith refused. Without Yaw's unit, they wouldn't do much good and would only join in Uduak's fate. Tau knew Hadith was right, but being right didn't help.

As they held back, Hadith stared wild-eyed at the fighting, at Uduak, who was last to fall. The big man did not claim the Goddess's mercy. The Indlovu beat him unconscious before he could. Then they continued to beat him.

The nearest officiant was a citadel umqondisi. It was his duty to call incapacitated men out of bounds. When Uduak went down, he turned his back, letting the Nobles do as they would.

Hadith, mind lost, ran in, shouting Uduak's name. That forced Tau and the rest of the unit into combat. It was nine Lessers against three times their number in Nobles. It was not winnable.

Runako, Kuende, and Mshinde were lost, and Tau called a ragged retreat. They ran and Tau had to drag Hadith away with them. The Indlovu gave chase, but the six Lessers evaded their pursuers, taking cover in a set of buildings.

As they scurried through the empty replicas, desperate to stay hidden from the hunting Indlovu, Themba cursed Hadith's hysteria. Tau grabbed Themba by the front of his gambeson and told him that by engaging the Indlovu, they had saved Uduak's life.

Hadith's attack had pulled the Indlovu away from the big man, and with the fighting moved on, the umqondisi officiant had been forced to declare Uduak and the other dispatched men in his unit out of bounds. Uduak had been carried off the battleground. Tau couldn't be sure, but he believed Uduak was alive. He had to believe it.

Themba quieted, saying nothing, and the six men heard combat. It was Yaw's unit. The fighting did not last long. That worried Tau.

Moments later, Chinedu pointed out the skulking forms of armored Indlovu circling the adobe longhouses in which they hid. The Indlovu walked single file, ducking beneath the building's windows, trying not to be seen. Tau saw them go past, their row of hunched backs reminding him of the stories his mother had told him when he was a child, the ones about the serpentine sea monsters said to hunt the open waters of the Roar.

Tau didn't believe the stories about enormous sea serpents, but monsters did exist. Twenty-seven of them were closing in on him and the five men beside him. Maybe four men. He wasn't sure he could count on Hadith if it came to more fighting. Their inkokeli hadn't been himself after seeing the Indlovu try to kill Uduak.

Tau let his fingers play over the hilts of his two bronze practice swords. There was no hope left. He had to admit it.

He'd come so far, done so much, and he'd not faced Kellan. Scale Osa's inkokeli was well protected and Tau had not been able to get to him. It burned, especially when he'd watched the murderous Greater Noble preside over Uduak's beating. Kellan had stood there, apart from the others, disdain on his face, as if he were too good to dirty his hands.

When Hadith lost control, Tau had been glad to go in. They went to save Uduak. That's what Tau had told Themba, but saving Uduak was Hadith's reason. Tau, shamed by the thought, couldn't be sure it was his. He'd gone to meet Kellan.

But the Indlovu had closed ranks. They'd blocked his way and Kellan had called for more men. Striving to reach Okar, Tau took his skirmish body count from five men dispatched to six, then seven, eight, and nine.

He'd terrorized the Indlovu until Kellan's actions stopped him again. The Scale Osa inkokeli yelled for the men standing against Tau to fight him together, to encircle him. Tau could not get through and the Indlovu almost had him. The only reason Tau was still in the skirmish was Chinedu.

Once they saw Uduak carried from the battleground, Chinedu and the rest of the unit ran to Tau's aid. With them beside him, Tau managed to escape, dragging Hadith along. They'd gone into the fight with nine men, come out with six, and, given the odds, they had to consider themselves blessed.

Still, none of it mattered. They'd trapped themselves in the crumbling buildings. The Indlovu couldn't be sure exactly where they were, but they were searching and the noose was tightening.

"It's over!" Kellan called from outside the buildings. "You're surrounded, outnumbered, finished. Come, take the Goddess's mercy, and put an end to this, with honor."

Themba nudged Hadith. "Say something, damn your eyes."

Hadith looked grim, distant, but he pushed hope into his voice and yelled out. "You want to do this honorably?"

Kellan laughed. "I will neither hear nor take offers from you, Inkokeli Buhari. The day is ours. You can take the painless path I've offered, or we come in there and..."

"You want to storm the buildings?" Hadith said. "Please do. We have sixteen men to your twenty-seven. We'll make a battle of it and end your chances to take the finals."

"Does the Common of Kerem count as ten men now?" replied Kellan. "There's six of you."

"You think so? Come and count."

There was no response.

Tau, hands shaking, growled to Hadith. "The longer we wait—"

Hadith shook his head, coming back to himself a little. "He thinks he's won, but he needs to finish us and keep enough of his men for tomorrow's finals. Our chance lies in the gap between where Kellan is now and where he needs to be."

Themba stared at Hadith like he'd begun eating dirt. "Chance? We're six Ihashe against twenty-seven Indlovu—"

"If we wait for Yaw—" Hadith said.

Themba sucked his teeth. "Hadith, come now! We heard the battle. Yaw and his men are gone."

"The battle was too short," Hadith countered. "Kellan didn't have time to get them all. I think Yaw ran, like we did."

"You think?" Tau looked away in frustration and saw them. The dark corner of the building held three kneeling demons, their yellow eyes locked on him, their sharp teeth shining in the gloom.

"Tau?" asked Chinedu.

Tau shook his head, blinking them away. "I'm fine but won't be for much longer. None of us will, if we stay here and let Kellan overrun us."

"He won't do it," said Hadith. "These buildings are bunched together and sound ricochets between them. He doesn't know which one we're in. He'll have to split his men to make sure we don't escape. If his men are split, he risks losing too many. That's why he's talking. He's looking for a better fight than this. If Yaw is out there and we wait, we can strike together."

"This is your plan?" Tau said.

"You have a better one?"

"Common of Kerem!" Kellan called. "Tau Solarin, I'm weary. Come out, if the rest of them won't. Come out and let us end what we started in Citadel City. My men won't interfere."

Tau's swords were in his hands and he was standing.

Hadith grabbed his wrist and yanked it. "Sit down, fool!"

"I'm waiting, Tau," shouted Kellan. "Will you stay in there, hiding from me? After all you've done, all you've accomplished, are you still that boy? The coward whose father had to fight for him? I expected more from you, given your father's bravery. Given the man your father...was."

Tau pulled away from Hadith's grasp.

"Tau!" Hadith said. "You'll lead them to us!"

Tau's hand was on the door. "He helped murder my father," he said, pulling it open and walking out.

KELLAN OKAR

Kellan Okar watched the Common of Kerem, as he was being called, walk out of the southernmost of the four buildings he'd ordered his men to surround. The Common was as Kellan remembered, dark as night, well proportioned, small. His face was scarred and otherwise unremarkable, except for his eyes. They were brown, which was typical, but they burned, which was not.

Kellan signaled his men to attack. The Lesser had no leather or armor. Instead, he wore slate-gray trousers, marking him as an Ihashe warrior, and a filthy patchwork gambeson. He held a sword in each hand and readied them, thinking Kellan's Indlovu were coming for him. They were not, and they did as Kellan had instructed. They passed Tau by, streaming into the open door from which he'd emerged.

The last man to pass Tau was the Noble who claimed to know him. Jabari Onai was his name. He had spirit, but like most Petty Nobles, he was limited by his natural talent, and Jabari had fallen on day one of the melee. Kellan had given him a spot in today's skirmish, in place of much better men, because of Onai's connection to the Common. Hadith Buhari, Kellan thought, was not the only inkokeli who could play mind games.

The Common watched the Indlovu running into the buildings, no doubt considering that he'd not only confirmed the location of

Scale Jayyed's men but also abandoned his sword brothers. Then he saw Jabari Onai and his face changed.

Kellan had been right to include the Petty Noble. Tau was shaken by his presence.

"I'm here, Tau Solarin," Kellan said, pulling the Common's attention back to him, "and this time your father won't save you."

When Kellan first heard the stories about the superhuman Ihashe warrior, he didn't connect them to the man he'd fought in Citadel City. That came later, when he learned the Lesser fought with two swords. Even then, Kellan ignored the tales. He had too much to do to spend time thinking about one unusually talented Ihashe.

Then, days before the melee, his newly appointed Gifted, a powerful initiate named Zuri, ordered him to the Gifted Citadel. It was their first official meeting, but he'd recognized her at once. She was the same Gifted who had enervated him when he'd fought the strange Common.

Already nervous about the meeting, he pushed the incident out of mind and walked over to greet her. He didn't get three steps before she accused him of murder.

She told him she'd have nothing to do with him and that if he did become an Ingonyama, she would reject her duty as his Gifted, jeopardizing his status. She would not enrage and empower a man like him.

Kellan had been lost. He'd murdered no one and she was threatening everything he'd worked for. He tried to calm her, begging her to justify her accusations. When she did, the episode with the crazy Common began to make sense. Kellan had explained himself, soothed the Gifted initiate, and considered the matter closed. However, the Goddess did not seem to see it the same.

The night after the Common dueled and beat Mayumbu, Kellan's patron, Guardian Councillor Abasi Odili, came to him. The councillor explained that Scale Osa would skirmish Scale Jayyed. He wanted Kellan to take care of the Lesser who fought with two swords.

Odili, Kellan realized, didn't know that Tau Solarin was the son of the man he'd ordered Dejen to kill earlier that same cycle. This was not personal. The Royal Nobles had simply had enough of Scale

Jayyed and their unprecedented run. Odili wanted the scale obliterated and Tau dead.

Kellan wanted to refuse. He didn't, though. He couldn't lose the councillor's patronage. Not yet.

It would have been different if his father hadn't been branded a traitor and hanged. It would have been different if losing the man she loved hadn't broken his mother, or if his sister were old enough to run the family's estates, or, after having seen all the tragedy befalling them, if Kellan's uncle had come to his kin's aid. It'd be different if wishes were worldly, but they weren't, and Kellan could look to no one other than himself to save his family.

He still needed Odili, and the man's money and influence, because he had to become an Ingonyama. It was the only way he'd ever get out from under Odili's thumb, his own family's debts, his uncle's disdain, and the shame of his father's cowardice.

Becoming an Ingonyama was everything and the only thing Kellan wanted, before seeing Queen Tsiora at the Guardian Ceremony. He'd seen her before, when they were both young and she was a girl, but she couldn't be called that anymore. Since receiving his guardian dagger from her, he'd thought about the queen more than any man should think about anything. It seemed destiny that the greatest service he could offer his people would also be his greatest joy.

Kellan's uncle could never be Queen Tsiora's true champion, and she would soon have to select another. It meant Kellan had a chance. His name was already spoken in the same breaths as many of the Omehi's legendary warriors, and he'd heard it was whispered in Palm that he was a possibility. It scared him to think it and yet he could hardly think about anything else. He longed to see Tsiora Omehia in more than just his dreams.

Everything Kellan desired was in reach, but a single stride in the wrong direction could burn his hopes to ash. So he told Odili he'd do it and, for the second time, harm a member of the Solarin family.

Kellan exhaled and even his breath seemed to boil in the heat. He pulled his sword from its scabbard and, ready to commit violence, still had time to wish things could be different. He'd played a part in the death of the Common's father, and there was no hiding from that or from the cruel work he was about to do.

Yet, he wanted to tell Tau he was sorry and that it wasn't fair. He couldn't, though, just like he couldn't have turned down Odili. There was so much more at stake than one Lesser's loss.

He called out across the space separating him from the Common of Kerem, taunting Tau with the things he'd learned from the Gifted initiate. "This day was fated," he said, loud enough for those in the stands bordering the urban battlefield to hear. He'd give Odili his show. "Twice we've met. The first time, your father gave his life for yours. The second, a Gifted wanted you spared. Today, it's the two of us, and I've spent my life training to kill men like you."

The world had gone silent, making it easy to hear the strange thing the Common said before he attacked. "You're wrong, Okar," he said. "There are no men like me."

Their blades met in a crash of bronze, and Kellan, much larger, weighing nearly twice what the Common did, planned to use his size, strength, and speed to overcome the smaller man. He'd make a play of it for the watching Nobles, embarrassing the Lesser. Then, after a time, he'd fake a killing blow that would, with the Goddess's blessing, do no more than crack the boy's skull.

It was cruel, but it was the best he could do, since Abasi Odili wanted the Common dead. After, Kellan would tell his patron that he thought he'd struck Tau hard enough to kill. He'd blame his dulled weapon for the error.

He slipped his sword away from the one held in Tau's right, no doubt the Common's better sword hand, and thrust his shield to blind him. As he did, he swung his own blade, planning to catch Tau in the arm or side. He didn't get the chance.

The sword in the Common's left hand moved faster than Kellan thought possible, hitting him on his helmet, snapping his head sideways and sending him stumbling with half the muscles in his neck wrenched out of place.

Head ringing and neck on fire, Kellan righted himself, only to be hit again. He raised his shield for cover and was struck below it. He whipped his sword at Tau's last position, slicing through empty air before taking a bone-numbing blow to the leg that ripped through the leather and cut him.

He reeled and limped back, swinging wildly. The Common, out of reach and eyes blazing, stalked him.

Kellan's heart hammered and his breathing was unsteady. He attacked anyway, but his swing was parried. He swung again and was blocked, repelled. He heaved himself back, desperate to make space, and heard the rumble of running feet.

He looked to the noise's source and his heart sank. It was the unit of Lessers, the ones he'd not been able to finish. They'd come to finish him.

There were eight, maybe nine of them. Too many for him to take alone. But the Common pointed them to the buildings. Kellan didn't dare hope they'd obey and almost wept when they did, running inside to help their sword brothers.

It made no sense, he thought. He'd sent twenty-seven Indlovu into those buildings. The Lessers had no chance against them all.

He grinned. This was it, then. All of Scale Jayyed were together, facing his men. The Lessers would be wiped out. That meant there was only one thing left to be handled. It was on him to eliminate the Common of Kerem.

"Blood will show!" he screamed, delivering a thrust for Tau's chest. The Lesser dodged and Kellan corrected, his blade blasting back the other way, hitting nothing. He rebalanced, spinning low, shield out like a weapon to break Tau's shins. It didn't connect, so he adjusted, ready to strike, and was clubbed to the ground by the flats of two swords.

He gasped. The pain was excruciating and, for a breath, he thought his back broken. It wasn't, but as the feeling in his body flooded back, it felt like someone had whipped hot coals into his skin. He tried to draw breath, but the fires webbing their way through his sides denied him a proper attempt.

"Get up, Nkosi Kellan," the Common said, his voice a rasp. "I'm not finished with you yet."

Kellan spat, tasting blood, and forced himself to his feet. He was hurt, feigned it was worse by wobbling, then flew at Tau. His desire to leave the Lesser unharmed forgotten, he let his sword soar straight for the throat. The Lesser sidestepped as if he'd seen the same sort of attack a thousand times, and Kellan careened past, crumpling, then collapsing beneath the pain and blow to his shoulder from the Common's sword hilt.

"Get up, nkosi," the Common said. "A man should die on his feet."

It was then Kellan realized the Common was toying with him. It was then he felt fear, clamping onto his neck like stone hands, filling his bladder, and making his legs weak. The Common wanted his life. The Common... Kellan tensed every muscle, coiling them, making them ready. He was not Odili's lackey and not a coward like his father. He was Kellan Okar, the best the Indlovu Citadel had ever produced, and fated to be queen's champion. His life would not come cheap.

He surged up, blade first, screaming obscenities, and the Common turned his attack, striking him on the upper arm. Kellan almost dropped his sword in agony, was attacked again, and, blundering away, he threw a desperate parry. It wasn't enough, and he felt armor rip and skin tear as he took a cut to the rib cage that made every movement a misery.

The Common lunged. Kellan swept to intercept with his shield, missed, and took Tau's blade between two of his armor plates, allowing a fingerspan of bronze to enter the muscle on his chest. He fell back, crying out, and wasn't given time enough to blink before the bastard shot his other sword out and low, burying a handspan of bronze in the meat of his left hip. The Lesser's blade pierced his side and ripped free, taking a flap of flesh and leather with it.

Kellan screamed and fell, the wash of sticky wet along his belt line telling him the wound would scar for life.

"Get up, Kellan Okar," the impossibility standing over him said. "Time to die."

ASHES

Tau waited for Okar to rise. The Noble had dropped his sword and was sitting on his rear. He was panting, one hand pressed against the gash Tau had torn in his side.

"Wait!" Kellan said, his free hand up, palm out.

"Greater Noble? That's what you're supposed to be?" Tau rasped, a fierce headache pounding in his head and thinning his vision down to slivers. "You're nothing, less than nothing, an insect to be crushed."

Tau felt tears coming and dashed them away with the back of his hand. He'd waited a long time for this moment. Here was a demon he could kill.

He heard the thunder of footsteps and looked over his shoulder. Several more demons had come out of the building. Tau snarled and blinked away the vision. It was the men from Scale Osa.

That was it, then. They had beaten Hadith and Yaw's unit. Scale Jayyed had been defeated and Tau was to blame.

"Strike him and you die, Lesser scum!" shouted the first Noble out the door.

Tau looked to Kellan. The Indlovu was back on his feet, sword in his blood-soaked hand.

"Get him!" Kellan ordered. "Attack, burn you!"

The men of Scale Osa ran for Tau, Tau made for Kellan, and

Kellan fled, making enough space so he could circle round and head for the safety of his men. Tau couldn't get to Kellan in time, and with dulled swords it would have been difficult to kill Okar before Scale Osa could stop him. To have the time he needed with Kellan, Tau had to kill everyone.

He launched himself into the fray, swords whirling, and the closest man took a dulled blade to the face, shattering his eye socket. The second Indlovu was fortunate. He took a foot to the chest as Tau pushed off of him, making room to careen his weak-side sword into the elbow of another. That man's arm made a sound like a thunderclap and then flapped loose, the bones connecting his upper and lower arm destroyed.

The rest of the men—there were thirteen, including Kellan and the one Tau had kicked—fanned out.

"Beg me!" shouted Kellan, who looked crazed and was still hunched over on the side where Tau had shaved his flesh. "Beg me for mercy!"

Tau attacked, and for a while he was winning, his sword snapping at them like a dragon's jaws. He cut four fingers away from the hands of one Indlovu, blood spraying into the hot Xiddan air as the Noble fell away. He smashed his fist and hilt into the throat of another, and that one went down without protest. Eleven left. It was too many. Tau attacked.

Their blades sliced at him from every angle. One of them cut away Tau's left earlobe. Another missed his hamstring but tore a string of flesh from Tau's calf.

As they harried him, Tau searched the ring of men for Kellan's face. If he was to die here, he would take that nceku with him, but Kellan had removed himself. He stood back from the circle and watched, his sword down and by his side.

"Okar, fight me!" Tau screamed. "Greater Noble? Standing behind your men, feared of a Lesser, a Common?"

Tau was struck from behind. He rolled with the hit, lessening the blow's damage, and avoided being impaled on the point of another man's sword. He snarled at the bastards surrounding him as he regained his feet, blocked one attack, then a second, before taking a sword flat to the gut that bent him double.

Refusing to be put down, he staggered and swung about with his blades, discouraging the rest from following up.

"None of you are worthy to lead us!" he seethed, waving his swords, keeping the Indlovu tentative.

"The Goddess judge you!" shrieked an overzealous Indlovu, diving after Tau. Tau spun off the man's killing line and brought his sword onto the back of the Noble's neck, breaking it. The Noble fell in the dirt, unnaturally still, whimpering, as Tau pretended to charge first one way, then the other.

"Hold the circle," yelled one of the Indlovu. "Hold here and we kill him."

Tau aimed his blades out to either side of his body, turning counter to the Indlovu's rotation around him. His teeth were bared and he was ready to break more men, draw more blood, when he saw Jabari.

"Jabari . . . ," Tau said, not knowing what he thought to find there, and his old friend did not answer. Instead, the Petty Noble tightened his lips and kept his eyes on Tau's sword, avoiding his face.

This was it, then. Tau readied himself. He'd charge Jabari, see if he could break through. If Jabari and the men beside him held, he'd cut the one to the left and spin to stop those behind him from ending his fight. The rest of the plan would follow from the reactions of his enemies.

It was a simple plan. He liked those best. It was also a pathetic plan. Tau sneered at the Nobles around him and gathered his breath. Eleven stood against him. There would be fewer before he died.

"In the name of Scale Jayyed, we surrender and submit to Scale Osa! We surrender and submit. Stand down! Stand down!" Jayyed, holding the gray-on-gray flag of the Ihashe, was running onto the battleground.

"No! I do not surrender!" Tau swung at the Indlovu around him. "I do not surrender!"

Running with Jayyed were two skirmish officiants. The Ihashe umqondisi with Jayyed was hurrying, but the one from the citadel lagged behind. No doubt he would have preferred to wait and see how things played out.

"It is not that Lesser's choice," Jayyed told the Indlovu around Tau.

"I am the scale's umqondisi and I surrender the skirmish. If anyone else is harmed it will be outside the protections of the Queen's Melee."

"Yes, yes," the citadel umqondisi muttered. "Back away, it's done. Scale Osa wins and progresses to the finals. Scale Jayyed is eliminated."

Swords held ready, the Indlovu backed away. Tau eyed them, still turning, expecting one of them to attack at any moment. The last man he turned toward was Jabari, who continued to avoid his eyes.

Kellan spoke from a distance. "Well fought, Tau."

"To ash with you!" Tau spat.

"You may not believe me, but I am sorry for this. I am sorry for your father. I wished no part in either event." Kellan sheathed his sword and joined his men, who were already walking off the battleground.

"Don't you speak of him!" Tau yelled to Kellan's back. "I'll kill you, Okar. I could have killed you today! Guardian dagger? Future Ingonyama? Go to your funeral pyre knowing I'm your better!"

"Be silent, Tau," Jayyed said next to his ear. "Be silent."

A ragged cheer was raised by the men of Scale Osa. They'd won. The crowd, though, come to see violence, were as voiceless as the sun setting overhead.

The Nobles in the stands did not speak. Worry gripped them. The Lessers in the stands did not speak. Rage had them. Scale Jayyed was eliminated and the tournament day had ended, but the bloodshed was just beginning.

CHAPTER FOURTEEN

SECRETS

Tau was injured, and instead of taking him to the Lesser infirmary, Jayyed and Anan took Tau to one of the small tents that served as private quarters for umqondisi in the Crags. Once there, they sent for a Sah priest to tend to Tau and bandage his wounds. Jayyed explained it was best to keep Tau out of sight until tempers in the Crags cooled. Already, several fights had broken out between Lessers and Nobles. Two Lessers, one from the Governor caste, had been hung.

Tau thought to ask why. He didn't. He was weary beyond belief, the cut on his leg ached, his ear burned, and his back was a giant welt.

The Sah priest, a short but curvy Governor caste woman, bound his cuts, rubbed foul-smelling ointment on his back, checked his head for injuries, and waved her hand over his eyes. She told Jayyed he'd be fine and that he should rest. Jayyed thanked her, and when he turned to speak with Anan, the doctor leaned close to Tau.

"You've shown us the truth," she said. "We're more than our caste. The Goddess blesses us equally." She patted him on the shoulder, like his mother used to do, and walked out of the tent.

Jayyed waited until she left. "What did she say?"

Tau was sitting on a cot, staring at the ground. "She said the Goddess blesses us equally. That we're more than our caste."

"Demons in the mist!" swore Jayyed, making Tau flinch. "Now the priests?"

"Why not, Jayyed?" said Anan in a hushed voice. "They've watched the same melee we have."

"Now is not the time."

"Because we're at war?" Anan asked.

Jayyed looked away.

"We're always at war."

"Come, Anan. Tau needs rest." Jayyed held the tent's flap open and they walked out.

Tau lay back and closed his eyes, but the pain was too much and he had to roll to his side. He reached for the oblivion of sleep. It would not come, chased away by thoughts that haunted him. Tau had hesitated. He had held back when he could have killed Kellan.

The tent rustled. Tau shot up, snatching the closer of his two swords as he did. It was Hadith.

"Put it down," Hadith said, as if they were still on the battle-ground, as if he could still deliver orders that Tau had to obey.

Compromising, Tau lowered his blade but did not put it down. "How's Uduak?"

Hadith grimaced. "He'll live and recover. He's already up and walking, Goddess be praised. But that's not why I'm here."

"Why, then?" Tau asked, the sword twitching in his hand.

"Put it away. Everyone knows you can fight." Hadith stepped up, standing a handspan from Tau's face. "I want to know if you can think."

Tau pushed him away. "Leave me be."

"You self-righteous cek, we could have changed everything. We had it in our grasp and you threw it away. You threw all of us away, to take your petty revenge."

"Petty? Mka!"

"Nceku! Your father died? Does that make you special? How many fathers have died in this war? How many more will die because the Nobles use Lessers like a break wall against the hedeni hordes? How many more, before Lessers have a say in the way our lives are spent?"

"A say? A say? We're Lessers. And you, that priest, and everyone else thinks I do this, for what? To upend the castes?"

"Priest?"

"Never mind," said Tau.

"Why do you do it?"

"To make them feel some of the pain I feel! To force them to see that my life, my father's life, is worth more than their whims."

"We're fighting for the same thing. Why do you keep trying to do it alone?"

Tau felt caught and didn't like it. "I'm not looking to change the Chosen," he said.

"Even so, the changes come."

"Then, they come too late."

Hadith narrowed his eyes. "What does that mean?"

"You were born too late to make a difference. We all were."

Hadith got right in Tau's face. "What does that mean?"

The tent's flap rustled and in came Zuri. "Tau! I came as... You have company—"

"Lady Gifted." Hadith backed away from Tau, bowing to Zuri.

"I'll come back," she said.

"Please, Lady. I was leaving." Hadith marched out.

Zuri seemed to forget him as soon as he was out of sight. "Goddess, Tau! Are you okay?"

"Hello, Zuri."

She ran into his arms and hugged him, making him wince when her hands pressed against the welt on his back.

She let go. "You're hurt?"

"I'm well. How are you?... You were watching?"

"Most of the Gifted Citadel was watching. It was horrible."

"I didn't kill him."

"Thank the Goddess."

Tau gave her a sharp look.

"Tau...I have something to tell you. I don't want there to be secrets between us."

Tau said nothing, aware that the day was about to get worse and unsure how it could manage it. Whatever came, he would face it with Zuri, without secrets, with nothing held back.

He decided he would tell her about how he had tracked Odili to the meeting with the Xiddeen. He would tell her about the surrender. She should know. He wanted her to know. "No more secrets," he said.

She looked nervous. She took his hands in hers, and she told him. "Days ago, before the melee, the Gifted Citadel learned that the queen intends to meet with the Gifted leadership and Guardian Council. She will do it the day after tomorrow, after she has declared the melee's winner."

"So soon?" Tau said, surprising her.

"You heard it too?" she asked. "The queen will call her war leaders to the Guardian Keep." She gripped Tau's hands. "I think they're planning a massive attack. I think they're going to graduate the Ihashe, Indlovu, and Gifted initiates early. I think they're going to join us with rest of the military, to take the war to the hedeni."

"You... you what? No."

"The signs are there. Tau, they've called me to active duty. I'll be an Enrager. I'll be an Enrager for Kellan Okar."

There it was. "Enrage? Kellan Okar?" His voice rose with every word, he pulled his fingers free of hers, and balled his hands into fists.

"I couldn't do it. I wouldn't. Not after what you told me. I confronted him, Tau. I ordered him to me and I confronted him. I accused him of Aren's murder. I told him it was you in the circle in Citadel City."

"You did what!"

"It wasn't Kellan's fault—"

"You did what!"

"It was Odili. He wanted Kellan to kill you, and when your father stepped in, he wanted Aren to die. Kellan thought the only way he could spare Aren's life was by taking his hand. He used the maiming as an excuse. He used it to claim that he had taken everything that made Aren a man. Tau, he was ordered by a guardian councillor to kill you and your father. He tried to save you both."

Tau's hands were shaking and he could see demons in the tent

with them. There were two behind Zuri and he could hear the slavering of another behind him. He slammed his eyes shut, tried to
calm down, but the demons were there when he opened them.

"Get out," he said, his voice trembling with strain.

"Kellan's father was killed for treason cycles ago. His family dis-
graced. Odili became his patron when he saw how well Kellan was
doing at the citadel. Kellan knows Odili's reputation, but his patronage keeps Kellan's mother and sisters from poverty." Zuri was trying
to read his face to see if she was getting through. "He had a hard time
telling me that, Tau. I don't think he's the man you believe him to be."

"You betrayed me," Tau said. "You betrayed me and gave that cur
the weapons he needed to defeat me and my brothers."

"I didn't. That was not my—"

"Get out!"

"No, I won't!" Zuri shouted back. "You're not listening. You're
twisting this."

"Twisting it? You come to me, tell me you're consorting with—"

"Consorting?"

"You spin tales of military attacks, hiding behind lies to mask the
fact that you'll be tied to the man who helped murder my father."

"He was trying to save you! Both of you!"

The two demons were standing right behind her. Leering from
over her shoulders. One of them showing teeth as long as Tau's
hands. "Get out!"

"No!"

Tau stood and retrieved his swords. "I can't stomach it, the filth
and lies spewing from your mouth." He stalked to the tent's entrance,
avoiding the demons, and paused there. "No more secrets?" he said.
"I know why the queen is calling the military leadership together.
It's not to wage war. She's calling them to arrange our surrender."

"What? No . . . No, that's not right . . ."

If Zuri said anything more, Tau didn't hear. He left her and her lies
in that demon-filled tent. He left to find Jayyed. No more secrets.

HORNS

Jayyed was in the scale's tent. He was sitting on the dirt floor with Anan. They had their heads together, talking. Tau moved through the room, ignoring the stares from his sword brothers. He went straight for Jayyed.

"Umqondisi, I need to speak with you."

"Tau? You should be resting and, more than that, you should not be here. Armed and full-blooded Indlovu have been wandering through the Lesser half of the Crags all evening. I have little doubt they'd love to run across you."

"It's important."

"Let it keep till morning. Let everyone's blood cool."

"Umqondisi," Tau insisted.

Jayyed sighed. "Join us."

"All respect, it's a private matter."

Anan's brow creased at that, but he acquiesced. "Have your talk."

"Umqondisi, here would not be a good place."

"Mmm...," said Jayyed. "The tent we gave you, then?"

"Somewhere else."

"It's been a strange day. This isn't helping. Follow me."

They left the scale's tent and climbed farther up the Crags. Neither man said a word until they left the fires and noise of the melee encampment behind.

"What is this?" Jayyed asked.

"I followed you and Odili to the Crags."

Jayyed brought a hand to his face, tugging the left side of his mouth like it itched. "You left the isikolo to follow me and a guardian councillor into the Crags? How many times would you like them to hang you, Tau?"

Tau said nothing.

"And today you abandoned your brothers so you could kill the nephew of the queen's champion."

"You know why."

"Have you learned nothing other than how to swing a sword?"

"When I first came to you, I came because it was my path to justice."

"You didn't hear me after Citadel City? Okar is a Greater Noble, and you know I have little love for them, but he's not an evil man."

"You're the second person to tell me that today, which I find strange, since I am neither looking nor asking for opinions on the matter."

"Do you trust the other person? The one who vouched for Okar?" Jayyed asked.

"I thought so."

"Until they told you what you didn't want to hear."

"I know who he is."

"No, you don't," said Jayyed. "You do know who I am. You do, I think, know who the other person is, the one vouching for Okar. Trust the people you know. Trust those who care for your well-being."

Tau shook his head. "This is not why I asked you here."

"I don't imagine it is."

"We can't surrender. We're Chosen," Tau said.

"If we lose the war, there won't be any Chosen."

Tau gestured with his hands. "What do you think happens if we surrender? How much do we give up?" He pointed to Jayyed. "Already, your daughter has been bargained away. I saw that. I saw Odili's face. I know he was part of that trade. He wanted you to suffer."

"It would be difficult for me to deny that," Jayyed said, his eyes locking on Tau's face. "With the arrangement between our queen and the Xiddeen shul, Abasi Odili loses everything. He wanted to pay me back for the small part I played in pushing for peace."

Jayyed paused, sighed, and continued. "When I was on the Guardian Council, I couldn't convince them that the war was already lost, but Queen Tsiora asked to speak with me privately. She believed me. She doesn't think our war with the Xiddeen is the one we should be fighting."

"Odili had you removed from the council after you spoke with her, didn't he?" Tau asked.

"The queen was too new to her throne to protect me, but before I left, she asked me to believe in her, no matter what came, and I did. I do." Jayyed smiled. "And she's done it. She's making peace, in my lifetime. These should be the greatest days of my life, but Odili couldn't have that."

"Jamilah."

Jayyed nodded. "I'm surprised the KaEid went along with it. She loves power as much as he does. It's hard for me to imagine her giving any Gifted to the Xiddeen, and I would have thought it impossible for her to let my daughter go."

"Your daughter is powerful," admitted Tau. "I was out of the line of fire when she hit the Xiddeen with her enervation and I could still feel the force of what she did."

With so much at stake, and Jamilah among the enemy, Jayyed's voice was still pride tinged when he spoke of her. "Enervator? Jamilah is one of the most powerful Enragers, Edifiers, and Entreaters in all the citadel." He looked down. "And she was given away. I thought the KaEid played for bigger stakes. Or, perhaps, in the face of what peace will bring to them, these petty punishments are all the Royal Nobles have left."

Jayyed fixed Tau with a look. "Tau, I would give anything to have my daughter safe by my side, but I want my people to live without war. If Odili is so small that he must put my child in the dragon's mouth, then I pray the dragon thinks Jamilah too wonderful to devour. Nothing Odili can do will make me forsake our chance for peace."

"Its results might."

"I won't pretend things will be the same, but the terms of our agreement are set to protect the vast majority of the Omehi people. They will protect the Lessers from having to send their men to die on the hot sands of the Wrist, from being raided by the hedeni in the middle of the night, from starving to death in cycles with a poor Harvest. This war has deprived our people of so much, and peace could mean a better life for so many."

"If that's true, why is peace not all we talk about? Why has it taken so long?"

"Because the Nobles lose. They fall under the purview of the Xiddeen shul, and he will not permit castes. The Nobles will farm like Harvesters, teach like Governors, work like Commons."

"Maybe," said Tau. "Or we give up our swords and they kill us all. Or we Lessers exchange one master for another."

"The Xiddeen are weary of war. They want peace and they want the Guardians gone, so the land can heal."

"The land?"

"We have Gifted, the Xiddeen have shamans. Their shamans believe that the Guardians pour evil from Isihogo into our world. They think the dragons are poisoning Xidda, that they cause the Curse."

"That makes no sense. We live closest to the dragons and the Curse begins at the edge of our valley."

"The dragons send their poisonous energies out and away from their nests. We are protected precisely because we live so close to them. Have you never wondered how we sailed the Roar? The ocean wasn't always as it is now. It could not have been. It would have been impossible to cross."

Tau was doubtful. "The Guardians cause the Roar?"

"They do. Unintentionally, but they do. They are nomadic. By moving, always, they do not destroy any one place."

"But they've found a reason to ignore their nature and remain on Xidda, with us," Tau said, thinking of the secrets piled on secrets.

"They have, and they have been our best bargaining tool. The queen pushed the Xiddeen as far as she could. The Guardians leave and we are given much in return. It's peace we're founding, not surrender."

"Peace..."

"Yes, after almost two hundred cycles, peace." Jayyed looked old. Perhaps he had always been so. "We should be getting back," he said. "Tell no one of this. We wait until a final agreement with the Xiddeen can be reached. The situation is fragile."

"I won't tell anyone," Tau said, worrying about what he had told Zuri. He hoped she would not tell it to anyone else. More, he wished he could take back his behavior.

"Thank you, Tau."

Tau didn't know what to say or how to feel. Peace...

"My hope is that, in the coming days, we'll discuss this openly," Jayyed said. "We'll look to a better future for ourselves, our kin—"

The war horns blew, drowning out Jayyed's hope. Tau had never heard so many. They came from high in the Fist, their call to battle belittling the night's stillness. More horns sounded, calling all Omehi to arms, and Jayyed's face went slack.

"Goddess," he said. "It's an invasion. We're being invaded!"

Jayyed ran and Tau followed.

PEACE

The Crags were chaos. There were people everywhere, watch fires had been lit to push back the dark, and full-blooded warriors, Ihashe and Indlovu, were arming themselves.

"We must gather the scale," said Jayyed. "Put on your gear, don't forget to bring water. Warriors new to a fight always forget water."

Scale Jayyed were already assembled outside their tent. Anan was bellowing orders, getting his men ready to kill, and to die. He tried to hide it, but the relief on his face when he saw Jayyed was palpable.

"Umqondisi present!" he hollered, and the initiates stood at attention. Tau ran into an open space in the lineup of men.

"My scale," Jayyed said to the men, "I know nothing more than you at the moment, but the horns are calling us to defend the peninsula from invasion." A few of the men muttered at that. "It appears you'll be graduating early, because every man that fights tonight does not do so as an initiate. They do so as a full-blooded warrior of the Omehi military!" A few cheered that. The rest, Tau included, were too chilled by the news to bring themselves to shout.

"Watch for your brothers," Jayyed said. "Keep them safe. They'll do the same for you. Fight hard. The only surrender in war is death's embrace, and I'd ask you to hold that cold touch away for as long as you can." Jayyed looked down the line, meeting as many of his men's eyes as he could. "March with me. We will learn our orders and then we execute them."

The men clapped their feet together, standing tall, and they saluted their umqondisi, who, in live battle, would be their inkokeli. Jayyed turned on his heel and led them to the Nobles' side of the Crags.

Hadith marched beside Uduak, and Tau joined them. Uduak had one set of bandages on his head and another up his shield arm. His face was puffy from a litany of bruises and his nose looked broken. He blinked at Tau in acknowledgment. Yaw was there too, next to Uduak. Chinedu must have been farther back in the marching line.

"By the Goddess, we are fortunate," said Hadith to Uduak and Yaw. It seemed, Tau thought, Hadith was no longer speaking with him.

"Fortunate?" asked Tau, ignoring Hadith's behavior.

"Think about it," he said, tapping his head. "The hedeni have launched a major invasion from the ocean. They must hope to race over the Fist and then on to Palm. They're trying to avoid our military by going over the water. They want to take the center of our valley and lay siege to our capital before our forces in the Wrist have time to react. And, with enough hedeni warriors, they could do it on any other grouping of days except for this grouping."

Hadith smashed a fist into his palm. "They've picked the worst possible time to invade. They're coming to take the center of our valley when every initiate and more than two dragons' worth of full-bloods are gathered here for the Queen's Melee. They're invading and, by the Goddess's blessing alone, we have an entire army here to block their path."

"Fortunate . . . ," said Tau, mulling over the strange timing.

"Impossibly so. A quarter moon earlier or later, and the hedeni would have an unshakable foothold in our valley. They'd reinforce and we'd be wiped out within a moon."

So, it was to be genocide instead of peace, thought Tau. He placed his hands on the hilts of his swords, their presence comforting him. Peace. It had been a short dream. Time to wake up.

"You," said a full-blooded Indlovu to Jayyed. "Take your scale and join up over there." He pointed to a mass of men, Indlovu and

Ihashe. "We're forming several claws to head up the Fist. We'll push the hedeni back."

"Nkosi, what are the Edifiers saying?" asked Jayyed.

Talk of Gifted brought Tau's mind to Zuri. He scanned the crowd of people, seeing Gifted among the Indlovu. He did not see Zuri, but spotting her among the hundreds would be no simple task. He did not see Kellan or the rest of his scale either. Zuri might already be with him and Kellan might be headed for a fight. That worried him.

"The Edifiers have nothing good to say," said the Indlovu. "The hedeni are coming over the mountains in the North, the South, and they're attacking through the Wrist."

"They're really doing this? Invading?" said Jayyed. He sounded bewildered, and Tau understood. Jayyed knew how close they had come to peace. The Noble, however, read Jayyed's tone as fearful.

"Hedeni!" the Noble said. "You'd think two hundred cycles of facing us would have taught them. Well, tonight we'll make the lesson take hold!"

It was meant to be the bold and aggressive talk that builds men's spirits, putting them in a fighting mood. Scale Jayyed did not react. The night's occurrences were too odd and it was too soon after the schism that the day's skirmish had caused between the castes.

The Indlovu glowered at them, wanting to say something derogatory about their bravery or character. To his credit, he held back. War was upon them and he must have been aware that many of the men in front of him wouldn't see the dawn.

"I'm with this wing," he muttered. "It has a full complement of men and will hold the Crags. You need to find your place in the wing over there. Goddess go with you. I mean that. They're putting a Royal Noble, fresh from Palm City, in charge of that lot and they're going into the Fist to meet the hedeni head on."

Jayyed pointed to a wing of full-bloods who were already geared up and about to march. "What about them?"

"Them? They're for the city. They'll keep our people safe if the hedeni break out of the mountains. "

Jayyed's eyes narrowed. "That so?"

"It is. Move out!"

Tau took stock of the defensive wing. It didn't take long to spot what had thrown Jayyed. The Omehi military was as caste oriented as the rest of Omehi culture, but all war groups tended to have a mix of Lessers and Nobles, and Tau did not see a single Lesser in the defensive wing.

"You heard. March!" shouted Anan, giving Tau no more time to consider it.

"Who are you, then?" the tall inkokeli of their new wing asked when Jayyed strode up, scale in tow.

"Jayyed with Scale Jayyed."

The inkokeli was young, thought Tau, and pretty enough to be the type more familiar doing battle amid a woman's skirts than in a skirmish. Tau could tell he'd recognized Jayyed's name, though, and Tau hoped that would mean he'd recognize the umqondisi's experience as well.

"You're Jayyed Ayim, former adviser to the Guardian Council?"

"I am."

"With your scale too? Yes, yes, it is. I see the Common of Kerem. The scar gives him away. Very good. Glad to have you here. We're going up into the Fist. Could be a half-decent fight."

"Could be," said Jayyed.

"Yes, yes. I'm Inkokeli Oluchi. We're breaking the wing into three claws. We'll climb the Fist in a prong formation. There are flatlands up there. If we move fast, if we stay in time with one another, and if we catch the hedeni on the flats, we can pincer them there and crush them."

"Lot of 'ifs,'" whispered Hadith.

"Jayyed, you and your men are with me and my Indlovu. We'll form the center prong. We have a Gifted assigned to us as well." Tau listened close. "She's good. An Enervator with experience. Seen combat in the Wrist."

Tau exhaled. It wasn't Zuri. Almost as bad, the inkokeli of their wing was less than new. He had to be fresh from one of the Royal Noble academies in Palm. He'd probably never seen live combat, even in a skirmish.

"This is it!" Oluchi said, walking up a small rise so he could be seen by the whole wing, unknowingly continuing where the other

Indlovu's speech had ended. "We are Omehi, the Goddess's Chosen. What we do this night will shake the halls of history. We go to meet the faithless hedeni, and where we find them, we fell them. Where they find us, they find death! Follow me! Follow me to victory and glory!"

Oluchi turned toward the Fist and went. The wing went with him and, for a full span, the only sound was men's feet falling in concert.

"Not bad," said Uduak.

"What?" asked Hadith.

"Speech," Uduak said.

Tau had been lost in thought, but Uduak's remark had to be commented on. "That was over a span ago."

"Not bad," the big man repeated.

"He's going to get us killed," said Yaw.

"Not me," said Hadith. "I didn't come all this way to die under some blue blood just days off Palm's teat."

"Quiet, there," said Anan. He was coming up from the rear of the scale and moved past them to march alongside Jayyed. The men hushed, Chinedu coughed, and Scale Jayyed marched to war, to fight, to kill, to die. And Tau realized he couldn't keep up with his emotions. Just spans ago nothing had been more important than the melee, than facing Kellan Okar, and now—

"Swords out!" screeched their inkokeli, his cry chased by the sound of an entire claw, one hundred and sixty-two men, clearing bronze from scabbards.

"I'm Omehi! I'm Omehi!" said a voice from up ahead.

"What is it?" said Tau. He was too close to the middle of the column.

Uduak, tallest among the Lessers, told him. "Indlovu. Bleeding. A lot."

"What's going on?" demanded Oluchi. "Who are you?"

"I'm Scale Osa, under Kellan Okar. We were with Inkokeli Odihambo's wing. We were with Prince Xolani."

"The prince? Where?" asked Oluchi.

"Ambush. The hedeni must have a dragon's worth of fighters. Odihambo's dead. . . . Half the wing is dead. You have to help!"

ROUT

"You have to come now," the injured Indlovu from Scale Osa begged. "They're dying, all of them. The wing is torn to pieces. Only Scale Osa held. Inkokeli Okar was enraged by his Gifted and fought, but it won't be enough."

Tau, who'd begun pushing his way through the column when he heard Scale Osa was involved, was near the front. "Kellan," Tau said, "he's your inkokeli? What did the Gifted who enraged him look like?"

Jayyed was beside Tau. "Stand down," he hissed.

"Who the char and...," started Oluchi. "Oh, the Common of Kerem."

The bloodied Indlovu from Osa showed no surprise at that. He was in shock. "You have to come. My scale...the prince, they die if you don't."

Tau turned to Jayyed, desperate.

Jayyed nodded, his mouth a grim line. "With respect, Inkokeli Oluchi, it is our duty to aid our prince."

"Yes, yes! The prince is in danger. Hurry now, men. We go to kill slough-skins! You, there," Oluchi said, pointing to a full-blooded Indlovu. "Pick six men. Three run to the claw south of us and three to the claw that's north. Tell them to abandon the march to the flats.

They have new orders. They will join us in turning back the hedeni that slew our Noble brother Odihambo."

Oluchi reached into his belt and handed the man two wax seals with the Oluchi family name pressed into them. "Go now." Oluchi turned to the wing. "We've marched for long enough. Now we run. We run to the defense of our queendom and our prince!"

The bloodied Indlovu from Osa led the way, and the wing ran, racing over uneven ground in the dark, racing to save their brothers from being cut down by the treacherous savages, the faithless hedeni. They did not go far before running headlong into the remnants of Wing Odihambo, in full retreat.

"Inkokeli," called Jayyed. "We can hold here. We can form ranks and use this rise as cover." Jayyed pointed to the incline that faced them. They were approaching a large gully that erosion, time, and an ancient and dried flow of water had cut into the mountainside.

Jayyed explained his strategy. "When the hedeni come over it, we'll be waiting to turn the tide."

Tau had no intention of waiting. Zuri could be over that rise. She could be fighting for her life. He would not wait.

"No, Jayyed," said Oluchi. "Our prince could be over there. We take the fight to the hedeni. They will crumble against us!" Oluchi waved the wing onward. "Up and over, men! We'll slake our swords' thirst on hedeni blood."

Oluchi and his scale charged the hill.

"Burn his tongue," cursed Jayyed, ordering his scale to follow.

The Indlovu, taller and longer-legged, topped the rise before Scale Jayyed. By the time Tau crested it, there were already close to two thousand women and men fighting and dying on the path that ran through the shallow gully.

Some of Scale Oluchi had run down to the fighting. The men who did that had gone past their inkokeli, who stood staring.

"Goddess wept," Oluchi said. "What is this?"

The battle was a mess. There were no lines of combat, no true distinction between Xiddeen and Omehi. The gully was a hundred pockets of smaller skirmishes, and in each of them, an outnumbered group of Omehi was in the process of being surrounded and cut down.

"Lost," growled Uduak beside Tau. "Already lost."

Tau wasn't listening. He was scanning the tumult for any sign of Zuri, feeling hopeless. He didn't see her. He'd have no chance of finding her.

"There," Uduak said, pointing near the middle of the gully. A group of twenty Indlovu had their backs pressed to a boulder and were being harried by a much larger Xiddeen force.

Tau looked. He didn't see Zuri but understood why Uduak had called for his attention. Relief flooded him. Zuri was there. She was alive. She had to be. Who else could be keeping Kellan Okar enraged?

"Okar fights there," Tau yelled to Jayyed.

Jayyed saw the situation for what it was. "He's trying to hold the center of the gully, give the remains of the wing time to retreat. He'll die there."

"He stays alive long enough and he saves most of the men in the gully," said Hadith. "They're holding the shortest path. The hedeni need to get past Okar's line to finish the wing."

"He won't hold long enough, and going down there to help kills us as well as him," countered Jayyed. "Look."

Jayyed pointed to the gully's opposite side. A massive force of Xiddeen warriors was gathering on its ridge, preparing to run down and into the gully. Many of the hedeni were mounted on creatures Tau couldn't understand.

They rode lizards as tall as a Lesser's shoulders that, from muzzled head to barbed tail's end, were the length of two men. The creatures flicked their tongues at the air, smelling blood in the night, and their eyes glowed, reflecting what little light there was. The Xiddeen riding the beasts held spears that were much longer than the ones they used in hand-to-hand combat. Tau glanced to Hadith and Uduak to see if his friends saw them too.

"Big lizards," said Uduak.

"The hedeni in the gully are the vanguard," Jayyed said, ignoring the creatures' presence. "The rest of the army is still gathering." He pointed to the Xiddeen on the far ridge. "They've seen our claw. They're waiting. When we commit, so will they. When they join the fight, it turns from bloodbath to massacre."

A massacre. Zuri. Tau knew he should think about it more, but there was no time. He ran into the gully.

"Tau!" Jayyed shouted.

Twenty strides were all it took for Tau to be in the thick of the battle. A Xiddian holding a spear stabbed at him. Tau batted the clumsy strike away and thrust his razor-sharp bronze through the man's chest. The man gasped as the life drained from his eyes. Tau yanked his blade free, felt his bile rise, swallowed it down, and ran on.

He was accosted by two more hedeni. One held a purloined sword and the other was a woman who had lost her spear. Her only weapon was a dagger. She saw Tau coming; he tried to go around her; she gave a cry and lunged. She was dead before she hit the ground.

Her companion, the one holding the stolen sword, swung it like a child. Tau's counter ripped out his throat, and as Tau ran past, the dying savage scrabbled at his neck, his fingers too few to staunch the red river.

Tau took two more steps, and two more Xiddians died. Not wanting to be slowed, he curved around a swathe of slaughter, Omehi men dying to a crush of hedeni and their spears. And then, by the Goddess, there she was, Zuri.

She was a hundred strides away, her back flat against a boulder some avalanche had deposited at the bottom of the gully eons ago. Kellan's group had gotten lucky. The fallen rock gave them a wall to which they could put their backs, and that saved their lives in two ways. It prevented the Xiddeen from encircling them and it allowed Zuri the protection she needed to enrage Kellan.

Fully enraged, Kellan stood head and shoulders taller than Uduak and must have outweighed Tau three times over. His sword dripped with gore and he roared with every swing, his blade coursing with equal ease through the air and through the bodies of all who faced him.

Not to be outdone, Kellan's men played their part in the carnage. They held the line against the Xiddeen advance, dancing in and out of the fray, supporting their enraged inkokeli by ensuring the Xiddeen could not mass in enough numbers to overwhelm him.

Tau had grudging respect for the Indlovu's bravery and tactics, but their efforts wouldn't change the outcome. The citadel warriors were outnumbered, and with every breath, more hedeni boiled into the gully. The lizard riders were coming, skittering down the ridge on the backs of their fiends.

The Xiddeen, it seemed, had thinkers as clever as Hadith. They had not tracked straight from the ocean to Citadel City. They had gone the long way round the Fist, bypassing the plateau where Oluchi had hoped to engage them.

It was poor fortune. Given the prince's presence, Wing Odihambo had hoped to serve as a rear guard to Wing Oluchi. They were not prepared for a fight like this. Tau moved closer, ready to fight his way past more Xiddeen and into the lines of the embattled Indlovu.

"Tau!"

He whirled and saw a furious Jayyed. Anan, Uduak, Hadith, Yaw, Chinedu, Themba, and all the men of Scale Jayyed were behind him.

"Jayyed."

"Nceku! What do you think you're doing?"

"I have to get Zuri," he said, pointing to her.

Jayyed saw her and the anger fell from his face. It took Tau a breath, but he understood. Zuri wasn't much younger than Jayyed's daughter.

"Get her and we leave," said Jayyed. He ordered his men into a fighting formation. "We'll push through, bolster the Indlovu lines, but can't stay. The gully is lost. That's already determined. What isn't yet determined is how many of us need to die in it."

Tau nodded and pushed on, not waiting to see if Scale Jayyed followed. He killed a hedena, got to the Indlovu line, blocked the overzealous thrust of a terrified citadel initiate, shouted that he was on the half-wit's side, and made his way into the ranks of Scale Osa.

Zuri saw him, and through the drain of maintaining Kellan's enraging, he saw her surprise. Tau tried to smile, to reassure her. She did not look reassured.

Kellan and his red-stained sword flashed past Tau's line of sight. Okar was doing as well as was possible given the circumstances. He was also taking hits that would have disabled or killed a normal man.

The enraging protected him, but there was a cost. Every blow Kellan took weakened the flow of energy coursing through him,

and Zuri had to reinforce that energy by drawing more from Isihogo. The more energy she took in, the harder it would be for her to
maintain her shroud. Already, she was rocking on her feet, her face
wan, her eyes dazed. She couldn't continue for much longer.

Tau had to get Zuri out, and the only sure way to do it was to
make Kellan call a retreat. The gully was filled with Xiddeen, and
Scale Jayyed didn't have enough men to escape the battlefield without help. Tau needed these Indlovu, and they would listen only to
Okar. Tau looked for the clearest path to Okar's side and took it.

Wing Odihambo had not expected a fight, and the fight they'd
found was with the entirety of the Xiddeen invading force. From its
outset, the gully battle had been a lost cause. Tau knew this, as he
knew the Xiddian in front of him would feint high and stab for his
chest. He knew it with the same certainty he had when he leaned
away from the thrust that the fighter had not yet thrown. And when
the spear was thrust, Tau punched his sword up and through the
hedena's armpit, into his heart, killing him.

Kellan was close, but a Xiddian threw herself in Tau's way. It was
a warrior woman with full lips, caramel skin, and astonishing green
eyes. She moved like an ocean storm, her bladework brilliant. He
took her hand off at the wrist and she gawped at him, as if to ask
why he'd done it. He wanted to tell her he wasn't sure, but his
bronze was hilt deep in her breastbone and there was nothing to say
that would have meant a damn.

"You!" Okar bellowed at Tau.

Tau wasted no time. "The battle is lost. Call a retreat."

Okar stove in a Xiddian's skull with the edge of his shield. "No."

"We can't hold."

"They killed him," Okar said, teeth clenched, his sword wheeling
this way, then that, demanding that those who opposed him either
leap back or die.

"Who?"

"The prince!"

"Prince Xolani?" Tau said, unable to imagine Omehi royalty
being killed in battle. It made no sense.

Okar grimaced at the name like the failure was his. "He's dead."

"Us dying won't bring him back."

"Giving time for the rest to escape," Kellan grunted, still swinging.

It wasn't true. Well, it was true, but it wasn't Kellan's real reason. Kellan wanted to die here, and Tau wanted to accuse him of that. That wouldn't get Zuri out, though. "You've done what you can. Leave now or the rest of your men die. Your Gifted dies."

Kellan swung his sword, clearing ground between him and those pressing forward. He spared Tau a glance and cast his eyes across the battle, which had long ago become a rout.

"Inkokeli Okar," Tau tried, "you need to save the ones in your care."

That got through. "Retreat!" shouted Kellan. "Retreat!" But it was too late.

Down the line from them the Xiddeen backed away, revealing the horror their press of bodies had kept hidden. Chinedu was closest, and Tau called out, screaming his sword brother's name, not knowing if Chinedu heard him or if he noticed on his own. Either way, Chinedu turned and faced the enormous and enraged Xiddian warrior.

Chinedu froze. He coughed. Then, bravely, he brought up his sword. It would, Tau knew, make no difference.

DAASO HEADTAKER

Daaso, headtaker for tribe Taonga, feared no man and had feared no man since beating her father bloody. Daaso had been young, her father drunk, and her mother had been in her father's way. Her father struck her mother and Daaso struck her father, several times. After that, there had been only one more fight between them to settle the order in the house. Daaso, not yet a woman, ruled and her father followed.

This was unusual, even among the Taonga, who prized strength, but Daaso was unusual. She was bigger than everyone she'd ever met, and stronger too. She'd lost wrestling matches, but never twice to the same fighter. She'd lost spear fights, but never to the same warrior, man or woman.

Daaso had risen to be a great warrior of the Taonga. Everyone knew her name, and those who didn't had heard of her deeds. She had fought in the fire-demon desert against the invaders and their black-robed witches. She had faced their small warriors, garbed in gray, and killed them by the dozens. She had battled their leather-and-bronze-armored men as well. They were tougher, faster, and used their swords like they were born holding them. She'd killed her share of them just the same.

Daaso had more than two lifetimes' worth of honor, a handsome husband, and birth-paired daughters, both of whom she could see becoming ferocious spearwomen one day. Daaso was blessed, and her blessings had multiplied when she was chosen at the Conclave to be bound to a shaman who had learned the invaders' magics. The shaman and Daaso had trained, and Daaso, who had already lived a glorious life, knew what it was to be one of the gods when the magics worked through her. They made her stronger, bigger, and faster than any mortal had any right to be.

Daaso, headtaker of the Taonga, feared no man, and with the shaman's help, she stood just below the gods. She thought that fitting, since she would take a god's vengeance for the evil the invaders had unleashed upon her homeland. She would cut her way through their stolen valley and uproot these vile people from the earth that their presence poisoned.

Daaso raised her spear. One of the small men was in her way. He was slim, he had a pinched face, his eyes too close together, and he coughed as if with illness. He looked surprised to see Daaso. The invaders had not expected the tribes to have their magics, and they always hesitated when faced by a woman.

The invader leveled his sword, moving faster and with more precision than most of the small men in gray. It didn't matter. Daaso lashed out with a god's strength, sweeping aside the coughing man's sword and, with the same blow, taking the man's head from his shoulders. The stupid look of surprise was still on his face as it spun through the air.

Someone shouted and came at Daaso. Foolish, she thought, to rally to the defense of a man already dead. Foolish, she thought, to come against Daaso Headtaker.

Daaso swung her spear at the running man, another small one, and was impressed when this swordsman ducked beneath the swing and came up attacking. Here, at last, was a challenge. Daaso jumped back, avoiding the small one's thrust, spun her spear, grabbing near its point, and rammed its haft into her opponent. She hit him, breaking ribs, and the invader flew back, slamming into the ground. Daaso came to finish him off and heard another man calling to the one she was about to kill.

"Jai-ehd!"

Daaso looked over to the man who had cried. It was another small one. He was standing near the invader who had been magicked as Daaso was, but unlike the magicked invader, or any of the others, this small man carried two swords.

Even across the distance and death struggles separating them, Daaso felt Two Swords' hate. It was palpable. Daaso made herself hold the look with the small invader. She smiled at Two Swords. Daaso feared no man, and if Two Swords cared for Jai-ehd, then Two Swords could watch him die. Daaso adjusted her spear grip and went to finish the good work she'd started.

The one named Jai-ehd scrambled to his feet. He was leaning to one side, unable to stand straight because of the ribs. He was older, Daaso realized, brave too. Daaso could admire that, even in an invader.

Daaso attacked and the wounded man blocked, staggering under the weight of Daaso's crushing blow. Daaso darted her spear in and out at the swordsman and landed no killing blow. The man was good, better than any small gray Daaso had fought. He defended Daaso's first two strikes with his blade, blunted the third on his shield, and countered with a straight thrust that took Daaso in the shoulder.

For a moment, Daaso worried the invaders' magics would not do as the shaman had said. She worried that Jai-ehd's blade would dive into her shoulder and deaden her arm, but the magic held and Daaso's skin was like stone. The swordsman's blade bit into Daaso's flesh, but instead of losing the use of her arm, Daaso was left with little more than a cut.

Still, a lesson was learned. This small one should be taken seriously and the shaman had warned Daaso not to take unnecessary blows. Each time Daaso was struck it weakened the shaman.

Daaso swung at Jai-ehd with enough force to take his head. The small one danced back and out of reach. Daaso fired spear thrust after thrust at him and he dodged and pranced, or batted Daaso's spear away. The battle between them was taking too long, and Daaso dashed forward, sending her spear ahead. The small one slipped to the side and Daaso reached out with one of her long arms, snatching up a handful of the small one's tunic, so he could no longer scurry like a lizard on hot rocks.

Daaso, holding the small one still, thrust her serrated spear into and through the meat of the man's leg. The small one, with terrible speed, brought his sword down onto Daaso's forearm. The blow should, by rights, have cut the limb away, but with the magic flowing through Daaso, the blade bruised instead of severed.

With no desire to test the shaman or his limits, Daaso tore her spear free from the small one's leg in a shower of blood. The invader shook Daaso's hand off his tunic and tried to step back, a mistake. As weight came down on the leg, with half its thigh muscle detached, it buckled.

The man fell, his expression a mask of fear and pain. He did not cry out, though. He had not when Daaso ripped his leg, and he did not when he fell. Daaso respected that, and Daaso knew the invader would cry soon enough.

Daaso raised her spear high, and with all the speed and strength the magic gave her, she slammed its point into the swordsman's gut, out his back, and into the dirt beneath him.

The swordsman screamed, dropped his sword, and curled up around the wound, reaching for the spear impaling him. Daaso wrenched her weapon clear, its serrations doing more damage on the way out. The man gasped, fell back, and vomited blood.

Daaso declined to take his head. Leaving him as he was would make for a worse end. He'd linger and he'd suffer, which was as it should be. Cruel, but better than any of them deserved.

Daaso stepped back and turned in the direction where she'd last seen Two Swords. Two Swords was coming. Daaso had known he would and Daaso had just enough time to make a mess of him. She'd kill Two Swords and then retreat, allowing her shaman to rest.

Only, there were too many Xiddeen between them. Two Swords would never cross the distance without taking a dozen spears in the back. Daaso thought to go to Two Swords. They could come together, like in the old myths, and settle their spear feud, but the magicked invader was over there and Daaso had taken an oath.

The Xiddeen warriors chosen to be imbued with this invader magic had sworn to Warlord Achak that they would not face the similarly magicked invaders. There were too few Xiddeen who had been trained to be magicked, and the warlord did not want any of them to die because they had decided to test their honor.

Daaso felt frustration. She was not afraid of the magicked invader. She would kill him as she had killed a hundred others. However, she had made her oath and her word was bone.

Daaso backed away from the front lines, ready to leave the battle, for now. She had wanted to kill Two Swords, but there was no point waiting. The small man would be lucky to make it halfway to her before some spearwoman or man punched holes through him.

No, Daaso would go, allow the shaman the rest he needed. She would take a drink of water and return to behead more invaders. Her mind was made up when Two Swords cut a spearman in half and called out to Daaso.

Daaso chuckled. The small one had spirit, and she stayed to encourage the fool, to see how the little man would die.

Two Swords threaded his way through several spear thrusts and killed three warriors as quick as Daaso could count them. The invader paid the dead and dying no mind, coming on fast. Daaso blinked and another was cut down. There was something strange happening here, and Daaso, experiencing the first stirrings of discomfort, tightened her grip on her spear.

There were still too many Xiddeen between them to think the gods would grace Two Swords with a glorious death by Daaso's hand, but Daaso was fascinated. She watched as Makara, one of tribe Taonga's best spearwomen, faced off against Two Swords. Makara's spear was legendary and she had two other Taongans with her.

She came at Two Swords from the side, lashing out without warning. She'd always been fast and aggressive. Somehow, Two Swords had seen her. He swayed to the side and lunged at Makara. Then he spun, extending his other sword and catching the second spearwoman, who had gotten too close. Without care, Two Swords turned his back to Makara and killed the third spearwoman, finishing that warrior with a sword through the neck. Daaso had no idea why Makara waited. The invader had his back to her. He was defenseless.

Makara dropped to her knees, the back of her tunic soaked in a pool of blood. She collapsed, dead. Daaso had not even seen the blow that had taken her life, and once again, Two Swords was coming.

A young spearman, who was not so young that he should not have known better, leapt at the small invader, shouting his war cry. Two Swords killed that poor fool without changing the pace of his stride. Then, finding Daaso again in the crush of bodies, Two Swords broke into a sprint.

He was yelling. Daaso had no idea what he said or what it meant, but the commotion drew the attention of the nearest spearmen and women. Two Swords killed the closest four in less time than it took for Daaso's heart to beat. With those last gone to the gods, Two Swords was close, close enough for Daaso to see his eyes, to see the demon in them.

The invader yelled to Daaso again, the string of words unintelligible, their meaning unmistakable. It was a challenge. It was a call to fight, to settle their spear feud.

Daaso felt the magic flowing through her. It made her skin hard as stone, amplifying her strength and speed, making her bigger and heavier than three small men, and Daaso, headtaker of tribe Taonga, who feared no man under all the gods, readjusted her spear grip, breathed deep through her nose, turned, and ran.

The small one screamed his frustration at Daaso's back. Two Swords could not follow. Pushing further into the Xiddeen and away from his own people would mean destruction.

Daaso was safe. She kept running. Daaso Headtaker feared no man, but she knew the truth. Two Swords was not a man.

CHAPTER FIFTEEN

CONCLAVE

Tau screamed at the hedena who had speared Jayyed, unable to believe the warrior woman had run. The Xiddeen in front of him seemed surprised too, and for a moment the fighting stopped. Tau didn't notice. He was numb. It had happened again. Someone he cared for had been hurt, and in spite of everything he'd done, nothing had changed. He'd been unable to stop it.

A Xiddeen warrior, the first to start fighting again, stabbed at him. Tau killed the man and took a step forward. Another Xiddian, fighting an Indlovu, was pushed too close. Tau ran him through and took another step. He could do it. He could chase the warrior woman down. He could—

"Common of Kerem, no!" ordered Kellan Okar from behind him.

"Don't call me that," Tau said, struggling to control himself.

"You will throw your life away. Go to your umqondisi. He's dying and we can't hold."

"Jayyed..."

"He's still alive. Will you let him leave this world alone?"

Tau glared at Kellan but left the front lines, running to where he'd seen Jayyed fall. He found him, face ashen and eyes half-closed. Tau went to his knees and took his hand. "Jayyed."

"Tau?"

"It's me."

"I thought... I thought it was possible. Peace."

Tau was back to the day his father died. "Fight, Umqondisi. Keep fighting. We'll get you to the Crags and a Sah priest will make this right."

"Take it... Ta..." Jayyed shoved something into Tau's hand. It was his guardian dagger.

"No, you'll want it when you're better," Tau told him.

"Get the scale... out." Jayyed pressed Tau's fingers closed around the rare weapon.

"Simple plan, like I've always liked. We're leaving, all of us."

Jayyed wasn't listening, and his eyes slid past Tau. Tau hadn't heard anyone approach, but Jayyed's gaze was so certain that Tau checked.

The collapsing front lines of the battle had pushed closer, but there was no one over Tau's shoulder. He looked back. Jayyed's eyes were focused, clear.

"Jamilah?" Jayyed asked. "You're already here?" He struggled, desperate to breathe and unable to take in air but wanting to say more. "Jamilah," he said. His daughter's name. His last word. Jayyed died there, in the dirt.

Tau heard heavy footfalls. He swung round and saw Kellan. The Greater Noble was no longer enraged and Zuri was with him. The battle had taken a unique toll on her. She looked bone weary and ill. Yet, she was caring enough, loving enough, to share his hurt.

She went to Tau and held him. She hadn't known Jayyed but could see what he meant to Tau. Her pity swept away the last of Tau's self-control and tears blurred his sight.

"He's dead," he told her, voice flat.

"Our battle lines have collapsed," Kellan told him. "We go now or never."

Zuri let go of her hug and Tau tucked Jayyed's guardian dagger into his belt before slipping a hand beneath the sword master's body.

"He can't come," said Kellan.

"I'm not leaving him with them," Tau said, waving his free arm in the direction of the hedeni.

"Tau, we'll have to run," Kellan said. "More of us are going to die before this is over. You carry his body and you risk yourself, as well as those of us who won't leave you behind." Kellan glanced at Zuri as he said the last part.

Tau wiped at his face, clearing tears. He stood. "Where's my scale?"

"Fighting to clear a path out of this for us," Kellan said. "If they can manage it, it will not stay clear for long."

Tau nodded, closed his eyes, and sent a prayer to the Goddess. He took Zuri's hand. Kellan looked like he wanted to say something about that but must have changed his mind. Instead, the Greater Noble bellowed to the Indlovu still fighting, ordering a retreat. The Indlovu, disciplined even in defeat, broke away from the disintegrating front lines, fleeing before the Xiddeen.

They ran, abandoning the mountaintop gully, past Inkokeli Oluchi, who had died surrounded by the bodies of a dozen of his men. They ran from the place where Jayyed Ayim and close to two wings of Chosen had breathed their last, and they did not slow until they were a thousand strides away.

They caught up to the remaining men of Scale Jayyed, Scale Osa, and what was left of Scale Otieno, the third scale that had made up Oluchi's wing. To Tau's relief, he spotted Hadith, Yaw, and Uduak. Yaw's shield arm was wrapped from wrist to shoulder with filthy cloth crusted with blood, but other than that, his friends had been fortunate.

"Tau!" Uduak said, coming over.

"Chinedu and Jayyed—" Tau said, his throat closing as he spoke their names.

Uduak stepped back, coming no closer. Yaw turned away, shutting his eyes, and Themba, near enough to hear Tau, was speechless.

Hadith came forward, speaking more to the ground than to those around him. "Anan too. He saved me."

Themba spoke then. "Runako and Mavuto are gone."

Mshindi, the twin, stepped forward. "Kuende is dead. I cut down the mka who slew him, but my brother is dead."

"You avenged him," Yaw said.

"I should have saved him. He's back there now, lying in the muck, my brother. I've never been away from him. We came into this

world together." Mshindi turned away, speaking the last to himself.
"Always thought we'd leave it that way too."

"They're coming," Kellan said, indicating the way behind them.
He had his hand on the hilt of his sword.

Tau looked. The night was dark, but the path behind them was
long and level, and he'd been born with sharp eyes. He could see
them.

The Xiddeen had reorganized themselves. They were marching.
At the front of their column was a group of lizard riders.

Hadith pressed his forehead to Mshindi's, speaking to the bereaved
brother. That done, he turned to the group. "We have to stay ahead
of them."

Kellan was standing nearby. "Yes, if anyone is still in the Crags,
we need to warn them, and if not, we need to warn Citadel City.
They have to know that our defense of the Fist failed."

Hadith raised his voice, speaking to the remnants of two wings.
"Help the wounded, no one gets left behind, but know that we cannot slow our pace. Citadel City may stand or fall on our speed."

Kellan eyed Hadith, unsure how to deal with the Lesser's pre-
sumption.

"Leave it," said Zuri. Kellan grunted but left it, and the fighters,
Ihashe and Indlovu, moved as fast as they could down the mountain.

"Tau," Zuri said, "there will be no peace?"

"Peace?" Kellan and Hadith said together.

Tau addressed Kellan. "You're the champion's nephew."

"And?" said Kellan.

Tau hesitated. It felt strange to give up the secret, but it was
more strange to imagine it meant anything but ashes. "Before the
melee, I followed Jayyed and Odili. They joined up with the queen's
champion, the KaEid, a few Gifted, and a couple Ingonyama. They
climbed the Crags and met a party of Xiddeen in the Fist."

"They did what?" said Kellan.

"You really want us to believe that you didn't know your uncle
was holding peace talks?" asked Tau.

Hadith almost choked on the words. "Peace talks?"

"I wouldn't know," said Kellan. "Abshir is more queen's champion than uncle. The man refused to come to my father's funeral. He said he could not, in good conscience, attend a coward's burning."

Tau could hear the bitterness in Kellan's voice.

"I wouldn't know anything that I was not, as an Indlovu initiate, supposed to know," Kellan said.

"What happened in the Crags?" Zuri asked.

"I only know what I overheard," Tau said.

"Then, tell us that."

"The hedeni came to the meeting with a captured Gifted, an Enrager. She'd been their prisoner for almost a full cycle. She was tortured. They made her teach them how to enrage."

"Impossible," Kellan said. "The races of man cannot learn each other's gifts. Besides, the Goddess burned out the Xiddeen's gifts when She cursed them."

Tau's voice was tight. "The hedena enraged, who killed Chinedu and Jayyed, would have a word with you on that." Kellan had no reply, and Tau told them the rest. "At the meeting, the hedeni returned our Gifted. Their warlord's son came too. The son is meant to manage our military's surrender, as a beginning to peace. In turn, we gave them an Enervator. She will teach her gift. Then, to complete the terms for peace, the dragons must leave Xidda and Queen Tsiora must marry the warlord's son."

"No, she can't!" Kellan spluttered. "Why would we accept this?"

"Jayyed doesn't think…he didn't think the war winnable and tried to prove it to the Guardian Council. For doing so, he was removed from their ranks and stripped of his role among them."

"If they found his evidence so lacking, how did we come to peace talks?" Kellan asked.

"Your uncle sits on the council. He heard Jayyed speak. He must have told the queen."

Kellan spoke slowly, placing emphasis on each word. "Your position is that secondhand words convinced our queen to sue for peace?"

"Jayyed spoke with her directly and it seemed to him that the queen already knew we were losing. But maybe his testimony to the council, along with whatever else she knows, pushed her toward peace."

"As you say," said Kellan, watching Tau from the side of his eyes.

"The talks I overheard were not the first ones. Queen Tsiora has had her champion, council chairman, and KaEid working to see if peace is possible. She found out it was, and, earlier tonight, Zuri told me that the queen planned to meet with the Guardian Council after the melee." Tau looked at the faces of those around him. "I think that meeting's goal is to inform the council that terms for peace have been accepted. If the queen knows that war with the Xiddeen ends in our destruction, she has to stop it."

Themba interjected. "Stop the war? Surrender it, you mean."

Themba's words, so near the ones Tau had spoken to Jayyed, seemed naive when voiced as the tatters of their fighting force raced down a mountain in the heartland of their queendom, fleeing an army of invaders they could not stop.

"You think it was easy for Jayyed to argue for peace?" Tau asked. "He spent his whole life fighting the hedeni. He sacrificed so much, and in the end, the Nobles took more from him than the Xiddeen ever did. Odili and the KaEid used Jamilah to hurt him. They placed his only child in the hands of our enemy!" Tau's voice had gotten louder. He didn't hear Zuri when first she spoke.

"No," she said. "Goddess, no." Zuri had stopped moving.

"Lady Gifted, we cannot dally," Kellan told her.

"We gave them Jamilah? Jamilah is Jayyed's daughter?"

Something in the way she said it made the rest of them stop.

"She's not just an Enervator," Zuri said. "Jamilah is one of our most powerful. She's an Entreater."

"We really should keep moving," Yaw said, looking back. The hedeni were lost to sight on the Crag's twisting paths, but they would not be far behind.

"Jayyed told me that she knew how to call to the Guardians," Tau said, "but she won't be able to do it. They blindfolded her, then covered her head before taking her into Xiddeen territory, to a gathering they call the Conclave. She can't direct the dragons there. She'll have no idea where she is and she's alone, no Hex."

Zuri was breathing too fast, like she'd been sprinting. "That's not how it works," she said. "Remember, Tau, Entreaters send out a youngling distress call. The Entreater doesn't need to know where she is. The dragons come to her."

"The Guardians can sense where this Gifted is?" Hadith asked.

"Yes," Zuri said to them both. "Yes."

"Must go," said Uduak, placing a large hand in the middle of Zuri's and Tau's backs, encouraging them forward.

"She was taken alone," Tau said, marching again. "She needs a Hex to call a Guardian."

"Only if she means to survive," Zuri said.

"Wait, the plan was to have Jamilah call down a Guardian attack on the Conclave?" asked Kellan.

"Why won't she survive?" asked Hadith.

Zuri turned to him. "If Jamilah calls a Guardian to the Conclave, it will come, it will attack, and when it realizes its youngling is not the source of the distress call, it will hold Jamilah's soul in Isihogo until her ability to hide from the demons fails. When that happens, the demons will find and kill her."

"Ah . . . ," said Hadith.

"No. I can't accept this," Kellan told the others. "It means my uncle negotiated in bad faith. He's many things but would never broker a false treaty. Not for war, peace, or surrender."

"He doesn't know," Zuri said. "Don't you see? It's a coup."

"A coup?" Kellan shook his head. "Lady Gifted, this path twists too much."

"And yet, she's right . . . ," Hadith said. "When the queen chose peace, she went against the Royal Nobles. Peace doesn't just end her reign; it ends them too."

Kellan spoke to Hadith. "You think the Royal Nobles have conspired to make sure a doomed war continues? Why? So they can hold on to privilege? Power? What good is it, if they're dead? There's no coup or conspiracy. For one to exist, the Royal Nobles have to believe we can win."

"That is what they believe," Tau said.

Kellan rounded on Tau, towering over him. "Then maybe they're right!"

"No," Tau insisted. "Jayyed was certain. The queen is certain. There are too many hedeni, and that was before they had our gifts."

"So," said Themba, "peace is our only hope and the hedeni are invading....Unfortunate."

"There's no need for talk of coups or conspiracy," Kellan said. "In war, the simple answer is often the correct one. The savages lulled us with hopes of peace and launched a surprise attack when we were vulnerable."

Zuri grabbed Tau's and Kellan's wrists, squeezing tight, her sudden movement making Uduak draw his blade.

"Zuri?" asked Tau.

"She's already done it," Zuri said.

Kellan pulled his wrist out of Zuri's grip. "With respect, Lady Gifted—"

"The hedeni...This isn't a first strike. We attacked them."

Kellan threw his hands in the air and marched away.

"A Guardian attacked the Conclave," Zuri said to his back. "It destroyed it and Jamilah is dead."

Kellan turned to her, incredulous. He was about to say something, but Tau was no longer listening. Zuri's words had completed the picture he'd been struggling to form and, finally, he could see it.

He saw how well Odili and the KaEid had planned this. He saw how patient Jamilah was to wait for the right time. Jamilah would teach enervation to the Xiddeen because those she taught would never be able to use it against the Chosen. She would train the shamans until it was time for the Queen's Melee. Then, during the melee, when both the Northern and Southern Isikolo, the citadel, and much of the Omehi military were in the Crags, Jamilah would call a dragon.

It had to be done then. The melee was the only time when enough of the Omehi military could be ordered into the Crags and Citadel City without raising the champion's or the queen's suspicion.

Tau could see it. He could see the whole horrifying picture. He saw the colossal black dragon that Jamilah would have called and, in his mind's eye, he saw it swoop down from the sky, blowing fire before it. He saw it boil the earth and blast a million souls to char and ash.

Kellan questioned Zuri. "You can sense this? The dragon? Jamilah?"

"No," Zuri said, "but it's why the hedeni are invading. We burned their Conclave and everyone there to ash. We are the ones who betrayed the peace."

They were in the Crags, near its cliffs. They could see all the way down to Citadel City. In the city's center, with its massive domes, stood the queen's stronghold, the Guardian Keep. The domes glowed with the scintillations of several hundred torches, fiery brands held in the hands of those outside its walls.

"Where would the queen be, right now?" asked Hadith, eyes locked on the scene before him.

"She's in the keep, isn't she?" said Tau.

Kellan was staring down at the city. He looked like a man with his head in a noose. "She's in the keep," he said.

The keep was surrounded—surrounded and under siege by an army of Indlovu.

"It's a coup," Kellan said.

YOUNGLING

K ellan ordered everyone down to Citadel City. Those too
injured to travel at speed were given a few guards and told to
leave the path, so they could hide from the Xiddeen. The rest ran.
Tau stayed beside Zuri, who was wearied from her time in Isihogo
and unused to using her body so harshly.

Running, they reached Citadel City in short order, finding its
gates and walls guarded by full-blooded Indlovu. One of them
raised a war horn to his lips, ready to send out an alarm. When the
guard realized they were Omehi, he lowered it.

"My name is Kellan Okar, third-cycle initiate of the Indlovu Cit-
adel. We have fought a battle against the invading hedeni in the Fist.
I demand entry for my men and my injured. We have news for the
Guardian Council."

Tau noted that Kellan did not say the champion or the queen.

The Indlovu with the war horn looked down from the low wall.
"Well met, Okar," he said, emphasizing Kellan's family name. "The
Omehi military, under the direct command of Inkokeli Odili, has
taken charge of the city's defense. You may enter but must proceed
directly to the Indlovu Citadel. It is the only place we can guarantee
your safety."

"With respect, nkosi," said Kellan. "I have already battled my enemy tonight. I have no need of protection. I do need to meet with members of the Guardian Council, or Odili in particular, to give them news of the battle and how it was lost."

"Lost?"

"The hedeni are invading in force."

"Are they?"

"Nkosi, time is being wasted and I have important information—"

"The inkokeli has the information he needs. I will send escorts to guide you to the citadel."

"I know the way."

"You do me injury, Okar. I seek your safety."

Kellan grew agitated. "We are being pursued by an invading force and they come in large numbers."

"The Goddess smiles on her Chosen. We happen to have large numbers of full-blooded military men and Gifted in the city."

"I do not see them."

"You will," said the Indlovu.

"Coming down from the Crags I saw fires in the city."

The Indlovu's eyes narrowed. "Did you?"

"They appeared to be coming from its center. Are we under attack?"

"I had hoped to avoid troubling you, Nkosi Kellan, but a seditious faction has, for the moment, taken the Guardian Keep. They are traitors demanding that when the invaders come, we surrender."

"I see..."

"Do not let it concern you. It's a few fools, traitors. Inkokeli Odili will burn them out."

Tau was about to say something. Zuri must have been able to tell. She elbowed him, urging silence.

"Nkosi," the Indlovu said, smiling, "you should proceed to the citadel."

"My thanks," said Kellan. "One last question, if it please you. Do we know the names or identities of these traitors?"

The warrior's smile grew grim. "Can it matter? They are traitors. They will be caught and hung. We are Omehi, the Goddess's Chosen. We do not surrender."

Kellan hesitated. "From your lips to the Goddess's ears," he said.

The man nodded at that, then waved a hand at someone behind him, and the gates opened. They entered the city, the glow of the distant fires lending a bizarre sense of warmth to the otherwise dark night. The lead Indlovu sent three full-bloods with them. They were told to go the Indlovu Citadel and nowhere else. This was a directive from Inkokeli Odili himself. No one was allowed to be on the streets of Citadel City until the enemy coming for their gates had been repulsed.

The full-bloods took up positions at the front, middle, and rear of their party.

"What do you believe now, Okar?" Tau whispered, saying Kellan's family name in the same way the Indlovu at the gates had.

"I've admitted it, Lesser," Kellan said. "Odili seeks to overthrow Queen Tsiora."

"He's filled the city with military loyal to his cause," said Hadith.

"It's not over," said Kellan.

"It's not?" Themba said. "Seems over."

"It's not," Hadith said. "Odili's wing are still sieging the keep, and that means the queen is alive. They wouldn't waste time fighting for anything or anyone less. Killing her is the only way he can secure the queendom under his control. He'll have to get it done quickly, though."

"The hedeni," said Themba.

Hadith nodded. "Odili has to kill Tsiora soon. He has to end the siege and set his men to the defense of the city."

Tau didn't think the odds made sense. "Is Odili that stupid? The Xiddeen are invading. He can't stop them with a few wings of full-bloods."

"That's not all he has," Zuri said. "The KaEid will be with him. Once the queen is dead, she'll command the Gifted to call Guardians to our defense. Odili only needs to hold the hedeni back until the dragons arrive."

"So, we all die tomorrow or the next day, instead of tonight," said Tau. "If Jayyed was right, we cannot defeat the Xiddeen in an all-out war."

"We have to save the queen," Kellan said, looking from face to face. "She needs us."

"Kellan's right," Zuri said. "Queen Tsiora is for peace and was betrayed by the same women and men who betrayed the hedeni. If she can convince their shul and warlords that she had no part in the attack on the Conclave, then peace might stand."

Hadith frowned. "More 'ifs.'"

Tau agreed with Hadith. "This is our hope? Would we honor peace if the Xiddeen destroyed Palm or Kigambe? Would we forgive them if they murdered every woman, man, and child in Kerem?" Tau's question cut hard because it was easy to answer. The Omehi would not forgive.

"The queen is the hope we have," Zuri told Tau.

"I'll fight," said Kellan. "I'll go to her aid."

Tau was incredulous. "Fight who? With what? The Indlovu have the keep surrounded."

"The queen has her guards. The queen has my uncle," Kellan said.

Tau hated feeling so helpless, but their helplessness was a reality. "They can't hold against a wing of full-bloods. We have no way to break the siege or get to the queen."

"That's not true," said Zuri. "The youngling."

Tau did not like where this was going. "The youngling beneath the Guardian Keep?"

Kellan looked lost. "There are Guardians in the Guardian Keep?"

Zuri nodded.

"Why are there Guardians in the Guardian Keep?" he asked.

Zuri didn't answer that. "The youngling tunnels. We can bring fighters through the Gifted Citadel and into the keep."

"Excuse, Lady Gifted," Yaw said, "but we're not being taken to the Gifted Citadel."

Uduak grunted, drew his sword, and leapt onto the back of the full-blood leading them, bearing him to the ground. The full-blood called out and Uduak knocked him unconscious. The full-blood near the middle of the line pulled his blade free of its scabbard, but so had most of Scale Jayyed. He looked at the sharp bronze aimed at his chest and dropped the weapon.

Scale Osa made up most of the rear, and they did not understand the confusion, but the full-blood with them had seen enough. He took off running.

"He'll tell the ones at the gate!" said Yaw.

"It won't matter," Hadith said, pointing to the unconscious Indlovu. "When Uduak hit that one, we chose sides."

Uduak brushed himself off. "Right side."

"Fighting for the queen, a Royal Noble, is the right side?" Themba asked.

"We have to hurry," Zuri said. "We don't know how much time the queen has. If Odili kills her, this is for nothing."

"Eh, we'll also be hanged as traitors, don't forget that part," Themba said.

"Themba," muttered Hadith, "always seeing the sunlight."

"Just want to make sure everyone understands the urgency, is all," Themba told him.

"Kellan!" One of the initiates from Scale Osa, a bulky brute with a block for a jaw, had marched his way through Scale Jayyed and up near the front. "What's the meaning of this?" He pointed at the unconscious Indlovu. "Have you turned traitor too?"

"Chidubem, these full-bloods are working with Odili to overthrow the queen," Kellan told his sword brother.

"Guardian Councillor Odili, you mean?" Chidubem said.

"They're sieging the Guardian Keep. We need to get to the queen before Odili can—"

"No! I don't want to hear this."

"It's a coup!"

"It's Royal Noble business."

"You can't be serious," said Kellan as the rest of Scale Osa and Scale Otieno came within earshot. He raised his voice, speaking to them. "Odili seeks to murder our queen. This Gifted knows a way that we can come to her aid. Brothers, you are needed, called to—"

Chidubem shouted him down. "Shut it, Okar! I'm not fighting against Odili and full-bloods on your word and the word of Lessers. Who knows why Odili has chosen to siege the keep?"

"The queen—"

"We heard," said Umqondisi Otieno, moving through the men

and standing nearby. "She wants to surrender." Then, raising his voice, he pointed to Chidubem. "Hear me! Like this initiate, I will not fight against my own. However, I will not hinder Okar or these Lessers either. Go your way and I will go mine, with my scale."

Kellan tried again. "Who will join me? Who will fight for the queen?"

A voice called from the crowd. "Chosen don't surrender."

Otieno walked away. "I'm for the Indlovu Citadel, as I was ordered to do on the authority of the chairman of the Guardian Council."

He left. So did the Indlovu. All but one of them. Jabari Onai held back and tried to make them see sense.

"Tau, don't do this," he said. "It's madness. Kellan, come with us. This is not our affair."

Tau said nothing, but it was disturbing how different Jabari seemed. He was still bigger than Tau. He always would be. It was just that he no longer seemed that way.

Kellan answered. "This is exactly my affair. I'm valuing my life and honor in the best way I know how."

"That's it, then?" said Jabari.

"It is."

Jabari sighed. "I would be no kind of Noble to leave my inkokeli to this task alone." Jabari joined them, though he did not look happy doing it.

"Nobles," said Hadith. "They've abandoned you. Such loyalty."

Kellan looked down and away. Tau saw it and could imagine what he was feeling. These were the same men Kellan had led for a cycle, the ones he'd taken to the melee.

"Are we sure we're doing the right thing?" Jabari asked.

This time, Tau responded. "I'm going," he said. "I need to speak with Odili about my father."

"Very patriotic," Hadith said. "I'll go too. Not for revenge, but to try and save my people from annihilation." He turned to what was left of Scale Jayyed, fewer than thirty men. "The Indlovu Citadel is that way," he said, pointing toward it. "I'm going this way with Tau, this beautiful Lady Gifted, my close friend Nkosi Kellan Okar, and this other Indlovu initiate. I'm going to fight with them because, in spite of our differences, we would all like to see an end to this war that has taken our mothers, sisters, fathers, and brothers from us.

"We go to save our queen and queendom from a tyrant who'd happily let all of us die so he can call himself a Royal Noble for a few more moons. That's what I'm doing, because it's the right thing, and because it's what Jayyed would have wanted."

Hadith put his hand on the hilt of his sword and drew it from its scabbard. He held it aloft and examined the blade, blood still on it. He nodded to the weapon, as if to say it would serve, and he began walking toward the Gifted Citadel. Tau, Zuri, Uduak, Yaw, Kellan, Themba, and Jabari went too. Following them was every man left in Scale Jayyed.

KEEP

The city had obeyed Odili's curfew. They saw no one along the paths, and every house was shut tight. The citizens of Citadel City were afraid. The Xiddeen were coming and Odili would let half the city burn so he could finish the queen.

"We're almost there," said Zuri. "Wait here, I'll go around the corner and ask to be admitted. When they open the gates, rush in. Try not to kill anyone."

"We'll try," said Themba.

"I mean it," she told him. "These are our people."

Zuri went around the corner and Tau heard her speaking. The voice that responded was gruff, male, an Indlovu. No doubt one of Odili's men, which meant he had already stationed fighters in the Gifted Citadel. Tau wondered how many and if their small party could take them.

He heard the gates creak. It was time. Hadith, who was in charge since the men were almost all Lessers, signaled the charge, and everyone rushed the gates.

Kellan, Jabari, and Uduak, using their long strides, got there first. Tau, Hadith, Yaw, and Themba were right behind. The lone Indlovu opening the citadel's bronze gates yelped as Kellan cracked him across the head, and the scale streamed into the citadel.

Tau had expected the Gifted Citadel to look like the isikolo. It did not. Its adobe buildings had been painted black, and at night they looked more like shadows than structures. Many of the buildings had a second floor and many were domed. Most of the buildings appeared to be interconnected, and Tau guessed an initiate could travel much of the citadel without having to venture outside.

"Weapons down!" Kellan hissed at the four remaining Indlovu on guard.

"What's this, then?" one of them asked.

"Respectfully, nkosi, there is little time to explain. We're here on orders by Abasi Odili," Hadith told them. "The siege is taking too long and we're to join the attack. We'll use the tunnels that lead from this citadel to the keep."

The Indlovu looked at Hadith but spoke to Kellan. "We have Lessers fighting with us?"

"We do," said Kellan.

"Why do we need more men? Why did you hit Alinafe?" The Indlovu had not lowered his sword. "And did you say you spoke with the inkokeli? Odili has already gone through the tunnels."

Uduak looked at Tau. Tau nodded. They attacked. Tau had two of them down, including the talker, as Uduak, Kellan, Hadith, and Themba took on the last two.

"I didn't kill them," Tau told Zuri when it was over.

She looked at the others. They all nodded, except for Themba, who looked down at the Noble by his feet and shrugged.

Zuri closed her eyes for a breath. "This way," she said.

"Close the gates and you five stay here," Hadith told a few of Scale Jayyed's fighters. "We can't leave the citadel completely undefended. Actually, one of you come with us to find these tunnels. If the citadel is overrun, gather up as many Gifted as you can and take the tunnels to the keep. Hopefully it'll still be standing."

The plan set, they carried on. Zuri led them deep into the grounds, to a small common area, a circle in the citadel. The buildings surrounding the circle looked alike enough to be replicas; there were many doors, and several paths leading out of the circle. Zuri chose one of the doors and they went inside.

Tau had never seen anything like it. From the outside he'd thought the building had two floors. He was wrong. It was one floor, but the ceiling was two floors high. It made him uncomfortable and he felt as if the whole thing could come crashing down at any moment.

The room was also larger than anything he could remember being in. They were in a rotunda; the edges of it had columns and hallways leading into darkness. The space had no adornments and the floor was pristine. It was the statues that held his attention, though.

In the rotunda's center was a statue of a familiar and beautiful woman dressed in black robes. Towering over her, its head reaching past the height of the building's two floors and extending into the rotunda's dome, was a dragon. The statues were made from bronze, lifelike, and the woman stood twice as tall as the average Noble, but the Guardian, no doubt due to the limitations of space, was a fraction of the size of an actual dragon. Still, the proportions on both woman and dragon were perfect.

Of course, there was no way to capture the eye-bending effect of a dragon's scales, but the artist had created a reasonable facsimile by bending the bronze this way and that in minute variations. It must have taken an eternity. The result was worth it. Light hitting the dragon statue reflected at a thousand angles and the thing's beauty and power stole Tau's breath.

"The Goddess?" asked Yaw, whispering.

"No, it's Queen Taifa and the Guardian that burned back the hedeni after we made landfall," said Zuri. "Quickly now. If they're expecting the hedeni attack, the preceptors and Gifted initiates will be in this network of buildings. They could hear us and come...."

"Lead on, Lady Gifted," said Hadith. "I have no desire to meet a scale's worth of angry Gifted."

Zuri guided them across the rotunda to a heavy door.

"Is it wood?" asked Tau, touching it and pulling his hand back. It was wood, but unlike any he knew. It was heavy, dark, and solid.

Zuri pulled a necklace from her black robes. "It's wood from the *Targon*, Queen Taifa's warship. It's wood from Osonte."

Tau returned his hand to the door, letting his fingers press against it, feeling its warmth. Wood from Osonte, he thought, from the motherland.

Beside him, Zuri manipulated the bauble on the end of her golden necklace, one of the ones all Gifted wore, revealing a key. The key slid into the door's lock, Zuri turned it, and the door opened onto a dark passageway with stairs descending into the earth.

"This will take us to the tunnels, and they will take us to the Guardian Keep," she said.

Kellan pushed his way to the front. "Let's go. The queen needs us."

"I'll guide you to the tunnels that go up and into the keep, and that's where we'll part," Zuri said.

"What? No," Tau said.

"You need to get to the queen as fast as possible. Nothing matters if she dies. But even if you save her, we cannot hold the keep against Odili's Indlovu."

"That's what I keep thinking," piped in Themba. "It's all I keep thinking."

"The keep will fall to Odili's men or, failing that, it'll be taken by the hedeni. We need to make sure we have enough time to hold talks with the hedeni, to tell them we're innocent of Odili's betrayal."

"And," Tau said, "our odds don't change if you're with us or not. So, stay."

"Our chances do change. I'll go to the coterie. There are enough of them to form a Hex. There are enough to call our Guardians."

"A Hex?" asked Tau. "I wouldn't have thought a Hex could be formed without its members having trained together."

"When it's necessary, we do what we must."

"Coterie?" asked Kellan.

"They tend the youngling beneath the Guardian Keep," said Zuri. "The youngling is the link between us and the Guardians."

"The Guardian here is immature?" Kellan asked, locking eyes with her. "Lady Gifted, is the youngling a captive?"

Zuri looked away. "Yes."

"Why? The dragons are our guardians."

"Not by choice," she said.

"How does any of this help us against Odili and his Indlovu?"

asked Hadith. "The Guardians nest in the Central Mountains. They can't get here in time."

Since looking away from Kellan, Zuri hadn't faced any of them. Instead, she kept her eyes forward and into the gloom of the tunnels ahead. "Sometimes, a Guardian in flight will wander closer than the Central Mountains. We'll look for and entreat the closest one. We'll call it to our purpose. It's the only way."

Kellan added his voice to hers, bolstering her argument. "She's right. We can't defend this keep with just a half scale of Ihashe and whatever is left of the Queen's Guard."

Tau shot a look at Hadith, hoping his sword brother had another plan or objection. Hadith opened his hands, palms up. He had nothing.

"Zuri, promise that you'll do the entreating," Tau said. "You can't be just one of the Hex. Promise."

"Tau—"

"Promise."

"I promise, Tau. I promise."

Tau nodded.

"The queen," said Uduak, and they began their descent.

The tunnels were rougher than Tau would have imagined. They were hardly wide enough for two to walk abreast, the ground was bare dirt, the ceiling low, and the walls coarse and uncolored adobe.

Torches burned every twelve strides. They lit the way but couldn't banish the tunnel's murk, and in the flickering light, Tau's mind turned heaving shadows into lurching demons.

"How much farther?" he asked, growing anxious so far beneath the surface. The walls, he thought, kept closing in, getting tighter, restricting the space and his ability to breathe. "How much farther?" he said again, panting.

"We're almost there," Zuri said, taking his hand and holding it. "Focus on your breathing. This happens to some."

"What does?" Themba asked, watching Tau.

"The tunnels, some find them disorienting."

"I'm fine," Tau said, trying to stop the ground ahead from tilting and his hands from shaking.

"Shhh!" hissed Hadith. "Voices."

"Indlovu," Kellan said. "Around the next bend."

Tau looked ahead. The tunnel did bend; he couldn't see more than thirty strides off before the torches disappeared.

"Odili came through the tunnels with men," Hadith said. "He knew a siege would take too long. These tunnels were his insurance."

The voices of the Indlovu grew louder and Kellan broke into a trot. "Hurry! We may be too late!"

Tau slid his hand from Zuri's and ran after Hadith, stumbling like a drunk. He had to get out of these Goddess-cursed tunnels. The scale ran with him. They made no cries of war, but the clamor of twenty-five-odd fighters with armor and weapons was more than enough to alert the Indlovu.

The scale rounded the bend, coming face-to-face with six of Odili's men. The narrow tunnels made the difference in numbers mean little. At most two could face two.

Ahead, the lead Indlovu was one of the fattest Tau had ever seen. He had shiny beetle eyes that his face seemed to be trying to swallow and a thick-lipped mouth that was curled like it had tasted something sour.

"Hold there!" he ordered.

Kellan pushed his way to the front, past Hadith and Tau. "There's treachery here. Guardian Councillor Odili means to murder the queen. Stand aside."

"Tsiora the surrenderer? She's no true queen. If you're loyal to the Chosen, return the way you came."

Tau couldn't take it anymore. He had to get out of the tunnels. "Out of the way!" he said, throwing himself at the fat man.

The earth beneath his feet seemed to shift, and he almost fell, righting himself just before the fat Noble swung for his neck. Tau threw himself to the side, banged against the tunnel wall, and fell back. He heard the scrape of bronze scuffing adobe and, stomach churning, he crawled away from the Indlovu as fast as he could. He felt hands grip him by the shoulders and was about to swing his sword when he heard Yaw call out and drag him back, away from the fighting that Uduak and Kellan had joined.

"What's wrong with you?" demanded Hadith, looming over him.

"It's the tunnels," Zuri said. "Their closeness bothers some."

"The closeness?" Hadith said.

"He'll be fine when we reach the surface."

Tau dry heaved and began to shake. It was like the storage barn in Daba. It was like his first few times facing the demons in Isihogo, the fear, the tension. He tried to adapt. It wouldn't take. He had no experience with this, no clue how to conquer it, and realizing that made it worse.

"It's clear!" Kellan shouted. "Let's go."

Tau was pulled to his feet and his arms were thrown around Hadith's and Yaw's necks. They half carried, half dragged him down the tunnels. His head was down, dangling loose, so he saw the fat Indlovu. The man was dead from a thrust through the chest. They ran on for a hundred strides and Tau tripped on the ground when it began to slope upward.

"I leave you here," Tau heard Zuri say to the scale. "But, I need a few fighters to help me convince the coterie of my plan."

"Of course you do." Hadith picked five men to go with her.

"Sharp bronze does make good arguments," Themba said.

"Continue up this tunnel," Zuri told them. "It will take you to the surface."

Zuri went to Tau. Hadith and Yaw stepped away, giving her space. "You'll feel better soon. Be careful, Tau." She hugged him. "I love you," she said. "I always have."

Tau groaned. He heard her. He wanted to tell her to stay. He could protect her. He had learned all he had so he could do so. He hugged her with arms as firm as seaweed, trying to hold her to him, trying to make her understand that she needed to stay. He had to protect her.

"Let's go," said Hadith.

Zuri kissed Tau, touched his face, and mouthed the words again. "I love you," she said. Then she stepped out of the embrace, wiping at her eyes. "Goddess be with you," she said. "May She be with you all."

"And you, Lady Gifted," said Kellan.

"Help me with him," Hadith told Yaw. "We go!"

Tau managed to turn his head back to Zuri. She was watching

after him. She gave him a small smile before the curve in the tunnel took her from sight. Tau closed his eyes. She had told him she loved him. She had said that. He tried to orient himself on that, as the world swirled.

A few strides later they stopped. Tau kept his eyes closed but heard wood splintering. He wondered if the door on this side was also made with Osonte wood.

"We're out," Hadith said. "You can open your eyes."

Tau did, dropped to his knees, and threw up. He could hear fighting.

Hadith squatted beside him. "Get yourself together. We're here."

Tau lifted his head, breathing in the sweet scent of fresh air, opened his eyes, and gasped. They were at the end of a corridor. The floor was tiled in a patterned mosaic; the walls were smooth adobe painted in brilliant colors and they soared up for four floors. Tau had found the dignitaries' quarters in the Southern Isikolo to be opulent. The interior of the Guardian Keep made those rooms look little better than his hut in Kerem.

Tau struggled to his feet, his head muddy. "Zuri…"

"She goes to get us dragons," Hadith said. "Pray it works or none of us live to see the sun."

"The fighting is this way!" yelled Kellan, dashing down the hallway and past row after row of enormous tapestries.

"Fight?" Uduak asked Tau. Yaw was beside the big man, looking worried.

"He'd better," said Themba. "We're outnumbered."

Tau nodded.

"Right." Hadith said, hefting his sword. "Let's go make peace."

STATUE

The hallway opened up into the keep's enormous anteroom. The open space was circular and had a third-floor balcony that extended around its circumference. Offering access to the balcony were two wide staircases that clung to the curved walls. Supporting the balcony were thick sculpted columns around which scattered and isolated groups of men fought for their lives.

The majority of the fighting was focused near the exit to a hallway on the far side of the anteroom. That was where Tau saw most of the armored Queen's Guard in their distinct maroon-stained leather. Abshir Okar, the queen's champion, was leading the defense as the guard tried to hold the hallway against several units of full-blooded Indlovu.

Abshir was incredible. He darted this way and that, his sword whistling through air, flesh, and bone, as he called out commands and slew those who stood against him. Tau found himself both impressed and worried. The champion was a brilliant fighter, but it would not be enough, not against the odds he faced. The Queen's Guard lost two men for every one they killed.

Kellan, seeing his uncle, charged.

"After him!" ordered Hadith. "Save the queen!"

Tau didn't see any queen, but he saw his enemy and that was

enough. He shook his head, willing the fogginess of the tunnels to leave him, and, swords out, he ran with the scale.

To get to Champion Abshir Okar, Tau would have to fight his way past a group of Indlovu doing battle with scattered members of the Queen's Guard near the fountain that centered the anteroom. Tau ran over to engage the men, unable to ignore the tall bronze statue of Tsiory that stood in the middle of the fountain.

The statue had to be Tsiory. It had to be Queen Taifa's champion and lover. It was almost as tall as the third-floor balcony, and Tsiory wore a suit of armor depicted in remarkable detail and intricacy. The statue's face was turned to the dome above and the sky beyond. Tsiory's sword, held with both hands, was placed point down into the fountain's bloodred waters.

At first, Tau thought some of the day's dead must have fallen into the fountain, tainting the waters. As he got closer, he realized that wasn't the case. The water had been colored the red of blood and it flowed from the hilt of Tsiory's sword, down the length of his blade, and into the fountain's bowl. It seemed gory, thought Tau, twisting past an Indlovu's swing and driving a sword through the man's lungs, to anchor Tsiory's memory in an ever-flowing pool of red.

Up ahead, Kellan had cut a path through Odili's men and was stampeding for the hallway that his uncle strove to defend. Scale Jayyed had chosen to fight the Indlovu by the fountain. They couldn't all go to the champion's aid. The Indlovu they left behind them would attack and they'd be pincered. On the other hand, if Tau let Kellan go alone, the Indlovu at the hallway's entrance would cut him down.

Unsure what to do, Tau crossed blades with a snarling full-blood. The Indlovu was good. The man's shield had a supernatural sense of where to be and his sword moved more like a twisting chain than a blade of solid bronze. The full-blood came on hard, with no fear of a Lesser in Ihashe grays.

Tau dodged the man's first two strikes, then struck out, stabbing him but hitting one of his bronze plates. He thought to finish the Noble but had to dart away before the man's follow-up swing could connect. The Indlovu was fast, as well.

"Tau, go with Kellan!" Hadith shouted, settling Tau's debate with himself.

Tau increased the pace of the fight, putting the Indlovu on the back foot and ready to finish him, when a roaring Jabari leapt into the fray. The full-blood slashed at Jabari's blade, knocking it from his hands, and seeing his chance to kill the Petty Noble, the full-blood lunged.

Tau threw himself forward, off-balance but on target. His weak-side sword caught the thrust and turned it up and away from Jabari's heart, as the blade of his strong-side weapon went into the full-blood's neck, bursting through the opposite side in a shower of gore. Jabari stumbled back, wide-eyed and aware of how close to death he'd come.

"Get your blade!" Tau told him, turning and running to help Kellan. He heard footsteps behind him and readied to defend himself. It was Jabari, sword to hand. Tau growled in his throat. He wasn't sure if Jabari's presence helped or hindered, but there was no time for discussion either way. He'd arrived and immediately had to block a sword aimed for Kellan's spine.

He caught the murderous cut on the edge of his blade at the same time as Kellan's shield.

"About time!" said Kellan.

"Fool!" cursed Tau. "Chasing after this fight."

"My uncle," Kellan answered, gutting the Indlovu who had tried to kill him.

Tau glanced back to the rest of the scale. The fighting around the fountain had intensified, and they wouldn't be coming to help anytime soon.

"Down, Jabari!" yelled Kellan, bringing his shield around to stop a blow that would have brained the Petty Noble.

Jabari was blowing air like a caught fish. "There's too many."

"Stay close," said Tau, putting his sword through a man's eye and dropping a level to spear another in the groin. Both men fell away, creating enough space for three more to take their place.

"Uncle!" called Kellan.

"To your left. Break their line," Abshir shouted to Kellan. "To the right," he ordered his own men.

Kellan moved left. There were only a few men between the Queen's Guard and him on that side, and at Abshir's order, more Queen's Guard had moved to help. Tau followed, fighting off three Indlovu and trying to keep Jabari alive, though it seemed his onetime friend was determined to skewer himself on every blade that came close.

"Stay near!" Tau told him again.

"I ... am ... near!"

"Quick, now!" Abshir said. "Let them through."

And, like that, they had joined up with the Queen's Guard. Tau looked past the press of bodies, shields, and blades. Beyond Tau's position, Hadith and the scale had been pushed back from the fountain. More of Odili's men were in the anteroom. They were coming in from the other hallways. The odds for Scale Jayyed and the men loyal to the queen had grown longer.

"Where's the queen?" Kellan asked his uncle.

"Behind us, but there are other ways in. Kellan, hold here. I must go to her."

Kellan nodded, his uncle stepped back, Odili's full-bloods flooded into the space he'd made, and several blades thrust for Abshir's face and body. He knocked a couple aside and Kellan stepped up, holding the line. An Indlovu dove in, his eyes bright as he swung for Abshir. Kellan split the man's skull, and Abshir shouted and fell.

Seeing the champion drop encouraged Odili's Indlovu. They pressed their full weight against the Queen's Guard, bowing the defensive line back and into the hallway. The guard were too few and had held because the mouth of the hallway meant they could stand united. The press of Indlovu threatened to snap the guard's advantage. Tau jabbed his blades everywhere he thought could do damage, but this wasn't his type of fight. It was like battling a wall of shields.

"Get him back," Kellan shouted to Tau.

Tau disengaged, calling for Jabari's help. They grabbed the champion and pulled him away from the defensive line. Abshir had been cut just below the armpit and the wound was deep.

"You'll be fine," Tau told him. He stood, meaning to go back to the fight, when Abshir clamped onto his wrist and pulled him down.

"Ihashe, the queen must be protected!" he told Tau. "The far end of this hall opens into the room known as the Goddess's Choice. Tell Kellan to take the gold door. He must find her before Odili. Tell Kellan!"

"Odili?"

"Go!"

Tau stood.

"I'm coming," Jabari said.

Tau wasn't listening. "Kellan," he said to the fighting man's back. "Your uncle is injured, but I know where the queen is."

"You go!" Kellan shouted over his shoulder. "I'll hold them back."

"The champion asked for you."

"Because he thinks I'm the best fighter," Kellan grunted between thrusts, shield blocks, and counterstrikes, "because he thinks I can be her champion in his place. But he's wrong. You're better. Save the queen!"

Tau shouldn't go. He knew he shouldn't. He wasn't thinking about the queen. He was thinking about Abasi Odili. He wasn't the right person for this.

"Let's go!" said Jabari, putting a hand on Tau's shoulder. "We can't let Odili get away with this."

Tau turned from Kellan and the fighting, looking down the long hallway. "He won't get away," he said.

CHAPTER SIXTEEN

ENRAGED

Tau and Jabari sprinted down the hallway. They ran past paintings of the Omehi queens who had ruled in Osonte and then in Xidda. They ran past the portrait of Queen Taifa, the Dragon Queen. They ran past the one of her daughter, Queen Tsiora I, and then past the portraits of queens Tau could not name. They ran into the room called the Goddess's Choice.

"Where now?" Jabari asked, turning in a circle.

They were in an octagonal room; each corner held a door, and each door was painted a different color.

"The gold," said Tau.

The gold door led to another hallway that opened onto a small courtyard with reclining chairs, tables, plants, and flowers. It was an oasis, a refuge from the city, the heat, the world.

Tau heard the sound of wood being chopped. He heard voices, but the thing that held his attention was the ground in front of him. It had been molded to mimic the peninsula. An artist had re-created their valley. The map showed everything from the Roar to the Wrist and all that was between. The peninsula's largest cities were there, each differentiated by depictions of their most iconic buildings. Tau saw Kigambe, Jirza, Palm, and Citadel City.

"Tau," Jabari hissed.

Tau knew why he was looking at the map. He knew he was stretching out the moment when he laid his eyes on them.

"Tau, what are you doing?"

Tau lifted his eyes and saw Odili, Dejen, the KaEid, and two full-blooded Indlovu.

"They're cutting through that door," Jabari said. "The queen must be inside."

"Yes," said Tau, walking forward.

"There's four of them and the KaEid. Tau..."

Tau was no longer listening. He was closing in on his prey like an inyoka slithering through tall grasses. He would go unseen until it was time to strike, time to kill. They wouldn't even know he was there until it was too late.

"Abasi Odili!" Tau yelled from twenty strides away. They turned to face him. "You murdered my father and destroyed my life. I am here to balance the scales."

Abasi Odili looked nonplussed. Then, regaining some sense of himself, he spoke. "Common, I have killed many fathers and destroyed many lives. You'll have to be more specific."

With a wave of his hand Odili sent one of the full-bloods at Tau. Dejen looked away, unconcerned, as he and the other full-blood continued to cut through the door.

The Indlovu came, and Jabari moved to stand beside Tau. The Indlovu had his sword up. "I am Abiodan Onyakachi of—"

Tau lunged, Abiodan jerked his sword to block, and Tau dropped, cutting through the man's calf with his blade. The Indlovu began to fall, and as he did, Tau drove his strong-side sword through his skull. The dead man collapsed onto the tiled floor. Tau jiggled his blade free and kept going. Jabari was no longer beside him. Jabari was staring at the dead Noble.

"Abasi Odili!" Tau called.

"Enough of this!" said the KaEid. "Abasi, have them killed and let's be done with Tsiora."

Dejen was first to react. He gave the thick and splintered wooden door a kick that came close to caving it in, before leveling his sword at Tau.

"Tau...," said Jabari.

"What's your name, Noble?" Odili asked Jabari, pulling his own sword free of its scabbard. "And what are you doing with this Common? What treachery against your kind is this?" Odili stepped away from Dejen, pulling the remaining Indlovu with him, putting the monstrous Ingonyama between them and Tau.

The KaEid raised her arms and her pupils shrank to the size of pins.

"Tau...," said Jabari.

Tau was ready. He would wade through her enervation, destroy Dejen, and kill her, then the Indlovu, leaving Odili for last. He would carve the flesh from his bones, pluck his eyes from his head, cut away his tongue, and force the point of his blade up the slit of the man's penis.

But KaEid Oro did not fire enervation at Tau. Perhaps something about him told her it would not have the desired effect. Perhaps she wanted to stretch out their suffering, see hopelessness on their faces. Tau did not know, would never know, but it did surprise him when Oro used her gift to enrage Dejen, transforming one of the Omehi's most feared fighters into a force of death.

Dejen roared as his muscles warped, stretched, and folded, thickening, multiplying. His loose-fitting armor-plated black leathers tightened, exposing the bloodred leather that the uniform's woven folds kept hidden until an Ingonyama was enraged. Dejen was not an attractive man, and with the KaEid's gift flowing through him, he was ugly, cruel-looking, an ogre.

In two breaths, Dejen the monster stood before them. He snorted air out of a nose as broad as Tau's palm, lifted his shield from beside the wooden door and smashed its edge against the door three times. The Ingonyama's speed caught Tau off guard. Almost as soon as Tau registered that Dejen was hitting the door, it had collapsed, kindling under his supernaturally powered barrage. From inside the room a woman screamed.

Dejen snorted again and turned to Tau, who had been rooted to the spot since the Greater Noble's transformation had begun.

"Some scales are too one-sided to ever be balanced, little gray,"

Odili said, stepping over the ruined door and into the room where the queen was hiding.

Tau let Odili's words pull his attention, a mistake that came close to costing him his life. Dejen dashed forward, his sword arcing. Jabari yelled, and Tau felt more than saw the attack. He dove to the side, heard the Ingonyama's bronze whistle past, and could smell its oiled metal as the blade ripped the air, a fingerspan from cutting Tau's face from his skull.

He crashed into the ground, rolled, and came back to his feet. "The queen—" was all he could say to Jabari, before Dejen's blade threatened him again.

Tau danced away from that swing and the next and the next. He shot a look in Jabari's direction. Jabari had his sword held high and was picking his way over the smashed door and into the room beyond.

Tau gave the Enraged Ingonyama his full attention. "Do you remember the Indlovu testing in the South?" Tau said. "Do you remember the man you killed there?"

Dejen grunted and swung. Tau backpedaled, using the courtyard as he would terrain in a battleground. He picked up a small side table with an empty rabba pot on it and tossed the whole thing at Dejen, who chopped it out of the air.

"Do you remember the man you killed there? You should, because he's the reason this night is your last."

Dejen charged and swung, his footfalls ringing out on the tiled floor. Tau dodged but didn't expect the Ingonyama to use his shield. Dejen turned it horizontal and swung it at Tau with a vicious backhand. Tau couldn't dodge that and had to block with his weak-side sword. He caught the blow, felt the hit reverberate through his body, and was lifted off his feet and thrown across the courtyard, banging his shoulder in the fall.

No time to waste, Tau sprang to his feet and threw himself out of the way of a lancing thrust from Dejen. He recentered, swayed around Dejen's follow-up, moved in, and stabbed up as hard as he could. He hit the Ingonyama's bronze plates and had to drop and roll to avoid being clubbed by the man's shield. He came up, flung himself at Dejen, and sliced for his belly. He felt his sharp bronze scrape across plate, leather, and skin. The attack would have cut a normal man in two, but the KaEid's power had hardened Dejen's flesh to stone. Tau sprang away and out of reach.

The Enraged Ingonyama looked down. The leathers around his stomach were torn to tatters and a thin trickle of blood leaked from one of the scratches.

"Kill him!" shrieked the KaEid, the strain from maintaining the enraging thick in her voice.

Dejen ignored her, speaking his first words to Tau. "I remember the Common from the testing. He died like all Lessers live, on his knees." Dejen charged and Tau ran to meet him.

Dejen swung at Tau's body, offering his slippery prey no opportunity to duck or leap back. Tau had no intention of doing either. He leapt on Dejen, his sword points soaring in for the sides of the Ingonyama's neck. The leap brought Tau too close for Dejen's blade to do damage, but the Ingonyama's hilt and guard blasted him in the side, and Tau heard his ribs crack. He did not feel the pain. The only feeling in him was rage, as the points of his swords punched into the Ingonyama's neck, just below the jaw.

"Die!" Tau screamed in the demon's face as his weak-side sword snapped in two, unable to penetrate the Ingonyoma's flesh. "Die!" he said again as his strong-side blade punctured Dejen's skin, skittered across the harder muscle beneath, found purchase in the enraged man's shoulder blade, and was jerked from Tau's hand as they both went down.

Dejen snatched up Tau's gambeson in his shield hand and Tau rammed his shattered weak-side sword, his father's sword, into Dejen's face.

"Die!" Tau yelled as the jagged bronze blade lodged itself a fingernail's depth into Dejen's lip, cheek, and eye, bursting the delicate orb in a gush of blood and ichor.

Dejen screamed and tossed Tau fifteen strides away with one arm, sending him flipping through the air like a straw doll to crash into the artist's mock-up of the peninsula. He landed on the raised ridges of the Central Mountains, on the same side as his cracked ribs, and this time he felt the pain. It burned up and through him like wild-fire, searing away all thought for several breaths.

"Get up, Dejen!" Tau heard the KaEid shout.

Tau forced himself into a sitting position and collapsed from the pain. Teeth gritted, he rolled to his good side. The KaEid seemed to be pouring as much energy as she could into Dejen, who had taken hold of Tau's broken sword and was pulling it out of his face.

The Ingonyama roared as the bronze was wrenched free, tearing out the last bits of eye and half his bottom lip. Dejen stumbled his way to his feet, touching a hand to his ruined face. He was panting and soaked in blood.

"Tau!" came Jabari's desperate voice from inside the room.

Tau shot a look that way. Dejen, with the eye left to him, did as well. Tau staggered to his feet. Jabari was losing his fight. He had a full-blood and Odili to contend with. Royal Nobles like Odili weren't known for their bladework, but they were still well trained, and that made it two on one. Tau was needed, but Dejen charged, sword leading the way, and Tau had no weapons.

He danced backward, throwing potted plants, small statues, and even a fire-blackened brazier at the Ingonyama. Then, risking death, Tau dove to Dejen's blind side, launching himself past the man and toward his fallen swords. He didn't have time to get them both. He snatched his grandfather's sword, came up blocking an unavoidable swing from Dejen, and almost lost his blade to the power behind the strike.

He shambled out of reach, placed a foot on his father's shattered blade, and dragged it back with him. When he'd gained enough space to grab it without dying, he snatched it, grunting at the peals of pain from his smashed ribs.

"Tau! Tau! Tau!" yelled Jabari.

And Tau went at Dejen, stabbing, swinging, and firing his swords at the enormous man as fast as he could, aiming as often as he could for the Greater Noble's remaining eye. The attacks alarmed Dejen, and for the first time the enraged man fought defensively, terrified of losing his sight.

Tau buried him under an unrelenting barrage of blows that could not cut Dejen deeply, but that was not their aim.

"The Goddess curse you, Dejen! Kill him!" the KaEid howled as Tau continued his assault, delivering attacks that forced the KaEid to pour more and more energy into maintaining Dejen's enraging.

"Release me!" the KaEid demanded, the alarm in her voice at a fever pitch. "Release me!"

Her shroud, Tau knew, was gone. The demons were coming. Tau increased the pressure, his ribs protesting every movement while his will drove him on.

"You will pay, Dejen!" Tau taunted. "You will die, Dejen! You will burn blind in Isihogo with Ukufa for eternity, Dejen!"

"Release me!" The KaEid stumbled toward them. "Let me go, you fool!"

Dejen would not do it. Tau could see the fear in the man's eye. Dejen knew that when the enraging left him, so would his life, because Tau would take it.

So Dejen did what he could to turn the tide of battle. He used his strength, his speed, his cunning, his training, to push an injured Tau back. He gave Tau a wicked but glancing cut to the thigh and came close to taking Tau's wrist, but Tau turned his father's sword in time to catch the brutal swing on the blade's hilt. The move saved him from amputation but broke three of his fingers.

Dejen pressed on, Dejen was desperate, and Dejen ran out of time.

The KaEid screamed with enough anguish to cause both men to jump away from each other. She fell to her knees and clawed at her neck, and blood erupted from her ears, mouth, nose, and eyes. She convulsed and seized, the skin on her face blistering, bubbling, rupturing. Those screams became gurgles and the KaEid choked on her body's fluids, going down to her hands, tossing this way and that, spattering them both with putrescence. With fingers clawed, she tore at her face, peeling stripes of flesh away in rolls. She opened her mouth wide, as if to give birth through it, and vomited a torrent of filth, her arms giving way as she did. She fell to the floor, no longer looking human, and she died.

Tau swung back to Dejen. The Ingonyama was no longer enraged. His black leathers hung loose and he was hunched from the pain of his many wounds.

"You killed my father," Tau told him.

"You do this because a Lesser is dead?" Dejen spat, the words muddied by his mangled mouth. "He was worth nothing. You. Are. Nothing!"

Dejen charged, his sword leading. Tau slipped the killing thrust and stabbed his father's broken blade through the Greater Noble's chest and into his Noble heart.

"Perhaps," Tau whispered, feeling the man's lifeblood pulse from the wound, through his fingers, and down his hand, "but you are dead."

Dejen gasped, trying to breathe. His eye fixed on Tau's face. Tau put a hand over the Ingonyama's shoulder and pulled him close, driving the blade deeper. Dejen's lips twitched, but he said nothing, and never would.

"Tau!" It was Jabari.

Tau ripped his father's broken sword from Dejen's body and let the Noble drop to the floor. He stepped beyond the dead man and staggered over to the room where Jabari fought for his life, and where the queen hid to preserve hers. Tau went to murder Abasi Odili.

ESCAPE

Tau burst into the room. He saw Jabari and the Indlovu first. They were facing off and the Indlovu moved like he was drunk. Jabari was bleeding from several cuts and having trouble holding his sword. The queen was there too. Tsiora, in a high-backed gown of purest white, had her back to the wall and was standing next to a lavish bed stacked high with thick pillows and silken blankets. She was not alone. There was a middle-aged woman with her. The woman had a stern but attractive face and, at that moment, she had her hands out to the Indlovu. She dropped them when she saw Tau.

She was Gifted and had enervated the full-blood. She was the reason Jabari was still alive. Tau went for the full-blood, when he heard a noise behind him. He spun, sword leading, and smashed the earthenware jug that Abasi Odili had thrown.

Abasi stood in the opposite corner of the room, as far as he could get from the Gifted and fighting men. Without a breath, the guardian councillor and architect of the Royal Nobles' coup ran from the room. Tau took off after Odili and heard Jabari cry out in pain.

Tau was at the door. He looked back. The queen had her eyes on him, locked on him, and the Gifted woman looked grim, lips pursed tight. She wouldn't be able to access energy from Isihogo for a quarter span at least. She was defenseless. Worst was Jabari. He'd taken a deep cut from forehead to chin that had just missed his eye. The floor was slick with blood, and as Tau watched, the Indlovu stabbed him in the biceps of his shield arm.

"Tau!" Jabari screamed, tumbling back and onto the ground.

Tau looked out the door. Abasi was getting away, but Tau could catch him. He took a step to do it, throwing a last look in the room and seeing the queen, who couldn't be more than a cycle or two apart from him in age.

It was madness to think she could lead them all. It was madness to place their survival in this girl's ability to renew peace with the Xiddeen. The effort would fail, and Tau could still catch Abasi. He could still…

Tau yelled his frustration and ran toward the fight. The Indlovu, hearing him come, swung to meet the attack, and they crossed blades. Tau feinted high with his broken sword and thrust low with his strong side, his ribs blazing pain the entire time. The Indlovu had no shield. He blocked the high attack and was run through with the other blade.

The man had spirit, though. With his free hand he pulled a dagger from his belt and went for Tau's chest. Using the sword embedded in the Noble's belly, Tau dragged the Indlovu in a semicircle, throwing off his attack and turning the attempt at a mortal stab into a glancing gash.

As they spun, the Indlovu tried to maintain his balance, yelling in agony. His lips were pulled back and his mouth was open, blood-tinged saliva sloshing around his teeth. Tau fired his left hand forward, planting his broken sword in the man's clavicle. The Indlovu sighed, the air going out of him, and then it was over.

Jabari, bleeding everywhere, slid his back up the wall behind him until he was sitting. He wiped at the cut on his face, smearing the blood and making it look like he was wearing a gruesome mask.

"You fight for the queendom?" Queen Tsiora asked, trembling.

Tau didn't answer. He had to catch Odili. He ran for the door and into three men. He jumped back, swords ready.

"Tau, easy," Kellan said, "It's me."

"Where's Odili?"

"Odili? We didn't see him."

Kellan was with Hadith and Uduak.

"My queen." Kellan dropped to a knee, facing the ground in front of his foot. Following his lead, Hadith and Uduak did the same. "We came as soon as we could," Kellan told her.

The stern Gifted woman spoke first. "Have we won the keep? Is the queen safe?"

"How is Abshir?" Queen Tsiora asked.

Kellan raised his head. "My queen…" He paused, mouth opening and shutting a time or two. "Champion Okar has been killed, fighting in your defense," he said. "I am his nephew, Kellan Okar, third-cycle initiate of the Indlovu Citadel."

"Abshir is dead?" Tsiora asked, still shaking but hands clasped tight, as if to hold herself together. "He was your uncle? I'm sorry."

The Gifted walked over to Kellan, pulling his attention to her. "Has the attack been repelled?"

"Vizier Nyah," Kellan said, addressing the Gifted woman, "the Queen's Guard holds the keep, but it is under siege by Odili's Indlovu."

"My queen," the vizier said, "we must rejoin the guard. We must see to the defense of the keep and ensure the safety of the warlord's son. Odili has shown his hand and will be punished, but if we lose the warlord's son, if Kana dies—"

"How did you not see him?" Tau asked a kneeling Kellan.

"Lesser," the vizier said, "when in the presence of Her Majesty—"

"He can't have gone far," Tau insisted. "I have to find—"

"Lesser!" the vizier shouted over Tau.

"Tau, kneel," hissed Kellan.

Tau did not. He rounded on the vizier, taking a long step in her direction. "Call me Lesser one more time."

The vizier seemed unable to believe her eyes. She gulped, opened her mouth, then shut it.

Tau spoke to Kellan. "I'm going to find Odili."

"Nyah is right, Ihashe," the queen told Tau. "We must go to the battlements. The men have to know that we are alive and that there is still value to this fight. We do not believe we can make it alone. Will you accompany us? Will you protect your queen?"

"We will, my queen," said Kellan.

Tau could not allow Odili to escape.

"May we know your name?" Queen Tsiora said.

He didn't want to admit it, but every time she spoke to him it was a shock.

"Name? My . . . Tau. Tau Solarin."

"Will you come too, Tau Solarin?"

Tau's pulse was racing. He'd come so close. So close and his chance was lost. He nodded to his queen.

"We thank you," she said. "Rise, Kellan Okar. Rise, men in his company. We ask that you take us to the battlements of our keep. We would see this coup crushed."

GATES

They marched past the bodies of the fallen Indlovu, Dejen, and the KaEid. The queen closed her eyes, letting Nyah guide her beyond the carnage. The vizier did not seem able to believe the scene before her.

"The KaEid is dead from a demon-death," Nyah said, describing what she saw to the queen. "Ingonyama Olujimi must have been enraged, but he...he appears to have been killed by a sword." Nyah turned to Tau. "He was enraged and you were alone. How did this happen?"

"The KaEid's shroud collapsed. She was first to die. Dejen was not enraged when the blade took him through the chest," Tau told her.

"Not enraged when the blade took him through the...you fought an Enraged Ingonyama until his Gifted's shroud collapsed? Is that what is being suggested here?"

She emphasized the word "shroud," bringing attention to the fact that Tau had used it first. Tau ignored that, saying nothing more, but could feel Nyah's eyes on him, her stare making his back itch.

As they rushed toward the battlements, Kellan told the queen and her vizier everything they knew. He told them about Jamilah and what they believed had taken place at the Xiddeen Conclave. The news seemed to age the vizier. Queen Tsiora was more stoic but also couldn't hide her alarm.

"Abasi and Taia have doomed us," the vizier said. "They've killed us all."

"We will tell the Xiddeen we were betrayed," Queen Tsiora said as they arrived in the keep's central courtyard.

Tau wasn't sure they had to worry about that. Throughout the courtyard was scattered fighting. The Queen's Guard were winning, and that should have been encouraging. It wasn't. The keep's heavy bronze gates shook and buckled every few breaths.

"Battering ram," Kellan said.

Hadith pointed to the battlements. "Up there."

There was fighting. A few Indlovu had scaled the walls, and the Queen's Guard, battling alongside the warlord's son, did their best to send them back down the way they'd come.

"Kana," said the queen.

"By the Goddess!" exclaimed the vizier. "If the savage gets himself killed..."

"They need help," Kellan said.

"Stay with the queen," Hadith suggested to Kellan, looking to Tau and Uduak. Uduak grunted his assent and the three men ran up the stone stairs to the top of the battlements, Tau's injured side torturing him with every step.

At the top, Tau looked out and down. Odili's men were everywhere. The keep was surrounded and it would not take long for the Indlovu to breach it. A swarm of them were using roped hooks to climb its walls, and there were two units of Indlovu driving a bronze-tipped battering ram into its gates. Behind the fighters manning the ram, a few hundred Indlovu waited, their weapons flickering with reflected torchlight. The hot night stunk of burning pitch, leather, sweat, and blood.

Tau dashed to the walls and cut at one of the roped hooks, doing his best to dislodge it. The rope was thick as an arm and taut with the weight of climbers. It was difficult to cut and Tau had to abandon the attempt to kill a man.

"Leave it!" yelled Hadith. "Get to the Xiddian."

Kana was fighting heavy odds. In pain, Tau staggered to his defense, splitting an Indlovu's face as he went.

Uduak got there first. He faced down a full-blood and they battered at each other's shields. Hadith joined the fight, coming in low, driving his sword through the crotch of Uduak's opponent. The Indlovu fell away, screaming.

Next to Hadith, a Queen's Guard died to a straight thrust, and Kana, the man they were trying to protect, stepped into the gap.

"Get back!" Hadith ordered.

Kana shook his head, his long braids flying around his shoulders like angry serpents. Then one of Odili's Indlovu swung for him. Tau was not close enough and Kana had his shoulder turned to the man.

"Watch!" Tau screamed, and Kana ducked, losing a braid instead of his head to the Indlovu's blade. Kana thrust his short spear at the man. The Indlovu blocked the attack with his shield and Tau buried his blade in the Noble's throat.

The four men, Tau, Uduak, Hadith, and Kana, along with a few of the Queen's Guard, held their section of the battlement, killing the remaining Indlovu who had made the climb. Uduak went so far as to disarm one man, then throw him from the walls, onto another climber, dispatching them both. Area clear, they chopped at the rope hooks, dislodging them.

"Battlement secure!" Hadith yelled to Kellan.

Three breaths later they were joined. The queen stood on the inner side of the battlement, the one closest to the keep. Down below, her guard had won their fight as well.

Queen Tsiora looked out at the massacre on the courtyard's stones. She was statue still and her head was held high. It was as if she was waiting to be painted. Tau did not understand what she was doing. Then one of the Queen's Guard saw her and cheered. The rest of the fighters, the ones in the courtyard and on the battlements, looked. They all saw their queen, their reason for this fight, and the loyalists gave a shout. Tsiora raised her royal hand and waved it at her men, like she was blessing them, and the ragged cheer grew louder.

Yaw came jogging up the steps with Themba. "Brothers!"

"Yaw, Themba," said Hadith. "Good to see you're still alive."

"For now," said Themba, eyeing the Indlovu outside the walls.

Yaw, seeing the queen, started. Then he bobbed his head up and down like driftwood on the Roar before dropping to his knees, pulling Themba down with him.

"You may rise," Tsiora said. They did and she spoke to Kellan. "Who leads our men now?"

Kellan pointed to the group of men behind the keep's gates. "My queen, the highest-ranking officer of the Queen's Guard is likely to be down there. When the gates fall, it will be the source of the heaviest fighting."

"You are a third-cycle initiate?"

"I am, my queen. Inkokeli of Scale Osa. I was to be trained as an Ingonyama, pending royal approval."

"We see. You are now an Ingonyama, Kellan Okar. You have received royal approval. You shall also lead the men upon the battlements."

Okar glowed with pride. "I will honor your name, my queen."

"Kellan Okar, Ingonyama, can we defend this keep?" she asked. "Can we hold, if we are clever and if we are lucky?"

Okar's face fell. He was unwilling or unable to lie to his queen, and so said nothing.

"We understand," Tsiora said, and for the briefest measure, Tau saw a frightened young woman with far too much responsibility. "Our challenge is significant," she said. "Thus, we command those loyal to the queen to be particularly clever and amazingly lucky."

Hadith chuckled, but, worried he might offend the queen, he pretended to be coughing. Queen Tsiora smiled at him, her eyes lighting up mischievously. Hadith lost the cough and smiled back.

Tau couldn't believe it. With a few words and a smile, this child queen had charmed the same Lesser who had worn Tau's ears thin with talk of Noble oppression.

"Betrayal?" Kana asked, speaking in halting and accented Empiric.

"It is," Queen Tsiora told him. "We were betrayed by the highest-ranking members of our nobility."

"Nobility...," Kana said.

Uduak pointed off in the distance, to the city's low walls. "Look!"

"Xiddeen?" Kana said, brows knitted. "My father comes."

Kana was right. The invading force had reached Citadel City and Odili had not yet taken the keep or killed the queen. The guardian councillor's plan was unraveling, and so was the Chosen's chance for peace.

"Why . . . my father here?" Kana asked.

"We have been informed that the Noble's treachery goes beyond us," the queen told him. Kana waited for her to say more, and Tsiora gathered herself. "It is likely that the Gifted sent to you was an agent of the coup. She was a . . . a caller of fire-demons."

Kana's face darkened. "She was covered and masked." He looked from face to face, and Tau knew he would find no comfort. "The Conclave?"

Tsiora held Kana's eyes with hers. "We are told that your father's presence may be an answer to what happened there."

Kana leaned in, disbelief etched on his severe features. "Fire-demon burn Conclave?" His body was tensed, and Tau prepared himself in case the Xiddian attacked the queen.

"My father," Kana said, "will kill you all."

"We will tell him we were betrayed," Tsiora said. "We will—"

"Queen," Kana interrupted, earning himself a growl from Vizier Nyah, "No. Achak, father, he kill everyone, all Chosen everywhere."

As Kana spoke, Tau heard the screech of wrenching bronze. It was almost human, the wail the gates gave as they ripped from their moorings and toppled.

Hadith swore, Uduak shifted his weight beside Tau, and the queen gripped the crenellations with so much force that Tau thought she might crack the adobe. The gates had fallen and Odili's Indlovu swarmed the Guardian Keep like a plague of locusts.

HEX

The Queen's Guard, the ones in the courtyard, died. After the bloodbath, one of the Indlovu noticed the queen, her cloud-white gown standing out in the dark, and many of them splintered off from the main group, rushing the stairs to the battlements. Kellan ordered the men with him to hold the stairs and asked Kana to stay back. Tau moved to obey, but the queen took his wrist. Her skin was soft, warm, like ash from a recently cooled fire.

"Will you stay with us, Tau Solarin?"

"My queen," he said, after a breath's hesitation.

She did not release his wrist. "Our thanks."

Feeling taut as a kora's strings, Tau stood by while Kellan and his sword brothers struggled to hold the stairs against a seething mass of full-blooded Indlovu. He flinched and tensed with every hit that his brothers took. And when Yaw was struck on his injured shoulder by a blow that sent him spinning to the battlement floor, Tau tested the queen's hold. Her grip was firm, staying him.

He looked at her, trying to convey his need. She saw him and looked back to the battle for the stairs. Her face was placid, but her chest heaved and her fingers were clenched.

"My queen," Nyah said, "you should leave the battlements. It won't be much longer."

Tau thought the same. It would not be much longer.

"Dear Nyah," Queen Tsiora said, voice steady. "There is nowhere to go."

Nyah moved her head like a wind vane, seeing Odili's men outside the walls, inside the courtyard, and pushing up the stairs. The queen was right.

"Tau Solarin, if the time comes, we would ask a favor of you," Tsiora said.

"My queen," he said, wanting nothing more than to join his brothers.

"When hope is lost, do not allow us to fall into our enemy's hands."

"Tsiora!" said Nyah. "Queen Tsiora, no!"

The queen shushed her vizier with a raised finger. "Tau Solarin, will you aid us in this matter?"

Kana watched the three of them like they had lost their minds. His spear was out and aimed toward the fighting, though he'd taken heed of Kellan and stayed out of it. He was waiting to hear what Tau would say.

"I cannot do this," Tau told her.

"Cannot?" she asked.

"I will die first."

She paused, surprised, but would not be dissuaded. "And leave us to be used, then killed by those who wish us harm? We would be at Odili and his men's mercy, such as it would be."

Tau could feel her shaking. Her grip was tight, but she was shaking.

"I'll not let them have you," he promised. "I'll stop them."

It shouldn't have worked. Anyone with sense could foresee the evening's end, and yet Tau's words settled her.

"We have faith," she said, "in the Goddess and in those loyal to us."

Silently, Nyah began to weep. Kana fidgeted with his spear. Kellan and the others had fallen back. Uduak was dragging Yaw with him. The stairs had been captured and Tau hated himself for making an impossible promise.

The end was coming and there was nothing he could do to stop it. He was not so powerful, he thought, as the ground beneath his feet began to writhe and the sound of a hundred thunderclaps tore through the night.

Indlovu were tossed from the stairs by the quake and Queen's Guards fell from the battlements. Tau pulled the queen away from its edge, forcing her down. It sounded and felt like he was in the middle of an avalanche. Tau had seen them before, in the mountains, but they were in the valley and, lying on the floor of the battlements, he couldn't see what had caused the furor. He heard the screams, though. He heard the horror in the voices of the men below.

Then a torrent of blazing fire, a column of twisting flame, lit the sky. Even behind the battlements' thick walls, the fire's blistering heat curled the hairs on Tau's skin.

"Goddess!" whimpered Nyah.

"Fire-demon!" said Kana, on the ground beside Tau and the queen.

Tau stood, helping the queen to her feet. He looked down on the courtyard. An entire section of it was gone, fallen away into a molten sinkhole from which the youngling had crawled.

The creature was, in turns, awe-inspiring and piteous. It was huge, but less than half the size of the dragon that had burned the hedeni in Daba. It had open sores on its body and many of its shimmering black scales were missing. Its wings were torn at the edges and its long, sinuous neck was collared, though the bronze chain that had held it in whatever prison from which it had escaped was snapped in two.

The youngling roared at the sky and turned its baleful look on the courtyard's invading Indlovu, who were stunned to immobility. It opened its maw and belched a river of flames, incinerating thirty men. Tau had to cover his eyes, the fires were so bright, and when they died down, Tau saw that Odili's Indlovu were attacking the beast. The stupidity and bravery of it made Tau believe that, perhaps, the Chosen were the greatest fighting force on Uhmlaba.

Tau's opinion, however, made no difference to the youngling, which caught a man in its jaws, snapped him in two, then snatched at another with the clawed tips of its foreleg and flung that man like a rock, smashing him to pieces against one of the keep's walls. The dragon roared again, and the Indlovu, brave as they were, fell back.

They knew what was to come. The knowledge did not save them. The youngling breathed fire, turning the courtyard into an inferno.

"No one should control such. No one," Kana said as Tau spotted the youngling's handler.

"Zuri," he whispered.

Zuri had her hands out, fingers splayed, toward the dragon, and from a hundred strides away, Tau could see the strain on her face.

"What did you do?" Tau said. "What did you do...?"

Kellan, Hadith, and Uduak had crawled over. Yaw was being tended by one of the Queen's Guard. His shoulder was a mess.

"That is not a Central Mountain Guardian," Hadith said.

"She freed the youngling," Kellan added.

"The coterie," Tau said. "Where is her Hex?"

Uduak saw them first. "There."

Tau followed Uduak's hand. The coterie were there, under guard by the five men Hadith had sent with Zuri.

"They're not drawing energy from Isihogo," Tau said.

"How can you know?" asked Hadith.

"They don't have the look, the focus," answered Kellan.

"Ah," said Hadith, bouncing his eyes from Zuri to the coterie and no doubt seeing the difference. "But, without a Hex..." Hadith paused, working it out. "She knew. There was no time to bring us Guardians from the Central Mountains. She knew from the start."

"What did you do...?" Tau whispered as the youngling blew fire at Odili's retreating Indlovu and Zuri stumbled, only just keeping her feet.

Zuri directed it to the stairs and the youngling scorched the Indlovu on them, leaving behind nothing but char and ashes. The Queen's Guard cheered, their voices holding an edge of hope, and the dragon whipped its head back and forth, looking for some unseen attacker.

The youngling had torn through the Indlovu and, no longer distracted, it was fighting Zuri's control, weakening her hold, demanding that she pull ever greater amounts of energy from Isihogo. It was collapsing her shroud.

"It's Odili!" shouted Kellan.

The wretch, along with four Indlovu, had emerged from one of the hallways leading to the courtyard. The youngling was between him and the destroyed gates. He was trapped.

"Kellan Okar," Queen Tsiora said. "We wish that traitor captured or killed."

"My queen!" Kellan signaled the men of Scale Jayyed and they headed for the stairs.

Tau had seen Odili. He didn't care. Zuri had begun to bleed from her eyes, ears, nose, and mouth.

"What have you done?" Tau said, going to his knees, emptying his mind, and flying to Isihogo.

EXPULSION

The youngling was there and its wings were not damaged; its scales were not missing. The youngling looked powerful, indestructible. Zuri was in front of it, holding her hands out and up. It had to be impossible, that someone so small could command such a majestic creature. Yet, the dragon heeled, though it would not for much longer.

Zuri's shroud was little more than smoke before a breeze—thinning, vanishing, gone. And there she was, beautiful, glowing like the sun at dusk, warm and filled with life. Tau had never seen her in Isihogo unshrouded. She was the purest, most magnificent of the Goddess's creations, and her light drew the demons in droves.

Tau ran to her through the blasting winds and gray-colored landscape. He ran to her side, pulled loose his swords, and steadied himself.

"Leave!" he yelled to Zuri, struggling to be heard over the underworld's incessant storming.

Zuri still fought the dragon for control. "Can't," she said, nodding at the youngling. "She won't let me."

"They're coming."

"I know. I'm sorry."

The first demon had emerged from the mists. It charged them on six articulating legs. It had two sections of body—an abdomen and a thorax, its head embedded where a man's chest would be. Its eyes, five of them, were fixed on Zuri, and its mouth, a gaping hole edged by bone-like pincers, stretched open. It snatched for her and Tau fought it back.

"I'm sorry," Zuri said again.

Tau yelled at the demon, slashing at it over and over, as the next monstrosity, this one slithering across the ground like some enormous worm, attacked. He cut for the new beast's head, but it avoided his blade and snapped back at him. Tau dodged and brought his strong-side sword crashing down on its back. It shrieked and retreated, giving Tau a chance to battle the six-legged freak.

"I'm sorry," Zuri said, her golden glowing face filled with sorrow and fear. "I can't... I hope—"

"No! Hold on," Tau screamed, wheeling out of the way of a third demon, which stood like a man but was covered in matted fur and had claws instead of hands. That one caught him, ripping into his upper right arm and tearing thumb-long gashes of flesh away. A fourth demon howled from the mists, snuffed the air, and careened on all fours toward Zuri.

Tau couldn't do it. Hard as he fought, he could not keep the demons off them both. So, he made them want him more. He reached for Isihogo.

"Tau!" Zuri shouted in a panic.

Tau pulled as much energy as he could from Ananthi's prison. He filled himself with it to bursting. He gorged until the power of it threatened to burn through him, until he shone brighter than a noonday sun.

The demons stopped in their tracks, no longer interested in Zuri. Tau heard the grunts, howls, roars, and hisses from a hundred others in the mists, and he stepped away from her, calling to them. "I am here for you, finally here in the flesh. Come, come if you dare!"

They came.

Tau lifted his swords and they blazed with the powers of the underworld, burning like they'd been dipped in tar and lit by torches, and with those fiery blades, he set upon Ukufa's thralls.

He whirled and spun, thrust and swung, moving as fast as he was able, striking with as much power as he could muster. His blades burned the beasts and they shrank back from his blows.

Tau felt triumph. Tau felt power. Tau felt he could kill these demons with his gift-infused swords, and if that was what would save Zuri, then it was what he would do.

He sliced the arm from one demon, chopped the legs out from another. He laughed. This was what it was to be a god. He swung again, connecting; he danced back, then came forward, and a demon, one he did not see, lanced him through the back with several of its dozen spear-like protuberances.

The pain coursed through Tau like a tsunami. It owned him, and when the thing he had not seen ripped its jagged limb out of him, the pain stole his senses. Tau stumbled away, swinging wildly. Through the haze of pain he saw Zuri, still there, still glowing. The dragon had not released her.

He looked down at his wound. The demon had him open from belly to groin. He swung about himself, doing what he could to keep the monsters at bay. He tried to shout for Zuri but didn't have the strength. His legs were going numb, his arms were heavy as boulders, and his breathing was labored. He was done, and a new demon had come from the mists.

It was twice Tau's height and covered in spikes from head to toe. It had no eyes and its head was horned. It could not see, but it knew where Tau was. It tracked toward him. Tau forced his arms up, his swords blazing.

"Do you bleed?" he spat, words daring and voice weak. "Shall we see?"

Tau staggered toward the demon of spikes, going to his death. The demon roared. Tau roared back and there was a flash that lit up all of Isihogo, briefly banishing its mists and revealing horrors and monsters beyond Tau's darkest nightmares. The demon hordes were endless, out there in the distance, endless, and then the light was gone and Tau was joined by a Gifted in the heaviest shroud he had ever seen.

"Tau Solarin," said his queen. "You will die here."

"Tsiora?" Tau spluttered, her honorific forgotten.

"The Omehi line has ever been Gifted." She raised her hand and blasted him with something that felt like enervation twisted in on itself. It sucked his insides out and pulled him away from Isihogo.

"Zuri!" he screamed.

"We will try to save your friend," Queen Tsiora said, as she increased the strength of the blast, ejecting him from the underworld.

LIMITS

uri!" Tau was on the ground. He didn't know why. He sat up and was assaulted by pain. Nyah came to his aid, holding him still.

"Don't move. You're hurt," she said.

Tau ran a quivering hand over his body. There was no wound to find.

"He went to spirit world! He was in nyumba ya mizimu, the Reflection," said Kana.

"He drew energy and was injured by a demon," Nyah said.

"How alive?" asked Kana. "Shaman? I think only your women have this power."

"He has no gifts. He's a fool who has put our queen in danger."

Queen Tsiora was kneeling in front of Tau, her eyes open but sightless, her focus in Isihogo.

"So many lies," said Kana. "You tell us your queens lost their power in the Reflection."

Tau had no time. He had to protect Zuri. He made a second attempt to stand but collapsed.

"Stop it!" Nyah said. "You've a demon wound. You took in energy, didn't you? The damage the demon did to you in Isihogo has come into our world."

Tau felt at his abdomen again; nothing.

"It is psychic damage. It cannot be seen, but it can kill."

"Help me," Tau said, reaching for Nyah.

Nyah recoiled.

"Help him, witch," Kana said, coming to Tau's aid. The men gripped wrists; Nyah glared, but helped; and they dragged Tau, groaning, to his feet and to the edge of the battlements.

Behind Tau, Tsiora let out a deep sigh. Nyah left Tau's side and he would have fallen if not for Kana.

"My queen!" the vizier said.

"We are well," Tsiora said. "We must warn everyone away from the youngling. It is no longer Entreated. It has been freed."

She was alive, Tau saw. She was on her hands and knees in the courtyard, tears of blood etched on her weary face, but Zuri was alive.

Not far from her, Kellan and what remained of Scale Jayyed were crossing the courtyard, making their way to Odili. They were careful to avoid coming too close to the youngling, which seemed confused. It snuffed the air and moved its head back and forth, as if searching for something that had vanished.

It was, Tau realized, still focused on Isihogo. It was searching for Zuri. It would not find her. Her soul was wholly in Uhmlaba.

Odili shared the youngling's confusion. He was searching for a way out of the noose tightening around his treacherous neck, but with Kellan and Scale Jayyed coming for him, he was trapped. Tau didn't care. Damn the man, he thought, as Zuri wobbled to her feet, looked up, and gave him a crooked smile. He had to get down to her.

Tau took a step toward the stairs, muffled a yelp of pain, and crumpled against the battlement's crenellations.

"You are damaged," said Kana at the same time that Odili began to yell orders to his men.

"What?" Tau asked, not willing to believe his own ears. "What did he say?"

Odili's men were hesitant, but his orders were their only chance and they followed them.

"He . . . he tell them attack fire-demon," Kana said as Odili's Ind-lovu set upon the youngling with their swords.

The creature's reaction was instant. It left Isihogo, returning its senses to the world, and lashed out, clawing one of Odili's men to death. It reared and blew flame into the sky, and when it came back down, Odili's men had retreated. They were running for the broken gates, Odili far in front.

Kellan and Scale Jayyed went to intercept. They would catch him. They were closer to the gates. The dragon roared and, seeing so many running men, it blew flame.

Kellan was in front. He saw what was coming, yelled a warning to the scale, and dove aside. Uduak was running with Hadith and Themba. The three men were focused on Odili. They did not see the twisting ropes of flame shooting toward them. Jabari, behind them and taller, did. He threw himself into the three men, knocking them down.

The rest of the scale were not so lucky. The youngling's blast exploded outward, smashing into a dozen of Tau's sword broth-ers, killing them instantly. He saw Mshindi explode in flames, and another man, half his body on fire, flailed around screaming. It took Tau a breath, but he realized the burning man was Jabari. He'd fallen on top of Uduak, Hadith, and Themba, and the edge of the dragon's fire had caught him.

The youngling roared, preparing a second blast, this one to kill the men who had survived. Zuri shouted, drawing attention to her-self. The youngling swung its head to her and she raised her arms, the sleeves of her black Gifted robes falling to her elbows. Zuri was back in Isihogo, drawing power, and the youngling stiffened, caught on a puppet master's strings. The second blast of fire did not come.

"It's too soon," Tau whispered, and it was.

Zuri cried out in Uhmlaba as the demons in Isihogo ripped at her, tearing her focus away and breaking the invisible strings that held the youngling in thrall. The dragon was free, had found its tormentor, and did not hesitate. It shot fire at Zuri, and there wasn't even time for her to flinch. One breath she was there, arms outstretched, robes bil-lowing against the incoming inferno, her skin glowing with reflected light, her eyes sparkling, beautiful, a woman beyond measure. Then the youngling's fire hit, incinerating her, blasting her from existence.

Tau's legs gave out. Kana couldn't hold him and he crumpled to the battlement floor, his whole body shaking. And without knowing he did it, he wailed, doing what little he could to release the suffering from a body and soul that had been handed too much too soon.

"Nyah, we must bind the youngling," said a voice Tau should recognize, but couldn't.

"My queen, you must not. Your shroud... We have no Hex."

"The coterie in the courtyard. Bring them to us. We will hold the dragon until they are here. Nyah, we are for Isihogo."

"Tsiora! No!"

And Tau wailed.

"My father, the warlord, he comes and the traitor flees with his men."

"We have the dragon. It is in our control."

"My queen, you will not be able to hold it."

"We will, for long enough. Hurry, Nyah, the coterie."

And Tau wailed.

"Warlord! Hear us. We, queen of the Chosen, must speak!"

And from a distance, shouting. "Demon whore! I will burn this city and all your cities. I will cut the hearts from every soul that shares your evil blood."

"Hold your warriors outside our walls, Warlord. We still pray for peace and do not wish our dragon to end that prayer with fire. We wish to tell of our betrayal."

"Father! The Omehi queen speaks truth. She was betrayed."

And Tau wailed, his mouth covered by a heavy and filthy hand that tasted of dirt and ash. Hot breath, close to his ear, shushing him.

"Kana, my son, have they told you what they did? A fire-demon set on the Conclave? It killed a hundred thousand, Kana! Women, children, our people. They died, every one, burning to death in a pyre three times the size of this city."

Tau saw Zuri vanish in flame again, burned away to nothing.

"The shul is dead," that distant and shouting voice continued, "and I will be our people's vengeance. I will scour Xidda clean!"

"Kellan Okar, we demand you take Kana into custody."

There was a scuffle.

More words from a nearby voice, accented and difficult to understand. "Tsiora? More treachery? You think this stop my father?"

"Warlord, we have your son and we offer a trade. His life and release for a season of peace."

"Witch! I'll slit your throat myself."

"Not before our soldier cuts your son's. A moon cycle, then. Retreat from our valley. Give us a moon cycle for your son's life. Enough blood has been spilled these few nights. We have a dragon in this keep and the rage are on their way. A moon cycle, Warlord of the Xiddeen."

Tau sobbed, wracking cries, as the big man, hand still covering his mouth, shushed and held him close.

"Swear it, Warlord. One moon cycle of peace and Kana is yours."

"Demon Queen! I'll cut the tongue from your lying mouth."

"Swear it. We cannot restrain our dragon much longer. Swear it or the first to burn will be Kana!"

"I swear it, witch! One cycle of the moon. I swear it. Give me my son! I swear it and swear I'll be back. I will come with every warrior of the Xiddeen and we will erase the blight of your people from the world."

Tau opened his eyes. He was crouched and his tears blurred the stone beneath his knees and hands, making the ground seem an artist's impression. He tried to stem the cries, halt the tears. He failed at both.

"Before your warriors and ours, we have made a binding oath. Kellan Okar, inkokeli of Scale Osa, send the warlord's son to him."

Footsteps, then a voice, accented, retreating. "Tsiora! I will speak with my father. I will try to make the warlord see sense. Tsiora, do not give up on peace!"

"Warlord Achak, the Conclave was not our doing. The man responsible is a traitor who sought our death. He has run from us, but you will have his head. This we promise, by the Goddess."

"A traitor's head? Demon whore, in my own time I will take all the heads I need."

Tau scrubbed his eyes clear of tears, and Uduak's hand lifted away from his mouth.

"Tau?" Uduak whispered.

Tau saw the queen standing tall. She had her hands behind her back, her shoulders squared as she looked out and down at the warlord and his army beyond her keep. She appeared imperious and it was a grand illusion, for Tau could see the panicked tremors in her hands.

"They're leaving," breathed Nyah. "My queen, the Goddess is great, they're leaving."

But not without a final word.

"We know your witches are dying," shouted the warlord, near the edge of hearing. "We know it as we know that, in the coming cycles, you will have too few to call the fire-demons. We know it and offered you peace. You saw that as weakness, paying it back with the blood of our innocent. Queen of demons, what you saw was kindness, not weakness. Queen of demons, what you will see is vengeance, righteous in cause and unholy in deliverance."

If the warlord said more, Tau could not hear it.

"The coterie is coming up." It was Hadith.

"We cannot hold the youngling," Queen Tsiora said. "Quickly, she must be re-bound before it is too late."

Tau let his broken swords fall from his fingers. They were as useless on the battlement floor as they had been in his hands. The people he loved died either way.

EPILOGUE

TSIORA OMEHIA

He's broken, my queen," Nyah said to her. "Demon-haunted, in the assessment of the Sah priests. He's been in that room since we held the burning for those we lost."

Tsiora turned away from Nyah and toward the closed door in front of her. "Have the warriors, his sword brothers, seen to him?"

Nyah, the woman Tsiora trusted above all others, the one who had risked her life to train her to use her gifts in secret, told her they had. "The men, his sword brothers, come. He won't speak to them or anyone else. And he has not gone to see the Petty Noble who survived the youngling's fire."

"How is the Petty Noble?"

"He suffers, my queen, he suffers." Nyah closed her eyes as if trying to block out some horrible sight. "My queen, you risk too much. You saw what he did to Odili's Ingonyama. You saw the way he fights. He's an animal, and was that way before losing the woman to the youngling. There's nothing left in him to which you can appeal."

"We disagree. You did not see him fight the demons in Isihogo to save the Gifted initiate. He took power into himself to draw them away from her. He fought demons while holding power . . . He is . . ." She didn't know what he was. "Nyah, he has lost loved ones. Their loss made him lose hope. We must return hope, if he is to be of use."

"As your vizier, I ask you to reconsider."

Tsiora would not. Her mind was made.

"Then, allow me to send guards with you," Nyah said. "We do not know how this man will react. He's unstable, dangerous."

Tsiora didn't want to admit it, but she was scared to be in a room with him, the Common of Kerem. She couldn't afford to behave that way, though. If her plan was to have any chance of success, they would need to trust each other. "You have seen him fight, Nyah. Do you know any guards he could not kill?"

Nyah looked helpless, flustered. When she was younger, Tsiora used to love doing that to Nyah, but since Tsiora had become queen, a flustered Nyah often meant Tsiora was about to do something of rare and impressive stupidity.

Unwilling to wait and lose her nerve, Tsiora reached out for the leather-wrapped package in her vizier's arms. "Wait for us," she told Nyah, taking the package and opening the door to Tau Solarin's room in the Guardian Keep.

He was standing beside his bed. His head had stubble. His face as well. He wore a loose tunic that could not hide the whipcord muscle beneath. He had on ash-gray breeches and was barefoot. He was staring out the window at the work below, watching the repairs. The gates were up, but the damage to the courtyard would take longer to mend, a lot longer.

Tsiora laid her package, lighter than she'd expected, on the bed, thinking it strange to see the man without his swords. The night Odili had tried to assassinate her, the Common's blades had seemed part of him.

"Tau Solarin, we need your help," she said to his back. He did not respond, this strange Lesser. Tsiora came closer. She could see out the window. She knew what he was looking at. Down in the courtyard was the place where the dragon had killed the Gifted he cared for.

"Tau Solarin," Tsiora said, hovering her hand above his arm and then, daring herself, letting it fall on his shoulder. He did not react. "Abasi Odili is in Palm City. He controls it now and has most of the Royal Nobles swearing fealty to our younger sister. It is claimed that, of her own free will, our dear sister has seen the righteous nature of Odili's cause. She has declared him her champion and herself the true queen of the Chosen. Queen Esi. It sounds innocent enough, don't you think?"

He still didn't speak.

"We have come with an offer."

"How did you do it?"

She jumped at his voice, at the metal in it.

"How did you push me out of Isihogo?"

Tsiora considered the question, wondering what to tell him. She settled on the truth. "We are of royal blood. Royal blood runs closest to the Goddess. We have greater gifts than all others. When we saw the danger to you, we used a type of enervation. Queen Taifa, though not the first to use this particular gift, named it 'expulsion.' With it, we can forcibly remove anyone, including those holding energy, from Isihogo."

"You could have saved her then," he growled, scaring her, though she didn't want to admit it. "You could have gotten her out, and she could have gotten away. She should not have been there. She should not have tried to—"

"We could not," Tsiora told him. "A dragon's hold cannot be broken. Expulsion, cast on Gifted Zuri, would have had no effect. We had to wait until the youngling released her on its own."

"Then, you should have let me save her!"

"You could not have done so and would have died in the attempt."

He faced her, his dark eyes and scarred face frightening in their intensity. Tsiora felt the need to step back. She locked eyes with him instead. "We need your help, Tau Solarin."

"I can't help you."

It wasn't said because he blamed her for the Gifted's death. The initiate sacrificed herself, and neither of them could have stopped that. Instead, she heard self-pity. He wallowed in his loss, set adrift. She would anchor him. "Tau Solarin, the queendom has been torn in two, and in less than a moon cycle, the warlord will return to commit genocide. The Nobles, led by our Royals, have divided the Chosen at the worst possible time. This cannot be allowed. Th

Goddess made us one people, and our survival rests on the Omehi acting as such.

"To accomplish what must be done, to reunite Noble and Lesser, we need a man like you. We need a man who faced Indlovu, Ingonyama, Xiddeen, demons, and dragons to be our champion. We need a hero to help us rebuild what has been broken."

"I'm no hero."

"You are to the Lessers. You are to the people who still fight for us."

"I am no hero."

Tsiora made her voice hard. "Then be a weapon."

That surprised him. She could see it in his rough-edged face.

"Our champion's first task is one of vengeance. Our champion will lead his closest men, and the armies that remain loyal to us, to the walls of Palm City. He will quell the rebellion and rescue our sister. He will right the wrongs the traitor has wrought on both our people and the Xiddeen. Our champion will kill Abasi Odili, in the name of the queen, in our name."

She gave him a breath to absorb it, and, unable to hide from what it would mean for the queendom and for her, she gave voice to the question she had come to ask. "Tau Solarin, will you be our champion?"

She shut her reservations away as best she could and moved to the bed, picking up and handing Tau the long leather package. Without curiosity he opened it, revealing the guardian swords she had had made for him. She heard his intake of breath as he saw the weapons, and, unable to help himself, he reached out, touching them, running his hands over the dragon-scale blades.

His hands stopped at the hilts, the hilts from his father's and grandfather's swords. With reverence, this strange and vicious Lesser took up the perfectly balanced and impossibly sharp weapons. He twirled them and the thought flashed in Tsiora's mind that he could kill her before she could call out.

Swords still in hand, he stepped close, so close she could feel the heat emanating from his body. They were the same height, she noted as his eyes bored into hers. She licked her lips. They'd gone dry. More, she wanted to know why she couldn't pull her eyes from his, why she felt ensorcelled by the fire in them.

"I will kill Abasi Odili," he told her.

It frightened her, the way he'd said it, but she would not balk. "We consider that a 'yes,' Champion Tau Solarin."

And, like that, there was no going back. A dragon had been called, and someone would have to die.

GLOSSARY

Ananthi, the Goddess—The one true deity, the creator of Uhmlaba, Isihogo, women, men, and all that exists. She is the source
of all gifts, and the Omehi are Her chosen people.

Aqondise—A leading warrior's most trusted companion; a
second-in-command.

Cek—Soulless.

Citadel City—The first true Omehian city on Xidda, Citadel City
sits at the westward base of the Fist and is home to the Indlovu,
Gifted, Sah, and Guardian Citadels. It is the primary training
grounds for the Noble warriors, the Gifted, the priesthood, and
it is the traditional base of power for the Royals who sit on the
Guardian Council and lead the military effort.

Claw (military unit)—Three scales operating together under a
single command.

The Crags—A large plateau in the Fist mountain range that has
been divided into several fighting areas that are used to train the
Gifted, Indlovu, and Ihashe. The Crags are the location of the
Queen's Melee.

The Curse—The massive and unexplored desert territory beyond
the front lines of the war. The Xiddeen live out in the Curse
though how they can survive in the poisonous wasteland
mystery.

Cycle—One rotation through all four seasons (Seed, Grow, Harvest, and Hoard).

Demon-haunted—A woman or man whose mind has been broken by time spent in Isihogo.

Dragon (military unit)—A dragon is three wings operating together under a single command.

Dragon's Span—A hand symbol meant to ward away evil thoughts, demons, and faithlessness.

Drudge—A Lesser made casteless for failing to serve the Omehi in combat.

Edifier—A Gifted capable of moving quickly through Isihogo to pass messages to other Edifiers in distant locations.

Enervator—A Gifted capable of temporarily incapacitating others by forcing their souls into Isihogo.

Enrager—A Gifted capable of pulling power from Isihogo and moving it through the blood of a Greater Noble or Royal Noble, making the target bigger, stronger, faster, and more resilient.

Entreater—A Gifted capable of binding their will to the will of another.

The Fist—The smallest mountain range on the Omehi Peninsula, it starts at the ocean and runs a short way down the center of the peninsula. Citadel City sits at its westward base. The Fist holds the Crags training grounds.

Gambeson—A padded defensive jacket.

Gaum—A potent intoxicant made from the poison in a scorpion's sting.

The Goddess's Curse—For fighting against Her chosen people, the Goddess afflicted the Xiddeen with a curse that corrupts their skin and bodies, giving them weeping sores and seeming to rot them from the inside out.

Guardian—The Omehi name for a dragon.

Hedeni—Women and men who have no faith in the Goddess and live outside of Her grace.

⋯x—A group of six Entreaters who work together.

Ihagu—The Omehi militia that makes up the front lines in the endless war against the Xiddeen. These men are not granted military status.

Ihashe—The elite fighters and soldiers of the Lesser castes. They are granted military status after graduating from the one-cycle training provided at either the Southern or Northern Ihashe Isikolo. They must serve six active cycles to complete their service.

Indlovu—The elite warriors of the Noble castes. They are granted military status after graduating from the three-cycle training provided at the Indlovu Citadel in Citadel City. They must serve six active cycles to complete their service.

Ingonyama—The Chosen's deadliest fighters, selected from the very best of the graduating military initiates. If the Ingonyama is a Greater Noble or Royal Noble they are teamed with an Enrager, who will use her gifts to empower the Ingonyama in combat.

Inkokeli—Leader of an Indlovu unit or Ihashe scale.

Inkumbe—A small grass-eating and four-legged creature from Osonte with small horns and cloven feet.

Intulo—A salamander/lizard. Also a description of a slippery person who won't stay still in an argument—their thoughts are loose, fluid, not substantial.

Inyoka—A poisonous serpent.

Isihogo—The demon world—a colorless, mist-filled prison, where time flows differently and Ananthi's powers are found.

Isikolo—A school or academy.

Jirza—The capital city of the northern province.

KaEid—The leader of the Gifted. Typically of Royal Noble blood.

Kigambe—The capital city of the southern province.

Kora—A stringed musical instrument.

Kudliwe—A small scurrying and flying insect that burrows into bags of grain and is difficult to kill.

Masmas—A frothy intoxicant made from fermented cactus juice.

Mka—The particular pungent and unpleasant smell of winds produced after having eaten bean- or onion-heavy meals.

Nceku—Soulless one

Neh—An Omehi interjection commonly used to indicate a statement of opinion or fact, a command, an exclamation, or a question, or to indicate that something went unheard.

Nkosi—An honorific used when addressing Nobles.

Olu—A pricey intoxicant made from crushed and fermented fruits.

The Omehi/The Chosen—The people, Nobles and Lessers, chosen by the Goddess to lead all the races of men.

Osonte—The original homeland of the Omehi.

Palm City—The capital city of the Omehi peninsula and the central province, and the seat of the queen and her royal family.

Preceptor—The one who instructs Gifted initiates in their training.

Proven—A warrior who has proven their mettle and worth in combat by sacrificing enough of their body to no longer be combat-ready. Proven maintain their military status and are required to serve out all time remaining in their six cycles of military service. Most Proven sign up for additional service.

Rabba—A fruity, bright, and floral aroma'ed stimulant drink made from wet-processed beans grown in the highlands of the Southern and Northern Mountain ranges.

Rage (military unit)—Three dragons (military unit) operating together under a single command.

The Roar—The unsettled ocean.

Sah Priesthood—The women and men who preach the word of the Goddess, maintain the Omehi's religious traditions, and help guide the Chosen ever closer to the Goddess's grace.

Scale (military unit)—The Omehi's most common and basic fighting unit, made up of fifty-four men.

Seasons—The Omehi make note of four seasons: Seed, Grow, Harvest, and Hoard. Each season lasts approximately three moon cycles.

Shul—The Xiddeen word for "great chief"—a leader whose powers transcend tribe.

Thmlaba—The world of the races of men.

ufa, the Insatiate—Ukufa the thief, liar, corrupter, divider, nslaver. Ukufa the creator of death, suffering, war, and hate broke the world with his hunger for more than the world could give. He is held in Isihogo by the body and spirit of the Goddess.

Umbusi—A fief's governor.

Umqondisi—A teacher, trainer, master, leader.

Wing (military unit)—Three claws operating together under a single command.

Xidda—The land the Omehi discovered after fleeing Osonte.

Xiddeen—The name the aboriginals of Xidda use for themselves.

NOBLES

THE
OMEHI
PEOPLE

LESSERS

THE CHOSEN CASTES

QUEEN AND ROYAL FAMILY

THE
RULING
AND
GUARDIAN
COUNCILS

ROYAL NOBLES

THE GIFTED

INGONYAMA
(ACTIVE AND INACTIVE)

GREATER NOBLES

INDLOVU
(ACTIVE SERVICE)

PETTY NOBLES

IHASHE
(ACTIVE SERVICE)

HIGH GOVERNOR
(ADMINISTRATORS)

LOW GOVERNOR
(CREATORS/EDUCATORS)

HIGH HARVESTER
(FARM ADMINISTRATORS)

LOW HARVESTER
(SKILLED FARM WORKERS)

IHAGU
(ACTIVE SERVICE)

HIGH COMMON
(WORKERS THOUGH CAPABLE OF
MANAGING OTHER WORKERS)

LOW COMMON
(WORKERS)

DRUDGE
(INDENTURED SERVANTS)

GRATITUDE

I want to say thanks.

I want to say it to Joey for being this book's first reader. His encouragement gave me the confidence to believe in my work. I want to say it to Malik for never being too busy to read a few more pages. He helped me realize this could be special. I want to say it to Anthony for making sure I never forgot the fundamentals of story-telling. He made me better.

Most of all, I want to say thanks to Helen Zdriluk, my high school drama teacher and friend. She taught me to believe in the value of creativity, gave me a chance to prove I could say something worth-while, and pointed out the path that has determined my life.

Mrs. Z, one of the last times I saw you, we were at a friend's wedding. I had just landed an executive job and was very proud of myself. I told you about it. You nodded, looked me in the eye, and said, "Yes, but what about the writing?"

I miss you, Mrs. Z. I miss you very much. I'm still writing. Thank you for believing I should.

THE SCALE

This story would not exist in its current form and, in all likelihood, would not have reached you without the efforts of many incredible people. Here are a few of them:

Brit Hvide Busse—my remarkable editor, whose sense of story, character, and world leave me breathless. Brit found this story, swore she'd bring it to the world, and she did.

Emily Byron and Nivia Evans—the editors working alongside Brit to make sure we never settled for anything less than our best.

Tim Holman—Orbit's publisher, one of this book's fiercest champions, and a fiery intellect whose work and life are nothing less than awe-inspiring.

Erin Malone—my literary agent, whose tireless work and dedication allows me to spend my days writing tall tales. Her industry knowledge and ability to translate it into something digestible is a magic trick unlike any other.

Caitlin Mahony—my foreign rights agent, who travels the world looking for new places where my words might find welcome.

Eric Reid—My film/TV agent, with the power to captivate you with the spoken word and a personality that makes every phone call an event to look forward to and to be remembered.

Alex Lencicki—Orbit's marketing and publicity director and the kind of person with whom it's a thrill to talk deep data and go-to-market plans. Alex makes marketing as exciting as any climatic battle scene.

Ellen Wright—Orbit's associate publicity director, whose marvelous work draws readers' attention to the fact that this story exists at all.

Lauren Panepinto—Orbit's creative director, responsible for this book's gorgeous cover design and, due to her amazing work, the look and feel of much of Orbit's oeuvre.

Karla Ortiz—illustrative genius, the hands and mind behind the cover image itself, and a lightning bolt of positive energy and verve.

Eileen Chetti—Copyeditor extraordinaire, she removed my extra commas, put in the ones I left out, and made the story stronger by keeping character wounds consistent, geography sensible, and universe terms comprehensible.

WWW.EVANWINTER.COM

Dear Reader,

Evan Winter here to say a heartfelt thanks. Life is the spans we're given and the choices we make in how to spend them. Thank you for sharing a few of yours with me. And, if you'd like to be the first to learn more about the rest of my work or hear a little about what I'm reading or doing, you'll find that and more at www.evanwinter.com.

Wishing you and yours happiness, health, love,

Evan Winter